FPL
SF

D 25.95

PIRATE SUN

KARL SCHROEDER

PIRATE SUN

Virga | BOOK THREE

A TOM DOHERTY ASSOCIATES BOOK **TOR** NEW YORK

This is a work of fiction. All of the characters, organizations, and events portrayed in this novel are either products of the author's imagination or are used fictitiously.

PIRATE SUN: BOOK THREE OF VIRGA

Edited by David G. Hartwell

A Tor Book
Published by Tom Doherty Associates, LLC
175 Fifth Avenue
New York, NY 10010

www.tor-forge.com

Tor® is a registered trademark of Tom Doherty Associates, LLC.

ISBN-13: 978-0-7653-1545-8
ISBN-10: 0-7653-1545-9

Library of Congress Cataloging-in-Publication Data

Schroeder, Karl, 1962–
    Pirate sun / Karl Schroeder.—1st ed.
        p. cm.—(Virga ; bk. 3)
    "A Tom Doherty Associates book."
    ISBN-13: 978-0-7653-1545-8
    ISBN-10: 0-7653-1545-9
    I. Title.

    PR9199.3.S269 P57 2008
    813'.54—dc22
                        2008022149

First Edition: August 2008

Printed in the United States of America

0 9 8 7 6 5 4 3 2 1

To the Tuesday night group,
for years of excellent conversation.

Acknowledgments

This series has been guided by the insights and suggestions of a number of excellent people. My first reader has always been my wife, Janice, and without her my manuscripts would probably be riddled with inconsistencies and errors. Many of my readers have contributed enthusiastic suggestions and even calculated the engineering feasibility of Virga (particular thanks to Vernor Vinge for "running the numbers"). As usual, the Cecil Street Irregulars, a weekly writing workshop started by Judith Merril more than twenty years ago, provided key insights into character and plot; and of course, this book ultimately owes its existence to David G. Hartwell, who suggested that I take the time to complete the full suite of ideas and themes first introduced in Sun of Suns.

VIRGA

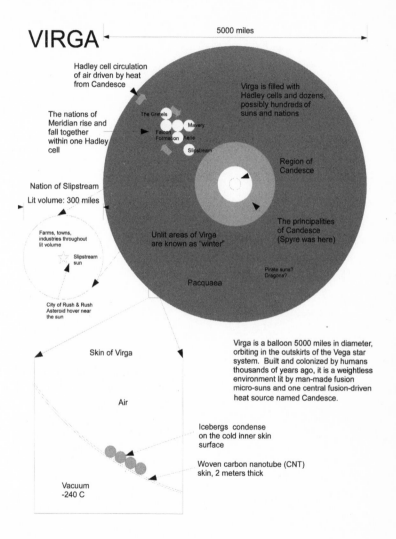

5000 miles

Hadley cell circulation
of air driven by heat
from Candesce

Virga is filled with
Hadley cells and dozens,
possibly hundreds of
suns and nations

The nations of
Meridian rise and
fall together
within one Hadley
cell

The Gretels

Mavery

Falcon
Formation   Aerie

Slipstream

Region of
Candesce

Nation of Slipstream

Lit volume: 300 miles

Farms, towns,
industries throughout
lit volume

Slipstream
sun

Unlit areas of Virga
are known as "winter"

The principalities
of Candesce
(Spyre was here)

Pirate suns?
Dragona?

City of Rush & Rush
Asteroid hover near
the sun

Pacquaea

Skin of Virga

Air

Vacuum
-240 C

Icebergs condense
on the cold inner skin
surface

Woven carbon nanotube (CNT)
skin, 2 meters thick

Virga is a balloon 5000 miles in diameter,
orbiting in the outskirts of the Vega star
system. Built and colonized by humans
thousands of years ago, it is a weightless
environment lit by man-made fusion
micro-suns and one central fusion-driven
heat source named Candesce.

"Nothing is more difficult,
and therefore more precious,
than to be able to decide."

—Napoleon Bonaparte

PIRATE SUN

Prologue

"ONE THING I *can* guarantee," said Venera Fanning. "There has never been a prison break like this one."

The barrel-shaped tugboat was so old that moss had spread continents over its hull, and tufts of grass jutted from its seams like hairs from an old man's chin. The powerful drone of the vessel's engines, as its small crew tested them, put a lie to any impression that it was feeble, however. In fact the bone-rattling noise of the test quickly drove Venera and her small group away from the dry-dock framework that enclosed the tug. Venera turned away from it and squinted past the light of Slipstream's sun. The city of Rush spread across half the sky, its gaily bannered habitat cylinders turning majestically among wisps of cloud. It was midday and the air was full of airships, winged human forms, and here and there cavorting dolphins.

One figure had detached itself from the orderly streams of flying people, and was approaching. Venera saw that it was a member of her private spy network, a nondescript young man dressed in flying leathers, his toeless shoes pushing down on the stirrups that drove the mechanical wings strapped to his back. He hove to and she admired the sheen of sweat on his shoulders as he saluted. "Here's the latest photos." He proffered a thick envelope; Venera took it, forgetting about him instantly, and tore it open.

Her fingers rose of their own accord to touch the scar on her jaw as she looked at what the pictures revealed: the planes and corners of a stone prison that hovered alone in cloudy skies. Not one building, but six or seven that had been lashed together over the decades, the blocky, boulderlike edifice hung half-wreathed in its own fog bank. The blocks, spheres, and triangles of the Falcon New Prison were of various architectural styles and colors, literally thrown together and hybridized with clumsy wooden bridges and rope-and-chain lashings into one cancerous monster whose only common element was that all its windows were barred.

With no gravity to flatten it, the composite prison was stable enough; storms were rare on the edge of civilization and there were no obstacles for the place to run into in its endless drift. The New Prison was a child of neglect, a forgotten mote on the fringe of the vast cloud of workers' dormitories, collective farms, and planned cities that was Falcon Formation. Most of the cargo delivered here was on a one-way journey.

Venera intended to make an unscheduled pickup.

She took a deep breath and smiled up at the courier. "Ask them if they're ready," she ordered. "There's no time to lose."

"Master Diamandis also sent these." He handed her another envelope. This one contained dossiers, but she only glanced at them briefly.

"I'll deal with them when we get back. I want to see this."

At that moment the tug's engines coughed and wound down. Venera spun in midair, a lithe movement born from a lifetime spent moving from freefall to gravity and back again. She glared at the crew, who were boiling out of the suddenly smoking vessel. "Now what have you done?"

"It'll work!" The chief engineer was practically wringing his hands as he flew around the curve of the ship. Like any sensible person he was afraid of Venera's wrath; she decided to show some restraint and merely shrugged to hide her disappointment. "I'll be back in two hours," she said. "See that it's ready to fly by then."

"THESE ARE THE players." Garth Diamandis laid out photos like playing cards across the tabletop. They sat under gravity, in a set of apartments Venera had rented (under the name of Amandera Thrace-Guiles) in one of Rush's more upscale town wheels. Garth, an aging dandy who had recently become Venera's closest friend and confidante, rearranged two pictures to overlap. "Martin Shambles is a key member of the Aerie resistance. Your friend Hayden Griffin apparently knows him."

"That's no surprise," Venera muttered. The nation of Slipstream spread in all six directions from its capital, this city; yet the thousands of cubic kilometers of farmland and township lit by Slipstream's sun had once been owned by a rival nation, Aerie. Slipstream had destroyed Aerie's sun, conquered the country, and assimilated its people—so naturally there were resisters. Griffin himself had been one when Venera had first met him.

"Since Griffin's reappearance and subsequent second disappearance, Shambles has been funneling supplies and money to a location in one of the sunless countries," Diamandis went on. "If that's where Griffin took the sun-making devices he acquired in the sun of suns . . ."

". . . Then that's where Aerie's new sun is being constructed," said Venera. She sat back. "Huh! That boy never ceases to amaze me. He was a good driver back when I employed him. Seems he's making an even better hero."

If Aerie could build and light a new fusion sun for itself, its people might be able to free themselves from bondage to Slipstream. Venera had married into Slipstream's nobility, but that didn't mean she had any loyalty to her new home. After recent events, in fact, her loyalties went in quite the opposite direction.

"So . . ." The deliciously intricate plot she had been gestating for weeks had taken a satisfying turn. "Granted the standoff between the admiralty and the palace, we already have two major players playing chess with one another's nerves."

"Three players, if you count the rioters," said Diamandis.

"Four, when you add in Aerie's various nonaligned malcontents." She held up several fingers. "Then five, if you add in Hayden Griffin and Shambles's people. All of their interests converging rapidly. I wonder when that new sun will be ready?"

"And then . . ." prompted Diamandis; he smiled in that way that had melted so many young ladies' hearts in his youth.

"Then there's us," said Venera. "All these contending forces are winding each other tighter and tighter. Rioters in the city, the admiralty and the palace facing off against one another, and then this Aerie conspiracy. What they all need is a spark to set off the powder keg."

She and Diamandis grinned at one another across the table. Then Venera rose, strode to the window, and twitched aside the heavy velvet curtain. She looked out over a sweep of rooftops that curved up in the distance, gradually becoming vertical. Many of the roofs were painted or shingled in patterns; when you lived on the inside surface of a cylinder, your roof was the most visible feature of your house, and Rush's citizens took pride in their houses.

Venera wasn't seeing the colorful vista. "A new Aerie sun!" she said, shaking her head. "This is exactly what we need. Garth, I want you to find out when it's going to be ready. We'll synchronize our own plans with theirs—establish a liaison, without revealing who we are."

Venera opened the window and leaned out; the rotational winds immediately lofted her black hair around her head like the wings of a raven. She closed her eyes at the freshness, feeling satisfied for the first time in many days. She'd been branded a fugitive in Slipstream, had been hiding in these few rooms since her return, but she was about to remedy that situation. A great trap was being set, and all she needed now was the trigger.

There was a discrete knock on the door. "It's ready," said a servant. Venera sat up with a jerk and swept the photos off the table. "Come on!"

It was satisfying, being just one mote of thousands crowding the city's airways, yet knowing that even the rioters who had burned the Grand Market in Cylinder Two were less a danger to the city than she. Venera watched out the bullet-shaped taxi's window as all the myriad details of the city's weightless neighborhoods flew by: food vendors and craftsmen selling their wares from inside wicker balls—a veritable cloud of these balls making up the farmer's market; big nets full of produce (a galaxy of cabbages here, a trove of engine parts there) being towed by straining jets or tethered albatross flocks; a quivering ball of water thirty feet across where some day laborers had stripped off their shirts and were dunking their heads and shoulders, laughing like little boys. All these details outlined in hard-edged brilliance by Slipstream's nearby sun.

At the moment Rush Asteroid was shading the drydock from that sun. The silhouetted asteroid was furred along its black outline by the trees that covered it. A cloud bank had formed in the cooler air of that long shaft of shadow, and tendrils of gray were closing around the drydock as Venera arrived. The tug's crew were making their final adjustments. While she hovered—literally—her eyes played across the panorama of infinitely receding cloud and sky that lay beyond the city. This maze troubled the eye in every direction. There was no up or down to Venera's world—save for what you made yourself—only the light of nearby suns providing any orientation at all to the tugboat's crew. Even that vanished at night. This lack of direction made journeys like this one hazardous for even the most experienced pilot. They made communication over international distances unreliable; sporadic, at best.

She had every reason to stay here in Rush to oversee the unfolding plan. That was the logical thing to do, and the safe thing.

The little tug's engines coughed into life again. "We're all set!" shouted the chief engineer.

Venera turned to Garth. "Well," she said. Suddenly she realized what she was going to do. "Take care of things," she said, kissing him on the cheek.

"You're not going too?" he asked incredulously.

"I'll be right back," she said in a tone that was simultaneously bright and defensive.

"But, this is when we're going to need you the most—"

"Oh, Garth, you've never *needed* me," she teased, and then before he could say anything more, she dove for the tug's open hatch.

"Contact Hayden! And Shambles! But keep it arm's-length, mind!" She waved from the closing hatch. "And spend some time with your daughter! She's still not to be trusted!"

Garth cursed lividly—but laughed anyway—as the tug spewed exhaust into the pristine mist and soared away. It cleared the girders of the drydock, leaving behind a slowly expanding galaxy of bolts and screws, discarded hull plates, and bent wires.

As it followed the long cone of Rush Asteroid's shadow away from the city, mist beaded on the ship's nose. Now the condensate rolled along the hull past booster rockets the size of a man that Venera's team had bolted to the iron. The droplets crept like a blindman's fingers along the links of a mile of heavy chain that the team had coiled around the tug's waist. Aft, the drops detached and quivered in the air like weightless jewels as the vessel faded in the distance.

Garth Diamandis watched his benefactress leave with much the same bemusement as he'd watched her arrive in his former home of Spyre, lo those many months ago. There was simply no predicting what Venera Fanning was going to do next and he'd given up trying. So, with a shrug, he turned to the rest of her planning team, who were milling about in confusion at the sudden vacation of their mistress.

Garth clapped his hands loudly to get their attention. "Stop gawking!" he said. "We have a lot to do in very little time. There's the Aerie underground to be contacted, and further infiltration of the pilot's palace accomplished. Everything has to be set up to topple in the right direction at the right moment.

"You can't overthrow a government by sitting around on your asses!"

Part One | THE ADMIRAL

THEY HAD PROVIDED him with two torturers today.

Chaison Fanning put out one hand to stop himself in the doorway, aware that the prison guard behind him would kick him into the room in a second or two. "Gentlemen," he said in as even a tone as he could muster, "to what do I owe the honor?" Neither answered, but it didn't matter; just hearing himself speak civilly counted as a victory. With luck, that brief moment might sustain him through whatever was about to follow.

Chaison flew the rest of the way into the interrogation room before the guard could kick him. "Against that wall," said the man who usually questioned him. Chaison didn't know this individual's name, but thought of him as *the reporter* because of the identification tag clipped to his uniform. The embossed white square announced that its wearer was part of the JOURNALISM DIVISION. A piece of tape obscured the name. At first Chaison had thought the tag was a joke of some kind; he had learned otherwise.

Curled up in the weightless black of his cell at night, Chaison's thoughts often turned to killing the reporter. They were fragile, weak fantasies—faint hopes, really, often shattered by panic as he awoke to find that he had drifted into the center of the little chamber. His flailing hands would find no purchase on wall, ceiling, or floor. In such moments there was nothing solid to be touched in any direction, no proof of his own existence but a scream; no face in his mind but that of his nameless torturer.

Yet he refused to scream, though other men in other cells did. Sometimes their voices brought him back to himself. A few nights ago he'd been drifting in the all-consuming dark when suddenly he'd heard a young voice calling out in the night. At first Chaison had thought his mind was playing tricks on him, because he recognized the voice. But he'd shouted in reply, and the other had answered.

That was how Chaison had learned that one of his crewmen was imprisoned with him. The knowledge had spread like fire in him, giving him a new sense of purpose. That knowledge had emboldened him to greet his tormentor just now.

"Put your hands in the cuffs," said the reporter from his position near the room's single barred window. Chaison wiped a smear of mold off the palm of his hand. In a building like this that had never known gravity, the stuff accumulated everywhere; this patch stood straight out from the doorjamb like fine white fur, just as it coated the walls of his cell. The new man closed the rusty rings over his wrists and Chaison steeled himself for a sucker punch or something that would soften him up for the coming questions. To his relief, the man just met Chaison's eyes briefly, then hopped lightly across the cell to position himself behind the desk podium with the pale-faced chief torturer.

The badge on his gray uniform read, HELLO, MY NAME IS. Underneath this somebody had scrawled 2629.

"Here's the one you wanted to see, Professor," said the reporter. He seemed a bit nervous. Flipping open a thick dossier, he held it out to the light from the window. "Chaison Fanning, former admiral of the fleet of Slipstream. Our most important guest."

"Hmmpf." The visitor took the file carefully and thumbed through it. He glanced at Chaison again, silver cloud light glinting off his wire-frame glasses. He seemed out of place here; he did, in fact, look a bit like a literature professor Chaison had once had.

Chaison cleared his throat. "I don't understand," he said, unable to hide the bitterness in his voice. "I've given a full deposition. You know everything."

"No, we don't!" The reporter glared at him murderously. "Did they clear you to read my articles in the *Intelligence Internal Journal*?" he asked the visitor. "He's been cooperative up to a point and I've been able to make most of my deadlines. But there's a crucial piece of information he's holding back. He's very disciplined, he exercises constantly in his cell, jumping from wall to wall, doing isometrics . . . Seems willing to die rather than give us this last thing he knows. I've had some trouble finishing the last article in the series. I assume that's why you're . . . ?"

"Mm, I'm not here to fault your work, you were always a good student," said the professor in a bland tone. "But let's start with the basics. It says here you . . ." He read for a moment, then raised his glasses and looked again. "Did this really happen?"

"Officially, no," said the reporter with a sigh. He watched in evident disappointment as the other flipped through the dossier with an expression of increasing incredulity. After a minute or so the professor pulled himself together and looked up at Chaison.

"You attacked and crippled our fleet," he said.

Chaison nodded.

"With six ships?"

Chaison shrugged modestly. He allowed himself a slight smile.

"How was this accomplished?"

"The better question," said Chaison, "is why you never heard anything about it."

The reporter reached behind himself and unclipped some nasty darts from the board next to the window. Chaison tried to swallow past a suddenly dry mouth.

"Hang on," said the visiting professor, putting a hand on the reporter's arm. "Let's all be civil for the moment. I presume that I wasn't cleared to know about this attack," he said to Chaison, "because it's a national embarrassment."

Chaison eyed the reporter, then said, "Your people launched a sneak attack on my country. I caught your fleet within your own territory and decimated it."

To put it this way was to sum up a gambit of high desperation, take the exhilaration of battle, the panic, and shouted orders on the bridge of a smoking ship that dripped blood into the sky as it maneuvered in pitch blackness at two hundred miles an hour—to take all of that and reduce it, obscenely, to simple history. Impossible; the remembered sound of bullets hitting the hull, thick as rain, woke Chaison every night. At random times on any given day, some quality of light might easily take him back to that bridge, where men's faces were lit only by the instruments and the roiling darkness outside the armored windows flashed into incandescence every few seconds, as this or that ship exploded in the night.

"Amazing." The new man was too absorbed in his reading to notice that Chaison had slipped into a reverie. "It says you used something called 'radar' to maneuver your ships at full speed in cloud and darkness. Apparently we recovered several working devices from the wreckage of your ships." Now he looked puzzled. "So why do we need you at all? Is there some secret to operating this radar that he's not telling us?"

"Well, no. And yes," said the reporter. "They work just fine. They just . . . don't do anything."

The professorial visitor sighed and tilted his glasses up to rub his eyes. "Explain, please."

Chaison had fought every inch against admitting even these details to the reporter, despite the fact that Falcon Formation's engineers already knew them. They had the wreckage of several of Chaison's ships to examine, after all; they could put two and two together. Yet even though Chaison had in the end bit the words of admission out one by one, in a blur of delirium and pain, he would gladly fight the questions again. There were still facts for which he would die rather than reveal.

The reporter seemed eager to show his former teacher his investigative skills. "Radar's a well-known technology," he said. "It just doesn't work. It's like those, what-you-call 'computers' and other electrical-onics things. Their operation is permanently jammed by the sun of suns."

In his life Chaison had met few people who knew that there were higher technologies than the simple steam- and fuel-powered mechanisms they'd grown up with. Fewer still knew that it was Candesce, the vast self-contained fusion sun at the center of the world, whose radiation rendered radar and similar systems inoperable anywhere in Virga. Chaison himself, nobly born and educated at the best schools, had only understood this in an abstract sort of way, until a year ago.

The visitor shook his head and frowned. "You're saying Candesce makes radar impossible. Then how did *he* get it to work, unless . . ." His eyes widened.

"Unless he's been inside Candesce," said the reporter with a nod. "Or knows somebody who has. Maybe the home guard . . ."

"But the home guard's neutral!" The professorial man shook his head rapidly, rubbing at his balding scalp with one distracted hand. "They exist to defend Virga from outside threats, they don't intervene in internal affairs!"

"That's what I always thought," said the reporter, with the air of a man who's recently come into possession of a great and secret truth.

Chaison almost laughed. Weren't interrogators supposed to keep their speculations from their victims? These two shouldn't even be talking in front of him, much less debating the facts of his case.

"This is what he won't tell us," said the reporter. "How did Slipstream get around Candesce's jamming field? Did they shut it off? Did they find a way to shield the ships from it? You see, I've been trying to wrap up my series for months with an appeal to the navy to develop this capability. It was no ordinary attack. If we knew this—if we had this ability—"

"Yes, I see." The professor met Chaison's gaze. It was odd, though: Chaison didn't see the lizard-like coldness in that gaze that he'd come to expect from the faceless apparatchiks of Falcon's brutal bureaucracy. Was this man here to try a new tactic—kindness, perhaps?—in hopes of prying these last, most crucial facts from Chaison?

It wouldn't work. If it had been a matter of saving his own life, Chaison might have told them everything. Even if it had been the integrity of his own nation, Slipstream, that was at stake, his will might have failed him; he was starting to hate Slipstream, or at least its government, for abandoning him to Falcon.

But the one whose life would be threatened if Falcon knew his secret was Venera, Chaison's wife. It was she who had discovered how to gain entrance to the sun of suns, she who knew how to temporarily shut down its suppressive fields. While Chaison had plummeted his ships into Falcon Formation's skies, Venera had entered Candesce during its night cycle and, at a predetermined moment, flipped whatever switch controlled the fields. Chaison's ships had one night and one night only to use their radar to ambush and destroy Falcon's invasion force. As Candesce shrugged itself awake, Venera had thrown the switch again and left.

At least, he assumed she had left. The plan was for them to meet up again at their home in Slipstream. Chaison had been captured after plunging his flagship into Falcon's new dreadnought like a dagger into the flank of a monster. He only hoped Venera'd had better luck getting out of Candesce.

He was rehearsing the lies and half-truths he would give these men, as he'd been taught in the admiralty, when something flicked past the window. He and the reporter both looked, but whatever it was, was already gone. Probably a bird or one of the thousands of species of flying fish that drifted through the clouds here on the edge of civilization.

Oddly, the visitor's eyes flicked to the window and then he said, rather loudly, "Well, we'd best get started with the serious questions, then."

The reporter grunted and turned to the wall of implements and devices behind the podium. The visiting professor chose that moment to grin openly at Chaison.

And then he winked.

"He really hates being burned," mused the reporter. "Too bad the furnace isn't working today. We could try . . ." Somewhere nearby there was a heavy impact, a thump that Chaison felt rather than heard. The building oscillated slightly.

The reporter frowned and turned just as something shot past the window. For an instant a blurred line hung there; then with a crunch and a snap of dust the blur resolved into a heavy iron chain. It stretched taut across the window, quivering slightly.

The reporter gaped at it. "What is *that*?" At that moment his mild-looking visitor tossed the dossier aside to reveal a wicked-looking blade in his hand. With well-practiced economy of motion, he plunged it into the reporter's back.

As the reporter pawed at the tools of his trade, twitching his life out in silence, his killer undid the manacles that bound Chaison to the wall. "He and his kind have debased our profession," he said to Chaison. "It's become diabolical, really. I'm told there was a time when we reported what we learned to the *people*. Can you believe it? So don't question my motives. —Not that a little cash incentive isn't a helpful motivator at times."

"What are you doing?" asked Chaison weakly.

"I should think it was obvious," said the professor. "Earlier, while I had the room to myself, I weakened your restraints. Let me show you." He yanked on one of the straps and it came out of the wall. "The story will be that you took advantage of the chaos to kill Kyseman, here. I doubt anyone will question that too much, after everything else that's going to happen."

Kyseman. The name rang in Chaison's head as he climbed off the rack. He rubbed his wrists. "What's going to happen?"

The professor just smiled. "Hang on," he said. Then he wrapped both his arms around the podium.

The unmistakable crackle of gunfire sounded through the window. Chaison jumped over to it and just as he touched the lintel another length of chain whipped past, tightening against the stonework and throwing chips and dust into the air. He looked past it.

A squat, barrel-shaped ship hove into view. It was peeling away from the prison wall, jets straining, as dozens of tracer rounds drew lines in the air around it. Chaison barely had time to say, "Oh—" before the ring of rockets around its waist lit and it jumped away.

The chain flickered out, an iron link between ship and building. The blare of the rockets was insanely loud; in seconds the little ship had disappeared behind billowing smoke and flame. And as the chain hauled on the stonework, the weightless prison began to turn.

"Do they have a toy called a yo-yo in your country?" asked the visitor. Chaison caught the windowsill as it began to move away from him. "It's very simple," continued the visitor. "You wrap a string around something and when you pull the string, the thing spins. It's a principle you can apply to anything, really . . ."

Chaison turned to him, grinning. "This place! It's not one building, it's five or six—"

The visitor was laughing now. "Make that eight. Various block houses and small jails that were towed here and nailed together to make a bigger structure. Not very stable. Prone to coming separated in strong winds—did you know that? Probably not, they don't advertise it to the prisoners. But your rescuers," he nodded to the window, "they found out."

The sky was spinning past, the little ship fast disappearing past the building's corner. Chaison craned his neck to watch it. "Who are you?" he asked. "And who are they if you're not one of them?"

"I told you," said the interrogator with a shrug, "I'm merely upholding the sanctity of my calling. I received a request to attend an interview, and at first I thought it came through official channels; by the time I learned otherwise, the cash incentives attached to it had . . . convinced me to do the right thing.

"As to who they are," he added, jabbing a thumb at the window, "I really don't know. All I know is that they were very specific about who they wanted broken out of this hellhole." From the hallway came shouts and the thud of men bouncing off the walls. Chaison and the professor both turned to look, but nobody opened the door.

Chaison turned back to him. "What do I do?"

"Just stay here. Your people will send someone along in a few minutes—when they circle back. This room is in one of the least well-secured blocks. We calculated it'll be the first to go."

Chaison nodded—then thought of something. "Wait—one of my countrymen is here too. One of my original crew. I can't leave without him."

The professor shook his head. "Oh, no. Absolutely not. I forbid it. You're to stay here, otherwise the plan won't work."

Chaison glared at him. "You don't understand. He's just a boy, and it's my fault that he's here. I can't leave him."

The clouds outside were moving past with startling speed now, and Chaison felt centrifugal force pushing him against the window. Creaks and groans sang through the prison's structure.

Chaison jumped to the door. He pulled it open. "Are you coming?"

The professor grimaced and shook his head. "That would be suicide. You broke out of your bonds, remember. I had nothing to do with it."

Admiral Chaison Fanning turned to go, then glanced back. "I suppose I should be grateful," he said, gesturing at the lifeless body of the chief torturer. The visitor smiled, but he hadn't caught Chaison's meaning; much of the satisfaction Chaison might have felt at his torturer's death had drained away the moment that the professor had said his name.

No longer a monster but a man, dead Kyseman rolled over in the air, seemingly to sneer at Chaison one last time. Chaison turned away and climbed into the slowly tilting hall.

CHAIN HISSED ACROSS stone and with a final twitch, let go. With grand gestures the whirling prison began to come apart: first its spidery docking arm flung itself out, piers grasping at cloud before it detached and sailed away; then hundreds of barrels and crates broke free of the simple twine that had tied them next to the service entrance. They flew scattershot, two smacking into the warden's catamaran just as a mob of outraged prison guards was trying to board it. One barrel shattered the windshield and the other knocked off an engine.

Chaison Fanning flinched at a sound like machine-gun fire, which seemed to be coming from all around him. It started at the far end of the building and raced toward him through the structure. It was the sound of nails exploding free of wood and cement. The place was creaking and groaning like some fevered giant, and the hexagonal corridor was visibly twisting as Chaison bounced down it. He knew every turn and straightaway of these institution-green passages and quailed at the thought of retracing the path to his cell. Only the giddiness of possible escape gave him the strength to climb up, hang on and turn over, then climb down, then hang on, then leap across twenty feet of air to the next junction. The centrifugal gravity wasn't much, but it was more than zero and zero was all he'd dealt with for months. Every day, Chaison had exercised single-mindedly for as long as his meager diet would let him, but even so he couldn't keep this up for long.

His little cell block was a bit more solid than the rest of the structure. Here the stone was silent, only the circular swing of weight indicating that something was wrong. Chaison bounded along, rounded the corner to his hallway—and ran right into an obese jailer who was having trouble with his footing.

The jailer sputtered for a second. "L-loose!" he shouted as the wall behind him became a floor. He flailed and sat down.

"I'll have those keys," said Chaison, leaning in. The jailer swung his baton wildly, rapping the former admiral on the elbow. He jumped back again, hissing.

"Help!" The jailer scrambled to his feet but kept going into the air as with a wrenching *bang!* the cell block separated from the rest of the structure. Daylight suddenly washed around the corner.

Chaison tackled him while he was gaping and managed to grab the baton out of his hand. He swung it two-handed and knocked the man's head into the wall. The jailer groaned and curled into a ball.

"Here! What are you doing?" Two more officers appeared silhouetted against the new sunlight. They had swords.

Chaison grabbed the jailer's keys and bounded away. The other two shouted and followed.

Now that the cell block had left the rest of the building it was weightless again. This might have given the jailers an advantage, but they hesitated at the pandemonium of enraged and excited shouting that had erupted from the cells. Chaison made it to the doors before they could catch him. He found the one he was looking for and slammed the master key into its lock, twisting it hard. Before he could get out of the way the door exploded open and someone shot out into the corridor. Chaison threw the keys to the slight figure who'd emerged from the cell, and turned to meet the two officers.

Both lunged, swords flashing. Chaison had rehearsed a moment like this for months—fantasies of escape had helped keep him sane—and was ready. He used the baton like a dagger in a hand-and-a-half duel, sliding it along the first man's blade and twisting, then doubling in midair and kicking him in the face. In a moment he had the man's sword in his own hand. He turned, too late as the other raised his hand and chopped—

—And missed as a ragged boy, no more than twelve years old, jumped him from the side. Before the jailer could turn his sword on the boy, Chaison leaped after him and stabbed, pinning his forearm to the wall.

As the jailer howled the boy turned, and Chaison was able to properly see him for the first time in months.

A scrawny gargoyle of a kid, cheeks sunken, eyes black beads in well-defined sockets, all framed by a wreath of oily black hair—for a second Chaison hesitated, sure that he must have opened the wrong cell. Then the apparition spoke in a familiar wheeze. "Sir! You look a sight, if'n I can say so."

Chaison laughed. "You should talk, Martor! Are you strong enough to handle a sword? There might be more."

Martor grinned hideously. "They been letting me out to run laps in the hamster-wheel, the fools. I'm good." He jabbed a thumb at the row of cell doors. "What about that lot?"

"Let a few out, I suppose. They'll make a good distraction while we get away."

"We? Who's this we you're talking about?"

Martor exchanged a wide-eyed look with Chaison. The voice had come from one of the cells, and it was familiar. Chaison went to the blank iron door and rapped it. "Excuse me?"

"Am I part of your distraction?" said the voice. It held over-
tones of power, as if the speaker had once been an orator or
singer—but it was thin now, and desperate. "After all this time, is
that the only role I can play in your escapade?"

Chaison blinked. "A-ambassador?"

"Who do you think I am, you ninny? I am the very Richard
Reiss whom you kidnapped from a life of privilege and luxury to
aid you in your suicidal little expedition. I'll have you open the
door this instant, unless you fear my quite-justified wrath at your
theft of my life and reputation. Open up, sir, if you love your
country and countrymen!"

"Sheesh, that's him all right," said Martor. He flung back the door,
and they were greeted with a vision of bushy gray hair and wild
eyes. Only the wine-colored birthmark on his cheek was familiar.

". . . Or were you just going to abandon me after all this
time?" Reiss, it seemed, was nearly in tears.

Chaison tossed him the baton and he caught it clumsily.
"Never," said the admiral. "I gave up a guaranteed escape to return for you. Now come with me if you ever want to see your
home again."

The two men and the boy turned and leaped toward the light.

THE LITTLE TUG hove next to the window of the interrogation cell. While men stood on the hull and laid down suppressing
fire against the few officers still in the building, Venera threw a
grapple across the short space and hooked the bars of the
window. At her order, a spring-loaded winch whirred into action
and the bars cracked, squealed, and then burst outward.

She stuck the barrels of two pistols into the room, and then her
head. She glared at the body of the chief interrogator, then raised
an eyebrow to the other man, who was still clutching the table
stand. He shrugged.

"Not here," he said. "But free, last I saw."

She cursed and withdrew. Seconds later the tug's engines howled into life and it shot away. The visiting interrogator watched from the window as it vanished in the mist.

He looked around at the thousand and one clouds that dotted the free air here at the edge of Falcon Formation. "Good luck with that," he said with a short laugh. Then he returned to his table to wait for his own rescue, and in the meantime thought about how he was going to spend the money the mysterious woman had paid him.

2

CHAISON AND HIS men spent the night huddled within the tenuous, lacy heart of a vast cloud. On their way out of the prison the boy Martor had nabbed a little pedal-fan used by the jail's gardener. The fan had a pair of straps that went over the shoulders, a seat on a short pole, and a pair of pedals mounted above a three-foot-wide propeller. To anyone watching they would have seemed a strange and pathetic sight: three prisoners inching their way between clouds the size of cities, one pedaling madly while the other two held onto his shoulders. To the left, the clouds were gray silhouettes framed by a bright blue sky that cradled a distant sun. Parades and banners of white vapor dotted the blue in swirls and walls that receded to infinity. On the right the clouds were white with reflected light, but their backdrop was a fathomless indigo. No artificial sun shone within those depths; there were no habitations within the daunting abyss known as winter.

They had argued about whether to go that way. "We ain't gonna get caught!" Martor had insisted. "We can sneak 'round the skirts of civilization, sticking to the twilight, until we reach the edge of Slipstream. Then . . ." He'd been interrupted by Richard Reiss's cynical laugh.

"We three, weak, starving prisoners, in our thin rags? You propose, lad, to consign us to the cold and the dark, where we will pedal this little contraption," he shook the fan's strap, "four or five hundred miles to safety? What will we eat? Hope?"

They had glared at each other and Chaison Fanning had to smile at the contrast between them. No one could have mistaken the wide cheekbones, broad brow, and august nose that Richard presented to the world for the compact cleverness of Martor's face. Being half-starved and begrimed seemed to make Martor more resemble himself—apprentice card-cheat, confidence man, and barracks trickster that he was. It was a standoff between a dignified if filthy Poseidon and every mother's nightmare child.

He let them bicker for a while because the activity seemed to be bringing them back to life. Eventually, however, Chaison said, "I have to agree with Richard. We need food and better clothing. — Besides, the police sharks will find us whether it's bright or dark, and they can range farther and faster than we can."

So as Falcon Formation's three suns flickered and dimmed, they whirred cautiously into a gray cocoon of vapor and prepared to sleep. They ripped their sleeves and tied the loose ends together; Martor, ironically the strongest of them, kept the straps of the fan over his shoulder. All made automatic checks in their pockets for anything that might drift away, though they had inventoried the stolen prison guard uniforms numerous times throughout the day.

Breaks in the haze showed shadowing clouds casting vast shafts of rose-colored light across the sky. The sight was familiar and reassuring; all three of these men had been born and raised in this world of air. The only gravity they knew was man-made in the rotating wheel-shaped towns that dotted the bright spaces around Virga's artificial suns. Chaison was acutely aware that these were not the skies of Slipstream, though, because he'd been raised in the city of Rush whose sky was crowded. No town-wheels lit as the light ebbed in this place; the air wasn't peppered with house-sized balls of water, the diaphanous nets of farms with their drifting galaxies of plant life, or the thousand-and-one vehicles and apparatuses of thriving commerce. There was no firm dividing line between civilization and winter, but if there had been he was pretty sure they'd be on the wrong side of it right now.

When full dark came, they tried to sleep. Quite unsuccessfully.

"What an irony!" Richard Reiss said after a while. Chaison started, and a tug at his shirtsleeve indicated Martor had done the same. "What?" he asked testily. He'd thought, just maybe, that he was drifting off.

Richard sighed heavily. "Months I spent dreaming about getting out of that damned hellhole. Months spent imagining what my first free night would be like. Oh, my fantasies were elaborate, gentlemen! Satin sheets, gentle gravity, warm candlelight. How I miss gravity! And yet, here we are, enshrouded in a directionless dark even more complete than the cells we left. If not for the fact that I can hear you breathing, and you, Martor, incessantly scratching—why, I would think I was still back there. These last hours . . . seem like a dream."

Chaison nodded. During nights in his cell he had sometimes lost the line between dream and hallucination. It was easy to do in weightlessness and dark.

Martor was lucky to have been allowed to use the prison's little centrifuge. Without gravity to struggle against even the most iron-willed inmates were doomed to weaken over time. Your bones would become brittle after a few months, your limbs barely able to move much less resist when the guards came for you. The simple omission of weight guaranteed Falcon Formation a quiet, riot-free institution.

Chaison had refused to succumb to that weakness. Every morning, as light returned the world to him, he would start bouncing gently from wall to wall, stretching out his limbs. The fingers of his left hand would touch concrete and push off, then, moments later, his right hand would touch the opposite wall. He would push with one foot, then the other. He would gradually increase the pace until he was kicking off with both feet and stopping himself with both hands—or failing to stop himself, and rolling into the impact with his shoulder. He had found every conceivable method for exercising against those walls and in the course of doing so had learned the contour of every knob and ridge left by the builders.

None of this exercise had helped the one part of him whose strength had been sapped over the months: his sense of purpose. Chaison's life had always been structured around duty and suddenly he had none. Without it, he had been dying inside.

Now he found himself clinging to these two men not for protection or companionship, but because they gave him a reason to be here.

He would see them safely home.

"Tomorrow should be eventful," he said. Richard scoffed, and Martor growled something at him.

Then the boy laughed. "Listen to me, complaining! I should be grateful."

"And who would have thought," said Richard, "that you would be grateful to be cold, shivering, and stranded in a cloud in the dark?"

For some reason this seemed hysterically funny, and they all laughed, a little bit too long.

"So, Martor," said Chaison after a while. Then he hesitated. "This is going to seem terribly inconsiderate, after all we've been through. Since I'm pretty sure I'm not an admiral anymore, I'd like you to call me Chaison. And I'd be honored if I could address you by your first name . . . but I'm ashamed to say I don't know what it is."

Martor snorted. "You been busy—and hey, you were the admiral and I'm just a press-ganged go-fer."

"Maybe so, but we shared an adventure few men could boast of. And I sent you—" *on a suicide mission*, he didn't say. But Martor had known it at the time, and had gone anyway.

"I got out okay," chuckled Martor, and a strange sense of relief flooded Chaison. Here was someone who had been there, who had experienced the battle just as he had. Small matter that Martor was the least significant crewman in the fleet, and Chaison its admiral. They had shared something.

After a few moments, though, he had to say, "I can't help but notice that you haven't answered me."

Martor shifted uncomfortably. "I don't like my first name," he said after a moment. "I always used to get jibed about it."

Richard Reiss guffawed. "We promise not to 'jibe' you. Well, don't keep us in suspense, lad. What is it?"

Another short pause. "Darius."

"But that's a fine name," said Chaison.

"Yeah?" Darius Martor sounded hopeful.

"Your name is a device, sir," said Richard in a lecturing tone. "You need to ensure that all your tools are appropriate and well kept up. —If you really think it doesn't suit you, you should change your name."

"Change it? But my father named me!"

"Ah . . . sentimentality." Chaison pictured Richard nodding in the darkness.

"Darius is damned well my name and I'm keeping it. And, and what about you?" asked Martor hotly. "Is that birthmark on your face a tool? Or just something you live with?"

"Now that you bring it up, actually I do find it useful. It makes it easy for people to remember me," said the former ambassador to Gehellen. "When I was a boy it was a great source of grief to me. The other children would mock me and I was beaten a few times. I learned to negotiate my way out of potential trouble, a talent that has taken me far. Perhaps I owe my career to this mark. As I said, you must employ all your devices."

It wasn't lost on Chaison that Richard had neatly deflected Darius's anxieties about his name while simultaneously bringing the conversation around to the subject of Reiss's own virtues. He added this datum to his mental fact book.

The following silence was a bit more companionable, though. Chaison actually smiled and (though he was sure there was nothing to see) looked around himself. To his surprise, he saw a faint red blur far below his feet.

"Do either of you see that?"

"What? Where?"

"Well, I'd point, but that's kind of useless right now. . . . I see a red light."

There was a pause, then the other two said, "Oh!" simultaneously.

"Not a town light," said Richard.

"Not a ship neither," added Darius.

"Nor a sun. I—"

"Shh!" Chaison waved a hand. "Listen!"

He had mistaken it for distant thunder—otherwise, he might have heard the thing's approach half an hour before. From the direction of the glow there came a deep, steadily modulated rumble, a ululation in the lowest register the human ear could discern. It rose and fell very slowly, but it was growing, and so was the light.

"That wouldn't be our mysterious benefactor, would it," said Richard Reiss nervously. Chaison had told them how the jail had been destroyed, giving what little description he could of the tug whose chain had spun the place to pieces.

"Whatever this is, it's much larger," he said unnecessarily. The red glow was beginning to permeate the cloud now; Chaison raised his hand before his face. He could make out his fingers against the umber light.

Now two vast crimson patches appeared, slowly turning in the night. They must be separated by a hundred yards at least, but were clearly part of one thing. What monstrous body lay invisible behind them?

Suddenly Richard laughed. "Oh," he said. "*That's* all it is."

Darius glared at him. "What? What's all it is?"

The foundry emerged from the mist like a photographic image appearing on paper. First to fade in were the platforms where men were working. Silhouetted against hellish flame, the figures were using long metal rakes to roil the chondritic coal in two giant kilns. The kilns were mounted upside-down with respect to one another, and the whole structure slowly spun to provide the gravity that the rendering process required. Now that the platforms were clear, the twenty-foot-wide scoops below the working platforms faded into focus. These were sucking in fresh air and causing one note of the foundry's continuous low roar.

Chaison shook out his clenched fists, willing himself to relax. Of course it was just industry, no monster: foundries and factories used prodigious amounts of oxygen, so they had to keep moving. This one was like a huge propellor blade—jet engines below the scoops kept the whole thing spinning—which hove through the clouds at a walking pace, harvesting air and spewing yellow smog behind it.

"That may be just what we need," he said, pointing to the clot of shacks and storage lockers at the foundry's central point. Ladders led from there past the angled stacks to various levels. Aside from allowing the scoops to bring in air, the furnaces' rotation gave a direction to the flame inside. In zero gravity, fire would otherwise expand briefly in a sphere then choke on its own smoke.

The shacks would contain supplies—spare overalls, maybe even something that flew better than this damnable fan.

"Is this a wise course of action?" Richard was frowning at the little human silhouettes that were slowly rotating around them. "What if we're seen? —Caught?"

Chaison looked at him levelly. "What if we're not? Besides, Ambassador, the men at those furnaces can't see anything beyond their own hands. They're flooded with firelight."

"Ah. Good point. But what if there's—" He didn't finish, because Darius was already pedaling madly. The little fan made a farting whir in the air below his feet, and they drifted slowly toward the flame-gouting behemoth.

Not the most dramatic charge I've ever led, Chaison thought wryly.

Something flickered at the edge of his vision. He whirled, just in time to see a slim gray shape vanish into the darkness behind them.

"Sharks!" Well, *a* shark, at least. If it had smelled them, the thing would be well on its way back to its pen in some police cutter. No way they could catch it, even if they'd had proper foot-fins or wings. The things were demoniacally fast. Sometime during the near-mythical creation of this world, their DNA had been sprinkled with genes from bees; even now the little bastard could be doing its directional dance in front of a police inspector. Writhing out how many people it had seen, their direction, distance, and speed.

The boy redoubled his pedaling. Chaison was afraid he was going to break the frail little contraption, but soon they were gliding up to the rope-and-beam tangle at the weightless center of the foundry. Chaison strained, fingers grasping at a rope—not necessary, they would get there no matter what now, but he was desperate for the touch of something solid. Then he had it and was hauling himself onto the hexagonal plank platform that fronted the shacks. He yanked his sleeve free of Richard's and drew his sword.

The foundry was basically a shaft of girders a quarter mile long, spun around its center. The smokestacks that topped the furnaces tipped back and vented into the air behind the foundry's direction of motion; they helped propel it through the air. At the very center of the beam, nestled among the shacks, was an unlit pilot house. Chaison flung open its door and entered, sword-first. There was no one inside.

The pilot house was a simple wooden box, eight feet square, that stank of smoke and iron. Under the open window at the front were a set of levers that controlled the foundry's speed and direction. For an absurd moment Chaison thought about using the foundry itself as their getaway vehicle. It was at least as fast as the foot-fin.

But the fact that there was nobody in here made him uneasy. "Surely they'd still want to watch out for lakes or boulders, even if there are no towns nearby," he shouted over the incessant rumble. "I would have thought a man would be on duty here at all times."

"You'd be right," said a gravelly voice. "—Careful," it went on as Chaison made to turn, "I've got a bead on your head."

Slowly, Chaison turned and looked behind him. Fitted into a shadowed corner of the pilot house was half a man; he was missing his legs, and in their place wore some kind of harness. But the wide-barreled scattergun in his hands made any other details unimportant. It was aimed now at the center of Chaison's chest.

"Get your two companions in here," said the man. Chaison could see Darius's face faintly lit in the doorway. He half-smiled.

"I don't actually control them," he said with a shrug. "If they decide to leave me here with you, there's nothing I can do about it."

"Tempting though that might be, sir, I at least am a man of honor," said Richard Reiss. He glided into the pilot house with as much dignity as his ragged appearance would allow. A moment later Darius followed.

"Ha!" The man with the gun edged forward a bit. In the ruddy light of the twin infernos Chaison saw that where his lower legs had once been, now he sprouted a three-foot metal spike, which was strapped to the stubs of his upper thighs. In freefall he would have no need for legs anyway, so Chaison did not make the mistake of assuming that he would be any less maneuverable or strong than the three men he faced. He had a leathery face and as he grinned displayed numerous gaps in his teeth.

"The secret police are looking for you three," he said with

satisfaction. "Also some other escapees, but three Slipstreamers in particular. Now, lest you think you might be able to take me, you'd better know that I rang the emergency bell before I bundled myself into that corner there. The boys'll be up any second now to see what the fuss is about."

He might have been bluffing. He wasn't. A few minutes later Chaison and his companions found themselves being shoved into a windowless locker by four sweaty, heavily muscled men. The foundry workers laughed and clapped the pilot on the back, and spat on their new prisoners for good measure before slamming the door shut.

Richard glared at Chaison. "Now was this a wise course of—"

"Shut up!" snapped Darius. "We had to try."

Chaison ran his hands over the back wall of the locker, looking for weak planks. "We have to keep thinking," he said. The workers had taken their two swords and Richard's baton. Without some means of locomotion, they were stranded here even if they did get the weapons back. "Did you spot any boats on the way in here?"

"Two," said Darius. He cocked his head. "I think I hear one of them leaving right now."

"Off to fetch our jailers," said Richard. "Wonderful! A short holiday this has turned out to be."

This made Chaison laugh. "Would you rather have spent the day in your cell? Pardon me for interrupting your valuable routine."

"It's not that," said the former ambassador sullenly. "It's just that . . ."

"What?"

Richard looked uncomfortable. "They're bound to punish us for this," he said, almost inaudibly.

"Don't get all schoolyard girly on us," Darius shot back.

"I haven't seen Richard act the coward yet," said Chaison. "Seems to me he has a healthy sense of caution, and there's no shame in fearing a beating. The question is whether that fear stops you from acting."

"He didn't want to come here," Darius pointed out.

"Well, he was right, wasn't he? It was my call, Darius."

Darius had no answer to that.

They passed the next hour in silence. The locker was small and uncomfortable; light entered it only through chinks between the stout planks. The faint illumination was occasionally blocked, indicating that there were men right outside the box.

There was little the three escapees could say to each other. They had been through a lot together, prior to their first imprisonment. All three had been aboard Chaison's cruiser when it attacked Falcon Formation's new dreadnought. They were taken separately from the wreckage, and it was only recently that Chaison found out that Darius Martor had survived and was imprisoned down the hall from him. Richard Reiss's presence was a surprise, and he wondered if there had been other survivors from the *Rook* in the prison. He would probably never know.

And what would happen now? Doubtless they would be separated. They might even be executed, though it was hard to anticipate the logic of Falcon's byzantine legal system. Certainly these few minutes together were likely to be the last they would ever see of each other.

The silence stretched.

The door banged and then opened a crack. It was the legless pilot, grinning at them through the gap. "Police ship's on its way," he said. "Just thought you might want to know."

"I didn't actually, but thanks," said Darius.

"Hey . . . sorry, you know?" said the pilot. "It's the fortunes of war—there's a reward for you and I'll be collecting it. Good for me."

He glanced around himself and then leaned closer to the door. "But I wanted to ask you fellows. Is it true? Did Slipstream really blow away half our fleet? Stop an invasion of your country?"

Chaison lifted his chin. "We did, and we did."

"Well . . ." The pilot rubbed his chin. "That's something. Good for you, I say. Don't hold with the government just stealing another sun. Wrong, is what it is."

Richard Reiss cleared his throat. "Sounds like you have a civilized sense of justice, sir. Why then are you turning us in?"

Chaison half-saw the shrug around the crack of the door. "Like I said, I need the money. Anyway, how was I to know how you would be? —Three starving prisoners with swords and me all alone on my bridge? I wasn't going to take the chance. Still won't."

"I assure you," said Richard, "we are men of honor."

"Too late for that."

"Then why in hell's name are you talking to us?"

There was a pause. "No reason, I guess," said the pilot gruffly. Chaison half-saw him jab his thumb in the direction of a light that had appeared over his shoulder. "Come on out. It's time." The pilot moved back and the door swung open.

Feathered sharks circled a knife-shaped police cutter with Falcon's bird-of-prey sigil on its side. The cutter was wingless, relying entirely on four barrel-shaped jets at its stern for motion and guidance. Both sides of its hull had windscreens and a seating area; a rectangular hole in the hull joined these two areas. Each side swarmed with black-uniformed men.

The cutter's spotlight slewed over the foundry until it caught Chaison and his companions. Then it fixed on them. Someone shouted, "Prepare to be boarded!" through a bullhorn.

The legless pilot glanced at Chaison nervously. Men like him often had reasons to work and live far from well-policed areas. Had some run-in with the law driven him here, to perch on this metal monster at the very limit of Falcon's sunlight? If so, it would have been useful to know that sooner. Chaison grimaced. It was too late to look for leverage on any of these men.

Someone threw a line out to the cutter, and several policemen started hauling on it. It bobbed closer while the sharks dove in and out of the spotlight's beam. Nobody spoke, and Chaison knew the strange paralysis that leads sane men to allow themselves to be led to execution.

Then there was a *whhf-bang!* and one of the sharks was suddenly an expanding pink cloud. Drops of cool blood sprinkled past Chaison. He blinked, and another shark exploded. A little white contrail led away from it, wavering into the dark.

He heard the tearing growl of a jet. It was headed away—no, it was coming back. The men on the cutter were scrambling for weapons, shouting and pointing. Something dove out of the cloud bank and suddenly everybody was shooting.

"Damn!" The pilot cringed back and the men holding Chaison's arms let go. The foundry workers were jumping behind whatever metal object was closest. Yet Chaison found himself still centered in the spotlight's glare.

Another bang and the light jerked to one side. Chaison and Darius dove for cover. Seconds later, Richard Reiss appeared to realize that he was the one remaining target on the foundry's superstructure. With a yelp he too scrambled for a hiding place.

An expanding oval of fire had appeared at the back of the cutter. Some of the policemen were squirting dead air into it from the ship's tanks while others fired blindly into the red-lit clouds.

"Over here!" That was a woman's voice. Chaison looked behind him and spotted a dark figure in the air behind the foundry. The figure waved an arm. "Come on! What are you waiting for?"

"This is that moment I'm told you're supposed to seize," said Richard Reiss. He leaped clumsily past the spiraling smoke spumes of the foundry. Chaison glanced at Darius, who shrugged. They hauled themselves hand over hand past the shacks at the foundry's center then launched themselves off the structure.

The dark shape became clearer: it was a slim figure dressed in black, sitting on a cloud-gray jet bike. The bike, a simple wingless jet engine with a saddle, was whining and spinning in a tight circle. Evidently it wanted to be moving. The woman kept her feet in its stirrups as she stretched out to catch Richard's hand. She drew him in then grabbed the handlebar of the bike and steered it over to collect the other two men.

"I shot one of their engines but it won't slow them down for long." The voice was definitely female, but Chaison barely had time to glance at her before she gunned the engine. He grabbed for something to hold onto, caught a metal ring on the side of the barrel-shaped bike and then found himself hanging off it by one hand as the jet opened up with a roar and they shot away from the foundry.

They shot through clouds and jet-black air for ten long minutes while Chaison did nothing but try to keep his grip against the battering headwind. Little lights glinted in the distant skies, some solitary, some in the glittering circles of wheel-shaped towns. The night would have been beautiful were it not that Chaison was wrapped in exhaustion, anxiety, and pain from his strained muscles.

Dawn was coming, an irregular pulse of red somewhere far below, when Richard Reiss finally let go and fell behind them. Instantly their unknown pilot throttled back. Idling, she circled them around to where Richard stood on the air, arms crossed indignantly.

"See here," he said. "How much of this abuse are we to endure in the name of liberty?" Faint rose light was touching the limbs of the clouds behind him, making him look incongruously angelic. "I demand a rest!" he continued. "And an explanation! Who are you? Did you break our prison?"

Chaison climbed up the side of the now-drifting bike. The pilot was slim, dressed in a sharkskin leather coat with a flying helmet on her head. She reached up now to slide this off. Chaison heard Darius grunt in surprise.

Her eyes were startling: huge blue ovals above a very tiny nose and mouth. Her hair was a black pageboy frame for this extraordinary face.

Darius swore. "A winter wraith!"

The woman showed white teeth in a wide grin. "I'm so much more than that." She laughed. Her voice was a strong and confident alto.

The bike was close enough to Richard now that he could reach out and grab Chaison's hand. The admiral drew him in until he could get a grip on the bike again.

"Surely you weren't the one in that tugboat?" he asked her.

She hesitated, then smiled broadly and nodded. "Pretty neat trick, huh? But then I lost you again in the chaos. Took this bike out 'cause it's faster."

Richard and Darius looked openly skeptical, but Chaison put out his hand for her to shake. "Then, accept my thanks for taking such risks on our behalf. I am Chaison Fanning, admiral of Slipstream. These, my companions, are Darius Martor and Richard Reiss."

She might be lying—but he'd seen his wife perform greater feats. He wasn't going to take the chance—yet—that she wasn't what she claimed to be.

"Well met," she said, shaking his hand firmly.

"But why would you risk yourself for us?" asked Darius bluntly.

"Because," she said as she gunned the engine again, "I am Antaea Argyre, and I am a scout for the Virga home guard."

Before Chaison could say another word she had opened the throttle, and away they shot.

3

"QUESTIONS, QUESTIONS," LAUGHED their rescuer when they finally stopped, an hour later. It was full day now but Chaison had no idea where they were. The hazy sky was dotted with farms like green clouds and spherical groves of fruit trees, punctuated with the occasional blocky building and crisscrossed by the miles-long ropes that served as roads between town-wheels. They had fled farther into Falcon Formation, rather than to sunless—and empty—winter. That fact was surprising.

Antaea Argyre had a leather-clad toe hooked through one of the bike's foot straps; that was her only contact with the machine. They hovered near the white wall of a cloud, miles from the nearest solid object. Chaison and Darius had joined her in weightless postures next to the bike, but Richard Reiss stubbornly clung to its solidity.

"First," said the long-limbed winter wraith, "you've all asked whether your nation remains safe. I can say that it does. You've won your border dispute with your neighbor Mavery. There is some unrest in your capital, Rush, but I really don't know the details of that so don't ask me.

"To answer your question, young master Martor, we are going deeper into Falcon because they are searching for you in winter—the other direction." Darius nodded grudgingly.

"As for what you muttered under your breath earlier, Mr.

Ambassador, yes, winter wraiths are real and not mythical. —And we're perfectly human, though the ancient anime-mods that make us look different from you make us shunned and persecuted by all. I am a Pacquaen, just as you are Slipstreamers." She gazed coolly at Richard until he nodded.

"Have you any food?" interrupted Darius. She smiled, and reached for one of the bike's saddlebags.

"I was wondering when you'd ask that. But as to your question, Admiral, I truly am a member of the home guard. I'm surprised that you've heard of us."

Chaison wanted to snatch the bread from her fingers. Instead, he let the other two take theirs first. It was the duty of a commander to eat last.

"I met one of the guard in the Virga tourist station," he said. "Some months ago."

Her eyes widened. "You've been there? You're a remarkably well-traveled man."

Chaison examined her discreetly as she spoke to the other two. He was trying to make the sort of assessment of her that he routinely did with men under his command. The first thing he noticed was that her eyes were the most exotic thing about her. The rest of her face, though strangely childlike, wasn't entirely outside the norm. Her flying leathers were of a typically Meridian design and could have been bought anywhere in Slipstream, Falcon, or Mavery. Ditto for the flying helmet, the bike, and its panniers. She did have a faint accent, but he couldn't place it.

The one striking exception were her split-toed, high-heeled leather boots. They laced up to just above the knee, and both were heavily scarred and scraped. The six-inch heels were blue steel, sharpened to a point. These weren't shoes. They were weapons, and well-used ones.

Antaea was nearly six feet tall but had the slenderness of some-one raised under lower than standard gravity—or of someone who had spent a considerable part of her youth in freefall. Those long limbs were strongly muscled. Her breasts were not so large that her loose jacket had to visibly accommodate them.

She glanced at him and he found himself looking away quickly before he could help himself. Damn.

"Tell me about this home guard," he said as what remained of the bread finally made its way to him. "I was told you were defenders of Virga—of the whole world. Defenders against what?"

She grinned. It made the sides of her oval eyes rise, creating for an almost demonic expression. "You know, I couldn't even con-vince most people that we exist. Your average farmer or city boy believes that Virga is infinite. They think this," she waved around at the skies, "is all there is. It's so nice to meet people who know differently."

"Any civilized man could tell you that the world of Virga is an artificial construct," sniffed Richard. "It is a vast balloon, adrift in empty space."

She eyed him. "That just tells us all that I spend very little time around civilized people."

"That's not what I—"

"No matter." She shrugged. "The thing is, our world is very small. It's—what, five or six thousand miles in diameter? Would it surprise you to learn that our ancestors built far larger structures elsewhere in the universe? Or to learn that most of those struc-tures are still inhabited?"

"You defend us against people from other worlds?" Darius's voice fairly dripped skepticism.

"You describe my job most precisely, sir."

Darius stared at her in disbelief, but Chaison frowned for a dif-ferent reason. "Have you traveled outside our world, Antaea?"

She hesitated, then shook her head. "Those who have, do not recommend it."

She didn't elaborate on that. Chaison wondered which of several lines of questioning he could pursue with this strange representative of an unknown power. He decided to venture one that had been eating at him ever since he'd heard of the guard. "Just how can the guard defend us against powers capable of building whole worlds? Surely not with guns and swords."

"Ah, Admiral! Such professional curiosity." She waggled a finger at him. "My masters have decreed that such knowledge is not fit for the ears of Virga's citizenry."

"Really? Why not?"

She hesitated again. He watched her carefully, trying to read her subtle expressions. Was she doubtful of what she was saying now? "Because of the potential for harm such knowledge brings," she said at last. Then she smiled, in a rather cunning way. "I could give you an example."

"Please do," said Richard before he saw Chaison's warning glance. The admiral already knew where this was going.

"Something happened some months ago," said Antaea. She pretended to examine a distant flock of fish that was nosing around the outskirts of the cloud. "We call it the outage. The outage hit the guard like a lightning bolt—shocked us out of our complacency. We'd come to rely on Virga's built-in defenses rather too much, and then one day, those defenses simply stopped working. The outage lasted less than twelve hours, but it threw my masters into a panic that has yet to subside."

Now Darius was trying to catch Chaison's eye. The admiral kept his face as neutral as he could, merely nodding politely for Antaea to continue.

"I had been enjoying a much-needed vacation in the skin of the world," said the Pacquaean. "I was flying with dolphins when the base sirens went off. When I got back to the installation the whole place was in an uproar. The protective field produced by the sun of suns had failed. And in the frozen vacuum outside the world, some things were uncoiling from a very long slumber.

"There was a battle. I was mercifully not involved—but we lost a lot of people that night. When the field was restored just as unexpectedly, we took stock. Many members of the guard had lost their lives trying to prevent the engines of the enemy from piercing Virga's skin and entering the world. Most had succeeded—but some of the enemy's devices had gotten in."

Chaison was thunderstruck. Had he known that his actions would have such dire consequences—threatening the very world—he would not have embarked on his desperate mission to save Slipstream. He would have found another way.

Antaea eyed him. "Mmm. Some of our agents were dispatched to locate the infiltrators; they're still searching. My team and I were sent in for another reason: to find the cause of the outage, and ensure that there isn't another."

"And did you find it?" he asked.

"Not yet." She looked him in the eye. "But I'm close."

"Well, the best of luck in that," said Richard jovially. "But we have more pressing concerns than your 'outage,' I think." Richard reached for the bread. "Lady, my companions may be graceless, but I appreciate a good rescue and therefore, thank you from the bottom of my heart. Sadly, however, I find myself compelled to hurry our little party along. As in, where can we find some less incriminating clothing, a decent meal, and beds to sleep in?"

Antaea was obviously not sure how to take Richard's trumped-up charm. She looked down her diminutive nose at him. "Is it not enough for one day that you be rescued, you need some luxury items to be satisfied?"

"One man's luxury is another man's necessity," he said mildly.

Chaison watched this exchange, smiling. "Richard is right,

though," he said. "We're of no use in these stolen uniforms. And without some gravity to condition our muscles, we'll be of no use in a fair fight either."

"Gravity I can give you," said Antaea.

SHE MADE GOOD on that promise later in the afternoon, when they stopped at an out-of-the-way farm. While deep inside Falcon, near enough its suns to bask in good growing light, the place was far from any town. Its owners were the perfect customer for an itinerant gravity seller, and Antaea just happened to have an official-looking work permit that said she was one. Nothing happened in Falcon without a permit, "So," she said, "I carry a good supply." All forged, as it turned out.

The three men hid in a nearby cloud while Antaea rode the bike over to the farm. The place consisted of a cubic house tethered to a heavy water tank and several carefully managed crop balls. Each ball was woven from the stalks of a thin but stiff vine, and was about two hundred feet in diameter. Thousands of clods of earth floated free inside the loose structures, each one invisible within a sphere of leaves. This farmer was growing soy.

Gravity selling was a good cover for an agent like Antaea. As the owner of a bike, she could travel freely to the more remote corners of the nation without causing comment. The more remote the area, the more welcome a seller was; after a few minutes of negotiation, she received enthusiastic consent from this particular farmer to give him some weight. The two could be observed testing the chains that tied the house to the water tank, then they let these out until the two objects had a few hundred yards of line between them. Next, Antaea flew out to pick up the Slipstream fugitives.

"Turns out he's hoping to make a trip to one of the towns in a few days, and wants to get into shape," she said. "He's willing to look the other way if you keep to the tank. You've got weight for the day. Use the time well."

She dropped the three men off at the rust-painted water tank, then returned to lash her bike to the side of the house opposite the chain mount, and at right angles to it. She settled into the saddle and gunned the engine. As the jet strained and pulled, the house began to drift away, the chain unraveling behind it. A few minutes later it snapped taut, and then because her bike was pulling at right angles to the line joining house and water tank, the whole assembly began to rotate.

For a few hours, the farmer would enjoy the centrifugal gravity allowed by the rotation. He had weight as long as he didn't step out his front door; Chaison, Darius, and Richard would have to stay atop the windblown surface of the water tank to gain the same benefit.

It was worth it. As the headwind from their rapid spin grew to a gale, Chaison felt a sensation he hadn't had in months. His head drooped, his shoulders slumped as he sat on the tank. After a few minutes Antaea had reached the safe rotation rate for the chains, which provided more than half a gravity. Up in the house, the farmer would be testing his legs; Chaison needed to do the same. He stood, carefully keeping a grip on the chain.

"Oh, that hurts!" The other two were also standing up. They grimaced and laughed as the deficiencies of their weightless exercise made themselves apparent. There were muscles essential to walking that Chaison had not been able to tone in all his cell-bound bouncing and isometrics. He wobbled on his feet.

Richard had it worst. Apparently his discipline had broken down early in their incarceration; he would need extensive rehabilitation to regain his gravity legs. Aside from the weakness, there was the little problem that the authorities would be looking for three Slipstream men crippled by chronic weightlessness. If they could spend a week or two in a town, he would at least be able to stand up and walk a straight line; the irony was that they couldn't visit a town until he could walk. The police knew this. If Richard could get his legs before they visited a town, their chances of getting caught might diminish—a little.

Chaison gazed out at the swiftly turning sky. He had no idea where they were relative to their home. Their fates were in the hands of a complete stranger. Almost out of habit, he began to form plans—half-conscious decision-trees like the look-ahead moves in a chess game. What if Antaea was an enemy? What if the guard were friends? Could they commandeer a ship from somewhere? Or could they fly all the way to Slipstream hanging off of Antaea's little bike?

Darius was frowning into the sky as well. They stood in a small circle all gripping the same chain, and for a few minutes he seemed to be thinking of something clever to say. Finally he said, "Well? When do we give her the slip?"

Chaison glanced up the chain at the upside-down house far overhead. "I'm not sure we do," he said.

When Darius returned an incredulous look, he shrugged. "Her intentions aren't clear, but I don't think she's our enemy. If she were, she wouldn't have admitted to being a member of the home guard."

Richard snorted. "You believe that drivel about her being the one who freed us?" He was trying valiantly to keep his knees from buckling.

"If not her, then who did it?" said Chaison. "As to the home guard . . . She knows too much to be making it up. The 'outage'— clearly she's referring to our shutting-down of Candesce's defensive systems. It never occurred to me that it would be noticed so easily. But then, it never occurred to me that there might be a real and present threat outside Virga that the system was keeping at bay. If I'd known . . ."

"If you had known, your wife would still have talked you into it," said Richard Reiss. Chaison glared at him, but it was true. The plan had been her idea, and she could be very persuasive. In fact, she had committed a minor case of blackmail to guarantee that Chaison would adopt the plan. He hadn't really had much choice.

Remembering that made him smile. She was an unstoppable force, that was for sure. But it had been months now that they were separated, and for all she knew he was dead. Venera was nothing if not practical. What if she . . .

He pushed the thought away. Against all expectation he'd been given a chance to return home; there was no use in speculating on what disasters might befall him when he got there.

Richard groaned and sank to his knees. "This is hell," he whined. "I need a soft bed."

"Rusted iron will have to do," said Chaison. "Be glad that you have that to lie on."

"I don't trust her," said Darius. "She's led us further into Falcon, not out of it. And she knows we caused the outage! How do you know she's not bringing us to some hall of justice crammed with home guard judges and lawyers and juries?"

"We don't," said Richard from his now prone position. "But the admiral is right. We have no choice but to go with her. She is being very systematic, isn't she, Fanning?"

"Yes . . ." He squinted upward again. "She looks childlike, but it's a dangerous disguise. Her easy manner through all of this suggests that we're not the first ones she's rescued from a tight scrape. That may be her job, in fact."

"I still can't believe she were the one who freed us," said Darius. "Maybe it was . . ." He fell silent.

Chaison thought about it. Who else could have done it? The admiralty? —No, they would never officially sanction an operation like that. And Chaison had been going against direct orders in undertaking his preemptive attack on Falcon. The pilot of Slipstream could not be publicly pleased by Chaison's gambit, however he might feel privately. But perhaps a cabal of loyal officers . . .

He shook his head. The officers most loyal to him were all dead, killed in the savage battle that had ended Falcon's invasion attempt. He had seen their ships destroyed.

This train of thought was as depressing as his speculations about Venera. Shifting from foot to foot, he forced himself to concentrate on the here and now. "Antaea wants information," he said, "but she's come to us alone and made no attempt to signal anyone else since she found us. As long as she's unable to compel us to tell what we know, we have a bargaining position: we know exactly what caused the outage, and if Venera returned safely to Rush, we have the means to cause or prevent another one." *Provided Venera hasn't thought up some other plan involving the key to Candesce.* It was the key—an innocuous white wand you could put in a pocket—that had made the outage possible. It had given Chaison's little fleet access to the interior of Virga's oldest and most powerful sun, Candesce, which had operated without human intervention for centuries. While the key was in play, another outage was possible. And if Antaea was right about the consequences of even a few hours of defenselessness, Virga itself could be destroyed if Venera chose to use the key again.

They talked more about what to do—how to sneak back into Slipstream and what to do when they got there—but eventually drifted into silence again. There was too much unsaid between them. There was the pain of long isolation and deprivation, of months living with the near-certainty that they would never see their homes and loved ones again. There was their complete ignorance of conditions back home; what had Antaea meant about "unrest" in Rush? Had any of the ships in Chaison's expeditionary force returned home safely? Did the people even know that Falcon Formation had tried to attack Slipstream? And if and when they returned, would they be hailed as heroes, or hung as traitors?

It wasn't that he was ungrateful at having escaped, Chaison decided as Falcon's suns began their evening fade; it was that everything in him had been suspended for months, both joys and, it turned out, worries. Both were returning to him now in equal measure, and he was unused to dealing with either. He was in emotional turmoil, and so must Darius and Richard be.

By evening their gravity began to fail. Unless Antaea ran her jet constantly, air resistance would slow down the rotating bolo of house/tank in just a few hours. As the frantic rush of air slowed to a trickle, and weight became a barely felt tendency, Antaea launched herself through the open air, foot-fins flickering in the golden light, to alight on the tank with elegant grace. "He's agreed to two more days of weight," she said without preamble. "You're going to need every second of it to get yourselves into condition."

Chaison nodded. "You mean to take us to a town."

Darius scoffed. "Why not make a straight run for Slipstream?"

She shook her head. "Your border is hundreds of miles from here. The air is thick with habitation and clotted with everything from garbage to trees. I couldn't get the bike above fifty miles per hour in clear air, ten in a cloud. And there's a lot of cloud lately, unusual amounts apparently. If we tried to go by night we'd barely crawl, the air is so full of hazards. And we'd be heard for miles."

"Four people hanging off a bike is bound to cause comment," added Chaison. "We're just going to have to be patient, and do things a bit differently."

She nodded approvingly. "Right. So here." She held out some bundles of clothing and a rolled-up shaving kit. "Make yourselves presentable. You can use some water from the tank you're sitting on. Any look that's different from what you had as officers will do. — But get rid of those beards, for God's sake."

Richard Reiss eagerly took the shaving kit from her. "Beards are not common in Falcon, I take it?" he said.

Antaea shrugged. "I don't know. I just don't like them."

She kicked off toward the farmhouse. Chaison couldn't help

but sneak a look at her kicking legs and leather-sheathed backside as she moved off. He noticed Darius noticing and sighed, turning his attention to the pile of clothing, but his visceral reaction to Argyre's presence made him think of Venera. Was she safe? How had she taken his disappearance? She was as brave as any soldier. She would be all right.

He lay down on the cold metal to sleep, repeating it as a sad mantra: she would be all right. She would be all right without him.

THREE DAYS LATER they found themselves waiting in a cloud again, this time within sight of a town-wheel that glittered in the distance like a hoop of gold filigree. Antaea had gone ahead with the bike; she was visible for a while but soon became just one dot among dozens buzzing around the axle of the wheel. She disappeared, and time dragged.

"I ache in every possible place," said Richard. "I seriously doubt I'll be able to stand when we get there."

Chaison had been counting how many seconds it took for the great wood-and-rope wheel to make one revolution. "From the place's size and rate of rotation, I'd say they're doing a comfortable point-six gee at the rim. Not a full gee, thankfully. You should be fine, Richard."

The wheel was like a very long plank bridge rolled up so that the two ends connected. Rope spokes crisscrossed the interior circle, suspending a set of buildings at the "axle" as well as a few dozen platforms at varying heights above the rim. Some of these hanging streets held halfway houses of streamlined shingle where people unused to gravity could conduct business and even lodge at lower gravities—point-three, point-one and so on up to zero at the axle. The buildings were connected to the outer rim by stairways and elevators.

Boats, bikes, and cargo nets hung off the rim of the wheel; the nets rippled in the wind from the town's rotation. Every now and then jets along the rim growled into life, rumbling for a few minutes as they kept the wheel spinning at its standard rate.

Several hours passed, with nothing to do but stare at the town and maintain station with the foot-fins Antaea had provided. Suddenly Darius exclaimed, "Where's the bike?"

He pointed. Chaison looked and saw a big pair of midnight-black wings cupping the air. The figure was heading in their direction—it was in fact Antaea, wearing a pair of angel's wings and towing three more pairs. The wings had a span of sixteen feet and were strapped to her shoulders. Foot straps let you kick downward to wind a heavy spring mounted between the shoulders; after a couple of kicks the spring released and the wings would flap once. Angel's wings varied hugely in quality and efficiency, but these ones were painstakingly handmade using real feathers. They brought Antaea across the half-mile of air between the town and the cloud in only a couple of minutes. She pulled a strap to fan the wings for maximum braking and glided to a stop next to Chaison.

"Here." She was panting slightly, a thin sheen highlighting the muscled contours of her skin as she handed him the bundle of wings. "There's day laborers' clothes, too," she said, pointing to a smaller bundle amongst the feathers. "You should get into them."

Darius was indignant. "Where's the bike?"

"The bike had a bullet hole in it," said Antaea. "Didn't you notice that? It was bound to cause questions; plus the policemen I plucked you from knew you were rescued by someone on a bike."

"What did you do with it?"

"This town is called Songly," she said, nodding to the wheel. "A member of the home guard lives here. I dropped it off with him and used some of our ready cash to buy these." Richard and Darius were strapping on the wings. They both seemed familiar with them, but it was Richard who seemed most adept. —That made some sense, as they were rarely used by the military, and Richard had spent twenty years living in a city that was mostly weightless.

Chaison tested his own stirrups, doing a tight loop in the air. The wings made a satisfying *whoosh* as they flapped. "Ha! I almost feel like a man again."

"Good." She was smiling. "Now we should split up. I've reserved a suite for the admiral and me at Family Residence 617. You two can bunk in the hostel."

Darius looked like he wanted to protest, but by this time they had all come to understand the logic of the situation. They couldn't afford to fit the profile the secret police were looking for: three Slipstream men traveling together possibly with a companion. They would split up and converge upon the wheel at the end of the day, when the workers who had fanned out at dawn returned like bees homing in on a hive. Richard and Darius were going to avoid the lower-gravity buildings and go straight to the rim of the wheel. The police would not expect them to be able to walk yet.

It came as no surprise that Antaea wanted to keep Chaison close. He was her assignment, obviously; the other two men were of little interest to her. She might be trying to split him off from his friends, and maybe she had accomplices waiting to kidnap him in town. But he had no real choice but to trust her—for now.

An hour later he was tottering up the stairs to their suite, the now-folded wings on his back feeling like a bag of rocks. Antaea showed no sign of strain as she pattered ahead of him.

Residence 617 was a government-subsidized hostel for married couples. It was illegal in Falcon—as in most nations—to refuse someone a night's gravity, so all town-wheels made provision for visitors. Still, the furnishings in the little suite were spare. Once inside Chaison shambled to the window and looked out. They were high up here, in a low gravity zone; the wheel's rim lay hundreds of feet below. Way down there, the larger itinerant's hostel where Darius and Richard were staying was a gray rectangle on the thin brown ribbon of the rim. He wondered if they had made it there without collapsing.

"Oooh . . ." He sank gratefully onto the single bed, only noticing when he flung out his arm how narrow it was. Antaea was stowing their wings in the closet, feet planted wide and swaying slightly. This was the first he'd seen of her in gravity.

He rolled over and pushed himself to his feet. "I guess I'll take the floor," he said.

She had her head buried in the closet. "What?"

Chaison cleared his throat. "I said, I guess I'll take the floor."

A sly smile played across her face as she leaned back to look. "No you don't. You've been living weightless for months now. A night on wooden planks would put out all your joints, from spine to ribs to knees. Get on the bed."

"Ah, well. It's a bit narrow—"

Antaea made a face. "I'm sleeping on the floor."

"Yes of course."

"Your gallantry is going to be the death of you, Admiral." She pried off her toeless boots.

Chaison allowed gravity to guide him to the mattress. "What's that supposed to mean?" he asked, but he wasn't really listening anymore. The sensation of lying down overwhelmed him. In less than a minute, he was asleep.

ANTAEA WATCHED THE admiral until she was sure he was asleep. Then she lay down beside him and turned away. She forced her breathing to slow and her limbs to relax, though her mind was buzzing with anxiety and plans, scenarios, disastrous possibilities. She needed this rest, at least as much as the man next to her. She closed her eyes.

Ten minutes later, she sat up and cursed under her breath. She rolled off the bed and went to sit in the room's only armchair. She sat there for a long time, not moving, not seeing the wall her gaze was aimed at. Then, reluctantly, she dug in her jerkin for her locket. Unclasping it, she held the silver oval up to the shaft of sunlight canting through the window.

She flipped open the locket and gazed at the portrait inside it. Telen Argyre smiled out at her sister with a direct, clear gaze that spoke volumes about their childhood—how it had been spent in free airs, how she and Antaea had been encouraged by their parents to learn and explore as much and as often as they could. How they had learned courage, and when an extraordinary opportunity had presented itself, had jumped at it together.

After a moment Antaea pried at the edge of the portrait, and it swung out of the locket. On its back was another picture, this one a black-and-white photograph.

It would be hard to tell for somebody who didn't know her, but this was also Telen. She sat in a straight-backed chair, her arms painfully stretched behind it and tied at the wrists. Her feet were similarly bound and there was a cloth gag in her mouth. She stared beseechingly at the camera.

Fingers trembling, Antaea restored the original picture. She glanced at the unmoving figure on the bed. She nodded to herself.

She would need every advantage she could get. And sympathy for this foreign admiral was the one thing she could not afford, if Telen was to survive.

4

CHAISON AWOKE GRADUALLY. He should have relished the feeling of freedom and gravity against his back; but instead he found himself immersed in sad doubt. As his eyes started to open he clenched them shut against the light, vision darting left and right at the roseate emptiness as he struggled to locate the source of the feeling.

There it was: last night he had fallen asleep to the feel of gravity pulling at him, and thought it wonderful. Now all he could think was that the last time he had lain so, Venera had been beside him.

He could see her face, her brave smile, as they'd parted for the last time. He was on his way to Falcon Formation in the *Rook*, she on her way into the blazing epicenter of Candesce. Chaison had known that she had been able to enter the sun of suns and that she had caused the outage, because the *Rook*'s radar had operated flawlessly for twelve hours during his attack against Falcon's fleet.

Chaison opened his eyes to behold the plank ceiling of the couple's hostel. An unwaveringly steady wind rattled the windows. He let out a long, shuddering sigh.

Venera Fanning was cunning, ruthless, and pragmatic. In the heat of battle she had shot people without hesitation. She had even bartered with pirates for the lives of Chaison's crew.

Still, she would have had to escape Candesce after the outage, and evade the roving ships of Gehellen, a nation that had put a price on all the Slipstreamers' heads.

Was she languishing in some Gehellenite prison right now? It was a thought he'd managed to avoid all these months, but now he couldn't shake it.

He rolled onto his side and levered himself upright, then wobbled to his feet.

"Ah!" Antaea emerged from the suite's small privy. He blinked at her in surprise.

She had changed into a colorful silk blouse and loose pants, and a big pair of round sunglasses covered her gigantic eyes. After her flying leathers, this was an unexpectedly feminine look.

"Where did you get that?"

Antaea cocked her head. "From my luggage. You should buy a knapsack, you know. You'll be conspicuous traveling without it."

He looked down at the drab day-laborer's clothes he'd acquired at the farm: toeless boots, stovepipe canvas pants of dull gray, and a sleeveless suede shirt. There were several pouches attached to the belt; all were currently empty.

He struggled to shake off his depression. "Money," he said slowly. "And personal effects and . . . official papers, I suppose." What did they use in Falcon? He vaguely knew that it was a monumentally bureaucratic state where you needed a passport to go to the bathroom.

Antaea was holding out something: a sheaf of just such papers. "Already done," she said. "I've been up for hours. I thought you needed your sleep."

"I did, thanks." A little annoyed at himself for letting her get so far ahead of him, he took the papers, examined them, then slid them into one of the pouches. "Denarian. What kind of name is that?"

"It's our family name, *husband*, don't forget it," she said with a grin. "Do you feel up to a walk up the street?"

He eyed the door. This hostel was at about a quarter of a gravity, but even that made the exit seem miles distant. But, though gray, the light welling in from outside was full daylight. If he was supposed to have business in this town it would be suspicious if he kept to his room.

"We need papers for my men too," he said. "Where did you get those, by the way?" He took a cautious step toward the door.

"My contact," she said. Her cool fingers wrapped around his bicep to steady him. "The same one I got the wings from. We're going to see him, actually—just as soon as we find the ambassador."

She assumed she was setting the agenda; well, let her—for now. Then he realized what she'd just said. "Richard? You can't find him? . . . That means you did find Darius."

"He was waiting where he was supposed to be," she said, rolling her eyes. "Richard had risen even earlier than I, and staggered out the door somewhere. He's probably lying in an alley somewhere by now, unable to stand—so we'd better hurry."

Chaison cursed, and pushed open the door to the vision of a cloud-wreathed sky and the morning bustle of the town.

Songly looked like it might hold seven or eight thousand people, whose dwellings were mostly strung along or above a wooden hoop a mile and a half in diameter and one hundred feet wide. At four points around the circle, clustered jet engines stuck into the airflow beyond the wheel's rim. Chaison could hear their roar and feel their pull every now and then, as they strained to keep the town spinning fast enough to produce gravity on the hoop.

The wooden street holding the hostel curved upward ahead and behind him, ending in a tiny-looking railing about three hundred feet away in either direction. It gave the hostel the appearance of being at the bottom of a giant bow of planking and rope. He walked to the side-rail of the narrow street, reaching up to grasp a taut rope that thrummed in the steady wind of the town's rotation. He looked down a dizzying vertical drop to see the roofs of houses and other buildings that clung to the inner surface of the narrow strip of wood. The people had built them high here because there was no horizontal space for growth. As a result Songly's main street was shadowed at the bottom of a slot walled with buildings.

Overshadowing this main avenue other partial streets hung suspended in the rigging of the spokes. These lay at different heights and none of them were fully circular, but traced arcs of different lengths. The high streets held farmer's markets, micro-g rookeries and gardens, and bike warehouses. Ladders, stairways, and cage elevators connected them to one another, to the main street and up to the wheel's axle.

The travelers' hostels were located on one such high street, which hung in the quarter-g zone dizzyingly far above the main hoop.

Chaison and Antaea found a cage elevator, and in short order they were inching their way down to Songly's main street. He wasn't sure what he'd expected from Falcon Formation, something more regimented and sinister, he supposed, and there were some hints of that. People wore a sort of uniform, a gray affair of shirt, jacket, and slacks that had different kinds of lapels on it signifying different societal roles. On the other hand, most people seemed to have customized their garb, adding spots of color or bright scarves in apparent defiance of their attire's drabness.

Physically, the town looked like any other. The air around it was crowded with the usual free-floating buildings, cargo nets full of supplies, gigantic balls of water and waste, and boats. The boats were the only surprise: Falcon's dark reputation hadn't prepared Chaison for the bright colors of their flower-shaped vessels, typically just a big basket with anywhere from two to five big petal-shaped wings made of wicker stretched with cloth. People standing in the basket could tilt the petals or swing them up and down. They were typically flown by several people with their backs braced against the bottom of the basket, each using his or her feet to work the spar of a petal. Glimpsed from the elevator they looked like animate flowers, opening and closing, slowly pulsating their way across the sky.

The elevator touched down in crushing gravity and Chaison staggered onto Main Street. Darius Martor slouched out of a nearby doorway, looking about as guilty and self-conscious as it was possible for a boy to get. People were ignoring him, luckily; many of those striding to and fro here were day laborers or students as he was pretending to be, and many would be visitors. After breakfast they would leave the wheel in a swarm, dispersing to farms, foundries, fish farms, and all the other sundry industries that were easier to conduct in freefall than under gravity. Some left by simply jumping over the rail into weightless air; Songly was only rotating at sixty miles per hour or so, so the workers could unfold their wings into the rushing air stream and dart away with ease. Some kids were doing the same—not to leave the town, but simply stepping outside it to let it spin past before snatching a bungee rope to reel themselves back in half a mile or more away. The air around the town was full of swooping, diving forms.

Soon Songly's heaviest street would be deserted. It would be easier to find Richard then, but it would also be easier for the secret police to run them down.

Luckily gravity-challenged visitors were common here; canes were plentiful for those unused to gravity. Despite his sense of urgency, Chaison trudged slowly into the main street. Antaea's heels sank into the wood with every step, and made a slight pop when she raised her feet. Darius hesitated, shifting from foot to foot about forty feet away, until Chaison grimaced and gestured him over.

Chaison looked left and right, then headed right. "You think he went this way?" asked Antaea.

"He'll be driven to head downward," said Chaison with a shrug. Down wasn't a direction in any normal sense: if you walked opposite the town's spin, you weighed a bit less and felt like you were walking down a slope even though the street was level. Up the street meant in the direction that the wheel turned. It felt like you were climbing an incline if you walked in that direction; hence, many towns had public conveyances that traveled only in the up direction. Songly was not big enough for such conveniences. In his weakened state Richard would almost certainly have taken the easier way.

"Sorry I lost him, Admiral," said Darius. "We didn't bunk in the same room. Didn't want to draw attention to ourselves."

"Don't call me that, damnit." Chaison was having trouble concentrating; the sheer number of people, the gabble of voices, sudden gestures, and shouts were nerve-wracking. It had been months since he had seen more than two men at a time, and those he had shied away from. The market stalls were crowded together cheek by jowl, many with nothing but turning blue sky as their backdrop. He wanted nothing more than to totter back to the suite and collapse on the bed, so his thoughts about Richard Reiss were turning murderous when Antaea grabbed his arm and pointed.

"Look. The pols."

He shuddered involuntarily. There were four of them, "secret" policemen who were not secret at all but swaggering goons in the pay of the state. They were entering the town's market, a madcap tunnel of buildings and balconies and stairs that absorbed the street and houses a hundred feet ahead. Each policeman swung a baton loosely, and seemingly at random they were stopping people and demanding to see their papers.

One raised his club to rap a man on the shoulder. The citizen exclaimed in anger and started to turn—then, seeing who had struck him, he ducked off to one side, bowing slightly.

As he moved out of the way Chaison spotted Richard Reiss.

The ambassador was sitting cross-legged on the planking not ten feet from the oncoming policemen. He had a small wooden box in front of him and was doing something with his hands, waving them in the air. There was a crowd of children half-encircling him.

"What," Antaea hissed, "is the idiot doing?"

Chaison watched Richard's lips moving, and realized that he had been hearing him for almost a minute already. He hadn't realized it was Richard because the accent was perfect Falcon.

"Beware the wrath of my mighty Sword of Documentation!" boomed Richard Reiss as he raised one hand dramatically. "You shall not pass, lest you sign all these forms and in triplicate!"

The children were laughing.

The secret policemen walked up to the Slipstream ambassador.

One of them glanced at Richard; another nudged the first and pointed in another direction; and they all walked on.

"I don't believe it," muttered Antaea. Richard Reiss lifted the string puppets he had been manipulating, and managed to get them to walk on the box in perfect imitation of the secret policemen. The kids howled with laughter, slapping each other on the backs and pointing at the targets of Richard's jape.

Richard looked up and spotted Chaison. "The world is safe from the Undocumented—for now," he declaimed. The puppets turned and bowed to one another. "Come back in ten minutes for another show." The children dispersed, chuckling, and Richard grinned as Chaison and Antaea walked up.

"A small donation would be appreciated, citizens," he said loudly. Antaea gave Chaison a long-suffering glance, then dug in her satchel. Quickly she stooped and slipped something to Richard; Chaison caught a glimpse of white and knew it was his identity papers.

With difficulty, Richard levered himself to his feet. "I was trying to keep ahead of those chaps," he said, nodding at the policemen. "Didn't think I'd make it another ten feet, when I spotted these puppets for sale at one of the market stalls. Lucky thing one of those jailors of ours had a little loose change in his purse." He patted his stomach as if puzzled at how little there was to his waistline. "Alas, I no longer have enough for breakfast. I was hoping some of the children would be forthcoming . . ."

Chaison had to laugh. "Quick thinking, Richard. —And the accent—"

"A close observation of people throughout my life, and a somewhat unhealthy obsession with fitting in," observed the ambassador, "have over the years given me some useful skills."

"Come," said Antaea. "We have an appointment."

"Ah—with a friendly meal, I hope?"

CHAISON HAD NOT missed the prominent posters that festooned every wall in the market. Some were old, and said things like COMPLIANCE BREEDS SECURITY and REPORT STRANGERS. The only reassuring note was sounded by one big poster proclaiming the imminent visit of a circus, featuring Corbus, STRONGEST MAN ALIVE! This sheet was half-covered, though, with new pictures showing young men with chiseled jaws and perfect biceps holding guns aloft and gazing into some idealized distance. These had captions like JOIN THE FIGHT FOR FREEDOM and IF YOU HESITATE, WE ARE LOST. They suggested several ominous possibilities, so when Antaea rapped on the side door of a tall whitewashed building, he was ready with questions.

The door was opened by a lean man with sunken cheeks and a buzz-cut. He wore livery, and behind him the space opened out into an airy vista of green fronds and polished stone pillars. "Come in," said the servant. Then he glanced down, and saw Antaea's footware. "I'll have to ask you to remove those. For the sake of the floors . . ." She grimaced, but complied.

The first storey of the estate was one open chamber that wrapped around a courtyard garden. The tall arches surrounding the garden let plenty of light into the rest of the space; there were no outside windows. It was clear why the doorman had been leery of Antaea's heels: the floor was inlaid with mosaics, a sensible decoration for a surface that tended to flex with the town's rotation. There were stone statues here and there—all tastefully painted. The bustle of the street was completely extinguished.

The servant didn't bother to lead them, merely pointing to the garden. A man leaned on one of the pillars, his hands jammed in the pockets of a loose robe. The robe hung over a more conventional manager's outfit of tan suede.

He stepped forward as Chaison approached, holding out his hand. "Admiral, welcome. I'm Hugo Ergez. Have no worries, I'm a friend." He looked drawn and tired, as if he hadn't slept—and Chaison could see deep lines scored around his eyes and the sides of his mouth, indicators of someone who bore up under a great deal of physical pain. Indeed, as they moved past him Ergez picked up an ornate cane and walked not more than ten feet before easing himself into a high-backed wicker chair.

"It is useful," said Ergez as he placed the cane carefully to one side, "for allies of the home guard to be wealthy men and women. We are better placed to use our resources than the poor."

Antaea sat near him. Her expression was oddly neutral, as though she felt she needed to not comment on Ergez's statement.

"Thanks for the identity papers," said Chaison. He and the other two men found some benches on the other side of a low drinks table. He sat with relief. "You do know that all we seek is to return to our homes?"

"So Antaea told me." Ergez pointed to some cups on the table. "Please. . . . In truth, your mission, whatever it is, is not my concern. I am merely here to assist."

"Can you assist with answers to some questions?"

Ergez exchanged a minute glance with Antaea. "Insofar as I can, yes."

"Is Falcon Formation going to war with Slipstream?"

Ergez looked surprised, then laughed out loud. "Slipstream?

On the contrary! Falcon and Slipstream are fast friends these days. It's a, oh, what's the phrase—a 'new era of cooperation between our two peoples.' I believe that's how your pilot put it in the newspaper article. . . . Which is around here somewhere . . ."

Darius frowned, looking from Ergez to Chaison. "Yeah but I saw all those recruiting posters. The market's full of them."

"Quite." Ergez lost his smile. Having offered drinks to his guests, he proceeded to take up a cup himself and lean back in the enfolding wings of the chair. He pursed his lips above the cup. "It's the Gretels that's the threat, Admiral—our largest neighbor, happily for you on the far side of our country from your own border."

"Ah . . ." This was news. It answered many questions—not least being why Falcon Formation had put together a secret force to invade Slipstream in the first place.

Darius squinted at him. "Ah, what?"

Chaison smiled sadly at him. "I'm afraid the attack on us was a sideshow, Darius. They simply wanted to secure their flank before dealing with the Gretels."

Darius sat for a while, absorbing this information. "So," he said eventually, "now that one way of doing it's failed, they're trying the other."

"I'm afraid that it makes it all the more likely that you and I were sacrificed as pawns. We were never traded back to Slipstream because asking would have been . . . impolite."

Even as he said this, Chaison knew he was playing into Antaea's hands. She must have known he would see the recruiting posters and have questions, and now he saw how this interview with Ergez was supposed to go. Too late; he had walked right into her trap.

Darius was scowling off into space. "We can't go home again, is what you're saying."

"Certainly not under your old names," said Antaea smoothly.

Chaison nodded to himself. "But the home guard could help us," he said. Out of the corner of his eye he saw Richard Reiss glance sharply at him. Richard had also seen the vise Antaea was applying.

She thought that he had only two choices: slip back to his home anonymously and build a new life there under an assumed name; or take whatever deal she would propose. That deal would have something to do with his revealing the whereabouts of the key to Candesce. Wherever she was, Venera had it, but Chaison was not about to let anyone know that—not only to keep her safe, but because he knew nothing of this home guard's real integrity or mission. He believed Antaea was who she said she was, but beyond that all was suspect.

Chaison had a third alternative, however, and the fact that Antaea didn't see it marked her as someone whose origin was the lower strata of society. It hadn't occurred to her that Chaison could publically fight to regain his position. He had allies in the admiralty.

He would play for time. "We would be grateful for any help you could give us in returning home. As to what we can do for you—"

A shout interrupted him. The door to the street was open and several men were piling in. One slammed it behind himself and leaned on it, cursing. He was holding his elbow, and Chaison saw blood welling between his fingers.

Ergez levered himself halfway to his feet. "Sanson! What happened?"

The man winced. He was short but lean and wiry, the perfect musculature for a town rigger—which he probably was, judging by his toeless shoes and the utility belt around his waist. "So sorry to disturb you, Mr. Ergez, it's just that you did say, if any of us ever had any trouble with the pols that we should . . ."

"Yes, yes, and I meant it." Ergez made it the rest of the way to his feet. "I just want to know if you're seriously injured."

Sanson shook his head. "Just a cut on my arm and a rap on my head," he said.

Ergez turned back to Chaison and the others. "Sanson and his men have my confidence," he said. "You can speak in front of them."

Chaison stood and walked over to the injured man. "Hold it out," he said in a commanding tone. The rigger obeyed automatically, then started to pull away. "Who's—"

"You can trust him," said Ergez. He was watching Chaison with frank curiosity. Chaison probed the arm carefully, turned the wrist, and examined the cut, which was deep but hadn't hit any main lines.

"We can sew that up," he said, "but you'll be on light duty for a few days. That's your left arm," he commented.

"What of it?" said the rigger, who was clearly deciding whether to be sullen at Chaison's manner.

"It's a defensive wound," said the admiral. He raised his arm in a blocking motion. "You did this. Not wise. You could have lost the arm if he'd been of a mind to really hurt you. You're clearly not a trained fighter."

Sanson glared at him. "It's illegal for a plain citizen to train at fighting."

Chaison reached out, taking Sanson's reluctant arm again. He leaned forward and said quietly, "Does that mean you won't let me teach you?"

The man's eyes widened. He glanced at his still-bleeding arm, then shook his head.

Satisfied, Chaison stepped back and turned to Ergez and Antaea. "We'd be grateful if you helped us return to our country," he said again. "In return, we will teach these men how to defend themselves. We need to get back into shape anyway; it's a perfect arrangement all around."

Ergez smiled, and so did Antaea; but her smile looked more than a little wooden and he suspected she was seething inside.

5

CHAISON HAD BEEN standing at the window of his office one night seven months ago, and so by pure chance he witnessed the rocket attack that set so many events in motion. Lurid red lines had flicked out of the darkness beyond the glitter of the city of Rush—once, twice, three-four-five in quick succession. He stood stock-still, coffee cup forgotten in his hand, as blossoms of sudden fire swelled on the inner surface of one of the biggest town-wheels. Those were the houses of Slipstream's rich middle-class, not the neighborhood he'd grown up in but one just like it. More rockets shot out of the night. Chaison walked unhurriedly to the corner of the little book-strewn room and tugged on the bell-rope. He could hear shouts of alarm ringing through the house.

He returned to the window, but the rocket attack had already ended. Fires leaned into the Coriolis-winds among the buildings lining the inner surface of Rush's open-ended, can-shaped town-wheels. Searchlights sprang to life, their long pale cones darting everywhere, and the town-wheels dumped vehicles into the air. Many of those were converging on the admiralty. Chaison watched their firefly glows approach, mentally inventorying them. Doubt-less one or two of those approaching visitors weren't coming to see Chaison, but were Venera's spies on their way to report to her. Of the rest, though, some would be delegations from the town fathers, outraged that the admiralty hadn't protected them; policemen with reports for the military branch of the Exchequer; members of parliament desperate to appear proactive in the eyes of their constituents; naval captains on their way to him for orders; and of course, there would be someone from the pilot's palace, come to let him know whose head would roll for their failure to foresee this attack.

Only this last visitor worried him—not because Chaison had not foreseen the attack, but because, vocally and publically, he had.

"So, do you think it *was* Mavery?" He turned to find Venera standing hipshot in the doorway. She was dressed in a crimson evening gown but one strap had fallen carelessly off her white shoulder. He walked over to straighten it.

"Mavery's afraid of us," he said. "Why would they invite defeat and humiliation at our hands?" He shook his head. "Your spies were right. I just didn't want to admit it to you."

Venera smiled and reached past his waist, the action causing her thinly covered breasts to brush across his uniform. "I do so love to hear you say that," she murmured. "That I was right, I mean." Then she stepped back, holding up the photograph she'd retrieved from his desk. "Does this seem more real to you now?"

The black-and-white photo was grainy and blurred. He hadn't believed what it showed when Venera first brought it to him. Gradually he had been persuaded that Falcon's new dreadnought was real, was nearly assembled in their secret shipyard, and was more than capable of taking on the entire Slipstream navy. If it wasn't real, then tonight's attack was an insane provocation. If it was, then everything that was happening made a sinister kind of sense.

He shrugged. "So you're willing to admit that *this* is real," she continued, waggling the photo between them. "What about the rest of it?"

He shook his head. "This preposterous tale of a pirate's treasure trove that holds the last remaining key to Candesce? This *radar* technology that your pet armorer believes she can build? You know, it's not about the evidence, Venera; how can I *afford* to believe it? There's just too much at stake."

She stood there for a few seconds, idly tapping the photo against her cheek. Then she shrugged. "It may be," she said as she turned to go, "that soon you'll find there's too much at stake *not* to believe in it."

Venera swept out of the room, and a succession of frantic, outraged, and brisk bureaucrats swept in. War was being declared, the navy mobilized; the admiralty were agreed that Mavery was behind this attack and that an expedition should be mounted against it. Chaison sat behind his desk and listened to them all, nodded, made suggestions, and waited for someone to drop the proverbial other shoe. It didn't happen.

Finally, much too late in the evening, the pilot's seneschal arrived. Antonin Kestrel strode in unannounced, his dark brows beetled in a scowl. "He's not happy," he said without preamble.

"Good evening to you, too, Antonin." Chaison smiled at his old friend; grudgingly, after a moment Kestrel smiled back.

"I need something to tell him," he said after a moment. "You understand. How could they have attacked us like this, so easily? Why were we caught with our pants down?"

"*He* was caught with his pants down because this attack doesn't fit his neat picture of the world." Chaison leaned back in his chair, folding his hands behind his neck. "I told him this was possible, but he insisted on preparing for an attack that fit his preconceptions, and now he's got something else instead. It's that simple."

Kestrel crossed his arms and glowered. "This is not a good time for your rebellious side to surface, Chaison."

Chaison guffawed. "You had that 'side' back at the academy too, if I recall. But in those days, we didn't call it rebellious. We called it common sense. And patriotic."

"I'm not here to listen to another of your accusations about our sovereign's supposed dereliction of duty," said Kestrel. "And as to your theory that someone else is pulling Mavery's strings . . ." He hesitated, then very carefully sat down in the chair in front of Chaison's desk. "You've made no secret of your dissatisfaction, ever since the pacification of Aerie. That operation—"

"—Was a pogrom, and totally uncalled for," snapped Chaison. "And he made me the scapegoat for it!"

"Hero of it, you mean. You owe all this," Kestrel gestured around at the room, "to the fame you deservedly received for that mission. Why can't you be happy with it?"

Chaison snorted. "Be happy with a reputation as a ruthless butcher? The orders were all his, Antonin. He should have the reputation, not me."

Kestrel looked pained. "I'm telling you, as a friend now, that you need to watch your step. You can't publically disagree with his policies. Especially not when so much power is being thrust on you, so unexpectedly." He leaned back and waited.

"Power?" Chaison let a half-smile play across his face. "So he's okayed the mobilization, has he?"

"Against Mavery. You have no other target, not even a target of opportunity." Kestrel stood up, and cast Chaison the sort of severe look—guaranteed to freeze the blood of any civilian or lesser officer—that he and Chaison had once practiced together at barracks. "I'm not playing around, Chaison. This is serious. You have too much power and trust in your hands to be able to afford another slip up."

Chaison stared at him. "You mean I can't get away with being right?"

Kestrel brushed a stray hair off his coal-black sleeve. "Not if it means that he is wrong," he said as he stood to go. "Anyway, he isn't, not this time. This claim of yours that Falcon Formation is behind Mavery . . ." He eyed Chaison, then shook his head. "It's puzzling." He sounded disappointed, but that was all he said and he didn't wait for Chaison to explain.

Chaison sat in silence, perfectly still, for a long time after Kestrel had gone. Then he wrote seven names on a sheet of paper, and rose to tug the bellpull again. When a junior officer appeared he handed him the paper. "Summon these captains to me. Now. Tell them to come alone."

After the officer had left Chaison sat down and steepled his hands, scowling at the disordered piles of papers and books strewn across the desk.

The pilot's deliberate blindness was criminal. All of Slipstream was at stake now, and so quite unexpectedly, he found that he would have to believe in something unlikely—risky, even, if he were totally unlucky, preposterous.

Venera had been right so far. This time, though . . .

This time she had to be.

CHAISON WAS WAKENED by a loud crash. He sat up quickly, wrenching the long muscles of his back. Another crash came, then a series of thuds. Belatedly, the town's collision alarm began wailing.

For nearly two weeks he and the others had stayed out of sight, mostly hiding in a set of windowless servants' quarters on the manor's second floor. Officially they were part of a team renovating Ergez's home and so they could come and go as they pleased, but so far they had stayed inside the manor. After prison, it seemed luxuriously vast.

This noise was new; Chaison dressed quickly and ran down the hall, finding Darius already out of his room and Richard peeking around his own doorjamb.

"What's going on?" asked the ambassador peevishly. "The sun's not even on yet."

More thuds. Now Chaison could hear men shouting in the distance. "I don't know," he said, "but stay here and keep quiet. I'll investigate."

"Sir?" Darius was bouncing on his toes. Chaison nodded for him to follow.

On the way down the stairs Chaison stumbled. "I hurt all over," he said; Darius grunted in acknowledgment. They hadn't been idle over the past days. In fact, they had spent every instant trying to regain fighting trim. Yesterday they had sparred in the courtyard, to Ergez's vast enjoyment. When they weren't exercising they were eating.

The stairs let out next to the courtyard. The square space was lit brightly by gaslight and Ergez stood under its white illumination along with several servants. They were staring up hectically. Suddenly one of them pointed and all of them let out a shout. The servants bolted for the archways leaving Ergez tottering next to the fountain. He put his hands over his head and ducked just as Chaison reached him.

"What—" Chaison started to look up just as something bright flashed in his peripheral vision. There was a tremendous *whack!*, a slap of noise, and then he and Ergez were drenched with a spray of cold water.

"Oh hell," laughed Darius from the wings, "it's only a *storm!*"

Another ball of water shot into the courtyard. This one was as big as a table. It took out one of the statues, exploding into white mist and ricocheting droplets.

The tiled floor undulated and the whole building shifted, some pillars rising a bit, others lowering. Ergez frowned, watching. "About time," he said. Someone had gotten to the town's engines and was cumbersomely turning the giant wheel so that it cut into the oncoming cloud of water balls. "Why didn't they see it coming?"

Chaison shrugged. It had been damnably misty ever since he'd arrived; a strange phenomenon this far from winter. His flyer's instincts helped him picture a vast soft pillow of moisture, squashing its way slowly through Falcon Formation, origin and destination unknown. As long as that moisture was dispersed as cloud and mist, everything was fine. Something was making it condense, however, and the result was first raindrop-sized, then head-sized, and eventually house-sized balls of water. The less frequent but bigger spheres were a navigational hazard, for towns as well as ships.

"Nobody's going to be moving in this," he said. "At least not very quickly."

"I guess you'll be staying with us a little longer, then," said Ergez. He let Chaison help him over to a chair—one well sheltered near the manor's inner wall.

Ergez had some sort of wasting disease. He was fighting it by remaining under gravity as long as possible. Had he taken to flight he would have left the pain behind, but he was obstinate. Chaison liked and admired him for that.

"Every day we stay puts you at risk," he said. "Your hospitality has literally been a life-saver—but if I had my way we'd have left already."

Ergez shook his head. "You wouldn't have gotten far, weak as you were. Anyway, all I've done was put a roof over your head. It was Antaea who snatched you from the jaws of our so-called justice system."

They were silent together for a short while, both listening to the distant shouting and occasional smacking noise of a water ball hitting the town. Hopefully the yelling didn't imply any bigger objects headed their way.

"How is it that you know her?" Chaison asked eventually. "Or is she merely one of your many contacts in the home guard?"

Ergez chuckled. He stretched out one leg, helping it move with his hands. Then he did the other. "Antaea and I go way back," he said. "I met her the day the world was supposed to end."

Chaison barked a laugh. "You *have* to tell me more than that."

Ergez looked innocent. "It's not that we don't want to tell people our stories," he said. "It's simply that most people won't believe us. We get branded liars, heretics, or lunatics—and sometimes all three.

"The world was due to end. Everybody in the guard knew it. A good many citizens of the principalities of Candesce knew it too. They had been forced to move en masse when Mount Ogils plowed its indifferent way through their nations about ten years ago. Ogils is an asteroid much like the one your people have tied their capital city to. The difference is that Ogils is more trouble than it's worth. For centuries now it's unreeled its long orbit around Candesce in an inconvenient spiral, slowly inching its way farther out and farther in with every turn. It had been coming closer to Candesce on its inward swing, and nearer the outer skin of the world on its outward leg. We were afraid it was going to hit the sun of suns—but when the day came, Candesce picked itself up and daintily scampered out of the way."

He laughed at Chaison's expression. "Never heard about that, did you? That's because the sun of suns made its move during the night. Ogils sauntered by and Candesce returned to its place, flicked itself on in the morning and no one was wiser. —Well, except that the vast shadow Ogils cast over the whole world had switched sides, but few understood what that meant. All the principalities knew was that they'd been saved. And we," he smirked, "made sure they thought it was our doing."

Ogils had pushed its way through the crowding principalities, and they chipped and hacked away at it as it passed, harvesting as much of its rock and iron ore as they could. Then it left, and they forgot about it.

"But we were still watching. Having passed through the center of the world, Ogils was now due to leave the world altogether. When it reached Virga's skin, it would keep on straight through it—and this meant it was going to tear a hole a mile wide in the world itself.

"The home guard gathered, helpless. We had ridden our bikes and dolphins along the iceberg-shrouded skin of our world, keeping that jagged landscape in view to orient ourselves, shivering in the terrible cold that radiates from deep space beyond. After weeks of shouting matches and quieter arguments about how to minimize the effect of having a mile-sized hole punched into vacuum, we had cobbled together an inadequate plan. We were going to try to deflect Ogils by peeling icebergs off the skin and towing them into its path. But imagine our surprise when, a hundred miles from the spot where Ogils was supposed to hit the skin, we ran out of bergs!"

Chaison cocked his head, remembering the seemingly endless plain of rounded and pointed white shapes, millions of them huddling in the dark, that he'd seen when his own ship, the Rook, had visited Virga's skin. They had been so densely packed that nothing could be seen of the surface they were stuck to.

"Along a vast line—like the mythical 'shore' of a gravity-bound ocean—the icebergs simply stopped," said Ergez. "We rode up to the black, iridescent surface of the skin. It looked like smooth charcoal. I touched it and it was cool—but not cold.

"Nobody knew what this meant, but we had counted on there being local icebergs for us to harvest. It was while we waited helplessly that I met Antaea.

"We had orders to stay well back from the expected storm of suction that would follow the breaking of the skin. When Ogils went through, it was expected that a hurricane would be born, sucking everything into space and inexorably emptying Virga of its air, though that might take centuries. But as the asteroid approached a cold fog had begun to form, and soon we couldn't see anything. When it became clear that we were standing off too far to see what was happening, Antaea called for new orders. The word came down: hold fast.

"I still remember Antaea's voice," said Ergez, "as she said, 'fuck that, I'm going in.' She held out her hand to me. 'Coming?' "

"What did you do?" asked Chaison. He glanced around the courtyard. The water balls had stopped falling; curiously, Antaea herself had not made an appearance during the commotion.

"I went along," said Ergez with a painful shrug. "She was my ride. We skidded in alongside Ogil's great, scarred black side just as it reached the equally dark wall that separated air and life from vacuum and absolute zero. And Antaea—damn her—flew us right up to the contact-point to watch."

He held up his hands, shaping something in the air. "Here's what happened: Virga's skin stretched, and stretched some more. The air trembled with a powerful vibration that was not quite a sound. And then it snapped, with a sound like the loudest gunshot you could imagine, sharp, startling even though we were expecting it.

"Ogils had cracked in half, but it massed so much it kept on going, peeling back the black skin and grinding loose stones and boulders that flew backward in a cloud. It took a few minutes, because Ogils was moving so slowly, but then it was through."

He said nothing. "So?" asked Chaison. "What happened next?"

"Nothing.

"There it sat, a vast puncture wound a thousand feet across, dented in and utter blackness on the other side. And just a faint puff of air coming from it, where we'd expected a hurricane flowing into it." Ergez shook his head ruefully. "We just looked at each other. And then Antaea said, 'Let's see,' and flew at the hole."

He laughed. "I bailed out that time! While I tumbled in the air, waiting to get picked up by the dolphins, I watched her bike disappear into that black cavern and then, after a few minutes, reappear. She was frowning. 'What did you see?' we asked her.

" 'Nothing,' she said. 'Nothing at all, as far as the eye can see.' "

"That's strange," said Chaison for lack of anything better. Ergez laughed again.

"Yes, and I never found out what it meant. The guard put Antaea's superior officer, Gonlin, in charge of the investigation, but I didn't hear the results of it before I took this duty. And nowadays they don't tell me anything."

Chaison thought again about the brief time he had spent at the skin of the world; his own memories were chiefly of a surreal wall of ice lit by flashing explosions and the green sparks of drifting flares. His expeditionary force had battled pirates there, dodging in and out of clouds and dark. Only Venera's driver, Hayden Griffin, had come close to the skin, as he blew away the points where the bergs adhered to the wall. Griffin had sent a slow rain of icebergs into the path of the arrogant pirates, destroying at least two of their ships.

Funny thing; he'd thought about that battle many times over the past months. Until this moment he had never considered what a rousing tale it would make. "So," he said to Ergez, "does that mean you're no longer a member of the guard? Did you muster out?"

Ergez shook his head. "Once you join, you're in it for life. But you're not always going to be active."

"How does one do that? Join the guard, I mean?"

"We have no recruiting stations, if that's what you're asking," said Ergez. "Some of our people are exiles or the insatiably curious who've left Virga altogether, but decide to return. They find it hard to integrate after what they've seen in the wider universe. Some hear legends of us, and go on great quests to find us. And some are plucked out of dire circumstances by home guard members, and are invited to join." He gave Chaison a shrewd look.

Did Ergez think Antaea was recruiting Chaison and his men? This might be a misapprehension worth encouraging. Ergez had told Chaison that Antaea's mission was not his concern, but it seemed more and more as though he didn't know what it was. Perhaps Antaea's reticence was standard procedure, a secrecy intended to protect the network of operatives from traitors or torture. Or there could be more to it.

Chaison and Ergez chatted until it became clear that no more water missiles were going to hit. Then Chaison walked back to the servant's quarters. He found Darius and Richard Reiss sitting at a little table in Richard's room, talking in low voices. Darius waved him inside.

"It seems our Antaea has a history of being reckless, and of not following orders," said Chaison.

"Ah, a woman after your own heart!" said Richard.

Chaison let that comment slide. He retold Ergez's story, filling in some details about what the edge of the world looked like for Richard, who had never been there. He added his suspicion that Antaea hadn't explained her mission to Ergez.

When Chaison finished Darius leaned back, hooking an arm over the back of his chair (he had to reach up a bit to do this). He was frowning. "That just don't sound trustworthy."

"If Ergez told me that story in hopes I'd reciprocate, that would mean he's curious but can't or won't ask Antaea himself," agreed Chaison. "We should think about what her real agenda might be."

Richard looked from man to boy. "I can talk to her," he said. "In my younger days," he pretended to examine his fingernails, "I was really quite good at pumping people for information."

"You can try," said Chaison, "but I have a more important task for you, if you're up for it."

The ambassador looked up eagerly. "Yes?"

"Puppet shows."

Chaison relished their looks of confusion for a full five seconds before he said, "You seemed to hit it off with those boys the other day. Knowing what Antaea is up to is actually less important than knowing how we can give her the slip. Agreed?" They nodded. "The home guard—according to Antaea—is offering to ship us home through their secret network. Very kind of them, but I don't like the price they're asking: information about the key to Candesce and what we got up to in the sun of suns. Richard, I'd like you to find anything you can about alternate routes home. Small-time smugglers, revolutionary cells—anyone who might be able to help us."

Richard stared off into space. "They'll take me for a spy for the secret police," he said. "I think I know how to convince them otherwise . . ."

"Good. Darius, you and I will—" He stopped at the sound of footsteps in the hall. After a moment Antaea poked her head in the doorway.

"Ah, there you are!" She sauntered in. "Cowering from the storm, are we?"

"And where have you been?" asked Darius indignantly.

"Home guard business," she said. "Very interesting too; would you like to see?" Without waiting she dragged over the clothes chest which was the only piece of furniture in the little room other than the bed, table, and already-occupied chairs. Sitting with her knees high on either side of her, she laid a folded piece of cloth on the tabletop. She withdrew her hands and smiled around at the men.

Taking the bait, Richard flipped the cloth back to reveal several paper bills. It looked like ordinary money, complete with the image of a half-familiar, regal woman adorning one side. He picked up one of the crisp new bills and examined it.

Above the woman's head were the words RIGHT TO ASSEMBLY, 30+ PERSONS. On the other side was a paragraph of dense text, very fine and small. "It seems to say what you can do," he said, reading the fine print. "Organize meetings . . . rent out halls . . . it's like a teacher's permission slip," he glanced at Antaea, "like for a day-trip or special project."

She nodded. "Except that these bills describe very adult

projects—I'm told there's even a right-to-kill bill, but nobody's actually seen it."

"It looks like money," said Darius, fingering another bill. "Very high-quality printing . . . hard to counterfeit. This some kind of . . . initiative," he said, savoring the word, "by Falcon's government?"

Antaea shook her head. "It's illicit. But very, very weird, don't you think? I take it you've never seen anything like it before?"

"People trading rights like money?" Chaison shook his head. "These bills look new. I never saw anything like it before our capture. Who's trading these?"

"People in the lower classes," she said. "Day laborers, indigents, petty criminals, it seems. But there's hints that others are starting to use it too—there seems to be a pipeline feeding it into the country, but for what purpose . . ." She shrugged, obviously intrigued.

"You know," said Chaison speculatively, "we were just talking about how frustrating it is to sit around here idle. So we're going to move about the town a bit . . . make inquiries."

She shook her head. "We're trying to keep you out of sight, not parade you in front of everybody."

"But for how long?" Chaison jabbed a thumb at the blank wall beyond which fog and water swirled. "As long as this weather lasts we can't go anywhere. And believe me, we can be discreet. We just want something to do. I'm betting they need extra hands to fix the town's rigging after today's unexpected turn, right? I've rigged town-wheels. I'll volunteer—"

Again she shook her head. "It's a good idea, but there's an extra fly in the soup. The last ship in brought some sort of special investigative team. Secret policemen. *Extra* ones. You want to risk going out with them around? They may be here to find you."

Chaison didn't like the fact that she'd held back this information until now. Either it wasn't true, or she was metering out what she knew in order to keep a tight leash on him and his men.

"Who are you to forbid us from going about the town?" he asked. "Are we your prisoners?"

"It's not me who's likely to imprison you," she shot back.

"Thank you for your concern but my mind is made up," he said. "Anyway, people already know we're here; don't you think it's just as suspicious if we're *not* seen on the street?"

She made a face. "All right."

Chaison picked up one of the mysterious bills and waggled it. "Ergez's men can introduce us around, to build some trust with the locals. We can do some odd jobs. And while we do we will keep an eye out for more of these. Deal?"

She smiled slyly, taking back the bill. "Deal. But don't stick your heads out too far. I'd hate to have to rescue you again."

After she left Chaison smiled at the others. "Let's hope the weather doesn't clear in the next few days."

6

ANTAEA SLUMPED AGAINST the town's railing. She was impossibly weary, but wouldn't let herself rest yet. Memory and nightmares were lurking in the corners of her mind, ready to pounce the instant she stopped moving. Better to collapse than rest.

Her official task for the guard was to investigate the rights currency. So, she'd been dividing her time between that and attempts to pry information out of Chaison Fanning. She had to admit she wasn't very good at that sort of thing; her attempts to make the Slipstreamers trust her came across as false, and she had nothing credible to threaten them with. She'd look weak if she just hung around, so she had been spending more and more time out of Ergez's. It was intensely frustrating that she was getting nowhere with him, and that just added to her exhaustion.

The skies reminded her of home today. Pacquaea was a winter nation and its airs were frosty; warm fronts regularly sailed in from places like Meridian, and as they cooled they condensed. The droplets got bigger and bigger until they were gigantic. Unlike here, the water balls back home often developed a crust of ice on them, making them doubly dangerous. When these crystalline orbs drifted too close to the town they were dynamited—a bang, the puff of spray like black fireworks against the inky sky. But they were never as numerous as the torrent of drops, big and small, that filled Antaea's sight now.

Pacquaea's weather was just a hint of what you'd experience if you followed the slow drift of cooling air to the wall of the world. As she leaned against the wooden rail, the calm, the turning air, and her own exhaustion made Antaea's mind drift. Unbidden, memories came to her of half the sky paved with jagged white fangs—millions upon millions of icebergs, stretching from the infinite dark below to the infinity above and equally to each side. Luckily dark, for they would be blinding in the light of a sun, and might drive you mad if you understood the sheer scale of the sight.

"It's been six hours." Antaea started; the memory of Gonlin's voice was so vivid he might have been standing next to her. But no, that vast wall of ice had been his backdrop. They had clustered in a rough star pattern in the weightless air, Antaea and sixty others, listening with growing apprehension to Gonlin's report.

"Six hours. All across Virga, ancient devices that've been dormant for millennia are waking up. The field that suppresses transcendent technologies has collapsed. Something's happened to Candesce."

"Has it gone out?" someone asked, voicing the nightmarish thought on everyone's minds. If the sun of suns died, the heat it supplied to the entire world would stop flowing. It would get much colder out here—cold enough to freeze the air itself—and that cold would soon begin to work its way inward. Without Candesce, all Virga would die.

Gonlin had shrugged. Antaea could picture him clearly, his indigo uniform limned in purple by the arc lights behind him, his face lit sharply from the side. She couldn't see his eyes, just the curve of his cheek, the worry lines cutting sharply across his profile.

"The sun of suns went into night-mode normally, as far as we know," he said. "Then, several hours later, the suppressor field it produces shut down. As of right now, Virga is wide open to artificial nature."

Antaea had shivered, glancing at Telen. Her sister's face was pale in the unforgiving light. "Have they penetrated the skin?" she asked.

Gonlin hesitated. Then he ducked his head. "Yes," he said. There was a collective gasp from those assembled around him.

"There are things awaking out there in the dark. Uncoiling and on the move. Some have pierced the wall. Others appear to have been . . . here all along." He bit his lip. "Eggs, you might call them. They seem to have been scattered throughout Virga long ago. They're hatching now. We have to destroy them."

Antaea had heard a distant sound, then—cracking thunder, distinctive and sharp. Somewhere, an iceberg was breaking.

The sound came again, from a different direction. Suddenly everybody was turning, staring at the distant wall of the world where little puffs of white were appearing.

Antaea heard screams, shouts. Dimly she was aware of Telen clutching her shoulder and pointing. Over it all Gonlin's amplified voice repeating, "Calm down, calm down! *Those are ours.*"

All across the measureless vertical plain, glittering, mirror-bright things were crawling out of broken cocoons of ice. They shook themselves, sending man-sized splinters flying, then unfurled diaphanous, metal-ribbed wings.

Gradually Gonlin's words penetrated Antaea's superstitious terror. She looked at him, then back at the wall. The others were falling silent as well, waiting for an explanation—or any kind of reassurance.

"These are Virga's defenders," said Gonlin. "We've always known they were there; you may even have heard legends about them. Where I grew up, we called them the *precipice moths.*"

Telen gasped and turned to Antaea. She nodded. As children they had shared a wonderful storybook filled with fanciful illustrations. One was a drawing of a precipice moth, portrayed as a dragon-like sentry guarding the gates of the world. She had always suspected that it was this particular storybook that had inspired Telen to study archaeology. But, even with all the wonders they had seen since leaving home, Antaea had never dreamed that the moths might be real.

"As of now the moths are under our command," continued Gonlin. "Our ancient mandate to protect Virga isn't just words. It is backed up by power—power many of you doubtless never guessed we had. What you're witnessing now is something I've never seen, nor has any of our people going back centuries. But the leadership has always known it was there, waiting in case we needed it. I'm sorry it had to be under these circumstances, but as of this moment you are each entrusted with a portion of that power. To repulse our enemies."

As he continued to speak, explaining the capabilities of these unexpected new allies, the precipice moths hummed close and began to circle. Then Gonlin was saying, "Telen, take Flight twelve. Antaea, Flight thirteen." And rearing out of the night had come a nightmare of living metal, its limbs terminating in the snouts of massive guns, its head a scarred steel ball. Its skin still smoked with sub-zero cold from its long slumber in the glacial wall of the world.

The giant head twitched one way, then another. Then:

"Who here is Telen Argyre?"

It was as if the glacier itself spoke, a voice ancient, cold, and deep as thunder. Antaea's sister shrank against her, and Antaea held her tightly. Gradually, though, Telen began to push against her, until Antaea let her go and Telen drifted through the air to the monster. "I am she," she said in an almost inaudible voice.

"We are Flight twelve." The precipice moth reached out, scooping her into one weapon-fingered hand. Then with a flip of its wings that made a small hurricane around the watchers, it was gone into the night. Hundreds, then thousands of other moths followed its lead into the black.

Yet more thousands were waiting in the shadows of the world's edge. One of them was sliding forward on the air, majestic and silent. Antaea remembered the fatal tone of its voice as it shouted, *"Who here is Antaea Argyre?"*

Antaea came to herself with a start. She had nearly fallen asleep against the rail. Maybe she should return to Ergez's.

Maybe tonight she would sleep without dreams.

THREE AFTERNOONS LATER, Chaison found himself standing on a thin, deeply bowed cross-rope, holding onto a vertical line with his left hand while he repeatedly swung his body out into the open air. He was trying to catch the handle of a winch that hung tantalizingly out of reach.

It looked as if all there was in the universe was himself and these ropes. They faded into the gray above, below, and to both sides. The mist was moving past him quite quickly—actually, he was moving through the mist, since he was perched on one of the town-wheel's rope spokes. He could see the movement only as swirls and trembles of gray, but when he turned his face into the headwind, the mist soon soaked his cheeks and made him blink wild droplets into the air.

Faint shouts from the other riggers drifted to him. They were trying to determine, without benefit of clear sight lines, just how far off round the town-wheel had become. It was maddening, slow work, made even more dangerous by the threat of lightning from the swiftly churning clouds.

Maybe it was the isolation of the mist, but Chaison was feeling indifferent to the hazards, had in fact lapsed into a pensive mood. He had always expected a violent death, shot or stabbed or cut or blown to smithereens with some ship under his command; or to die in bed, surrounded by family, doctors, and officials waiting to announce his end to the press. Those deaths came with the role, they were the natural capstone to the persona he had constructed as admiral of Slipstream. And then, in the last few months, he had imagined dying of neglect in prison, which was also within his role: this time, as prisoner of war, nobly sacrificing himself for his people.

Instead of any of those things, his story seemed to be ending with him becoming just one of the crowd. He was a laborer, winching ropes to keep a town-wheel round. And if he made it back to Slipstream, what of his old self would await him there? Just days ago, he had been confident that he could call on his old friends and allies in the government, to salvage something of his old life.

But he'd thought further about his old acquaintances as he worked anonymously on the rigging gang. Had the men ever been loyal to him, or was it his position they respected? And his friends . . . was it him they had liked? Or his power and respectability?

For the moment Darius seemed to accept his authority, but there was no reason for this to last. Darius had every reason to resent Chaison, because Chaison was the man ultimately responsible for the tragic arc of Darius Martor's life. Press-ganged into the navy at a ridiculously young age, Darius barely remembered any other life. Now that he was out of prison and able to glimpse (however dimly in a dystopia like Falcon) what ordinary life might be like, he must soon awaken to how mean and downtrodden his own life had been. And he would look for the cause of it.

Chaison would see him safely home anyway; that ambition was practically all he had now.

Another shout came from below, this one closer than the rest. Chaison looked down between his feet and saw the head and shoulders of a man emerging from the mist about fifteen feet below him. It was Sanson. He quickly hauled himself up to a position just below Chaison, blinked at him for a moment, and said, "You'd best make yourself scarce."

"What do you mean?" He clambered down to hang next to Sanson. Momentarily, the gray silhouetting of the rigger was stripped away, revealing a vista of rooftops and rope spokes below him. Then more lacey clouds moved in and they were once again alone.

Sanson wiped black, matted hair out of his eyes. "It's the pols. They've called us down for inspection. This new man they have with them wants to see us all. Maybe he's looking for you."

"Why would he be looking for me?" asked Chaison innocently. Sanson began to climb down again. "He has your accent."

Chaison watched him fade into insubstantiality. His heart was pounding; what did this mean? Why would an inspector of Falcon's secret police speak with a Slipstream accent?

A brief horn blat sounded the call-in. Above him he could hear other riggers grumbling over their unfinished work. Chaison hung there for a while, thinking. Then he began to climb down.

For days he'd been trying to pick up trustworthy news about events back home. Something was happening in Rush, the capital of Slipstream, but nobody seemed clear on just what. He'd heard rumors of a siege, but who was besieging whom? No one had suggested that the government was in trouble. It was one more mystery to add to an already confusing situation.

He had no intention of revealing himself to this inspector, but he had to see him. So after descending a few dozen feet Chaison found a pair of cross-ropes and left the main line. He would find another way down and come up on the secret policemen from behind.

The town emerged as he descended, a silver sketch. He had been about a hundred feet up, a fraction of the way up the rope spoke. The highest buildings rose less than fifty feet above the ring of planking that was the town's official ground level—but that didn't mean that there weren't other structures in the heights. At different times entrepreneurs or town officials had hung smaller constructs from the rigging itself, everything from storage hutches to guest rooms accessible only by ladder. The pols had their perches up here too, crow's nests from which they could watch the street below. These were empty today, and it was simple for Chaison to half-open his wings and jump from the terminus of his rope bridge to one of these. He landed just as lightning jittered through the clouds along with the strangled choking of distant thunder. He stepped to the opening in the center of the round platform and quickly took the rope ladder down to the street.

The secret police had lined up his work gang in an alley that ran from the street to a high wooden wall that blocked any exit. There was only rushing air on the other side of that. Chaison saw eight policemen as he peeked around the corner; their backs were to him as they menaced the riggers.

"Where is he?" The voice was like a whip-crack, contemptuous and impatient. But it was true—the accent was familiar. Taking a chance, Chaison leaned out farther to see if he could identify the speaker.

He stood tall in the middle of the press of policemen, obviously different now that Chaison had spotted him because he wore a different uniform than they. In fact—Chaison swore quietly—it was the livery of Slipstream's royal service. What was such a high-ranking official doing here?

Maybe he hadn't been abandoned after all. Chaison leaned against the wall, blinking rapidly. Was Slipstream looking for him? Did they want him back enough to send officials to liaise with Falcon's most sinister institutions? It seemed strange, but what if it were true?

The Slipstream official's voice came around the corner again: "You have exactly ten seconds to tell me where he is." And Chaison swore again—because he recognized that voice.

Without hesitation he stepped into the mouth of the alley and said, "I'm right here, Kestrel."

His old friend turned, spotted him, and smiled. Then he raised his arm, pointing his baton directly at Chaison.

"Seize that man!"

Chaison was so surprised that they nearly got him. He left several hairs in the fingers of one of the pols before he reached the rope ladder to the crow's nest. His muscles were screaming before he was ten feet up, but the pols were fat and unused to actually chasing their prey.

The rope ladder swayed and danced, and the headwind pried at his wings, but there was nothing to see once the rooftops dropped below. He made it to the platform, rolling onto it gasping, and drew his sword. The first head that popped above the planks was going to get hacked off.

There was a hurried discussion below, then Kestrel's voice ordering the men aside. Chaison pictured them leaning out with one foot on the rungs, arm out for balance like dancers, as Kestrel pushed his bulk up the rungs past them. "It's me, Chaison," he said before his eyes appeared through the hatchway.

"What the hell was that all about?"

Kestrel grimaced. "Sorry about that, old man. I have to impress my hosts with my . . . zeal. Show them I'm not biased in your favor, understand?"

"No, actually. I don't." Chaison crouched, the sword still in his hand. He had a suspicion that the rest of the pols were sneaking up the spoke ropes, preparatory to dropping on him from above. It was what he would have ordered in Kestrel's place.

"Why are you here, Kestrel? And why are you here?"

The seneschal made a half-visible shrug. "Surely you're not going to play coy with me, Chaison. We both know what this is about."

Chaison ransacked his mind and memory for any clue as to what Kestrel was talking about. "I'm to remain safely behind bars here, is that it? Part of the pilot's peace pact with Falcon?"

Kestrel scowled in his familiar way. "Surely I deserve more honesty than that," he said. "With the situation in Rush balanced on the edge of a knife you have the gall to plead ignorance? I'm loyal to the pilot, you should know that. It's out of loyalty that I'm here; I've come to make sure you don't make it home, Chaison."

Chaison gaped at him. "But *why?* What situation?"

Kestrel stared back for a second. Then, "Fuck it," he said. "Now!"

Chaison was already in motion. Having already come to this platform from above he had some idea of where the spoke ropes were, even though he couldn't see them in the mist. So he unfurled his wings and leaped without looking. For a second the world disappeared into swirling gray; then there was the crisp image of a man—one of the pols—soaring past him in the opposite direction. The policeman cursed and swung his baton, but they were already by one another. Chaison saw the rope he'd been aiming at and lunged for it. He caught it with the tips of his fingers, lost his grip and fell—and caught another cross-rope ten feet below.

"Your betrayal runs deep, Chaison," Kestrel bellowed from somewhere nearby. A grumble of thunder lent punctuation to his words. "It's a cunning plot, but it won't work! This weather's got you cornered and you know it."

The tightly drawn cross-ropes came in pairs, one for walking on, the other five feet above it as a handhold. Chaison quickly walked the footrope over to a vertical line and shimmied up it. Twenty feet up he spotted another rope ladder along another set of cross-ropes. He made it to that ladder and went up it, even as dark shapes appeared on the line below him.

"I've got him! He's headed up!"

Chaison cursed and climbed faster, but his freefall-wasted muscles were at their limit. They were going to catch him in a minute or two. From what Kestrel was saying it sounded like he intended to kill, rather than capture, Chaison Fanning. He just wished he knew why.

He ran out of ladder and, moments later, ran out of cross-rope too. With one hand on a taut vertical line he balanced next to the knotted end of the footrope and watched four pols with drawn swords emerge out of the mist at its other end. Two proceeded to dance lightly along the footrope, their black wings half-raised for balance in the stiff headwind. Chaison kicked at the rope but it barely moved. He was too tired to climb the vertical; maybe he could slide down it . . . but there were shouts from below now as well.

He took a deep breath and turned to face the first ropewalker. The man grinned and fell into a fencing pose, his raised backhand clutching the overhead handrope. He inched closer.

Then he disappeared. Violent cold sprayed over Chaison and he nearly lost his footing.

Mirror-bright shapes shot like cannon-fire out of the mist to shatter into billions of cascading droplets among the ropes. Chaison hung on to the lines as they began to buck and sway under the onslaught of the sudden storm.

7

TWO MORE OF Chaison's attackers were swept off the ladder in the first seconds of the deluge. A third tried vainly to get down the ladder but a sphere of water bigger than he was hit him at a hundred miles an hour, and he was gone as though he'd never been there.

The town's alarm siren began to bray. Chaison swung around the ladder and stared into the grasping waves of cloud that had reduced visibility to nearly zero. He saw dancing, darting shapes, which resolved into a school of bright yellow fish. Their long fins were flickering madly as they tried to escape something; they shot past him leaving little glimpses behind—of lace tail, gelid eye, splayed gill. Then gigantic lurching motions in the cloud announced the arrival of the raindrops.

They hit the town like missiles. The wind was shifting and the sixty-mile-per-hour headwind caused by Songly's rotation quickly became a stinging gale. The storm hurled raindrops big as chairs, tables—houses—against the wooden walls and roofs of the town. He heard a distant crash that could be the sound of somebody's roof caving in, or of street planks heaving up. Seconds later the drops became a charging army of strange twisted forms, their shapes driven out of the round by the turbulent air so that some looked like amputated arms, others bedraggled spiders leaving trails of spray. They divided and recombined, jostling and tripping one another in their haste to wreck the frail town-wheel.

The rigging was being shot out from under him. Chaison stepped off the rope ladder and let himself fall until he passed a blindly lashing rope. He grabbed for it and swung in a long arc out of the turn of the wheel. If he let go now he would be one with the storm. Pailfuls of water doused themselves over him and he choked, blinded. Then the rope stretched tight and swung him hard, and at an angle, over Songly's street.

All he could think as the buildings swept by was, *Maritin's work will all be in vain.* Maritin was Ergez's masseur, who had worked after each sparring session between Darius, Chaison, and Ergez's friends to put their misplaced joints and locked muscles aright. After an extended sojourn in freefall, the body had a tendency to go out of wack at the least provocation. Here came a big provocation: he was about to hit the upside facade of the market.

The vision of harsh rectangles, planks, and nails disappeared in a white explosion as a huge quivering raindrop got to the street ahead of him. Chaison opened his wings, slowing too late, and hit the churn of water, which cradled him for an instant then lowered him gently onto the street. The frothed water was draining between the planks as he got to his feet and staggered in the direction of Ergez's manor.

He had to pass the alley where Kestrel had confronted his work gang, but both laborers and inspectors were long gone. There were few people on the streets, just a couple of men hurrying to their emergency posts at the town engines. The other riggers would be aloft despite the danger; hopefully they'd had time to don wings in case they were swept away by the storm.

The secret policemen would be huddling somewhere safe. This was not the sort of emergency that called upon their skills.

It took almost a minute of pounding on Ergez's door before someone came; the air was full of the roaring noise of the storm. The portal creaked open an inch, revealing the frightened face of Maritin. The man gestured frantically for him to come in. "Hurry,

hurry!" Chaison stepped in and Maritin slammed and secured the door behind him.

"It's a disaster!" Wringing his hands, the masseur fled leaving Chaison to find his way through semidarkness to the courtyard. It didn't help that gravity had become decidedly uneven: his weight would increase then decrease in long thirty-second pulses, while the rain-slick floor shuddered and swayed in sympathy with the assault of the water.

Chaison had seen storms before, but never anything like this. Growing up in Rush he was insulated from their effects anyway, since there the town-wheels were huge iron behemoths that would shrug off anything less than the impact of an ocean.

"There can't be this much water in the whole country!" The voice had come from over to his right; peering in that direction Chaison saw a little huddle of light from some oil lamps set on a table that was surrounded by wicker chairs. He walked over to find Ergez perching in one chair, with Darius, Richard, and Antaea in the others. On the table between the lamps was a cube-shaped tank of clear gelatine, which contained a seemingly random throw of little beads. This was clearly a map of Songly and vicinity. Ergez was leaned forward painfully to point to one side of the tank.

"It's coming from the Gretels." He looked up and saw Chaison. "Admiral! Did you hear? A ship staggered in to port at the axis," he jabbed a thumb upward, "just before this hit. They'd been running ahead of it for the past twelve hours. Said it looked like a giant hammer falling on them."

"From the Gretels."

"From our neighbor and enemy, yes. Is that not curious?"

The floor shook under them. Chaison had to smile. "I admire your poise, Hugo. I don't think your employees would call all of this 'curious.'"

"It can't take up the entire border," muttered Ergez, ignoring Chaison's comment. "There's not that much water in the region.

Of course, the Gretels have a couple of small seas. . . . It must be a jet, long but narrow, but where it's coming from . . ."

"The home guard will figure it out," Antaea said confidently. "Meanwhile we just hang on and hope the town holds together."

"Yes, but we should be prepared," said Chaison. "Pack up your things and keep them handy," he told Darius and Richard, "in case we have to abandon the wheel."

Ergez shook his head. "Oh, there's a ways to go before that—" The floor swayed under them and he fell silent.

Chaison was feeling decidedly lighter; the gravity gang must be running the town's jets in reverse, braking the wheel to a slower rotation. That was Songly's second line of defense against such violent weather, the first being to turn the town-wheel to cut into it. If both of these tactics failed, the wheel could be stopped entirely. It would then be a loose band twisting in the wind—a scarf with houses. But the stresses on the structure would become manageable.

Ergez was looking around, obviously judging which heavy objects would need tying down. "Come," Chaison said to his men. "Best get it over with now."

Upstairs, he grabbed Richard's arm as the ambassador made to enter his room. "Hang on. We have to talk."

Darius came over; Richard glanced at the stairs and Chaison nodded. Antaea was still down there with Ergez.

"This weather can't last," said Chaison. "We have to take advantage of it while we can."

"I was hoping for another day," said Richard. "The lads have promised to introduce me to—" But Chaison was shaking his head.

He recounted his run-in with Kestrel and the subsequent chase. "It won't take them long to find us here. They need only put the rest of the rigging gang to the question—"

Darius barked a laugh. "Anybody disturbs those riggers now, they'll be thrown off the town! It's the riggers keeping the place together."

"And they'll be heroes once it's over," said Richard.

"Nonetheless, Kestrel will find us. If I know him, it won't take long."

Darius grinned. "So we leave? Tonight?"

Chaison nodded. He turned to Richard. "Have you learned enough to give us an alternative to Antaea?"

The ambassador preened. "It takes a lot to earn the trust of these folk. I've had to be honest!" He shook his head in distaste. "So some outside of Hugo's household know that we're fugitives. That was good enough for a couple of them—these people hate their government with a passion I've never seen. Just to spite the pols, they gave me places and secret signs for hideouts in three cities. If a straight run for Slipstream's border turns out to be impractical, we will have places to stay."

"Excellent! Darius, have you secured some transport?"

The boy nodded. "There's a local merchant's been modifying his bike for speed. He ain't gonna report it if it's stolen. Better still, he's got it in this private shed with a trapdoor. All we have to do is get in, get on it, and drop out the bottom of the town."

"All right. Get ready, then. We'll leave after dark."

A hint of doubt came across Richard Reiss's face. "Going out in that will be very dangerous—"

"So is staying here."

SNEAKING AWAY WAS going to prove difficult. Ergez's men flitted back and forth like nervous hens, securing everything not already nailed down and arguing endlessly over everything else. They wrung their hands over cracks in the wall and jumped at every sound. All the rooms of the manor were lit. Chaison sat in his own small chamber, arms crossed, and frowned at the wall.

There was only so much panicked running around he could listen to; this crisis was nothing like some he'd been in. So his thoughts drifted, inevitably, to Kestrel's betrayal. He knew his friend was loyal to the pilot, despite all that had happened over the years. Somewhere in Kestrel burned a deep and ineradicable fear—a terror of the mindless mob he imagined was the only alternative to authoritarian rule.

Falcon Formation must believe that Slipstream was behind Chaison's jailbreak. Maybe they protested in strong terms, and in response the pilot sent Kestrel—and perhaps others—to help in the search. It seemed an extreme gesture of goodwill, and not at all like the pilot. And why should Chaison's breakout cause such a ruckus in the first place?

There was too much he didn't know; one thing he did was that Kestrel was now his enemy. That was a bewildering and saddening thought. It also implied that other former allies and friends in the admiralty might have taken the same turn.

Where would that leave Venera? Assuming she had made it home safely, did she now find herself the wife of a despised traitor? If so, how would she react?

Chaison realized that he had no idea what she might do.

Over the hours the thud and smack of impacting water lessened. The courtyard drained and someone optimistically mopped it dry. Gradually, the running and shouting trailed away as Ergez's people relaxed enough to snatch some sleep. Chaison sat and brooded.

Finally Darius rapped lightly on his door. "It's clear," he murmured. Chaison donned his wings, picked up the hip pack that contained his only possessions, and followed Darius into the hallway.

Lamplight showed a boy who still resembled the *Rook's* go-fer, but who had lost some of the feral look that had settled on him in prison. His face was starting to fill out. Richard Reiss had trimmed his beard to a civilized gray fringe, but it still covered most of his wine-colored birthmark. Man and boy were dressed well but conservatively and had long ago replaced their stolen military swords with a simple gentleman's épée in Richard's case, and a respectable knife in Darius's.

There was something else though, more important than their grooming or clothes: both Darius and Richard were calm and alert. They looked ready for whatever was coming. Seeing this, Chaison smiled.

"Which way?" he asked.

Darius pointed toward the courtyard stairs. He shrugged apologetically. "Doorman's sleeping by the servants' entrance, with his arms around a big bag holding all his worldly possessions." His grin turned him momentarily into the rodent he'd appeared just after the prison break. "Seems he's got little confidence in you riggers' ability to keep Songly together."

"Through the main rooms then." Chaison led the way past the closed servants' doors, to the top of the stairs. Gaslight cast a sharp coffin-shape of white across the bottom of the steps. He stepped down quickly, but paused when he heard voices. He held up a hand to stop the other two, and crept the last few feet to glance quickly into the courtyard.

Ergez and Antaea stood by the fountain. She was a study in red today, her arms crossed across a silk blouse, one leg splayed sideways below her cocked hip. She was wearing her boots despite the delicacy of the floor. Ergez stood half in shadow, his hands on his hips as he leaned forward to stare at her.

"You think the appearance of this bizarre black-market money somehow vindicates your position?" he was saying.

"No, it's not proof, Hugo, I'm not some fanatic who sees God in every shadow," she said. Antaea sounded defensive, which was a first. "It's just a fact," she went on. "Pardon me for grasping at facts! Hugo, you can't tell me that this world, where kings and dictators can enslave scientists and thinkers, is worth saving! You've seen the universe outside Virga; this place is worse than primitive, it's bar-

baric! Who exactly is the guard guarding, hmm? The bureaucrats of Falcon? The pilot of Slipstream?"

Ergez gave a growl of annoyance. "If we became political we'd be just like them—only worse. Our power—"

"Has to be given to the people." She let that statement hang between them for a long moment. "You know me, Hugo. I'm not preaching revolution, I don't believe in the violent overthrow of states. But I've seen artificial nature. I know what's possible for us. All that the guard keeps out."

"So what are you going to do?"

"What's going on?" hissed Darius from behind Chaison. He held up a hand for silence. "Wait."

Either Antaea had said something Chaison didn't catch, or Ergez had figured out the answer to his own question. "You surely don't think you can—"

"He did," said Antaea. "Ergez, he *did*. This is the man who caused the Outage. If he could do it, why not—"

"No! I forbid it. Antaea, I'll tell the others—" There was a scuffling sound, a low curse, a thud. Chaison heard Ergez gasp "No!"

Chaison swung off the last step and around the corner into the courtyard. He was met by a strange tableau: Hugo Ergez and Antaea frozen in mid-struggle, staring back at him. Antaea had her hands on Ergez's wrists, had half-bent his arms behind him. Weakened by his infirmity, Ergez was bowed backward over the fountain.

"What are you doing?" Chaison asked, keeping his voice pitched to the low tone he'd learned inspired the most fear in men he had to discipline. To his surprise Antaea let go of Ergez and stepped back, looking abashed.

"I—"

The town siren interrupted her. Chaison realized with a start that for some seconds he'd been hearing a distant pounding, like the impact of faraway rocket fire. But it was getting closer, and now the floor shuddered. He turned to make sure that Darius and Richard were behind him, in time to see a writhing torso of water twice his size hit the courtyard's roofline. Something dark and many-limbed seemed to be flailing in the sky beyond.

The warning keen stopped. They all looked at one another for a long moment, and then came a sound Chaison had only heard once before in his life. It was the bone-rattling wail of an evacuation siren.

The floor slid beneath him, then dropped away for a second. They all fell over and he heard furniture sliding. The gaslight flickered and went out. From upstairs came the confused shouts of the servants who had been tossed from their beds.

"The braking engines are on full!" Ergez's silhouette loped toward the front door. The others followed as best they could across the strangely animate floor. "What could make them—" Blackness gave way to a rectangle of gray as he flung open the door.

Gravity was gradually slackening, but it might not be in time to prevent the breakup of the town. Some huge force seemed to have seized it—but when Chaison reached the street with the others, he felt no appreciable wind. If it wasn't a hurricane tossing the structure, what could it be?

Lightning washed everything white; a fierce crash came seconds later. Richard Reiss's voice boomed into the dying echoes: "Did you see that? Did you *see* that?" He was pointing at the sky above the street.

Chaison didn't look—he was transfixed by the sight of Songly's people staggering and running out of their homes and into the single street. The mist had cleared; everything had a terrible clarity to it. More lightning banged across the sky, freezing instants here and there of frightened faces, fingers pointed at the sky.

Who was in charge here?

Richard grabbed his shoulder, was yelling something. Annoyed, Chaison shrugged him off—but then looked up.

Spasmodic flashes lit up a gigantic hand, bigger than the town-wheel, that was reaching down to crush the town.

Chaison gaped, lost for a moment in uncanny dread. Then the lightning flickered again, lighting blue and green depths in the sky, and he made out the one word Richard was saying over and over:

"*Flood!*"

Up until now the storm had been moving air, mixed with cloud and water drops in all sizes. Such dense storms were rare, but they did happen; gradually the vast cloud would pass, the droplets become smaller and less frequent. Normality would be restored. He'd thought that was what was happening in the past few hours.

It had just been a lull. Something must have stalled part of the storm, and the part behind had caught up. Huge drops had hit, merged, and become bigger still. And then more crowded in.

At some point the ratio had flipped: what Chaison saw approaching the town was not myriad shapes of water in air, but hollows and cavities of air in water.

He grabbed Darius's arm and pointed. "The main mass of the flood hasn't caught us yet. Can you see? Just a few arms have hit the wheel and knocked it off-round."

Darius gave himself a shake and visibly tried to focus on Chaison's words. He squinted up the curve of the wheel, then nodded. "Aye. Aye—but it won't be long before that big wall of water hits, and then the stuck part will slow—"

—And the parts behind would ravel into it while those ahead tore away. Gravity would fail catastrophically well before the town's engines could stop the wheel.

Tactically, this was perfect. The chaos would be so great that their escape was assured—provided they left in the next few minutes. So said the military planner in Chaison.

The man saw something else: people milling in helpless confusion, no one coming to their aid. No one in sight seemed familiar with command, nor did anyone seem to know what to do. If seconds counted for the escape of Chaison and his compatriots, they counted even more to save the lives of the people of Songly.

Chaison hesitated—and cursed himself for it. A real gentleman would see no dilemma here.

He ran though the crowd, heedless of the ache in his legs and back, until he spotted the rigger Sanson, who was hurrying his pregnant wife and young son into the street. "Who's in charge of evacuation?" he shouted as he reached them.

Sanson shook his head. "It's all under government control. I think . . . I think it's somebody in the political offices. But they don't tell us workers details like that. Security reasons."

Chaison shook his head in disgust. Even if the bureaucracy wasn't corrupt, the nearest official who knew the plan was probably a mile up the curve of the wheel.

"Sanson, we have to get the riggers together." Chaison pointed straight up. "The docks are at the axis. Everybody's boats—"

The rigger shook his head. "We can't get the whole population up there!"

"We have to get the boats down here. Cut them loose and lower them. The riggers will have to do it. Gravity's low enough we should be able to guide them to a soft landing in the street. Then get people into them."

Sanson sent an agonized look at his wife. She smiled. "We'll be all right," she said. "You have to do this."

Antaea, Darius, and Richard arrived. "What are you doing?" demanded Darius. "We gotta go." Chaison shook his head; to his surprise, though Darius and Antaea glared at him, Richard Reiss smiled.

"I think our admiral has wrestled with honor and lost," said the ambassador. "What are you thinking, sir?"

"I'm thinking that someone has to take responsibility for these people." He described the evacuation plan. Antaea scowled, but Darius reluctantly nodded.

"Come, then." They ran on, looking for the other riggers and anyone else able enough to help. Richard rounded up some of the boys he'd gotten to know and told them to relay the plan both directions around the wheel. "And if the pols try to stop you, kick 'em in the shins," he told them. "Their opinion doesn't count right now."

The town was about to be engulfed in what could only be described as froth. It was similar to any thick, bubbly mass of water, except that the bubbles were dozens to thousands of feet across, and the film of water between them was equally thick. Scattered through it all were smaller droplets, filaments, and clouds, and increasingly, debris. Chaison watched two riggers scamper up ropes as a full-sized tree sailed by little more than ten feet from them. The whole scene was lit in fragments by savage lightning that roared through the dark cavities of the flood.

While they waited for the riggers to lower the boats, Chaison, Ergez, and Antaea and his men organized the townspeople into groups. Each group would take a boat. It quickly became clear that there wouldn't be nearly enough vessels to evacuate all the thousands of people who lived here. Some would have to ride it out in their houses; many were unwilling to leave their homes in any case. Chaison shouted instructions on how to batten down the doors and windows to keep the water out in case they became inundated. "You'll have to wait for things to calm down before swimming out. The currents could drown you ten feet from an air pocket."

At one point Sanson put a hand on his arm and shouted something. The rigger was holding a small bundle of wax paper. "What?" Chaison put his hand to his ear.

"This is to thank you for your help," shouted Sanson. "Introductions! To the right people . . ." Then he pressed the package into Chaison's hands and hurried on.

Antaea stopped next to Chaison during a momentary lull.

Everyone had scattered to execute their parts of the plan. "What did Ergez do with your bike?" he asked her. She nodded.

"Still in his workshop. There's a floor hatch there, we can launch—" She started in the direction of Ergez's estate.

"Not yet! We haven't finished here."

She looked him in the eye. That hint of humor that was always present in her face looked more like superiority—or contempt—right now. Then her lips quirked into a half-smile, a kind of ironic compassion. She came up to Chaison and put a hand on his arm. "You've done it—the riggers know the plan, they'll take things from here. I know you're not used to letting go of a command, but this time, you have to."

He pressed his lips together so as not to yell at her. For a few minutes he had been the admiral again, coordinating an urgent action. Men had been running to obey, and lives hung in the balance.

But Antaea was right. This was not a ship. The townspeople were moving to save themselves. It was time for him to do the same.

"All right," he said, "let's find Darius and Richard and—"

She tackled him.

In the reduced gravity their fall was slow, but it was still fast enough that the sword-thrust missed. Chaison landed on his back and found himself staring up at Kestrel, who stood above him, lightning framing his drifting hair, a wild look in his eyes.

"Was this part of the plan?" Kestrel demanded as he raised his sword again. Chaison rolled, barely evading another blow.

He felt more than saw Antaea do a foot-sweep and topple Kestrel. Then he had regained his own feet. Chaison drew his sword as more silhouetted figures appeared from among the jumble of running people: the pols, coming to assist the seneschal of Slipstream.

Chaison grimaced. "I don't know what you think, Antonin. But somehow you've made me more than I am."

Kestrel made a sort of half-laugh of disgust. "Oh, really? And what about the spies you placed in the ministry—even in the palace itself? Are they a figment of my imagination?"

"Ah, as to that . . ." *They weren't actually my spies,* he wanted to say—but how could he even begin to explain that it was his wife who had created the network, and had run it for several years without even telling Chaison? Anyone who knew Venera well would believe it; but to Kestrel she was merely a casual acquaintance. She had always played the empty-headed court lady in his presence.

Damn her. "It's not what it looks like."

Kestrel shook his head in apparent disappointment, as his men arrayed themselves behind him. "Next you'll be telling me you've had no hand in the *Severance* fiasco."

Chaison stared at him slack-jawed. He was dimly aware that he was leaving himself open to attack but was having too much trouble absorbing Kestrel's words. "The *Severance* . . . survived?"

Seven ships had gone with him into winter, but one, the *Tormentor,* had been lost to attacking pirates near the iceberg-choked outer wall of Virga. Six vessels made it to the vast sargasso of Leaf's Choir, and six had participated in their ambush of Falcon Formation's fleet. As far as Chaison was aware until this moment, all six had been destroyed in the attack.

"It was clever of you to use that ship as a symbol for the people," Kestrel was saying. Chaison shook his head and fell back a step, trying to understand what the man was saying. "So publically besieged," Kestrel continued, "the pilot can't simply destroy it—he has to *take* it. And your friends in the navy have stalemated that. The *Severance* is a festering wound in the heart of Rush. Your supporters are waiting for your return. If you enter Rush as a free man, half the city will rally to your side. But if you enter it in chains—or dead—"

He attacked and Chaison had no more time to think. He and Kestrel fought beneath lightning and a collapsing sky of shimmering water, among shouting people and the splintering facades of twisting houses—but echoing through Chaison's mind were Kestrel's words. He retreated over popping boards and up a twisting street that fell away with each step, as Kestrel and his thugs shouted and tried to surround him and Antaea. Chaison killed a man with a thrust to the neck, but didn't see him fall; instead, lightning painted a dozen miraculous flowers that were fluttering slowly down to the street. The boats had arrived.

Far up the curve of the town, a wall of water touched the turning buildings. Planks flew—an entire roof flipped away—and the rope-and-wood wheel snapped. A long ripple whip-cracked down the surface of the street, ejecting houses, street boards, and citizens as it came. Antaea exchanged a glance with Chaison. As the hump reared behind Kestrel and his men, they both jumped. With a barking roar the street planks leapt up after them. Kestrel's squad were tossed up with broken boards and popped nails.

The street was missing half its planks as Chaison landed again. The broken wheel was toppling into free-fall, a wrenching collapse that followed the ripple by a few seconds. "Come on!" He grabbed Antaea's hand. Hopping over gaps in the street— glimpsing boiling cloud and surging water beneath their feet as they jumped—they made it to Ergez's door just as gravity failed completely.

Chaison clawed his way through Ergez's entrance into blackness, and for a horrible moment he was back in the blockhouse cell again. There was nothing to see, nothing to touch.

"This way!" Antaea's voice anchored him. He shook off the panic and climbed along the ceiling joists after her. In some ways it was easier now; he was used to free-fall and as part of the flood's jetsam, the house was no longer jostled as fiercely. But there was a bit of weight—a pressure that told him the building, maybe the whole street, was being pushed by the water.

They crawled like spiders along the walls of a pitch-black

hallway. "In here!" Antaea had another door open, and he followed her into more darkness. Something brushed his cheek and he shouted reflexively. Reaching out, his fingers found the head of a hammer. He swung his hand cautiously and found the air filled with drifting saws, bolts, and bundles of wire. "Why here?" he said, hearing his words swallowed by thunder and nearby smashing sounds.

"Look for a lantern," she said. For several minutes they made slow swimming motions, touching this or that object, grasping it long enough to find out what it was—or in many cases, long enough to know only that it wasn't a lamp—and then letting it go. Things drifted away, came back. Chaison was about to say that it was useless when the back of his hand brushed glass. He snatched at the unseen form, came up with the spindle-shape of a windup lantern. "Got it!"

He wound the thing's tiny fan and spun the flint wheel. The fan drew air across the wick, which would otherwise starve itself in free-fall, and a golden glow shone out. It revealed a bizarre galaxy of tools with himself at its center. Antaea was a pair of bright eyes and curves of clothing in shadow. Behind her loomed her bike.

They said nothing as they unmoored it; as Antaea mounted its saddle and kicked it into life; as Chaison found the floor hatch and yanked it open. But as she gunned the jet into the opening and reached for his hand, their eyes met.

He hesitated, looked to the door. Darius and Richard Reiss were still out there somewhere, but there was no way to find them. He had to hope they had made it onto one of the flower boats.

Chaison took Antaea's hand and leaped onto the saddle behind her. With a roar they shot out of Ergez's house, past sewer pipes and broken ropes on the twisting underside of Songly and into a maze of writhing water.

Part Two | THE STRONGMAN

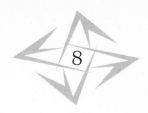

8

THERE WAS NO sky anymore. What surrounded the town was something like the inside of a cascading fall of cloth; or like the inside of some nightmare's closing mouth. This froth, this spray, held chambers a mile or more in diameter, caverns of air chained together into writhing tunnels threatened with being sealed at any moment by sloughing walls of water. The magnesium headlamp of Antaea's bike pinioned tumbling spheres like armless monsters, miniature spinning planets of water tossing off runnels and droplets with indiscriminate fertility. Any one of those could choke the bike if they hit it.

Chaison leaned back to take one last look at Songly. The town was a glittering arc of lights being torn apart by silver arms of water; still racing quickly, the ribbon of wood and rope holding its houses and market was shearing a mane of white spray off the grasping fingers. In moments it would be consumed—the market, Ergez's house, the workers' hostel—and perhaps Sanson and his family, and Darius and Richard Reiss.

Unable to watch, he started to turn away—but just then, lightning revealed a dozen bright flowers opening and closing in the air next to the ribbon. Some of the boats had escaped.

If he'd had another half hour . . . If he'd anticipated what was coming . . . He knew he was a good commander because being beaten filled him with intolerable anger. This time, there was no enemy to strike back at.

He had to turn quickly as Antaea put the bike into an insane series of maneuvers to avoid oncoming water. She was slim enough
that he could put his arms around her waist and still grip his elbows; Chaison had to lock his hands in this position, else he
would have crushed the wind out of her or been torn from the
bike by the rushing air. They weren't battling a headwind made by
their own speed, it was air being squeezed out of narrowing
chambers ahead of them that rushed past. The bike's engine
roared, flat-out, and yet for long seconds they made no progress.

Then with a kind of elastic snap they were flung ahead into an
undulating tunnel of water. Antaea leaned left and right and they
dodged boulder- and house-sized water drops. He felt the corded
muscles of her back flex against his abdomen and chest. The un-
dersides of her breasts tapped his forearms.

She swore fiercely as the bike coughed and shuddered. They
started to tumble but she righted them—barely—and Chaison
looked back to see a round white cloud expanding around their
contrail. They'd swallowed a head-sized drop and it had nearly
extinguished the engine. "We can't keep up this speed!" he shouted.

"You want to stop for that?" She nodded at the infalling walls.
Chaison gritted his teeth and hung on as she spiraled them
around tumbling drops and through hissing spray.

"Look out!" Ahead of them the long tunnel was suddenly con-
stricting. Antaea gunned it recklessly and Chaison was slapped by
hard projectiles of water until he was gasping and blind. Then the
bike slewed hard, he blinked away droplets and saw that they
weren't going to make it, and Antaea shut down the engine and
leaned back hard. Her body pressed him down, the bike rotated
with them and, hull-first, they hit the wall.

The impact slammed her against the bike and him against her.
Chaison expected to choke on water but instead as he raised his
head he saw that they were at the bottom of a conical splash-crater,

shockwave still expanding it as the bike slowed. Just before it would have come to a stop the water ahead of them simply parted like a curtain and they were through the narrowed neck and in another chamber of air.

Antaea reached down to restart the engine. Chaison twisted around to gape at the round hole they'd punched through the wall. It looked exactly like a bullet hole through soft metal, but it was six feet wide. The bike trailed droplets and spray as the engine caught and they raced away.

He turned back, securing his grip around her waist. "Have you done this before?"

Antaea laughed. "Thank you!"

They continued on, more cautiously, through a shifting world of transparency and shadow. Again and again they were forced to change direction, so that soon it became impossible to know where they were or what direction they were traveling. It wouldn't have surprised Chaison if Songly had loomed out of the dimness. Instead, they saw debris—boards, barrels, and snaking coils of rope, and once a complete grove of trees, their roots still intertwined—but no humans alive or dead.

The image of those fragile little boats had stayed in Chaison's mind. How were they going to make it through this chaos? They weren't, he decided. They would have to find high-pressure bubbles of air—areas that couldn't be collapsed further—and wait until they circulated into view of daylight, or were rescued. But the scale of the catastrophe seemed so vast that rescue was unthinkable.

Chaison had been nursing the magnesium headlamp, feeding in its long wick by hand as Antaea flew. There was only so much wick to feed it, and at last the lamp sputtered and went out, leaving them in utter darkness.

Antaea swore and cut the engine. For a second the shattering roar echoed back and forth, describing invisible spaces. Then there was nothing but a strange sighing, almost a groan: the sound of water capturing sky.

"This is bad," she said unnecessarily. He could feel her leaning this way and that, doubtless searching for some sort of light. He did the same, keeping his grip on her. The universe had become reduced to her body pressed against his, and the hot metal curve of the bike between his thighs. Once again he felt a momentary panic, remembering his cell, and without realizing held her tighter.

"Admiral . . . ?" Her voice was concerned, questioning. For a few seconds Chaison was confused by it. Just as he realized he was squeezing her breathless, something caught his eye. He let go with one hand and pointed. "There!"

He felt her reach back. Her fingers traced along his arm, found his hand. She twisted to look at the indistinct green patch he'd seen. "Yes!" Without consultation, they stretched their bodies and pushed with their legs, altering their center of gravity and turning the bike. Then Antaea reached down to start it.

Chaison relaxed his grip. Cautiously they drifted closer to the aqueous glow, which slowly resolved into a glasslike wall, its depths harboring a single wan shaft of sunlight that angled up from below. It seemed miles away.

Antaea rotated the bike and gunned it gently, stopping them a few feet from the surface. "How do we get through?" she asked. "It looks like a long way."

"We could swim," he said doubtfully. "It would be easy—" They could just hold their breaths and kick their way through.

Antaea shook her head. "If we abandon the bike, we'll be stranded once we reach clear air."

Once at a surface, they could stay half inside the water and slog their way up and around the slopes and intricate curves of the flood, looking for rescue or something to beat the air with. Chaison had to admit though, that when exhaustion claimed them they would have no choice but to exit the water, else surface tension would drag them slowly into it, to drown. Being stranded in empty sky was little better. "We need the bike," he admitted.

"We can push it through ahead of us," she said.

"A short distance, maybe. But that . . ."

"Yes—it would be too far. . . . Unless we give ourselves a head start." She twisted her body to turn the bike and he followed her lead automatically, before realizing what she was intending.

"Antaea, wait! We could destabilize the water ahead of us— close off whatever chink there might be, or push it away."

"Chance we'll have to take." She opened the throttle, taking them back into blackness.

Chaison bit his lip, trying to think the thing through rationally. "Not too fast," he said after a moment. "If you go too fast the water's surface tension will be like—"

"—Concrete, I know, I know. I took flying classes when I was a kid, Admiral."

"Chaison."

He could barely make out her smile as she looked back at him. "Chaison." Then they flipped over again, and she opened the throttle wide.

She almost misjudged their speed. At the last instant she flipped the bike sideways, not even bothering to choke the engine. There was a bone-jarring *bang!* as they hit the water at forty miles per hour; Chaison felt like his spine was being driven out the top of his head. He recovered enough to take a deep breath and then cold water reached out from all directions to claim him.

He exhaled slowly, as he'd been taught. Drowning was a very rare thing in Virga, but Chaison had once suffered through an academy training course that covered it. He was surprised that he remembered it. As long as he breathed out, the water wouldn't enter his nose; instead, a long bubble formed along his cheek and broke away behind him in the dark. Chaison kept his hands pressed to the cold flank of the bike and his body straight, kicking with his feet. Unfortunately the can-shaped jet blotted out any view of where they were going. That shaft of light could be ten feet away or a thousand, for all he knew.

The light *was* increasing, otherwise he would have turned back. After long seconds he began to see shapes in the wavering water: reflections and refractions of distant sunlight; the mirrorlike curves of air surfaces; bubbles. It was ethereally beautiful, like a model of the sky rendered in glass, with mirrored balls standing in for clouds.

When he spotted a bubble as big as himself less than ten feet below, he grabbed Antaea's arm and pointed. She nodded vigorously; abandoning the bike they swam over to the silvery oval and plunged their heads into it.

He faced her inside a quivering sphere half-lit in green. Antaea took him by the shoulders and laughed wildly. "Just in time!" she shouted. "I was about to kack!"

He didn't think this was a good time to joke, but her smile was infectious. "There may not be any more of these, so we'd better not waste this air talking."

"What, you've never done this? Sat with your head in a bubble inside a lake?" He saw she was serious. "I suppose Slipstream doesn't have many big water balls," Antaea went on, "and you grew up under gravity, didn't you? It was different where I come from. There's minutes of air in this bubble. We could have lunch here."

"The bike is drifting away," he pointed out.

"Ah. There is that." She began gulping great breaths of air. "Let's get back to it, then."

He took her offered hands, and together they swam back to the bike. Their kicking feet shattered the bubble, leaving its dozens of children to disperse aimlessly.

The light was plainly visible now. It came from a sheer wall that stretched into obscurity above and below. Beyond that surface lay brightness, even the crescent-curve of a cloud. But between them and it there were no more helpful bubbles—and it was a long way. As they positioned themselves behind the bike Chaison glanced at Antaea, who shrugged. Then they began kicking again.

In seconds the sense of adventure he'd gotten from Antaea was gone. This new desperation was physical, a howl of outrage from the body: breathe! It overrode any thought, any determination he might have had. Chaison fought toward the light, tossing his head back and forth, aware that the rest of his movements were becoming random as well. They weren't going to make it.

Antaea convulsed and let go of the bike. It turned under Chaison's hands and he found himself looking down the intake. Trapped there by the fan blades was a head-sized bubble of air. —Of course, it could be a head-sized bubble of toxic exhaust, but he didn't care. He jammed his head into the jet and gulped at the quivering sphere.

A moment later he was out again and holding Antaea with one hand while he pushed the bike with the other. Everything was closing in and graying; worst of all was a terrible loneliness he'd never felt before. He had never realized that in drowning, the body tells you that you've been abandoned. There is no one and nothing outside that can help you as death emerges from inside.

Air burst around him. Chaison gave a reverse whoop, putting all his strength into one breath. He hauled Antaea into the light, letting the bike tumble where it wanted. For a few seconds he could only gasp in long shudders. Then he turned to Antaea.

Her face was a horrible gray; she wasn't breathing. He forced her mouth open and swept it with one finger, removing a small gout of water. Helplessness overwhelmed him as he realized he didn't know what to do next. It normally took two people to do CPR in freefall, one to provide air via mouth-to-mouth contact, the other to compress the chest from behind. Chaison had learned where to place his intertwined fingers—midsternum—and to squeeze the patient's rib cage against his own chest. You couldn't do this effectively from in front because the person's back diffused the pressure. But he had no choice this time.

He removed one of his shoes and placed it under Antaea's small breasts. He moved his mouth over hers, then hesitated.

He shook himself; this wasn't a kiss, it was something he'd been trained to do to other men. He wrapped his arms around Antaea, squeezing her body sharply as he pressed his lips to hers and drove breath into her.

Despite his rationalizations, the sensation of Antaea's lips against his was shocking. He cursed himself for being weak and self-involved, and renewed his work. The shoe dug painfully into his own solar-plexus; hopefully it would concentrate the pressure in the right spot.

After just a few seconds Antaea coughed weakly, then convulsed in his arms. She reared back, sucking in a great wheezing breath. Chaison loosened his grip, but kept his hands around her arms until he was sure she wouldn't strand herself in the air.

Air . . . He looked past her for the first time. An empty sky, purple and clear, beckoned past water drops and twirls of mist. He and Antaea stood half out of a vast wall of undulating water that must stretch for miles. A distant sun bathed the whole scene in shades of gold and rose.

To their right a green arm of water hundreds of feet thick and thousands long stood out from the main flood. It was crooked as if grasping at the diffuse ribbons of cloud that surrounded it. Convoluted shapes in paler green and blue hinted at giant bubbles and caverns hollowed out of the flood beneath Chaison's feet.

Antaea was blinking at the spectacle. "Made it!" she croaked. "Where—the bike?"

"Here." He turned them so she could see it. The truncated spindle-shape jutted up a few feet away. It was a simple matter to wave his feet and bring them over to it. Antaea gripped its saddle with white-knuckled intensity, letting out several sobs before she got her breathing under control.

"You got us out," she said after a long moment. He shrugged.

"Turned out there was an air bubble inside the bike. Just enough to keep me going the last few yards."

She nodded, started to say something, then looked away. For the first time he saw something like shyness in her. The impression only lasted a few seconds before her usual brashness returned. She hauled herself into the bike's saddle and stuck out a leg for him to grab. "Give us a push, Admiral. I'll see if I can get this old bike to spit up some lake."

He thrashed his legs in the water, excavating a crater and throwing spheres and jets of it everywhere—but also giving the bike just enough of a push to get it clear. Then he climbed behind Antaea. Wrapping his arms around her he was even more aware than before of her body conforming to his. He was able to feel her trembling, and looked down to see her hand hesitating over the handlebars.

"Do you want me to fly?" he asked.

She nodded. "I . . . don't think I'm quite up to it right now." She swung herself around and he eased forward. It was her turn to wrap herself around him.

It took a while to get the bike going; there was a fair amount of water inside it which wasn't easy to dislodge. Chaison had to work the manual pedals to spin the fan in order to create a weak current of air to wash it out. He did this for long minutes, and all the time they drifted slowly across the drop-filled sky, drawing closer to the gargantuan arm that jutted out of the flood's main body.

The engine caught the tenth time he hit the sparker. Suddenly the pedals disengaged, the fan began to whine, and the bike coughed and hacked as it vaporized the last of the water inside it. Then he turned them in a tight circle until he found a fairly clear path through the drops. When he had it, he opened it up and they roared clear of the flood.

"It's so . . . localized," yelled Antaea. He glanced back. As the bike accelerated, back felt like down—so the sensation was of rising miles above a frozen and impossibly magnified splash of water.

There should have been an equally gigantic bathtub behind it, but now that Chaison could see the full extent of the flood he saw only sky beyond.

The flood was a chaotic twist of dense water, roughly cigar-shaped, and about four-by-eight miles in extent. Ahead and behind it were twisting funnels of dense cloud in which lightning still flashed.

"God's spit," shouted Antaea over the mad roar of the jet. Chaison had to laugh. It did look almost like a jet of saliva from something transcendently huge. But when he followed the trail of cloud and spray back, it became obvious where it had come from.

The jet had come straight out of the distant, golden sun.

He pointed. "Not Falcon's?"

She shook her head and leaned close to say one word.

"Gretels."

Chaison nodded. He didn't know how they had done it, but somehow Falcon's neighbor had used one of their suns to evaporate a lake and shoot it into Falcon territory. Probably they had used reflectors and heat baffles to concentrate the fusion device's heat, creating a long channel of lower-density air. The evaporate from a lake towed next to the sun would seek out that channel and run through it . . . and reappear as clouds and drops on the border with Falcon.

He forgot the speculation as something bright flashed in the middle distance between the flood and the sun. Chaison squinted, and saw another flash, then another. He swore softly.

"Do you see that?" He pointed. At first she just shrugged and shook her head—then suddenly she grabbed his shoulder.

"Ships!"

He nodded. "Dozens of them, at least." A whole fleet was massed in the turbulent clouds behind the flood. They were pouring into Falcon Formation's airspace behind it.

Looking past Antaea, he could see the bike's contrail was

feathering wide behind them. "We'll be visible," he said. There would be pickets—bikes like this one, with riflemen on them—running ahead of that fleet. They could pop out of a nearby cloud or use the sun for cover, and Chaison would never see them coming. Anxious again, he turned the bike so that the Gretels' sun was directly behind them, and opened the throttle wide.

This way lay the heart of Falcon Formation, but beyond it were the skies of Slipstream, and home.

Then Antaea's hand rose again, pointing. A spray of ships lay across the cloudscape ahead. These were coming from inside Falcon. Chaison swore again—loudly, this time—and turned once more. *Like a sparrow between two hawks,* he thought. He laid down a course at right angles to the incoming fleets, with the flood behind him. The fleets would engage around the flood; it was the perfect wall to keep at your flank.

He glanced at Falcon's ships and suddenly laughed. Antaea put a questioning hand on his shoulder. "Just wondering," he shouted back at her, "how many of those ships I put holes in?"

What would the airmen on those vessels do if they found out that Slipstream's admiral was cutting the air just a few miles ahead of them? He laughed again, then leaned forward to lay on more speed.

The only way to orient yourself in Virga's skies was by the light of national suns. Within three hundred miles of Slipstream's capital, Rush, home meant inward toward the light. Outside that zone, all suns began to look the same; confusion was easy, and beyond the light of nations lay the indigo darkness called winter. All that Chaison knew was that he was running parallel to the border between Falcon Formation and the Gretels. But on which axis? Dead ahead could lie some third nation, or just beyond the obscuring clouds, winter. That might be their safest destination right now.

Among dusky skies where the civilized suns were distant smears of rose and crimson, he and Antaea could skirt the nations of Meridian until they found Slipstream. The way would be dangerous, for among the purpled clouds you could easily miss rocks and water drops that could smash a bike or a pilot's head. There were pirates and madmen, desperate exiles and wily opportunists on the fringes of winter. And, if you strayed too far and lost the light entirely, it would be sheer dumb luck if you found your way back again. You would be adrift in the realm of legends.

Chaison was willing to chance it.

Occasional glances back told him that pickets from the two fleets were engaging each other. Bikes swirled like angry midges, their backdrop the vast hammerhead of the flood. He had no doubt that his contrail had been spotted, but he was clearly a civilian or a deserter. There was no point in chasing him.

He began to relax. At the same time, the air ahead of them was becoming more crowded, so he had to cut back their speed anyway. Many farms and villages on the edge of the flood had managed to see it and dodge out of the way in time. They now formed a donut twenty miles wide with the flood in the central hole. Lots of stuff had come loose as buildings, groves, and fish farms had flapped, jetted, whirled, or undulated from their normal stations. Chaison jigged the bike around loose trees, octahedral sheds, ducked flying hammers and sleeping chickens like feather balls. Contrails from other bikes scored the sky, and here and there flower boats pulsed. He was tempted to approach some of these to see if they were refugees from Songly, but he knew what Antaea would say, and she would be right: trying to find Darius and Richard right now would just expose them all to more risk.

Falcon's suns began to dim for the night. The clouds cast long gray capes of shadow through the air, and everything became touched with delicate colors. Sunoff should have been a peaceful time, but the jetsam of the flood made it dangerous to stay in the open. Anything—even stray bullets and rockets from the distant battle—might fly in and hit you in the middle of the night. So, Chaison heaved a sigh of relief when he spotted the road.

It was a simple rope, punctuated every half-mile by colorful banners jutting from mirrored buoys. It twisted and spiraled up from below and angled away from the dwindling flood. Traveling beside it in orderly streams were hundreds of vessels. The streams went in opposite directions, but one was much denser than the other. Only a trickle of people were heading toward the battle, though a lot of very fine craft—yachts and cabin cruisers—could be seen striking off into open air in the direction of Falcon's heart.

Chaison watched a lamplighter tether his bike next to a road buoy. With an economical and well-practiced motion, he leaned in and started the buoy's engine. The little two-stroke would suck in air for the buoy's beacon. The lamplighter shot off to the next buoy, and slowly he drew a line of stars across the sky. With relief Chaison fell into the heavier column of traffic where he could see by the light of others' headlamps.

They moved with a scarf of stars past graying clouds that framed deepening blackness. Behind them the ever-changing sky was lit by white lightning and the orange flashes of a fierce conflict. Chaison could hear nothing over the racket of the bike's jet, yet the evening seemed strangely watchful; the drone of the engine faded in his consciousness, replaced with nothing but the awesome majesty of the pirouetting clouds.

Those clouds had become black-on-black presences when they parted at last to reveal the road's destination. It was a city, one of the most beautiful Chaison had ever seen.

Neither he nor Antaea spoke as the traffic merged into a column of lights that drifted down the tunnel of a vast avenue. Windows cast warm amber light from all sides, their glows filtered and cupped by millions of leaves. The houses and mansions of the city were nestled among trees—millions of them—that stretched their branches here and there to clasp their neighbors. That light touch kept the buildings from drifting and, over the years, the city had acquired a stable shape. Chaison flew among green clouds full of lamplight that opened here and there into veins and arteries where flew winged men and women, children with foot-fins, cavorting dolphins, boats and bikes, taxis, birds, darting, huge-finned fish. After a while he cut the bike's engine and they drifted with the current. They listened to the growl of engines, the singsong of nearby conversations, the laughter and music of a city alive and vibrant.

There were some signs of the distress taking place in the skies outside. Doormen at hotels tiredly turned away families who clutched their few possessions and gazed around themselves bewilderedly. Vehicles were clotted together in darkened cul-de-sacs, their owners sleeping or cooking beside them. But on the whole, war had not yet touched this place.

Antaea touched Chaison's shoulder. "That sign—this must be Stonecloud."

He nodded. "You know it? No doubt the guard has a chapter-house here?"

She said nothing. After a moment he looked around at her. Antaea shrugged, grinning tiredly. "Can we agree not to talk about the guard for a while?" she said.

Chaison squinted in surprise—then remembered Antaea's confrontation with Ergez, just before Songly's breakup. "Whatever you want," he said. He crossed his arms and frowned into the stream of traffic for a moment. "Richard . . . was in contact with the local black market in Songly. He talked about smugglers in Stonecloud, though we really didn't intend to go this way."

She didn't ask him why Richard had been investigating smuggling routes. "Do you remember how to find them?"

"I think so," he said. He reached down to start the engine. "Somehow, I'd feel safer with them tonight, than outside."

She nodded. He turned the bike, and drew them down a side-avenue whose name Richard had mentioned.

9

THE SMUGGLERS' ADDRESS existed, all right, but the eight-sided building was a burnt-out husk wrapped in leathery police tape, no sign of life inside. Antaea and Chaison stared at it for a while; the bike pinged and creaked as it cooled. Finally Chaison said the obvious: "Now what?"

Antaea was hugely relieved by the desolation, though of course she wasn't about to show him that. "We should wait here for Richard and Darius," she suggested. "A day . . . two. There's only a small chance that they came this way, after all." *Provided they got out of Songly alive,* she didn't add.

Chaison's shoulders slumped. "I suppose so," he said after a while. His disappointment was palpable, but she steeled herself not to feel guilty. He was her responsibility, and they had been through a lot together, but he was not her friend. This relationship had a definite end.

Antaea couldn't quite admit to herself that it was getting harder to picture that moment. They had worked well together escaping Songly and, in retrospect, she had taken great comfort in having him at her side. She could think of few other companions she would have wanted in that situation. But *no;* thinking along these lines was futile. This adventure was taking its toll on her nerves, that was all. She had to find out when it would end.

So they tied their belts to hooks in the blackened doorway of the smugglers' building, and tried to sleep. At first staying here so openly seemed like folly: wouldn't the pols come looking to sweep up visitors? But watching the streams of people passing by, that seemed less and less likely. In fact, after a while Chaison muttered sleepily, "Where they hell are they?"

"I'm sure they're all right," Antaea said reflexively—meaning Richard and Darius.

"No, I mean, where are the police?"

"Yes," she said reluctantly. "It is strange."

From here the city appeared as a dense drift of buildings and cloudlike forest, lit by innumerable streetlights and the glow of windows angled in every possible orientation. The perspectives went down and up and across dizzyingly; and everywhere they were filled with people. The whole city was awake and about despite the lateness of the hour, and an electric tension filled the air. But there were no official vehicles in those throngs, no pols interceding in the increasingly common arguments and traffic jams. Stonecloud would have been an assault on the senses at the best of times, so in a way it wasn't surprising that it took so long for Chaison and Antaea to notice this strange lack. Now that they had, though, the city's wakefulness took on an extra atmosphere of menace.

They slept with the uneasy mutter of the city in their ears. Both were startled awake sometime late in the night by a nearby argument that had become a screaming match. They blinked at one another, then drew the bike farther into the doorway, sheltering behind it.

"Who's looking after this city?" muttered Chaison darkly. "It's dereliction of duty, I'd shoot men who did that under my watch." He glanced around the dark bowers that crowded their building. "This may not be the safest place after all . . ."

"We have no choice," she said. "Your men, remember?" He grimaced and closed his eyes again. "Chaison?" He opened them a slit. "I can't sleep. I'm going to go find us some food, and maybe some news if I can. You're all right here?" He nodded blearily. He knew she wasn't through with him; she'd be back. And she knew he wouldn't leave this spot until he was sure Richard and Darius weren't coming.

Antaea got a firm grip on her bike and pushed off. After she'd drifted a dozen yards into the air, she flipped into the saddle and pedaled the bike's fan up. It lit, and she was away.

Alone and responsible only for herself, her spirits immediately lifted. The adrenaline percolating through the city also affected her. Stonecloud was beautiful, a vast bowl-shaped forest embedded with jewellike buildings unlike any city she had lived in. The millions of trees that formed its skeleton were clustered into balls with their roots entwined in common around clods of earth. Some, notably elm and oak, thrust branches for hundreds of feet in all directions, and the city planners had twined young branches of neighboring trees together, like linked hands. Grown together, they formed walls and shapes far bigger than the individual trees making them up. Nestled among the branches were thousands of glass and stone structures, mostly houses in the theatrical style.

Stonecloud was a tourist city, of course; this beauty was deliberate and an exception among the otherwise drab and uniform cities of Falcon Formation. Stonecloud was a lie—a lure designed to lull visitors into immigrating. To Antaea, this was no objection to the place, because she couldn't imagine herself settling in any city, unless late in life she drifted back to Pacquaea, her home. She was an outsider everywhere, by choice, though seeing young couples drifting down the arteries of the city, she did feel the occasional wistfulness of envy for their more innocent lives.

Someone had to make those lives possible; that was the problem, and the reason why there was a home guard.

She paused, mind empty of thought, to admire some of the mansions. The theatrical style defined two parts to a free-fall room: an "audience" or area for people to congregate, and opposite that a window or large architectural space that served as the "stage." She saw houses with glass domes peeking out from frames of forest, wicker and velvet shapes nestled deep behind the glass. Lamplight backlit complex canopies of leaf and branch; she caught glimpses of men and women lounging in the air in some of these bowers.

It was easy, at first, to ignore the fact that many of the mansions were dark.

Presiding over the glowing forest were giant metal town-wheels—six, at least. They filled the bowl, stage to its audience, each wheel turning majestically inside a spherical cage of forested girders. At night they made a glittering galaxy that could bewitch you for hours. Near them was another bowl, a half-spherical amphitheater that cupped a smaller sphere made of wicker. This was floodlit even this late at night, to show the dozens of garish sets and props that had been built into it. A vast sign on the side of the sphere said:

PEOPLE'S CIRCUS
HOME OF CORBUS STRONGEST MAN IN VIRGA
ATTENDANCE NOT MANDATORY

Stonecloud was entirely different from the cities of Antaea's home, but the encompassing darkness and the bustle and commerce seemed familiar. Especially when she passed those windows, their glow hinting at intricate interior experiences, Antaea felt a pang for choices not made. She had to remind herself that the life she was living had a purpose, and that she might yet return home once that purpose was fulfilled.

Richard had given Chaison an address. Well, Antaea had one of her own, memorized along with those in a dozen other cities and towns. Ergez had given them to her, dutiful home guard alumnus that he was.

Navigating a city in three-dimensions came naturally to Antaea. She looked for street signs, which here followed the universal convention: they appeared as three arrows, red, yellow, and blue, joined at their tails to indicate the city's x, y, and z axes. Addresses were always strings of three numbers indicating the location's distance in yards from the city's official 0,0,0 point. She followed corkscrewing arteries, flew down parallel sheets of facade and forest, passed the knotted clumps of estates caged in ornate wrought-iron balls hundreds of feet across. She didn't get lost.

Despite the lateness of the hour, the bar Ergez had told her about was open. She tied up her bike and launched herself at the loops of rope that stuck out of the entrance, narrowly missing a banner that said LAUGH WITH CORBUS. Once inside her confidence ebbed, because the place was as crowded as a wasp's nest and she recognized no one. Then she spotted her contact, over at the bar.

The bar was literally that: a brass pipe festooned with cup holders. Patrons hung in the air on one side of it, and the waitstaff glided back and forth on the other. The baby-faced man she slid next to had about a dozen empty helix glasses in front of him and looked decidedly unfocused. "Raham," she said, shaking his arm. "I'm here."

He stared at her for a few seconds before saying, "Damn. I lost that bet."

"Gonlin," she said. "Is he around?"

Raham shook his head, which was apparently a mistake. He took half a minute to find Antaea again (she was less than three feet away), then said, "The whole damned pack leffft for Shlipstream yesterday. Do you have him?"

She nodded. Raham brightened. "Great. I'll . . . take it from here." He spun around, missed his footing, and flailed at the bar.

A passing waitress yelled, "Sick bag at fourteen!" The nearby patrons all reoriented themselves so they could keep Raham in sight.

"Sorry," said Raham. "Sorry. Wasn't really expecting to see you. Thought I was . . . left behind."

"Raham." She took him by the arm. "I don't understand. Why did they leave?"

He glanced away, the very picture of shifty discomfort. "Something . . . something came," he said. "From winter. We had to bug out before it caught up to us."

"What? Make sense, Raham, damnit." Something had come after them? Not, someone had come after them?

Raham hurried on. "Yeah, well, Gonlin said, better chance of rende-, rend-, of meeting you in Slipstream anyway 'cause that's where Fanning would be going. Also, no war there. So he moved the whole operation, 'xcept me of course I was to watch out for you." He nodded deeply, his eyes slipping shut.

She shook him. "*Where* in Slipstream? Damnit, Raham, what's my rendezvous?"

He roused enough to tell her, then drifted asleep. Antaea paid his tab and waved at one of the bouncers. "Get him under gravity so he doesn't drown in his own puke," she said. Then she flew back to her bike and, without a backward glance, shot into the light and chaos of the city.

ANTAEA FOUND HERSELF reluctant to return to Chaison. She needed to regain some sense that she was in control—if only in control of a bike and her own private thoughts—so she flew through the city in a widening spiral, taking in the sights, thinking about what to do next.

The problem was that any time she was idle, her thoughts inevitably drifted to her sister. Telen was the only family Antaea had; she'd taken care of her after their parents had died in an accident. She had learned to fight so she could defend Telen from the bullies who picked on them for being state wards. Telen had always been the thinker, the avid reader, while Antaea was the doer. Ironic, then, that Telen should be the one to decide at age twenty to leave Pacquaea in search of the legendary home guard. "I can't spend the rest of my life in this squalid little country," she had cried when Antaea tried to convince her of the foolishness of her plan. "I'd rather freeze or starve in the dark looking, than give up on the chance of finding somewhere better." And so they had left together. Against all odds, they had found the guard and in doing so, a new life. Even, Antaea had sometimes thought, a new family.

Antaea had trusted Gonlin with her own life. Gonlin had repaid that trust by promising to kill Telen if Antaea told anyone else in the guard what his group was doing.

So much for family.

Near dawn, she found herself on the fringes of Stonecloud, where vistas of open air came upon you suddenly as you turned a corner or looked up. At first everything seemed the same here as deeper inside, but then she rounded a tall cone of forest and glittering glass and nearly ran into a cloud of people.

Antaea swore and spun the bike to brake, nearly falling off in the process. She turned it again and tried to make sense of what she was seeing. There were hundreds of people outside here— thousands, maybe, their voices audible above the tearing noise of the jet. They all seemed to be shouting and talking.

People hung in windows and doorways, in pairs, threes, or gathering crowds at the intersections of the artery. Many were pointing and gesturing; she saw a woman scream but that sound was swallowed by distance. She followed the general gaze with her own.

Something puzzling hung in the sky beyond the city limits. A glow, a shape that, the more she looked at it, could not be what it seemed to be.

Antaea turned the bike to roar out of the city and into open air. She shot up and away, skirting a cloud bank that momentarily obscured the thing she'd seen. Perched atop the cloud for all the world as though it was solid, was another bike, its rider staring at whatever lay on the other side of the mist.

Antaea flew over and cut her engine a dozen or so yards away. Drifting close, she saw that it was a man sitting astride the jet, his hands folded over the handlebars. He was staring out into the night that enfolded the city.

"Hello," she said. He glanced over, then returned his gaze to whatever it was he saw in the dark. "What is everybody looking at?" she asked.

He said nothing, merely pointed. Antaea passed the last wisp of cloud, saw what he saw, and swore.

Miles high, miles wide, the malevolent face of a bearded god confronted Stonecloud, its mouth wide in a soundless scream.

Antaea felt a flood of cold come over her; her hackles rose and she hissed involuntarily. The moment of superstitious dread passed as she realized that the face—which really was there, and really was that big—was drawn on the night sky in lights. There were thousands of them, swathes and clumps forming the features of the angry god. As she looked closer, the individual twinkles resolved into windows and streetlights, cunningly lit in patterns: this arc of houses making a vast eyebrow against the darkened neighborhoods behind it; that circular pond, ringed by caged streetlamps, making an eye.

"It's a city?"

"It's called Neverland," said the man. "The Gretels have sent their regional capital against us. They mean to swallow Stonecloud."

Antaea looked back at Stonecloud. This apparition must have just appeared, because there had been no talk of it in the bar. People had been speculating about the result of yesterday's battle, but nobody knew anything—except that the pols were missing and the city's bureaucrats were nowhere to be found either. The rich and powerful had probably known about Neverland's approach for many hours, but nobody had seen fit to communicate the news to the public.

The tension ringing through the city made sense now. Stonecloud had been abandoned by its government, a pawn sacrificed to the enemy. And that enemy was about to arrive.

Antaea turned the bike and shot back into the city.

GETTING BACK TO the burned-out smugglers' den proved difficult. The city's arteries were boiling with people, an increasingly hysterical and aimless mob. Antaea's uneasiness grew. They should strike out now—before dawn—and take their chances in the open air. Better that than to be trapped here when Neverland arrived.

By the time she arrived at the smugglers' den she was calm because she had decided that this was the only sane course of action. So when she drew the bike up next to the doorway where she'd left Chaison, and saw that he wasn't there, Antaea swore and kicked the bike's cowling six times.

"Fanning! Where are you, damnit!" She circled the building, then stopped to climb inside it. He was nowhere to be found. Antaea's heart sank. Of course, he was a military man and as ruthless as she. He'd never had any intention of waiting for his men, he'd just waited until she left and struck out on his own.

Either that or Richard and Darius *had* arrived in her absence. Maybe they had convinced him to abandon her.

She preferred that version of events.

Depressed and full of self-recriminations as she was, it took Antaea a while to notice that the traffic around her had changed. When she did she sat up, startled, and looked around. Had Neverland arrived already?

People were streaming through the city, vast throngs of them headed in one direction. They weren't going out, so it wasn't to escape. They were on their way in.

She cut the engine and strained to hear the loud conversations, interspersed with shouts and waving hands that propagated up and down the stream of people. The voices blended together into a chaos of noise in which she picked out the words "Neverland" and "attack" every now and then. There was one word however that kept being repeated, like a mantra.

Corbus.

She burped the bike's engine so as to drift next to the crowd. "What's going on?" she yelled at nobody in particular.

"The pols are gone!" shouted a rakish young man with a buzz cut. He wore one of the uniforms that were common throughout Falcon Formation, but the shoulder patches that indicated his job and rank had been torn off. Now that she'd noticed that, Antaea saw that many other people in the crowd were missing their patches as well.

"The city fathers, the bureaucrats, the pols—they all left when the battle went against us," continued the young man. "Flew away like bats at dawn. The city's wide open to the Gretels!"

"So where is everybody going?"

He laughed, a bit wildly, and pointed ahead. "The circus!"

In the distance, the giant bowl of the circus stadium glowed under smoking arc lights. The golden wickerwork sphere it cradled was spinning with stately majesty, colored spotlights on it throwing arms of light into the depths and bowers of the clouding neighborhoods. Flocks of people converged on it from every direction.

"But—but why?" She burped the bike's engine again to catch up with the man who'd spoken to her. "What's at the circus?"

He laughed again. "Corbus!"

"The *strongman?*"

He nodded. "People were starting to riot, they were trashing the municipal offices. Somebody'd cornered an informer, they were going to tear him to pieces. Then Corbus shows up, he's carrying a bag of yarn. Apparently he knits! He throws it aside and fights the whole crowd! Knocks down twenty men, tells them to stop acting like babies. Then he jumps to a podium and starts talking. Tells jokes, gets the whole crowd laughing with him. And then . . ."

"What?"

"He organized them. Sent them to put out the fires, look in on the old people . . . He took charge!"

The cry was being taken up by the crowd now, drowning out the rest of what he said. "Corbus, Corbus, Corbus!"

Antaea sat back in amazement. The pols had deserted the city, and somebody had stepped forward to take responsibility. A circus performer! It was simultaneously pathetic and glorious, and she found herself drawn to follow these people—whom she didn't know and shouldn't care about—to the stadium. Yet she had to find Chaison.

Unless . . . A suspicion came to her. *He wouldn't*. He might. Chaison Fanning was a romantic, a man who took the notion of noble obligation seriously—an anachronism in an increasingly cynical world. It would be just like him to break up a fight, to put out a fire, command rioters to go look after the elderly . . . Corbus and he were kindred spirits. And if he'd heard about the city's power vacuum, and further that somebody was *taking responsibility* for these people . . .

She spun up the bike and headed for the stadium, which was a swirl of people like panicked schools of fish, darting this way and that unpredictably with flashing wings. There was a general movement into the bowl of the stadium, though, and she followed it, pausing to tie up the bike in a nearby grove.

Nobody was taking tickets at the stadium's lip, people were just pouring over it and hand-walking down the ropes crisscrossing its interior to find perches. The noise was incredible, just a continuing, mindless chant of "Coooorbus, Cooorbus." The mob mind could turn in any direction at any second and Antaea felt herself being swept up in it, in a way she hadn't felt since she was a child attending the city games at home. The feeling was terrifying and intoxicating and even as she fought against it she felt a crushing sense of loneliness come over her. Everybody here was with someone, it seemed, and even the solitaries were one with the city itself tonight.

Antaea shook off the feeling. She had come here to save her sister Telen's life. Everything she had done for weeks now had that as its aim. This crowd, this city, even the admiral were just steps along that road.

The chant faltered and an animal roar filled the stadium. Antaea found a perch on one of the ropes and looked up. The majestically-turning golden sphere in the stadium's center had stopped and spotlights were sliding over to focus on one patch of its surface. The whole ball was festooned with devices, she saw: trapezes, cannon, and nets, water sculptures and cages and twirling mirror-balls. The circus would have used all of that as an aerial playground, and if the ball was spun up to any high rate of turn, the performers would have had to do their stunts while hanging precariously over the heads of the crowd. That was a situation few in Virga ever encountered and for most people the sheer novelty of it would add a thrill to the proceedings.

A hatch opened in the side of the ball and the spotlights zoomed over to highlight it. A bald man climbed out onto the wicker surface. He waved his hands for silence and there was some cheering and a diminution of the overall chaos, but ragged elements of the chant continued. After a moment he threw up his arms in disgust and disappeared back up the hatch.

He'd been an odd-looking fellow, short and squat in a way Antaea had never seen. The opposite look was common enough, of people stretched out to almost spidery lengths by a life spent in low-gravity and freefall. This look, though, reminded her of something.

A few seconds later the hatch flipped open again and the man emerged, only now he was wearing an absurdly bright black-and-yellow-striped tunic. A massive cheer rose, shaking the stadium and making the taut ropes thrum. Again, he waved his hands for silence and this time, reluctantly, the crowd obeyed.

He waited until the noise had subsided, and then waited some more. Antaea had thought it was silent, but it became even more still. He waited, and the silence became as vast a presence as the roar of the mob had been minutes before.

"What are you *doing* here?" The words were startling because they seemed to come from behind Antaea, but she'd seen Corbus's mouth move just before she heard them. The acoustics of the bowl focused the sound back on the ropes, she realized. He was perfectly audible.

"What are you doing here?" he said again. His voice was very deep and gravelly, belying the clownish attire. "Please, it's not safe. I beg of you, return to your houses and look to the safety of your children. There's nothing for you here." He turned to go, but a wave of noise rose from the crowd, an animal hiss that made Antaea's scalp crawl. Corbus was pinned by it, halfway into the hatch. He turned to look at the crowd and though he was too far away to see clearly, she imagined that right now he must look deeply frightened.

He stood out from the wicker again, raising his hands in supplication. "Please! Our situation is impossible. Stonecloud has been isolated by the Gretels and our own forces have deserted us. What are we to do?"

"Fight!" someone in the crowd yelled. The mob rumbled assent.

Corbus shook his head. "How? This is insane! What army have we got? Are we going to push the Gretels back with our bare hands?"

"You're an Atlas!" a man shouted. It took a moment for the word to register with Antaea; then she blinked in surprise.

The Atlases were legends, or so she'd thought. (Ha! a little voice in her head said, *you thought the precipice moths were legends too, and the Gates of Virga, and* . . .) As a girl she'd heard stories of nations that built special town-wheels where the gravity was much higher than normal—up to three gravities, so it was said. They raised babies on these wheels, trained them as soldiers. Turned loose on enemies in freefall, they were practically unstoppable because of their titanic strength and endurance. Atlases were reputed to be short and squat, boulders of muscle with thick necks.

Corbus waved again. "I'm just an entertainer," he said. "A buffoon. What I might have been . . . it makes no difference now. The Gretels will be here in days, maybe hours. What do you want me to do?"

"Fight!" someone shouted. Others took up the cry. Corbus waved his hands desperately.

"Fight who?" he cried. "They've sent a city at us. Navies fight! Not cities. Not people. The people in Neverland are just like us— just like you. Women, children, old people who've earned nothing if not the right to die in peace at home. We fight them, we fight ourselves. Even if we won, we'd lose."

The chant continued rising in intensity: *Fight, fight fight fight!* Corbus hung in the air, his whole posture beseeching, defeated. He curled in on himself as if the words were blows.

"Get out of there, get out," she heard herself mutter. "Come on." She realized she was gripping the rope with maniacal intensity.

Suddenly Corbus burst into motion, throwing out his limbs to make a star shape. He had torn off his polka-dot shirt.

"Fiiiiight!" he roared. The sound filled the stadium and the chanting died instantly. The crowd gasped and Antaea felt as if she'd been slapped.

What had just happened? Had his reluctance just now been an

act? Or had he really undergone a magical change of heart before the whole watching city, buoyed by its passion and compliant to its will? The cynic in her couldn't believe it, but there was an electricity in the air suddenly, a hunger to believe. She longed to follow it.

"If fight we must, then we must fight the true enemy!" he bellowed. "The Gretels' navy leads that city. We can fight that navy and spare the innocent city that is being shoved like a sacrificial victim onto our swords. But understand this: if a fight is what you want, then you must fight. Not your neighbor there on the rope beside you. You, yourself! You must commit to it, you must be willing to die for your city if you are going to see it saved! Can you do that?"

Yeeeeesss!

"It can be done," shouted Corbus. "We can save Stonecloud and Neverland. Not for the fucking bureaucrats in their distant capitals, not so the pols can return to torment us for eternity. But for our own sakes! For the sake of our cities and ourselves! Are you with me?"

They screamed YES at him. Antaea's heart was pounding; she wanted to scream right along with them. But as she stared around wide-eyed at the crowd, she spotted Chaison Fanning.

Among twenty thousand shouting people, he stood out. He was perched on a rope near the top of the bowl, quite close to Corbus. And, seemingly alone in all the crowd, he wasn't cheering or yelling. He sat quite still, his faced turned toward Corbus, his expression serious and intent. *Studying.* Or, perhaps, judging.

Again Antaea's hackles rose, but this time it was because she was seeing an aspect of the admiral she had known, in an abstract sort of way, must be there. She'd met him as a refugee, but what she was looking at right now was a coldly calculating military leader. He was assessing the situation, deciding what Corbus might be capable of.

Swearing luridly enough to draw shocked glances from the people around her, Antaea began to jostle her way over to him. She had to step from rope to rope, flying little distances. People yelled at her to get out of the way, she was blocking the view. She kept on going.

"If we're going to do this," Corbus was saying, "I'm going to need experienced people. I'd like everyone who's got military experience to come up—in an orderly fashion!" He glowered at the crowd. "Assemble here." He pointed to the empty shark cages to his right. "We're going to need city workers, people who know where the sewage lines run, the emergency routes, and who have keys to the fire trucks. Assemble here." He pointed to his left. "And lastly, I'm going to need commanders. Military personnel of rank. I don't care how old you are, if you mustered out twenty years ago. The city needs you. Are there any captains in the crowd? Anybody who was a colonel in the last war? Join me now."

Antaea knew exactly what was about to happen. She was going to lose her admiral to this man. Once Chaison was ensconced with Corbus and his people, she would never get near him. She'd have to go back to Gonlin empty-handed and then her sister . . .

She put both feet on the rope and oriented herself, then leaped with all her strength into the air. Seconds later she turned, unfurling her wings to land just a few feet from Corbus.

Corbus was blinking at her in surprise. Up close he looked quite grotesque, everything about him squashed and compacted by the forces of his past. "Who are you?" he asked, not loudly enough for the crowd to hear.

"Home guard," she said. His slablike face split in a grin and he gestured at the stadium full of people. Antaea turned and saw Chaison; he was in the air not a dozen feet away. The expression on his face when he saw she'd gotten to Corbus first was priceless.

Antaea turned to the crowd. "My name is Antaea Argyre. I am a lieutenant in the Virga home guard!" A mutter went through the crowd. "Yes!" she laughed. "We exist. And I am here to help you!"

Chaison landed and introduced himself to Corbus. Others were rising from the crowd now, mostly older men who might have been leaders once, but had moved here to Falcon's pleasure city years ago.

Chaison shot Antaea an inscrutable glance, then turned to the crowd. "I am Admiral Chaison Fanning of the Navy of Slipstream," he shouted an authoritative voice. "I was visiting your city when all of this occurred. I . . . do not know whether you can fight the Gretels' military without touching its people, or save your city without sacrificing yourselves. But I believe you should try.

"My skills and experience as a military commander are yours— if you want them."

The crowd burst into screaming applause.

Others arrived and introduced themselves. Antaea hand-walked over to Corbus, and Chaison approached him from the other side. The former strongman—now defender of Stonecloud, sure to be crowned mayor in an hour or two—stared out at the throng, a look of awe on his face. "Well now," he said. "All we need is a plan."

Chaison smiled back. "That," he said over the rumble of the half-wild crowd, "you can leave to me."

10

ANTAEA ARGYRE GRABBED Chaison's arm. "What the hell do you think you're doing?" She looked furious, which he supposed was perfectly understandable. "You're going to get yourself killed, or maybe you always wanted a transfer from Falcon's prison to one of the Gretels'!"

The rally continued in the stadium, but Corbus had turned it over to some prominent local businessmen. His plan seemed to be to bore the crowd until it calmed down and left. Meanwhile, backstage, he was assembling his team.

"Backstage" was a series of plank decks in the shape of balls nested inside the outer, wicker one. The central sphere was sheathed in heavy cast iron and it had big steam engines clamped to its outer surface from which long driveshafts extended outward. These could be employed to rotate the outermost sphere during the show. Corbus squatted on the side of one, talking nonstop to the people hovering around him. He looked almost feverish, his broad forehead dotted with sweat, his eyes wide as he frequently licked his lips, staring at nothing. Yet when he spoke he seemed completely lucid, if unsure of whether he liked the position he'd been thrust into. He had listened to Chaison's story and shrugged off his political imprisonment. The two of them had then talked strategy for half an hour, and now the former admiral of Slipstream found himself in charge of mounting a defense of this foreign city, before even taking a tour of the place.

"Somebody has to do this," he said to Antaea. It was a hopelessly inadequate response, he knew; he couldn't explain to Antaea why he'd been driven to come here despite his exhaustion and the anxieties of being a fugitive. He had left his station at the smuggler's hideout because he hoped he could find some news from home. When he'd heard what people in the passing crowd were saying, however, he'd responded instantly: Corbus was acting, not reacting, in response to Stonecloud's crisis. Chaison had been tossed about by forces he had no control over for far too long, and felt a surge of adrenalin at the thought that he, too, might finally be free to act and not react. He joined the crowd streaming to the stadium. He needed to stop being the refugee and, if only for a night, be himself again.

"Somebody might have to do this, but not you!" Antaea was saying. "Did you stop to consider that these are the people who held you in a tiny cell for months, tortured and abused you, and fully intended to leave you there to die? How do you know they're not going to trade you to the Gretels?"

He shrugged. "I'm of no value to the Gretels. And these are not the people who imprisoned me." The pols were gone; these were civilians surrounding him now. Chaison had to admit he'd been impressed by the spectacle in the stadium—not by Corbus's performance, because the man was a professional entertainer and knew how to work a crowd. It was the crowd itself that had convinced Chaison to volunteer. He had always been taught that it was the hereditary ruling class who should make vital decisions in matters of politics and war. Yet no one of that class cared as much about Stonecloud as the people who had no choice but to live in it. Corbus might have manipulated them, but they really were loyal to their city and he had, in the end, bowed to their will; perhaps he had only manipulated them into seeing what their will really was. Their fierce pride had touched Chaison in a way that nothing political had in a very long time.

He was fed up with politics as usual; he supposed that was partly why he'd mounted the secret expeditionary force against Falcon to begin with. He had explicitly gone against the wishes of the pilot of Slipstream, and apparently Antonin Kestrel believed he was a traitor because of that decision. If Kestrel hadn't been lying then all of Slipstream believed the same . . .

He didn't want to face that possibility. "This is about loyalty to a principle," he said quickly. "It's about making a commitment to defend helpless people, rather than those who are in power." She was staring at him with a funny expression on her face. "I know you don't understand," he added.

Antaea shook her head, he supposed in disbelief. "The Gretels will be here in a day, maybe less. What are you going to do to keep them out?"

"I have a plan," he told her. He did, although it was a desperate one, more of a fallback position to delay defeat than a recipe for success. "I vouched for you to Corbus and he's sufficiently impressed that he's going to make you a line commander. You'll take my orders during this engagement, and in my absence you will act on my authority."

Antaea opened and closed her mouth. Again her expression was hard to read, but he figured she must be furious; he was not prepared to be sympathetic. It was true that they had narrowly escaped the pols, and the sensible course of action would be to lay low until they had a chance to flee the city. He had made this impossible, in fact he couldn't have made his presence here more visible if he'd sent a semaphore message to the Falcon capitol buildings. Her carefully orchestrated rescue plan was in tatters.

So was her mission to learn the location of the key of Candesce. Antaea must know by now that she could neither talk nor torture it out of him. Where Falcon's interrogators had failed, she would not succeed. She had absolutely no reason to stay with him at this point—so what would she do? He couldn't see any reason why she would remain; her loyalties were to the guard and she had never, as far as he knew, taken the oaths of honor that he had.

She didn't budge. "I'm sorry," she finally managed to say, "this is a lot to take in." Then she looked away.

Chaison stared at her. This mild submission was the very last reaction he had expected. What could possibly be compelling her to stay with him? —But he had no time to think about it right now. Corbus was waving him over.

Still, he felt her eyes on him as he flew away, and the sensation that she was accusing him of something he knew nothing about didn't leave him during the rest of the night.

CHAISON WAS SURROUNDED by the blare of saws and a swirl of flying workmen. One of twenty or more work gangs was cutting the street away from its neighbors, and he had finally taken a break from his planning sessions to come watch.

This street, which was very near the stadium, was made up of trees that had been joined to form the body of a woman, hundreds of feet long. Its hands were joined to two similar sculptures on either side of it. The workers were cutting its wrists.

Chaison frowned at the destruction. Everywhere he looked, he saw men and women shredding the work of centuries. Some were weeping as they worked, jewellike tears joining with the sawdust and torn leaves to make a fine mist that was slowly pervading the city. They were doing all this on Chaison's orders.

He knew the emotions all of this ruin should be causing in him, but he couldn't feel anything. Partly that was due to exhaustion, of course; but while Chaison was intensely busy, he had also found himself distracted all day. Memories kept assailing him, of significant moments in his life. Even during his darkest times in Falcon's prison, he had been able to cling to a faint hope that if the walls magically flew away and he was transported home by some miraculous force, he would be home. He had been suspended, per-haps, kept away from his real life by circumstance; but that real life was still out there, waiting, if forlornly, for him to return.

Now, as he drew plans and gave orders to the very foreigners who had imprisoned him, he recognized that on some level he was letting go of that life. If he were to return, things would not be the same. Kestrel believed him a traitor, and that meant that most, maybe all of his countrymen must too. He had gambled with that possibility but, at the time, Venera had been at his side and he had felt brave enough to risk a loss of country. He would, after all, still have her.

But if she believed he were dead? If she learned that his name was blackened beyond repair now? She was too much the prag-matist, and he was too much the realist to believe she would re-main the solitary widow for long.

Maybe he had been doomed from the start. On the evening that he had arrived to begin his very first diplomatic mission—more than ten years ago now—Chaison had found himself scrub-bing small droplets of blood off his face and hands over a gold-rimmed basin. His traveling companion was doing the same in the basin next to his. Around them the walls murmured faintly with the many comings and goings of the palace of Hale.

"I can't get the damn smell of gunsmoke out of my hair," said Antonin Kestrel. This had been his first mission for the pilot as well. The two men (so young they had been!) glanced at one an-other ruefully as they scrubbed.

Naturally there were no leads as to who had tried to have them killed earlier that afternoon. He and Kestrel had been led into an ambush in an alley by their official guide, and only good swords-manship and the intervention of a passing stranger had saved them. (He had no idea at the time, but that passing stranger had been his future wife, Venera.) The local authorities professed to be outraged, and were, he'd been told, torching the neighborhood where the attack had happened, just to be safe. Chaison imagined someone in a sumptuous palace lounge planning the whole thing, offering the destruction of an undesirable block of buildings as a bonus to the paranoid king of Hale.

They continued cleaning up, and neither spoke for a long time. Then Chaison said what was on both their minds. "Do you think we were sent here to be disposed of?"

"By Hale's king?" asked Kestrel, scowling at the lemon-yellow wallpaper. "Or our own pilot?"

"I hate to say this," Chaison said with a grimace, "but it could be either—or both."

Chaison Fanning's crimson dress uniform did not mark him as coming from a family that had any hope of succession to the throne of Slipstream. This might not matter; the wandering nation he called home was kept together more by external threats than internal cohesion. Chaison represented the admiralty—was their bright young hope—and the admiralty's power was the pilot's chief worry. Kestrel was from the civil service. Did the pilot see them both as future threats? He had claimed that sending only Chaison and one companion to Hale would be seen as a gesture of trust by the king; it also made it easier to kill them once they got here.

Kestrel gave up on his hair. "The problem, old man, is that we have to play our parts, no matter what. Even if it means walking into more traps."

Chaison had nodded stoically. His "part" on that occasion was to tell the paranoid king of the backward little nation that Slipstream had no intention of altering the trajectory of two cities, holding half a million people between them, that were on a collision course with Hale. While air moved quickly within Virga, massive objects like asteroids, lakes, and cities tended to maintain majestically slow orbits, circling around Candesce and rising and falling in the fountains of air that the great sun of suns propelled outward. Unlike most nations, Slipstream had tied its fortunes—literally—to a mountain of rock that obstinately steered its own course around the world, indifferent to politics or economics. Slipstream was about to brush past Hale. The friction of its passing could be minimal, or huge. This was the message Chaison was to deliver to the crabbed old murderer who sat uneasily on Hale's throne.

In retrospect, it was almost obvious that the most convenient outcome for both Slipstream and Hale would be the messenger's death. Just as it was obvious in hindsight that the pilot of Slipstream had known about Falcon's imminent attack, and had been prepared to allow it to happen for some reason—perhaps as a joint operation between Falcon and Slipstream to intimidate the Gretels, with no real conquest and some stronger alliance to come out of it. Maybe Chaison hadn't been set up to fall this time, but he'd made himself a convenient patsy anyway.

He'd always thought he was a realist. It was starting to hit home to Chaison just how much of a dreamer he'd really been.

THE DISTANT SUNS were shutting down again, the sky painted in tones of mauve and amber, when Antaea's troublesome admiral finally stumbled into the circus dormitory. Antaea had arranged for them to be given the same room—pinioning the place's self-styled concierge with a withering stare when he objected—and was already here. She had even managed to sleep a couple of hours, but the fear of him walking in on her as she slept kept waking her up. That, and drifting thoughts about the things he'd said after their ridiculous revivalist induction into Corbus's defense league. Chaison had talked like one of the heroes from the storybooks she'd once read for Telen (and herself). She'd never believed that heroes like that existed in real life, but you could be wistful and dream sometimes. Yet here he was, the noble admiral, sacrificing himself to save a city. It was romantic, and ridiculous, and extremely confusing.

With Corbus's defense league only hours old, there was no reason Chaison should receive the message telling him where to sleep, so Antaea was both surprised and relieved when he stalked down the little centrifuge's narrow flight of steps and came to a halt in the center of the living room. He looked dazed.

"So," she said brightly, "how was your day?" She had changed into a black silk robe with long-necked birds embroidered on it. He didn't seem to notice either her irony or her attire as he rubbed a hand across his brow.

"This is going to be a disaster. I tried to convince them to posture—mount a credible-looking defense and then negotiate for better surrender terms. They want to fight. I don't understand why they insist on doing it, they'll just lose more that way."

"I understand them," said Antaea. She stood up, feeling the Coriolis and centrifugal forces of the dormitory cylinder pulling the different parts of her in different directions. He collapsed on a couch under a huge set of crossed circus javelins, and she came to sit on a yellow-and-red star-spangled drum, draped with blankets, that served as the room's only other seat. "You need to spend some time out in the streets. Then you'd see."

He grimaced. "I was out for a while. It's a beautiful city, aye. I'm not sure the Gretels would dismantle it. It's exactly the sort of prize they're after."

"I'm not talking about the beauty," she said. "Think about Corbus and his volunteers. A self-styled mayor, army veterans whose glory days are long past—all these unexpected heroes who were, well, clowns! and servants yesterday. These people have been given a tiny glimpse of a new world, one in which they are masters of their own fate, and now the Gretels are going to come in and take it all away from them. That's why they're fighting."

"That's crazy," said Chaison with a shake of his head. "If they beat back the Gretels, the pols will return in a week and they'll be back where they started. It's either Falcon or the Gretels for them."

"I don't think they believe that," she mused, staring out the ever-changing window at distant city lights. "I'm not sure I do either."

He looked surprised. "You're more of an idealist than I thought."

"Idealist? You don't have to be an idealist to see that our world is frozen in midnightmare. It's a world of despots and tyrannies, full of premature death and lifelong misery. And why? Because the energy field Candesce uses to keep alien forces from invading Virga, this field also suppresses the very technologies that might pull us out of the barbarism we're sunk in!

"You had in your hands the means to change things. And what did you do? You frittered it away to win one trifling battle in the name of one trifling little pirate state out on the edge of nowhere. How pathetic!"

That was her frustration talking, but she couldn't stop herself. Chaison seemed unmoved, however. He leaned back in his chair and rested his hands on its arms. "You're obviously not used to having power," he said mildly.

"What's that supposed to mean?"

"You think I didn't know what I could do with the key?" He gazed at her coolly. "Or, more precisely, what it *looked like* I could do?" He shook his head. "Using power and controlling outcomes—those are two different things. You learn that when you lead something like a navy. You can aim it, you can let it fly, but after that it's all up to the gods. The one thing you can be sure of is that you'll cause chaos.

"The key to Candesce unlocks absolute power over every man, woman, and child in Virga. With it, you can heat or cool the whole world, change the winds, still them completely; freeze your neighbors and let your own country bloom. Or you can—" He paused, squinted at her—"Cause another outage. Let artificial nature into our world.

"You can unleash Candesce; but you can't control it."

Silence hung momentarily.

Antaea pushed down on her anger. She made herself smile. "Oh, but you can." She sat down again, leaning forward and clasping her hands. "You wielded Candesce like a hammer to smash your enemies. But the sun of suns is a much more subtle instrument than you know. It's true it wreaks havoc with electrical devices; you probably don't know that it also limits the amount of data that can be processed per cubic centimeter in Virga. The way you used it, I'll bet you think the suppression field is a kind of switch that is either *on* or *off*. But it's not like that at all. It can be dialed up or down. It's just that right now, it's dialed all the way up."

Chaison steepled his hands and leaned back. He gazed at her over his fingertips (and a brief up-and-down flick of his eyes told her that he'd finally noticed how she was dressed). "How do you know this?" he said.

"Because I work for the guard. They have knowledge of things everyone else in Virga has forgotten. I've seen Candesce's design."

His eyes remained fixed on her from behind the peak of his fingers. If he was impressed, he gave no sign. "This is all very interesting," he said slowly, "but beside the point. Let me summarize our situation. You want me to tell you where the key to Candesce is, so that you—*you*, not the home guard—can use it to dial back the barrier that prevents artificial nature from infecting Virga. Not to the point that A.N. can enter Virga, but to some point near that."

"Well. Yes," she said. "And you think my motives are selfish, and everybody's selfish until the unthinkable happens to them. And when that happens, some of them stay selfish—but some come to realize that they're just like everybody else. What happens to others matters as much as what happens to them."

"So what unthinkable thing happened to you, Antaea, to make you so unselfish as to risk your life for this?"

He was too close to it. She had to put him back on the defensive, and quickly, so she leaped to her feet and stood over him, hands on her hips. "I might ask you the same thing, Admiral Fanning. Why are you risking your life for these people? And don't give me that noble claptrap about responsibility. You don't believe it any more than I do.

"This is about fear, isn't it? About you being afraid to go home."

He sputtered and half-stood and Antaea knew she had struck home. "You're afraid that you have no home to return to. No house, no position, no wife—"

Chaison was on his feet now, standing nose to nose with her, his fists bunched. She could smell him, feel the heat rising off his body. Suddenly Antaea didn't know what to say.

They stood like that for seconds too long, neither speaking. He moved; and she had a moment of anxious anticipation—and then realized he was sitting down, looking away.

Angry, she sat as well. The awkward silence lengthened; it had to be broken somehow, so she said, "Have you looked out there? Thousands of those people—the people behind those windows you see now—are going to *die.*" She didn't want to continue this argument, but it was all she could think of right now. "And why?" she rolled on. "Oh sure, because the Gretels are going to attack the city, that's the surface reason. But the real reason is that the people have no control over their own destinies. Yet they could. They could!"

He glanced back at her—and damn him, was he smiling? "Yes I want the damned key to Candesce!" Antaea said desperately. "So does the guard, but they just want to lock it away somewhere, against the day. They're afraid of its power. I want to give that power to the people. So that they can save themselves."

Now for some reason her face felt hot. Antaea threw up a hand up in frustration, stood, and stalked toward the little bedroom. "Why am I even talking to you? You don't want things to change. You're an aristocrat!"

He was on his feet in a second, his hand clamped around her upper arm. "I don't want to be here," he hissed. "But I don't have the luxury of making choices, Antaea. All my choices were made for me the day I was born. Which boys would be my friends; where I would go to school. Who I could talk to, who I had to ignore. What I would become. Even the decision to go against the pilot's orders, even that had to be done. The only time I ever did anything for myself—on my own—was when I married—"

He let go of her arm.

He stepped back, his expression troubled.

Here was her only chance, Antaea realized. Persuasion had failed. He had faced down the torturers. She was left with seduction, which had been on her mind anyway since the moment she met him; and so she rallied her courage, moved close and started to raise her mouth to his—then saw his face.

It held an expression of defeated resignation. She saw infinite patience there, the look of a man who has long ago abandoned himself to his role in life. It came to her that he knew what was coming, had plotted out each of her moves as on a chessboard, long before she spoke or acted. He knew what she intended, and thought he knew why she would be doing it. If he responded, it would only be as a countermove in a game he obviously took no pleasure in playing.

"Fuck it," she said, stepping away from him. "Listen, Chaison, it's late, we're both exhausted . . ."

He watched her, eyes wide.

"I was going to demand the bed, but let's be fair about this, why not?" She went to the table and rummaged in one of the belt pouches lying there.

Antaea turned and held up a bronze coin. "I'll flip you for it," she said lightly. "Loser gets the couch."

He laughed.

They flipped.

She lost.

11

DAWN FOUND THE city transformed. Antaea couldn't be-
lieve what she saw from the spinning windows of the circus dormitory; she went outside and stood in the air, and it was still
there.

Work gangs coordinated by Chaison's lieutenants had spent the
previous day and all of last night sawing Stonecloud apart. Now the
city was in pieces, each a neighborhood a thousand or more feet
across comprised of green forest, gray stone, and flashing glass.
Straining jets and propellers on all manner of tugs, taxis, trucks,
and buses struggled to rearrange the blocks in a new order.
Stonecloud had been a bowl-shaped city before, in keeping with
the theatrical style of architecture. Now that bowl was exploded,
transforming over the hours into an expanding, medusa-shaped
cloud. Its farthest reaches were made up of bikes, catamarans,
market craft, and anything else that had its own engine; inside this
were individual buildings, then whole blocks, and at the center of
it all the majestically turning town-wheels. These at first appeared
untouched. As Antaea looked more closely, she realized they had
slowed their rotation. Over the hours they slowly edged to a stop,
and then thousands of odd objects, never made for freefall or
intended to be tied down, rose up and drifted into a cloud in the
wheels' centers. Chairs, ornamental pots, statues, bookcases,
books, and whole wardrobes full of clothing lofted out of windows and doors, exhaled into the air like mist in winter.

"That's deliberate," said Chaison when he returned from the planning session he'd attended before daybreak. He sat on her bike in some bizarre circus outfit/dress uniform they'd cobbled together for him ("it's not meant to be pretty, just visible," he'd said with a grimace) and pointed to different features of the shattered city with the rifle he held.

"The airspace inside the town-wheels is full of hazards to stop bikes or missiles—or battleshops—getting in there. If they're going to fire upon the city, they'll have to do so from outside."

"And this . . . obscene destruction?"

"Move maneuverable items to the periphery. A cloud formation to make it hard for them to surround us. Most delicate objects at the center." He pointed again. "Semaphore stations to relay orders from the command center. I'm going there now, I came to pick you up."

She jumped and he grabbed her ankle, lowering her into the seat behind him. They shot into a chaotic airspace filled with contrails, unattached ropes, families pushing huge nets containing their worldly possessions; under, over, and around zipping bikes, undulant dolphins, and bewildered, winged people. Shafts of sunlight lit the turbulent flocks unpredictably as forests and buildings drifted about.

A shrill siren cut the air and vessels and people darted away from something happening just ahead. Chaison brought the bike to a stop, turning it so she could watch.

They hovered near what had once been a beautiful park. Spherical, its outer shell a delicate filigree of intertwined tree limbs, it held a water drop two hundred feet across—a small lake. The park had been peeled like an orange, and the work gang who had done that work were fleeing. The only man left near the lake was a burly hard-hatted laborer hiding behind a metal shield. Wires trailed from something in his hand through the air and into the water. Just as Antaea realized what he was going to do, he twisted the thing he held.

The lake exploded.

First, a sphere of white appeared at the very center of the greenish ball, then the sphere expanded with lightning speed and the surface disappeared into an expanding cloud of mist.

Chaison twisted the throttle and they raced ahead of whirling, shuddering drops. "What the hell was that for?" shouted Antaea over the noise of the engine.

"They'll tow the water to the outskirts to make a missile barrier," he said. He pointed as they shot past another gang that was stripping the branches off some beautiful, ancient oaks. "Those will be sharpened and tied into a wall formation. We'll put riflemen behind it."

A catamaran—two spindle-shaped hulls connected by an engine nacelle—pulled next to the bike. One of the men aboard waved his arms frantically. Chaison pulled over and cut his engine.

"—Barricaded inside their mansions!" the man yelled. "They're firing on our people!"

"Just for the hell of it?" asked Chaison. "Or are we doing something to provoke them?"

"Well, we did turn off their gravity."

It emerged that some of the wealthier citizens had stayed behind when the apparatchiks and industrialists bailed out of the city. They were hunkered down in their estates, with private security forces patrolling their perimeters. Having little contact with the rest of the city, they doubtless assumed that Stonecloud had fallen into some state of mad anarchy. After all, the whole place was being torn apart around them, and the wheels themselves had stopped turning. They were shooting at any work gang that came near.

"They're terrified," said Chaison. "Leave them alone."

They sped on. "There is a lot of looting going on," Chaison commented, "but it can't be helped. I need every able-bodied man and woman on the barricades."

"Then it really is anarchy!"

He shrugged angrily. "I have a couple of photographers moving through the city. They're taking pictures of the looters. There'll be a reckoning—just not today."

They pulled up next to Corbus's "command bunker"—which was actually just the circus ball, towed from its position at the focus of the amphitheater to a place where most of the exploded city was visible. A number of semaphore men hung from the wicker now, some waving their bright flags, others watching distant precincts for incoming messages.

Antaea didn't know whether to be impressed by the energy of it all, or laugh at the absurdity. "You did all this overnight?"

Chaison laughed as he reached for a mooring rope. "It's the circus, believe it or not. They were organized on paramilitary lines and travel as an independent unit. They're used to putting up and striking sets on deadline."

Antaea wasn't sure what she'd been expecting in the command bunker—salutes, at least. What she found as she climbed into the building after Chaison was pandemonium. Men and women flew to and fro, or argued in midair, clipboards flapping. The circus ball was a maze of little chambers, most of them crammed with brightly colored circus gear. Somebody had strung painted ropes through the place in an attempt to organize it; little signs were tied to these every thirty feet or so. Chaison and Antaea followed a blue rope that was marked COMMAND CENTRAL by various hands and in various creative misspellings.

The central sphere was one big room that had until recently contained machines, if the unpainted squares of wall, rivet holes, and bent stantions were anything to go on. Most of the room was now taken up by a passable model of the two cities, made up of little wooden blocks that slowly rotated like a madman's mobile in the middle of the chamber. Any blank spot on the walls was festooned with photos, many annotated in red pen or flagged with brightly feathered darts. Corbus's new defense staff tumbled slowly through the air, most cross-legged and writing furiously on their lap-desks.

Corbus himself sat overflowing a metal chair that was mounted above the floating map. She'd been hearing more about him, not all of it good. For years now, he had been a kind of ghost figure at the circus, despite his place at top billing. The other performers only saw him during his shows; in between times he hid away in his little cabin, which was walled, ceilinged, and carpeted with books. He was unfailingly polite when he spoke to people, but terribly quiet as though he didn't quite believe he had the right to speak.

He was nothing like that now. "We need sixteen of those, not eight!" he roared at an elderly looking man who had been showing him something. "My God, I made a simple request, how is anything going to get done around here?" He looked up and saw Chaison and Antaea. "Admiral, how does it look out there?"

"Good," said Chaison. "Things are coming together."

"Coming apart, I hope you mean." Corbus beetled his brows expressively and turned his attention to Antaea. "Our home guard ally. I trust you slept well while the pirate admiral here took apart our city around you?"

She smiled. "Pirate?"

"Oh, haven't you heard?" He hesitated—for an instant she saw a hint of the reticent, shy man who'd been described to her. Then he plunged on. "This fellow conquered a country! His people took over Aerie, now they're plundering it, and when they're done they'll drop it behind them like a gnawed fruit. Slipstream's a pirate nation, and this here's the chief pirate." He grinned wolfishly at Chaison. "Which is why I'm glad he's on our side."

Chaison looked like he wanted to argue and had even opened his mouth when Antaea cut in with, "I'm sure he's just what the city needs. But how about you, have you had any sleep?"

"Me?" Corbus looked surprised at the question. "I . . . don't re-call. Don't think so." Then, before her eyes, he seemed to crumple in on himself as if he'd suddenly lost a hundred pounds. He squinted, rubbed at his eyes. "It's hard," he said quietly, "keeping the brave face on hour after hour. How do you do it?" She realized he was addressing Chaison now.

Chaison frowned. "I delegate."

Corbus gave a gravelly laugh. "Yes, well, as you can see there's little chance of that happening here." He blew out a sigh. "I feel like a prisoner, can't take a damned crap without somebody knocking on the door. The people put me here and I'll be damned if I do anything to disappoint them, but it's hard.

"Which brings me to your plans to fire incendiaries at Never-land's suburbs." He waggled a sheet of paper accusingly at Chaison.

"I have to consider all scenarios," Chaison said. "It's not a choice I would make lightly—"

"Enough!" Corbus splayed his great, muscled arms. "I know all about hard choices. Just look at me. I took orders once and I gave them; and afterward, I ran and hid from the world for twenty years." He glowered at Chaison. "You know, Fanning, I'd rather do without you entirely. Your kind brought us to this point. I'm not un-grateful for your help, it's just . . . this isn't really your fight, is it?"

"I'm interested in the safety of the people who live here," said Chaison. He didn't sound particularly defensive, merely matter-of-fact.

"I'm sure you are, but you're not trained to protect people, are you? You're trained to slam ships and soldiers together until so many people on the other side have died that their commanders' nerves break."

"Isn't that what you need me to do?"

Corbus shook his head. "No, because ultimately it's not going to be the navies or their commanders who decide how this siege ends, nor aristocrats like you. It'll be the people."

Chaison blinked, opened his mouth, then closed it again. That was all Antaea saw of his dismay, but it was enough. "Your job—and your only job," said Corbus in an intense, almost strangled voice, "is to checkmate the Gretels' ships. The cities you must leave to me."

Now Chaison looked puzzled. "What are you going to do?"

"You won't understand it," said Corbus. "But you'll see."

He rubbed at his eyes again, then pushed himself back in his seat, looking cornered and haunted. "So forget your incendiaries—come talk to me about your plan to stymie their ships. Explain these darts to me again."

THE CITIES CIRCLED warily. Stonecloud had transformed from a green bowl cupping spinning town-wheels, into something like a giant claw, smudged with diesel and jet smoke, its shattered fingers made of buildings and tipped with the sharp prows of ships. It made slow grabs for the nebulous suburbs of Neverland, which reared back and soughed around it.

Neverland was fully disarticulated, a nimble armada of buildings and ships. Its own town-wheels waited miles behind the main body, a nervous baggage train that presented Chaison with a tempting target. He might be able to get a few missiles past the nets and gravel clouds in the intervening space, but it probably wasn't worth the effort. Attacking Neverland's wheels would not slow the assault.

A steady stream of reports and fresh, sulfur-smelling photographs poured into Command Central (or Command Centril, as it said on the sign outside the door). Despite the chaos, the level of competence in the room was actually pretty high, because Stonecloud, like any large city, boasted its share of veterans as citizens. Some of these were elderly, but some were young and many were stubbornly loyal to Falcon Formation. Chaison had no idea how they were reconciling their situation with that patriotism—since the government they believed in had shamelessly abandoned them—but he didn't care all that much as long as they did their jobs. Chaison scanned reports, talked to people, pointed to this or that part of the drifting cloud of buildings, asked questions, and occasionally issued orders. Mostly, he sent suggestions to Corbus and the former Atlas did the actual commanding. This was fine by Chaison.

None of it was going to do any good anyway. Neverland's strategy was clear: the best way to take a city was to absorb it, and Neverland was simply bigger than Stonecloud. However beautiful the Falcon regional capital was, its identity would not survive. Its neighborhoods would be dissolved into Neverland like grains of salt in a glass of water—and if they couldn't be, they could be split up and distributed throughout the rest of the Gretels' cities.

As night fell, a new set of photographs came in. "What does it mean?" asked the boy who handed Chaison the prints. He had obviously been rifling through them as he flew up here. Chaison ignored the lax discipline and held up one picture, then another.

Half-hidden behind the swarming buildings of Neverland was a huge cloud of people, all in the open in a three-quarter's sphere formation. There must have been twenty thousand or more bodies in that cloud. At its center, bright lights silhouetted several tiny dots.

"It's a rally," he said absently. "A public rally. Those aren't soldiers." *I hope those aren't soldiers.*

Shuffling through the rest of the pictures, he found another showing a similar formation elsewhere in the city. All the images had been taken through telephoto lenses, and were blurred from atmosphere and engine smog. "Damn! It must be half the city . . ."

He whistled loudly, turning heads up and down the room. "I need somebody who knows Neverland. Who's lived there." After a minute of consultation a middle-aged woman edged out of the drift of people. Chaison gestured her closer, and showed her the pictures.

"They hold these all the time," she said. "Indoctrination rallies, to make sure everybody understands whatever fairy tale they're modeling current policy on. It would be good to know which tale they're using today . . ." Then she shrugged, and handed the pictures back to Chaison. "Attendance is mandatory, but because of that the rallies have lost their punch. Nobody cares; you'd be hard pressed to find a more cynical bunch than Gretel townspeople. The government's always crying wolf, so if they're hoping to whip up mass enthusiasm from the people with this, it's not likely to work."

Chaison refrained from asking what a crying wolf was. He was not reassured by her words. "They expect their citizens to become conquerors," he said. "They'll have prepared for this over a long time."

"Maybe." She shrugged again. "But nobody believes the government."

Preparations didn't slow for nighttime, but Chaison had reached the end of his strength. As he let himself be flown to a new, larger apartment on one of the town-wheels, the image kept going through his mind of Neverland's people pouring into Stonecloud bearing swords, knives, and homemade truncheons. What had they been told about the people they were supposed to subdue? Chaison had been taught to mistrust and fear the people of Falcon; he had only just come to see them as they were, as ordinary folk struggling to maintain sane lives under the heel of an oppressive system. The Gretels were past masters at distorting reality. Had they told their people that Stonecloud was full of trolls and wicked witches, all of whom deserved to die?

His handlers dropped him off at the axis of the two-hundred-foot apartment wheel. He found himself thinking of freedom in clear skies as he climbed into a railed slot at the top and bounced his way into vertigo and increasing weight. It would be good to be flying, a new man with a different name, in some far corner of the world . . .

He found the little apartment at the end of a quiet, carpet-lined hall, entered, and closed the door gratefully.

It was very dark in here. He strewed his clothes indiscriminately as he made his way to the half-seen bed. It was only as he climbed in that he realized Antaea was already in it.

She chuckled. "Hello."

"Hello." He smiled into the blackness, feeling her warmth next to him. It would be so easy to just turn over and enfold her in his arms; but somehow—when exactly he wasn't sure—they had come to an unspoken agreement. Whatever attraction they felt for one another was off-limits to the game Antaea was playing on behalf of her guard masters. Knowing this made him feel hugely relieved, and relaxed to be around her. Somehow, chastity had become a little island of trust on which they both could shelter.

"When?" she murmured; he knew what she was asking.

"A few hours at most," he said. "By dawn tomorrow, it'll have begun."

Then he turned over and, sensing her relax beside him, fell instantly asleep.

FOR THE GRETELS, dawn came three hours early. As startled sentries in Stonecloud blinked at the sudden day, four fast cruisers leaped out of Neverland's jostling towers, batting aside a few Falcon bikes that tried to intercept them. They roared to within hailing distance of Stonecloud's outer neighborhoods, and broadsided them.

Work gangs had been at it all through the night, strewing rubble from the dismantling of the city into the surrounding air. The idea was to create a no-fly zone for bikes, ships, and missiles. The problem was that the rubble eventually drifted off-station, so in the end it was easy for the Gretels to find breaks through which to fire. Sixteen, twenty, forty rockets slewed through the inevitable gaps in Chaison's defenses, impacting deep within the city.

Chaison was standing on a T-bar atop the circus ball. The rumble of the explosions momentarily drowned out the flutter of semaphore flags from behind him. Orange blossoms of flame peeked between the crowding neighborhoods.

"They mean to sow confusion in the heart of the city," he commented to Corbus, who watched silently, gnawing his calloused knuckles. "They'll also block our sight lines."

Behind the bombardment, Neverland was moving. The two cities had played out a ponderous dance throughout the night, with Neverland trying to line up its neighborhoods for strikes into the heart of Stonecloud, and the Falcon city eluding its grasp like some deep-winter jellyfish, drawing strings of buildings in and whipping them out again at a mile per hour or less. Stonecloud's fuel reserves had run out late in the night, the thousands of trucks and private vehicles that were towing the buildings disengaging one by one. Houses had begun to collide. It was this deep grumble, the sound of a giant grinding its teeth together, that had finally awakened Chaison and Antaea.

More missiles arrowed into the city. Chaison had nothing comparable to fire back. He was gratified, though, to see that most of the explosions were taking place in dense clouds of forest; leaves and twigs flew, but so far nothing had come close to the town-wheels.

These were the strategic target. The Gretels' plan was obvious: to absorb the zero-gravity sections of the city directly into Neverland, and to dominate the town-wheels by placing heavily armed cruisers inside their spokes. The plan would succeed as long as their navy led the attack; without those cruisers Neverland might end up being assimilated by Stonecloud instead. Much of

Chaison's time over the past twenty-four hours had been spent working on how to cause that hesitation.

A young page jumped up to the T-bar from a nearby semaphore station. "They're firing into the debris cloud on the outskirts. Lots of rockets, lots of explosions!"

He nodded. "High-explosive charges, no doubt. The shock waves will clear the debris. They're making a hole they can pass through. I need to know if the gauntlets are ready. Send reserve gangs there, there, and there," he pointed. "And alert the winter wraith's team to start lining up the sticks."

Stonecloud didn't have conventional rockets; but that didn't mean the city didn't have missiles. He shook his head at the folly of the plan. The Gretels would be laughing about it tomorrow.

The Gretels had split their naval force into two; one squadron of ships headed straight into the gap they'd blown in the city's defenses while the other could be glimpsed as bright flickers of light passing behind building and cloud, far too fast for the gauntlet gangs to follow. They were circling around the city at high speed looking for a second way in.

The first squadron nosed through the last flinders of drifting debris. Bullets pinged off their metal hulls, but the five cruisers were battened down, their own machine-gun snouts poking out of steel domes. They peppered the buildings ahead of them with bullets, easily suppressing the defenders' uncoordinated rifle fire. One launched a rocket into an apartment wheel, which convulsed and flew apart, filling the arteries behind it with flying masonry. The cruisers shoved past the smoke and into a wider artery, a kind of cave formed of massive, essentially immobile municipal buildings that opened out after a quarter mile into the central space of Stonecloud. The air here was clear, the buildings static; the cruisers sped up.

The other squadron had found an opening on the far side of the city. Rockets erupted from their sides in startled lines as they spiraled through the broad gap in the buildings. The town-wheels beckoned through divergent clouds of forest, lake, and housing.

Chaison yelled "Now!" and the semaphore men waved their flags in grand gestures against the backdrop of shattered city. Simultaneously, two very different attacks unfolded.

The first squadron suddenly found the artery closing in around them. The government buildings were too heavy to move; but they had been spaced in such a way that dozens of smaller houses could be fitted between them. All through the city the obvious avenues had been similarly lined. Now, gauntlet teams consisting of hundreds of bikes, trucks, and other vehicles were converging on the houses from behind and pushing them into the artery. Before they could react, the cruisers found themselves boxed in—with houses ahead, mansions behind, and more closing in fast from the sides. Two of the cruisers opened fire but at such close range their rockets just blew the houses into fragments that rebounded toward them.

A spindle-shaped metal monster bristling with rocket ports and machine guns tried to turn; its captain had spied a narrow alley between the heavier municipal blocks. It was too late. Two stone mansions hit it from opposite sides, folding around it in a puff of masonry dust. Behind and before it, two more ships were bumped by passing houses—and then the artery became one slow crash, with cubic, octahedral, and spherical buildings shearing and breaking and five Gretel ships being chewed in their midst.

Across town, the other squadron had better luck. They had circled around faster than the gauntlet teams could react and now found an avenue of empty air that led straight to the vulnerable wheels at the city's heart.

Antaea had seen them coming. She waited, mouth dry and heart pounding, near the wheels with several dozen men on bikes and a small cloud of tree trunks. These had been chosen for their size and straightness, and had been pruned and sharpened into vicious spikes. As people shouted and pointed at the four cruisers, Antaea nodded at her wingman and they set to work.

The bikes were tied together with heavy cable—some in pairs, some by four in a cross formation. Antaea and her wingman had brought their bikes in close on either side of a pole, with the cable trailing out behind them to wrap around its flat base. For many long minutes they had sat in the air, each holding a metal hook that gripped the splintered trunk just behind the sharpened point. Now with the help of a third bike they nudged the pole into a turn, until it was lined up pointing straight down the artery the Gretels were coming up. Then they opened their throttles wide.

For long seconds, nothing happened. Then, impelled by two howling jet engines, the sharpened log began to move. On all sides, other poles were inching forward, their acceleration slow but inexorable.

Bullets drew a cage of tracer lines around Antaea. The incoming cruisers could obviously see that a small cloud of bikes was headed their way. Odds were, though, that they couldn't see the poles, which were end-on to them. Antaea leaned into her saddle, willing more power into the bike.

When they had the poles up to thirty miles per hour, she signaled her wingman again. As one they turned their bikes out and away from the pole. Now the cable was acting like the string of a bow, and the pole was its arrow. The two diverging bikes shot their missile as the cable snapped and rebounded. Antaea had a moment of terror as she watched the steel whip lash straight at her; the bike lurched under her and then the world started spinning.

Twelve sharpened logs met four armored cruisers at the mouth of the artery. The first pole bounced off the curved prow of a ship and shot spinning through the air. It took out a two-hundred-year-old house, casting sculptures and broken frescoes into the sky.

The second pole rang another cruiser like a bell and left a deep dent in its side. Another log hit the scored plates and went straight through them. Bright metal flew as the thirty-foot needle disappeared entirely into the cruiser. Pithed, the ship began to drift.

Antaea saw some of this, but she was flipping head over heels through the air as her bike wove a drunken contrail in the opposite direction. It shuddered as machine-gun fire caught it, then blew up.

She spotted a cruiser with a huge shaft jutting out of it, gouting smoke and tumbling; then she flew through the clawing branches of a tree and out into open air again. Stunned by blows from the branches, she could only watch helplessly as the pipe-choked underside of a town-wheel got closer second by second.

SHARP BANGS ECHOED through the city, punctuating the faint sound of cheering from Stonecloud's residents. Chaison frowned, listening to the irregular popping. It came from the direction of the first Gretel squadron and made a pattern. The pattern repeated twice.

"They're signaling somebody, probably the other ships," he told Corbus. Lacking the wireless technology Aubri Mahallan had once shown him, the Gretels were using percussion-charge strings, a common enough way of messaging in cloud or darkness.

"It's almost time," Corbus said suddenly. Chaison turned to him, frowning; he wasn't watching the Gretels' ships at all, but had his eyes fixed somewhere beyond the edge of the city. "I'm going to leave you for a while," said the Atlas. "You're doing fine, Fanning. But it's time for the real action to commence."

"What real act—" But Corbus was already gone, bounding away to the row of parked bikes near the circus ball's door. Several men were there waiting, and they shot away from the ball in formation.

Chaison felt betrayed; whatever Corbus had planned, he hadn't seen fit to trust his prized admiral with the information. This couldn't be good—but he had no time to think about it right now. Chaison needed to know what was happening in the dust-choked artery where the first Gretel squadron had disappeared, as well as in the vent far down the curve of forest and building where the second had run into Antaea's logs. The first squadron still had not emerged; they seemed to be stuck, though he had no illusions they had been destroyed. Of the four ships in the other squadron, one was disabled, another had hove to in order to help it, and another was drifting as its crew labored to remove the beam in its side. The fourth cruiser was circling slowly, laying down covering fire for the others.

Suddenly it changed direction. He saw a purposeful flare of exhaust blur the air around it as it went from a distant, short line to a dot. It kept this shape as the seconds lengthened.

Chaison glanced around. Absurdly, he found himself hesitate—the semaphoremen were intent on their tasks, the pages were flying about on angels' wings, equally focused, and a steady stream of photographers and other reconnaissance personnel were hopping on and off bikes at the circus ball's entrances. At last they were starting to look like a team.

"All vessels to your fallback posts!" he yelled as loudly as he could. "Everybody else—inside! Now!" Chaison dove off the T-bar and yanked the flags out of the hands of a startled semaphoreman. "Now!"

There was no time to turn and look, but his imagination served him better than sight: flares of light would be appearing now around the expanding dot of the distant cruiser. Each orange star would last just a few seconds, but in that time the missiles would approach the speed of sound. They would be here just . . . about . . .

Something flickered in his peripheral vision, and an explosion scraped half the wicker footing off the circus ball.

A wall of shocked air washed Chaison into the sky.

THE UNDERSIDE OF the motionless town-wheel had become a wall. Antaea blinked and shook her head, then realized she was flying at it at more than a hundred miles per hour. She would hit the tangle of pipes, struts, and guy wires in seconds.

Cursing, she reached down to unclip her wing restraints. The feather-lined wings snapped out and back, nearly dislocating her shoulders. Instantly she went into a spin—the wings were designed this way, to create a stable shuttlecock for rapid braking. Antaea threw out her arms to moderate the motion.

Something struck her hip, and before she could react, her arm was knocked numb. Antaea hit herself in the face with her own bicep. Her feet struck something solid and she crumpled as best she could, hitting shoulder, jaw, and ear in turn.

Dazed, she hung in the air for a while, vaguely aware that she was surrounded by gigantic gray limbs and birds' beaks. A forest and birds made of . . . metal? She groaned, spat blood, and turned her head cautiously.

She was tangled in the understructure of the town-wheel. These big metal ones routed all their plumbing under street level and the pipes and pump stations were streamlined, which explained the strange birds' heads: metal teardrop-shaped bunkers where men could work were mounted under the wheel.

Thunder tore the air. Antaea grabbed a taut cable with her right hand—her left arm was still numb—and pulled herself past the pipes. The formerly empty airspace where she had lined up her squad was speckled with clouds of smoke, debris, and the instantaneous red lines of tracer fire. At the heart of it all were four ships, one drifting, another aswarm with men who were pulling a tree-sized dart out of it; and two more with their engine wash facing her. These were making straight for Chaison's bunker and were firing rockets as they went. Through the heat-distorted air she glimpsed explosions in the distance.

The nagging, rational part of her mind—the part that never shut up—told her that she still had leads. If she'd lost Chaison Fanning, she might still track down his men, Darius and Richard, and find the key through them.

She hated herself for thinking this way.

Using her feet and right hand, she monkey-swung her way through the forest of pipes until she came to an egg-shaped pump house. This had a little hatch on it, probably never used before based on how hard it was to open. Prying it back, she climbed in and found, as expected, a shaft and ladder leading toward street level.

Antaea swam along the shaft, trying not to hear the coughing rumble of distant explosions.

12

THE CITY OF Neverland made its move. All morning it had closed its suburbs like the claws of a giant hand, encircling and devouring Stonecloud; but it had paused, its boxy houses a hundred yards from the nearest Falcon dwellings. People of both cities fixed frightened gazes on their sudden neighbors from behind curtains and hastily hammered barricades. The vista stretched for miles: a thousand cornices and shingled walls turned to present now this, now that glass surface to the sunlight—and from behind all of them, eyes watched.

The military was elsewhere. In the case of Falcon Formation, it had never been here. There were rumors of a new city council, of some famous general or admiral guiding the work gangs that had broken up the city. Out in the arteries that fed the local neighborhoods, bikes and cargo haulers moved purposefully; few of the residents knew who they were answerable to or what they were doing.

The citizens of Neverland knew the Gretel navy was there . . . somewhere. They could hear the battle progressing—everyone could, it crashed through the clouds of housing like close thunder. Many of Neverland's people had attended the rallies, knew they were expected to subdue their new neighbors, by force if necessary. They were to take up makeshift weapons, whatever was at hand, and pound on the doors or smash the windows of the foreign houses, demanding surrender. The prospect was terrifying.

The navy had promised to be here. There were supposed to be lieutenants on bikes to direct them but apparently they were stretched too thin, or distracted. As the first neighborhood began its final move, some people crawled out onto the sides of their houses, clutching their broom-poles and knives, and stared around, looking for leadership. The houses were being pushed forward by fans, jets, and other contrivances, but the men running these were simply following distant semaphore instructions. They had no authority nor any idea of what to do if they lost sight of those faraway flags.

By chance it was two apartment blocks that came into contact first. The Falcon building was brick shaped and made of unadorned concrete, the Gretels' a windowed torus festooned with gingerbread carvings. As the buildings closed the last few yards their windows began opening and men appeared at them, armed with whatever was at hand. They stared at one another—and for miles in every direction, every eye, and every binocular and telescope was trained on them as well.

There was a gentle bump as a corner of the rectangular apartment touched its donut-shaped counterpart. Attackers and defenders were close enough now to see the fear on one another's faces. For long seconds, nobody moved.

Then someone stretched up out of a window on Falcon's side. He held no weapon, just a white cloth that he waved ahead of himself as he swung onto the side of the building. It was Corbus. With a gentle push of his feet he let go of his home and drifted into the small angle of open air that remained between the facades.

A murmur of recognition spread down the side of the flat-sided apartment. As everyone watched, the squat, heavily muscled Falcon man took a deep breath and bellowed, "The people of Stonecloud have no quarrel with the people of Neverland!"

Another murmur spread, this time on both sides. "We are the

same!" continued Corbus. "Pawns in the hands of men who would destroy our two great cities!

"Do you really believe," he asked the people peering at him from Neverland's apartments, "in your heart of hearts do you believe, that Neverland could swallow a foreign city and yet be unchanged?" He shook his head. "You know better. Whether you win or not, your great city will be annihilated in this change. Hasn't it already been, in large part?"

He'd struck a nerve there. Neverland's former arrangement—even its traditional locale in relation to its neighbors—had been erased for this attack. Corbus had judged correctly the resentment this would cause.

"But this need not be." He rolled each word out, like a line of heavy stones. As in Stonecloud's stadium days before, he thrust out his arms and legs to make a star shape, and said, "Join us, your neighbors! Not as conquerors or slaves, but as equals! Together we can say no to this pointless war. Restore our cities to their former glory. Live in peace together!"

His words echoed out then died in the distance. For a long moment there was silence, and stillness, up and down the plane of converging buildings. Then a window opened opposite Corbus.

An old man emerged. He too was weaponless, and held a single small scrap of paper in his hand: a bill of the mysterious rights currency that had recently begun circulating in both cities.

He drifted out. The two men came together in the air, and slowly each reached out. They clasped hands.

A gasp went up; a light of hope appeared in the eyes of those who moments before had been cowering behind their windows, awaiting an attack. Hesitantly, they began to gather, and point and murmur.

Then: "*Traitor!*" someone screamed. A lone figure erupted from a window on the Gretels' side, rifle raised. A shot sounded and the old man convulsed and let go of Corbus's hand. More shots, and

Corbus roared and put a hand to his ear, where a spray of blood was darkening the air. He grabbed a rope and hauled himself back toward the apartment window.

Shouts and roars of fury washed away from that central point like ripples on a lake. Suddenly there was gunfire everywhere; and as the rest of the buildings crunched together, chaos and madness descended on the cities of Stonecloud and Neverland.

ANTAEA EMERGED INTO a weightless street. As she climbed up the access shaft she'd imagined she was moving horizontally, gliding over the rungs of the ladder; that meant that when she pushed aside the metal street-cover and poked her head out, she found herself looking down (or up) a vast wall of cobblestones. Bereft of a ruling direction, the street was as vertiginous a surface as she'd ever seen.

Behind the shop window across the street, baguettes and bread loaves hung in the air like some magician's trick; the shingles on the shop's roof had risen up like the raised hackles of a frightened animal. A little ways down the road, a rocking chair hovered four feet above the cobbles; and everywhere, a haze of dust, pebbles, and grit that had accumulated on every horizontal surface over the years, was breathing itself slowly into the air.

She closed her eyes, concentrated, and imagined a new up and down, one in which the street was laid out flat and everything just happened to be weightless. It helped a bit; when she opened her eyes she was able to pretend she was stepping onto an ordinary road, but with the added ability to fly.

Everything was groaning, popping, and creaking as it eased out of the gravity-bound state it had been in for so long. What with this and the distant thunder of explosions, Antaea almost didn't notice the sliding sound behind her. She turned to find a rifle being aimed at her from an open second-story window.

She raised her hands. "I'm with the city," she shouted.

There was a pause. Then a slightly panicked voice yelled back, "Which city?"

"I'm defending Stonecloud," she said slowly and loudly. She kept her hands in plain sight.

"You're not from Falcon," said the other. "You're a winter wraith."

Antaea's natural wryness asserted itself. "How astute of you to notice," she said. "But that makes me just as much a foreigner to the Gretels as you. And I'm trying to help you."

"Why?"

That one stopped her. She opened her mouth to laugh and say, "I have absolutely no idea," then thought better of it. As she drifted into the air she got a better view of the man behind the window; he looked like he was in his mid-forties. The bedroom behind him was wallpapered with yellow floral designs.

"My man is from here," she said at last. This wasn't the case, but the truth was near enough that it felt like she was confessing something true. It wasn't a comfortable feeling.

"He insisted on staying and fighting," she said. "What could I do? Leave him?"

The rifle wavered. "Where is he then?"

She jabbed a finger over her shoulder. "Do you hear those explosions?"

There was another pause while he thought about that. Then: "You'd best be going to him, then."

"Yes. Thanks. Um . . ." She was now hovering at rooftop height and the streets were becoming a strange maze below her. "Where can I get a bike?"

The house's defender waved his rifle to the right. "I saw some of our boys go that way a little while ago. Somebody said there's a rich fellow holed up in his house that way."

"Ah. Well, thanks." She cast about for something clever, or at least reassuring, to add. "Good luck!"

He snorted and slammed the window.

Nursing her sore arm, Antaea flapped in the direction he'd indicated, wondering at what moment she had decided that, yes, it was Chaison she was going to try to find, rather than some means of escaping the city.

CHAISON AWOKE TO the sensation of a small hand on his wrist. He blinked into alertness, and found himself staring into an abyss of fire and twirling debris framed by incongruous forested park-balls. The hand tightened and he was pulled in the other direction; he looked up and met the gaze of a page-girl, no more than twelve years old, who held his arm in one hand and a rope in the other.

He grinned at her but she was all business, hauling on the rope so they sailed back through smoke and drifting grit to a half-open door on the half-peeled circus ball. Chaison managed to make it through under his own steam, although out of respect and gratitude he let her keep her grip on his arm until they were inside. Then he gently disengaged himself.

"Thank you," he said, resting a hand on her shoulder. Now that they were indoors she indulged an impish smile, then hopped away. Chaison would have said more but the place was losing another layer of decking under renewed rocket fire. Splintering chaos raged through the inner levels while men and women covered their ears and cowered.

Chaison made his way to the iron-sheathed central chamber, where the carefully constructed model of the city had turned into a drifting cloud of wooden blocks. Men and women were crowded in here. Minutes ago they had been a functioning military organization; now they had returned to what they'd been two days ago—citizens, mothers, workers. Panicked and still, they turned their eyes to Chaison as he entered.

"It's not safe in here!" Chaison shouted. "You have to escape while you can." There wasn't more than a couple minutes' time to get everyone out of the building safely; after that the approaching cruisers would be able to circle the building and pick off anyone coming out the back.

"No!"

Corbus had appeared in the doorway. The former Atlas, strongman, and now ad-hoc mayor of Stonecloud was bleeding from a cut over his ear, and his pale face held an expression of horror. The men who'd left with him surrounded him now, all of them grim. One of the circus acrobats held a repeating rifle in his hand, and it was loosely pointed in Chaison's direction.

Corbus spread his huge hands, his face projecting an expression of eloquent, tragic sorrow. "Our city," he cried. "No one but us can save our city."

"You can't do that if you're dead," said Chaison, speaking as bluntly as he could to try to puncture Corbus's theatrics. "Staying here is bad tactics."

Corbus shook his head. "Look at them," he said, pointing past Chaison as if he could see through the blockhouse walls. "There's only two ships inside! Only two! The rest have been destroyed."

Shaking his head, Chaison climbed down the wall to join them. "Not destroyed," he said, pitching his voice so that everyone could hear. "They're just bottled up. We might have disabled two, if we're lucky. Meanwhile, Neverland's suburbs have us surrounded."

The acrobat peered at him shrewdly. "What do you suggest we do, then? Surrender?"

"There are degrees of surrender," said Chaison. "That's the only advantage we've ever had in this fight. Their navy's taken some losses—probably more than they expected. Now is the time to ne-gotiate a settlement. Keep your neighborhoods intact, ensure that Stonecloud remains a distinct city rather than being absorbed—"

He was interrupted by one of the semaphore men bursting into the chamber. The man's flags were stuffed into a pack on his back, and they danced in the air behind him making it look like he'd been pierced by a dozen absurdly big and bright arrows. "The squadron we hit with the houses . . . it's free," he shouted. "And undamaged."

Chaison nodded. "They'll be on us in minutes. We have to leave now."

With great dignity Corbus drew himself up and stared down his nose at Chaison. "Admiral Fanning, thank you for your help. The citizens of Stonecloud will take it from here."

"Take it where?" was all Chaison could think of to say. Realizing he suddenly looked foolish, he scowled and said, "At the very least, a tactical retreat to a new command center—"

But it was useless. Chaison heard the sound of big jet engines closing in, and knew that everyone would be hearing them too. At least two cruisers were now circling the blockhouse.

"We have to take that ship!" shouted Corbus. "Destroy the ships and the cities—the cities will . . ." He seemed to remember something with a start, and for a moment his expression was deathly. Then he frowned, as though abandoning all sympathy for his own thoughts, and thrust a fist in the air. "For Stonecloud! For our city! Join me now, and save our city!" A tentative cheer came from a few throats, and as he turned and vanished down the cor-ridor some men followed him.

The acrobat watched him go, then turned to look sadly at Chai-son. "Keep them safe," he said. Then he jumped after his mayor.

Chaison waved the remaining people closer. "You need to get into the most defensible chambers, close the door, and stay there," he said. "One way or the other, this will all be over soon."

"Then we've lost?" asked one of the pages.

"We won't win."

THE ONLY AVAILABLE bike was bright canary-yellow and festooned with iridescent stickers that proclaimed BEST SPICE POCK-ETS IN TOWN! The stickers glittered like beacons in the shafts of sunlight penetrating the sky-high wall of buildings. This visibility was a shame since Antaea was flying straight toward the Gretels' cruisers. It was only a matter of time before she drifted into the crosshairs of some slow-witted but sharp-eyed gunner. The prospect made her hunker closer to the hot curve of the jet.

Luckily, after the Gretels had pulled the wooden lances out of their ships they had then shot everything in sight, so the air was clotted with debris. She had to weave a complicated line through the space around the town-wheels because a stray rock sucked into the intake could ruin the bike. She didn't stop for leaves and twigs, though—a few of these belched flaming out the back of the bike as she flew.

In any case the Gretels were distracted by a small but conse-quential firefight taking place around Chaison's command cen-ter. It looked like some fools were making a last stand there; her pulse skipped as she wondered if one of those distant figures was Chaison. But he couldn't possibly be so stupid . . . She accelerated, squinting into the headwind—and almost immedi-ately hit something.

The bike shook between her legs making a huge *braaaap!* noise as it began to yaw out of control. She caught a glimpse of sparks and smoke flailing behind her and then let go, consigning the damned machine to whatever fate awaited it—this putting her right where she'd been a few minutes ago, namely falling out of control.

She billowed her wings which yanked her feet-forward. Right

ahead of her (below her, according to her inner ear) was a cloud of drifting rocks; she was going to pass right through it. Antaea kicked a fist-sized stone, then landed with her heel on one the size of her head, spinning it off to the left. For a few seconds it felt like she was hopping down a slope, from rock to rock to rock, then she was through. Behind her, gunfire.

The circus ball was just ahead. It had shrunk, and was furred with splintered planking. A cloud of Gretel troops surrounded it, some beleaguered defenders huddling behind shields near the main door. As Antaea feathered her wings for normal flight, she saw one of those men stand up out of his crouch. It was Corbus the strongman. He was screaming something, swinging his rifle over his head in a tremendously dramatic gesture.

Then he coughed and drifted back under the impact of dozens of bullets. Antaea turned sadly, and kicked into the stirrups of her wings. They gusted her around the curve of the ball, away from the sad carnage, and she alighted on the bullet-pocked decking. She gripped it with her toes and looked up.

Eight airmen on bikes were closing on her. Four had their rifles aimed at her head. Antaea put up her hands while, in foolish parody, her wings rose on their springs as well.

A big shape hurtled over the blockhouse's horizon and scattered the tight knot of bikes. Two went twirling away. Antaea put her hands to her ears to block the deafening roar of a jet at full thrust, almost losing her grip as hot exhaust washed over her. Then the attacking catamaran spun in mid-arc and for a mere instant, stopped in the air.

It was a battered thing, two twenty-foot-long spindle-shaped nacelles riding on either side of a big industrial-strength fan-jet. That jet was now screaming as it aimed the boat at the bikes.

The Gretels were firing but it was close-quarters now and as the catamaran swept in the engine throttled back. A small figure carrying a big sword leaped from one of its nacelles; one of the airmen blocked a thrust clumsily with his rifle but was propelled off his bike by the force of the attack. The short swordsman put both feet against the smoking side of the bike and kicked off. His target was the next bike, but its pilot was too quick with his rifle.

Antaea threw her sword. It caught him under the shoulder, not digging in but throwing off his aim so that his shot missed, and the small man was on him in the next instant.

Antaea slipped off the wings and launched herself from the wreckage. She had no sword, but in such tight quarters what she had was better.

Two of the bikes were drifting about six feet away. Antaea fell between them and as their riders swung around to strike at her she lashed out. The long spike of her right heel caught the first rider under the jaw; she was already spinning and kicking out with her other leg, pinning the other man's calf to his bike. As he hissed with pain and reached for her ankle she crouched and put both boots into his chest. Since she'd leaned to the left as she did this she began to spin and so was able to grab his shoulder on the way by. She planted her feet again, carefully this time, and jumped.

There were two of them left and both were good swordsmen. Her ally—whoever it was—was engaging the first recklessly. He had one leg jammed down the intake of the airman's bike, preventing it from starting. The airman had equal leverage, with his feet in the stirrups of the bike.

Antaea's own adversary met her with a wicked thrust of his rapier, but was astonished as she parried it with one heel-spike and slid the other boot down the blade, twisting. He was nearly disarmed and reared back with a curse. Antaea smirked at him past her poised feet.

He tried a cut. She blocked the blade with her ankle though it split the leather enough to reveal the steel greave beneath. He cut again and she caught the blade between left boot-sole and heel-spike. Again she twisted and again he nearly lost his sword. Now his blade was stuck.

She brought her knee to her chin, which drew her to him. Before he realized his mistake she lashed out with her other leg, punching a hole in his forehead with her right heel. He convulsed once and drifted away.

Antaea pirouetted, catching one handlebar of the bike with her toes. Blood dotted the air between her and the last jet, and perching on it was Darius Martor. He was gaping at her in frank astonishment.

"It's a weightless fighting style for women," she said, shrugging modestly. "Taught in my country. Our legs are better weapons because our center of gravity is lower—"

He snapped out of his trance. "Come on!" He reached out to take her hand.

"Chaison is inside," she said, nodding at the circus ball.

He shook his head and for a second or two she was furious with him. Then he said, "We got him already. There's no time for this! The Gretels will be all over us."

Hand in hand, they timed a jump from the last bike and as it tumbled into smoke and fire, they sailed up to the waiting catamaran. She flipped herself through an open hatch and into Chaison's waiting arms.

"DON'T *ABUSE* ME. I've never flown one of these things before." Richard Reiss put the tip of his tongue between his teeth and squinted at the controls. While he did this, building blocks, tree limbs, and swirling leaves scudded past the plastic windscreen.

Chaison stared at the ambassador. "Richard, why are you dressed as a clown?" Ballooning pantaloons and a polka-dotted top spilled out around the edges of Reiss's seat; he had red smudges on his cheeks that he'd obviously been trying to rub off.

The ambassador turned with great dignity, fixed Chaison with a steely eye and said, "It is a very long story, and one I find I would rather not relate."

Darius grabbed his shoulder and shouted, "Zero by forty! Right now!" Richard turned back and spun the control ball to zero degrees latitude by forty longitude, and the vessel made a long, sickening arc that ended with them entering a debris-chocked artery leading away from the town-wheels, the blockhouse—and hopefully, the Gretels.

The hum of the engine was reassuring; even the sound of Darius and Richard bickering made Chaison smile. He could finally let himself relax a bit. "Think this will get us back home?" he asked no one in particular.

The Gretels had been literally pouring into the smashed circus ball when Darius and Richard appeared, swords bloodied, from the other direction. "Well met, friend!" Richard had boomed. Chaison was almost alone, having ordered the remaining citizens of Stonecloud into a set of fairly defensible rooms. He had hoped the Gretels weren't in a mood to make examples of people, but it was better for the townsmen to take their chances on a negotiation, than to try to escape through open air. Chaison knew what the nervous tail-gunners on a military cruiser were like.

"Ship's fully fueled, Admiral," said Darius, not turning his head. "Even has sleeping bags in the other nacelle."

This nacelle was about twenty feet by six, made of thin ribbed metal, and divided into two compartments. The nose was transparent plastic and there were several portholes behind it. The pilot's cradle was in the nose; that was where Richard Reiss was currently sweating and swearing.

A square door separated the front compartment from the back. "What's in there?" Chaison asked, jabbing a thumb at it.

Richard looked back and grinned. "A present for you, good sir," he said. "And a bit of a surprise, I'm sure."

Chaison narrowed his eyes but Richard was immune to the sort of haughty upper-class glare that worked so well on lower-level staffers. "I'm not sure how you could surprise me after that rescue," he commented, easing his way to the hatch. He made sure he kept at least a hand and a foot pressed against the fuselage at all times; Richard was performing unrated maneuvers at unpredictable moments.

"Let's see this 'present,'" he said, and opened the hatch. He immediately swore and slammed it shut again.

Antaea was staring at him. "What?"

Chaison flipped the door open again. Crammed among fuel barrels and supply boxes was Antonin Kestrel. He was tied quite thoroughly, his eyes accusatory over the oily rag stuffed in his mouth.

"This is *not* funny," said Chaison. Richard and Darius were giggling like schoolboys. He fitted himself into the awkward space and pulled the gag out of Kestrel's mouth. "Hello, old friend."

"Friend!" Kestrel glared at him. "You have no friends anymore, Fanning. Only dupes."

"—Then give me the controls!" Darius was shouting. Chaison glanced back to see Richard and Darius trading places at the pilot's chair. Beyond the windscreen scattered buildings and a small flaming forest punctuated a blue sky.

"Are we out?" Chaison called.

"Yes!" Darius waved a hand over his head as he took the yoke with his other one. Richard preened. "I took us out, Admiral," he said.

Chaison pushed past Kestrel to press his nose against a porthole. The city of Stonecloud was a sky-spanning, slow-motion explosion of masonry and forest, its suburbs being pierced with visible speed by the long talons of Neverland. He spotted occasional flashes of gunfire, but whatever was really happening in there was obscured by distance and smoke. The sight wavered, blurred with white, and then disappeared as the catamaran entered a cloud bank.

Chaison felt a wrench of sorrow. He'd been right all along: there had been nothing he could do for the city. Corbus should have surrendered peacefully before anyone could be killed, and if Chaison had been a better diplomat he might have persuaded him to do that.

Stonecloud was an unfinished sentence, an interrupted excuse. Chaison wanted to go back there and undo everything that had just happened.

Just visible through the hatch, Richard Reiss, former ambassador to Gehellen, was strapping himself contentedly into a seat. Chaison frowned and looked for somewhere else to rest his eyes. He turned his head and found Kestrel watching him.

"Tell me, Chaison," said the seneschal smoothly, "was that a dry run? Practice for our next stop?"

He shook his head numbly. "Next stop? What are you talking about?"

Kestrel nodded to the cockpit. "This boat has enough fuel for several days. Can you doubt that the lad there is going to take us straight into winter?"

"And, from there, it's a straight run back to Slipstream."

Part Three | THE PILOT

13

"HE'S RIGHT," SAID Richard Reiss. "We have no time to lose if we want to save the others."

"Others?" Chaison turned back to Kestrel. "Back in Songly you said something about the *Severance*—"

"You're not going to convince me you don't already know everything," said Kestrel. He turned his head away and closed his eyes.

Chaison climbed through the hatch, momentarily debating whether to slam it on Kestrel's smug expression. "Yes, the *Severance!*" said Richard, reaching forward to pat Chaison's knee as though he were some bright schoolboy. "That's what this is all about."

Puzzled, Chaison nodded past the hull. "You mean, the—"

"No no, not the Gretels' invasion, though it may have been indirectly triggered by it. I mean Kestrel, our imprisonment—our abandonment by the pilot! We got the story out of Kestrel on our way to find you."

Antaea came to perch with them. She was doing her best not to meet Chaison's eye. "But how did you come to be with Kestrel in the first place?"

"Oh that." Richard dismissed the whole subject with a wave of his hand. "That's another story."

"I'm sure it's an interesting one—"

Chaison shook his head. "I want to hear about the *Severance*. And about whatever's happening back home."

Antaea discretely backed away into the cockpit.

"Well," Richard said with some relish, "let me tell you—"

"Rehearsing your propaganda!" shouted Kestrel.

Richard shrugged, and began the tale.

SEVERANCE WAS QUITE possibly the ugliest ship in Slip-stream's navy. Chaison had wondered once or twice whether he chose her for his expedition simply out of embarrassment—to get her off the roster for more public battles. Plug-shaped, little more than sixty feet long but forty wide, *Severance* boasted an outer hull of steel and concrete, few portholes but a plethora of gun ports. Her engines lined the inside wall of a shaft that ran down the ship's center, like parasites in a section of vein; thus protected, they were invulnerable to anything but a direct shot from fore or aft, and huge hatches could be rolled across the ends of the shaft if the moment was desperate.

The features that made her a good blockade vessel were keeping *Severance* alive now. She had sloughed back into port shortly after Chaison's sneak attack, billowing smoke and covered in black scars. It being late afternoon, the citizens of Rush had seen her coming from miles away, and crowded the air waving banners and speculating. Some blasted horns in exuberant welcome. It was assumed by all that this was part of the main naval force that had left weeks earlier to engage Rush's other neighbor, Mavery. That little nation wasn't considered much of a threat and the deployment of the navy was locally seen as more a reply to an insult than a war, for Mavery had started things by firing several rockets into the heart of Rush. Almost no one in Slipstream knew that it was Falcon Formation that had put Mavery up to it.

"Ha!" interrupted Kestrel at this point in Richard's narrative. "Your first lie!"

"I am merely laying out all the facts for the young lady, as I understand them," said Richard with great dignity. "You, of course, have a different story."

"Absolutely," said Kestrel. He strained forward against the ropes. "The truth is, Falcon never intended to invade Slipstream. Their navy was on regularly scheduled maneuvers that day."

"Of course," commented Chaison wryly, "it being an exercise, they felt it essential to fill their troop carriers with men . . . as . . . ballast?"

Kestrel sneered. "There were no men in the troop carriers."

Chaison closed his eyes. He remembered when one of Falcon's carriers had burst from rocket fire scattering men to the six winds. There was a brief moment—it could only have lasted a few seconds—when the *Rook*, under his command, shot through a cloud of twisting human forms at two hundred miles per hour. He wished he could forget the sound of them impacting the *Rook*'s hull like so much heavy hail.

"Continue," he said to Richard Reiss.

Severance's captain was Martin Airgrove, who had been assigned this ship, some said, because of his personal resemblance to it. Airgrove was short, squat, and foul-tempered. The grand irony of the present situation was that Chaison knew he was a loyalist. He would have proudly laid down his life for the pilot, and had assumed he would have to do just such a thing when he joined Chaison's expeditionary force.

Chaison had told the captains of the seven ships that the pilot had sanctioned their secret expedition. The fact was, the pilot had vetoed it. He did not believe Falcon was about to attack.

Chaison did.

"You've got that part right at least," said Kestrel. "You went against the pilot's express wishes. Treason."

"It would have been treason to stand by and do nothing while Falcon Formation conquered my country," said Chaison. Despite himself, he felt hurt by Kestrel's accusations.

Coughing to a stop in a cloud of smoke, *Severance* had disgorged Airgrove and his senior officers, who had gone straight to the admiralty. "This decision," explained Richard, "was what saved their lives, for it was strictly according to protocol. The junior staffers were all for taking the news straight to the pilot; had they gone to the palace first, they would never have left."

As it was, Airgrove entered the offices of the admiralty and was briefing the senior staff before the pilot even knew he was back. Meanwhile, *Severance's* crew had spilled out into the airways and streets of Rush. They told a tale so strange and powerful that it had spread through the entire city by nightfall.

Richard began to talk about events in the admiralty, but Kestrel interrupted. "I was there," he said. "The pilot sent me to find out what the commotion was. I entered the briefing room to find Airgrove half-collapsed over the podium, a hundred senior staffers and rear admirals poring over his every word. He was describing a battle and at first I was excited to hear of the gallantry and ingenuity of our men. We had prevailed! I was proud. Proud!" He shook his head mournfully. "Then gradually I realized something—that peppered throughout Airgrove's description were the words *Falcon Formation*. Not Mavery, not . . . anybody else within reason. This battle he was talking about, it was against an *ally*. You can't imagine the horror that crept over me as I stood there. I felt like gravity had failed, because it was *you* doing this."

Kestrel had sent a page running for the docks, and meanwhile interrupted the briefing. "The pilot needs to hear this!" he'd shouted over the objections of the staffers.

Thus began the first standoff of what was to become an escalating crisis.

"It would probably have all ended right there, too," said Richard, "if the pilot had chosen to come in person. He could have closeted himself with Airgrove and arrested him right there. But by then the men were disembarking from the *Severance*, telling their story to anyone who would listen. And the pilot chose to send the honor guard to the admiralty. When these armed men burst into the briefing room, the staffers rallied around Airgrove."

"It was a fiasco," admitted Kestrel. Sixteen men in plumed helmets had leveled their rifles at the most respected leaders of the Slipstream navy, and demanded they turn over Airgrove. "It wasn't my order, but I was bound by honor and law to execute it." Airgrove would have gone, too, had he not been dragged bodily out the other door by two captains and a commodore.

When Airgrove didn't reappear, the word went out to arrest the *Severance*'s crew, most of whom were either with their families, drinking, or trying to hawk the most extraordinary treasures that the Rush pawnshops had ever seen. So scattered, they were hard to find. The standoff in the admiralty had gone on for more than twenty-six hours before Airgrove calmed down from his initial fury (expressed in equal parts against the pilot and Chaison Fanning) and ordered them recalled.

"That was the line," said Kestrel. "When he did that Airgrove crossed from being a misguided dupe of yours, to an active traitor. His men trickled back to the docks under cover of night, with help from the dockhands themselves, and reboarded the *Severance*. We got wind of this just as *Severance* tried to cast off, and intercepted her with the city's police ships."

The citizens of Rush awoke to a new and very visible stalemate, one taking place in the very air of the city. It was impossible to ignore or cover up what was happening. When the story leaked out, the riots began.

"Half the people in Rush aren't even Slipstream citizens," Kestrel reminded them. "They're from Aerie—they're conquered people and they hate the pilot. So now, the *Severance* is under siege and propaganda's floating about that tells how you and the admiralty resisted the invasion of Aerie and how the pilot vetoed your attack on Falcon. The admiralty sustains the ship by shooting supply rockets to it. We catch the ones we can, but some always get through. Airgrove is bottled up inside—has been for months now."

"But why?" asked Chaison. "What is he waiting for? Surely the story is out now. He can have nothing further to gain by staying there, unless he's just out to save his own skin, which doesn't sound like him at all."

"Oh, come now," snorted Kestrel, shaking his head. "It was only a matter of days before the rumors began to circulate. And when they were confirmed . . . it just spiraled out of control after that."

Chaison was puzzled. "What rumors?"

"Why," said Richard, "that you were alive, of course."

Kestrel nodded in disgust. "Airgrove is waiting for *you*, Chaison.

"The whole damned city is waiting for your return."

14

THE TRANSITION TO winter wasn't well-defined—at least in most countries. Light from the several suns dimmed as the catamaran accelerated on a tangent to Stonecloud and the Gretels' border. Initially the Gretels' two suns were off to starboard, Falcon Formation's to port. Gradually, they fell behind and reddened with distance. In nations like Slipstream, people would still sometimes set up farms or manufacturing in this permanent dusk; those raised out here often moved back, claiming a love for the subtlety of color that played on the clouds here. Crops wouldn't grow when the light became too dim but most governments would let their people homestead as far away as they were able.

Falcon Formation had strict laws about such things. "There's no more houses," Richard Reiss commented suddenly, after they had been flying for several hours. Chaison glanced out a porthole and saw nothing but an endless abyss of royal purple air dotted here and there with peach-colored clouds. Richard was right; a few beads of light glittered far back where the catamaran's contrail curled into turquoise skies, but to the sides and ahead there was nothing.

"They're not allowed to build out here," said Antaea. She and Chaison had not exchanged a word since Kestrel began his story. She had been sitting quietly, repairing her boots for the past hour. Now she leaned over to look out the porthole as well. "It's a pretty distinctive sign that you're approaching Falcon. You can *see* the regimentation from here."

Chaison looked ahead, into the azure of winter air. Keeping his voice carefully neutral, he said, "I take it, then, that the spaces ahead will be empty?"

"*Very* empty," she said. She still wouldn't meet his gaze. "Falcon patrols a zone at least fifty miles deep, and they shoot anything on sight unless it's between the channel buoys. And anything flying in a channel gets boarded."

"So we should hurry."

She shrugged. "We can safely assume they're distracted right now."

Chaison went forward anyway and strapped himself into the copilot's seat. Darius appeared to be enjoying flying the cat; watching the boy, Chaison saw a hint of what the grown man would be like. It made him smile. "We're actually going home," he said.

Darius yawned and stretched luxuriously. Ahead of them there was nothing but deepening blue. " 'Long as we don't get lost," he said.

"We're not going all the way into winter." Then Chaison sat up straight. "Are we?"

"No no." Darius shook his head with a laugh. "Antaea said to keep Falcon's suns on our port side 'til we find ours, then make a straight run for it. After all, we haven't got Gridde to navigate for us."

Chaison grinned, remembering the old man, so passionate about his map boxes with their fine jewels, strung on finer hair, that represented the cities and suns of Meridian. Gridde had died of natural causes hours after his greatest triumph: he had guided Chaison's flagship to the legendary treasure trove of the pirate Anetene. The effort had cost him his last reserves of strength, but Gridde had died happy, and fiercely proud.

Chaison and Darius shared a sad glance. Then Chaison said, "Falcon sweeps this area for pirates and smugglers. We should have clear air ahead of us, if you'd like to open the throttle a bit."

"Sure," said Darius, "but I'll need someone to spell me in an hour or so."

"I'll go take a nap, then." Chaison started to get out of the seat, then said, "First though, you have to tell me how you found me. And how you escaped Songly, and how you captured Kestrel."

Darius laughed. "Just that? Nothing else you want me to talk about?" He smiled at the infinite blue outside the canopy. "But it's simple enough to tell. We didn't catch Kestrel. He caught us."

The fight with Kestrel and his thugs had ended as Songly came apart under them. Darius and Richard had become separated from the pols, and barely made it in time to one of the boats.

The impromptu gang of riggers, boat pilots, and laborers cast off their flower boats just as Songly disintegrated. Buildings and streets, ropes and houses had tumbled every which way, some smashing against huge water drops that themselves burst into showers of rain. As dark walls of water began closing in, the boat pilots threw lines back and forth, lashing themselves together. Women, children, and the elderly huddled in the bowl of Darius's boat as it twirled like a mobile in the wind; he had hung onto a belaying pin and watched as sheeting water separated them from their neighbors, snapping one of the ropes.

"Row, damn you," their pilot screamed over the giant slamming sounds of colliding water-mountains. Darius braced his back against the inside curve of the boat and pushed against an oar shaft alongside three other men. He'd felt the oar's big wing slap the water, shoving it back and turning the boat into a dark cavity of relatively free air. Four other boats followed, tugging one another at the ends of their ropes. It was a tiny fraction of the town's population, but there were many other avenues of escape from the town; he was, he told Chaison, "pretty sure most people got out."

Lightning, refracted into shards of blue and green through the tissues of the flood, showed a long sinuous cave stretching ahead of them. The boats surged ahead, frantic to find an escape from the water. Darius pushed against the oar until his legs ached and his back was rubbed raw. Then, by luck as much as the skill of their pilots, they found a chink in the flood and popped out into open air.

The boats hung amid cloud banks, their oarsmen exhausted, nobody speaking. Then, still without speaking, the boatmen on all five vessels tugged their ropes, and the boats drifted together.

Four of the flower boats were crowded with townspeople. The fifth was nearly empty, except for a dozen secret policemen—and Kestrel. They had ejected the men and women who had taken refuge in it, and hadn't been rowing at all for the past hour. They had let the other boats do all the work. Now, at gunpoint and with drawn swords, they asserted their authority over the tired, distraught people who had saved them.

"They found Richard and me right away, of course," said Darius as he steered the catamaran around a medusoid cloud. "Since we had plenty of rope Kestrel used some to tie us up. Then they proceeded to lord it over everybody else. I don't think Kestrel much liked what his pals were doing, but he didn't try to stop them."

"He was a foreigner," shrugged Chaison. "What could he have done?"

"He could have *said* something." Darius scowled blackly at the controls. "Anyway, they got us rowing again. They wanted to run for the inner cities where they could be safe from the Gretels."

Now he grinned. "But the Gretels found us first."

As evening fell the sky filled with ships. The Gretel invasion force was huge, a navy easily capable of conquering Slipstream had they turned their attention that way. The ships were bizarre, of course, like everything Gretel—festooned with decorations, banners, and paintings depicting scenes from the ancient fairy tales that the Gretels used to make sense of their lives. An iron cruiser covered with images of half-mythological beasts called *bears* hove to and demanded that the flower boats surrender. None of the thugs was inclined to argue with the behemoth.

"They'd taken a good long look at us before they swept us up," said Darius, smiling at the memory. "The captain was quite sympathetic. 'Got no quarrel with ordinary folk,' he told us. 'But these are a different matter.' These being the pols, of course."

The secret policemen surrendered with that air of martyred happiness men adopt when they feel they're fulfilling some noble destiny. Kestrel wasn't having any of it, though. "Pardon," he told his captors, "I'm a foreigner here. I was extraditing these criminals back to Slipstream when I became caught up in your war." He pointed to Richard and me.

The Gretel captain had mused, tugging his beard as he looked from Kestrel to us and back. "Criminals, are they?" Then he turned to the rest of the refugees. "*Are they?*"

There was a resounding "No!" in response.

That was how Kestrel came to be Darius and Richard's prisoner. The Gretels kept the pols but let the rest of the refugees go, and the flower boats had trawled their slow way through crowded airs to Stonecloud, arriving just in time for the city's battle with Neverland.

CHAISON BASKED IN the light of home. Every sun had its own, subtly different spectrum, and this was the light he had grown up under, that had shone into his childhood bedroom, on his boyhood schoolbooks, his first love's face. It was ineffably familiar, even reddened and smeared with distance as it was.

He paused for a moment on the little ladder that led between the catamaran's hulls. They had pushed the boat's single engine hard throughout the night as they followed the faint distant specks of navigation beacons. Early in the morning the radiance of Mavery's sun had lit the far distance, fully a quarter of the sky fading to purple, a brighter zone obscured by clouds at its center. Mavery's day was slightly out of phase with Slipstream's, and when that far glow appeared Chaison had, for the first time, begun to feel real anticipation.

Now they hovered on the edge of home, and he was faced with a number of hard decisions. Most of them had to do with the political situation back home, but what weighed most heavily on him was the question of what to do with Antaea.

He tapped on the hatch of the catamaran's second nacelle. "Come in," she said from inside it.

He had watched her climb here eight hours before, the headwind tearing at her clothes and pack as she clutched the rungs of the ladder. Chaison had nearly ordered Darius to cut their speed, but they were shooting between cloud banks that totally obscured the navigation beacons, and were relying on momentum to keep them going in a straight line. If they slowed now they risked turning without knowing it, and then when they started again they might fly straight into winter. Nothing was easier on the edges of civilization than getting lost.

With Slipstream in sight, they could afford to relax, so the headwind was light as Chaison climbed into the second nacelle. Antaea had one foot hooked around a crossbeam and was sewing feathers into one of the bullet holes in her wings. Little fluffs of white ringed her head like inquisitive pixies.

"Admiral," she said neutrally. "Are we there?"

"Slipstream?" He held his hand up to the familiar light streaming in the portholes. "Nearly. I spotted some mushroom farms a ways back." She nodded; there was a little pause, then he said, "You knew all along."

"I knew about the *Severance*, and the riots." She nodded. "I knew somebody was on their way to break you out of jail, though I swear I don't know who it was. Your loyal staffers, probably. That's how I happened to be in the area."

He nodded. Chaison had long since figured out that Antaea was traveling alone, and it would have taken the resources of more than one person to pull off such a spectacular jailbreak. He'd been hoping she could verify who it was, but he didn't think she was lying about not knowing that.

She grimaced. "Chaison, is it really necessary for me to tell you why I kept those facts from you?"

"No," he said. "I'm just disappointed."

"Why?" Irritably, she threw her darning into a knit bag. "You've kept our relationship adversarial from the start. I came to you for information and you've refused to give it to me. Why should I give you any?"

He hesitated, then said, "Antaea, everything changes from here on in." Outside, he heard the jet whine into a higher pitch.

She looked at her wings glumly. "We had a little holiday from being enemies, you mean," she said. "And now it's over."

"Enemies?" He raised an eyebrow. "Is it that bad?"

"No, no, I don't mean . . ." She shook her head. "Did you come over here to kick me off the ship? Or just to tie me up like Kestrel?"

"I came to be reasonable," he said. "The key to Candesce will still exist tomorrow, and next week. It's not like your dream will cease to be possible in a month, or a year. I'm asking you to give this mission of yours a break. Let me return home and do what I have to do and then, when it's all over, we can talk about what's to be done with the key. You, your people, and me."

"Ah," she said. Her eyes were wet and she wiped at them furiously. "If it were that simple . . ." For a while she looked around at everything but him, seeming to be on the verge of speaking yet saying nothing. Then: "It was quite a little holiday, wasn't it?"

He had to smile. "You're pretty good in a tight spot." As he said this he realized the possibilities for innuendo in that phrase; now

she looked him in the eye and her mouth quirked into a smile—
she'd clearly had the same thought.

He heard himself say, "We're not home yet."

Antaea's huge eyes widened even further. "We're not, are we."
She examined him thoughtfully. "You know, Chaison, there *are*
moments in your life when you can act solely for yourself—be
just yourself."

"Back at the dormitory," he said, "you were planning to seduce
me." She shrugged. "Yet you didn't. Was that one of those moments?"

"You know it was." She hesitated. "It was the one time we were
honest with each other, wasn't it?"

"And now?"

"You said it yourself. We have a couple of hours."

Her gaze was direct, and intense.

Chaison reached for her.

AFTER THEY MADE love, Chaison slept. He was exhausted,
not just physically, but emotionally. His sleep was pervaded by the
thrum of the catamaran's engine, and the gentle swaying motion
of its path through the clouds. At times he thought he was back
on the *Rook*, expecting to wake to the sounds of a warship in full
flight; at other moments he feared he was back in the cell, and
clung to the engine noise as a lifeline.

Then it stopped, and he was immersed in cold choppy air. Reflexively, he threw out his arm as he had often done in the cell
when he drifted away from the wall during sleep. —That is, he
tried; his hands were behind his back and wouldn't move, though
wind flittered through his fingers.

Chaison opened his eyes. He was falling through a sky dotted
with green spherical farms and the distant glow of houses. Ahead,
in the direction of his fall, Slipstream's sun was reddening as it

prepared to shut down for the night. Cutting across its face was a long dove-gray contrail. He heard the fading scraping sound of a departing jet.

He yelled, and again struggled to bring his hands around. Now he felt the ropes that bound them. Cursing wildly, he tumbled over and over.

Then a hand clamped onto his shoulder, steadying him. Antaea hove into view, her wings twin strokes of magenta against the darkening sky. She was frowning, and wouldn't meet his eye.

"Holiday's over, Chaison," she said quietly.

For a moment he sputtered, all manner of protests and accusations on his lips. But he kept silent because Chaison suddenly realized his own mistake: he had believed he knew all that was motivating Antaea Argyre, and he had been wrong.

"Where are we?" he asked, through a tight throat.

"We bailed out early," she said. "Hopefully the others won't find out in time to find us. Don't worry, we're on our way to Rush, too. Just not to visit the same people."

All his effort was wasted. His worrying, his hopes about getting home; the breakout, running from Kestrel, the defense of Stonecloud—Antaea had wiped it all away. Close as he was, he wasn't going to see his home after all, and it was a woman he had cautiously come to trust and care about who had taken it all away. The realization stuck in his throat like ashes. He couldn't speak.

Antaea sighed heavily. "You're not even going to ask why? Well I'll show you why." She unclasped something around her neck. She opened the locket in the fading sunlight. Inside was a nice but perfectly ordinary miniature of a perfectly ordinary-looking young woman. She had the same skin tones as Antaea . . . and the face was similar.

"My sister Telen," she said. "As she was two years ago." Now Antaea did something to the locket, turning the portrait aside to reveal another picture.

"My sister, as she is now. Or was, three weeks after the Outage." Antaea held the locket in front of Chaison's eyes until he had to acknowledge that he understood what he was seeing. This time she did meet his gaze.

"Who has her?"

"In a way," she said heavily, "that's the most terrible thing. It's *friends* who have her. Men and women, anyway, whom I believed were my friends. . . . Come, we have to get out of the clear air in case Darius and Richard see that we're gone."

"They'll feel it," he said as she grabbed his shirt collar. "The cat will fly differently."

"I was counting on them being too tired to notice." She began kicking the wing stirrups, and with him in tow flapped laboriously in the direction of a peach-colored cloud bank.

As she flew, Antaea seemed to be composing her thoughts. "I was telling the truth when I said I believe Virga has been trapped by its own technologies," she said. "We paid too high a price to keep artificial nature out; we sacrificed the ability to keep people free from robbers, and demagogues and . . . pilots. Pirates. I thought—oh, for two or three seconds—that you might be sympathetic too, and decide to give up the key freely. I forgot that Slipstream's a pirate sun. You're no better than Falcon, or the Gretels."

"You don't know what I might have done."

"I know you weren't about to give up the key. But . . ." She was silent for a long time, and during that silence they entered the chilly precincts of the cloud. "The fact is I wouldn't have given it up either," she said at last. "Not to *these* people."

"They're not the home guard, are they?"

"Oh, they are! Members of the guard who have been outside Virga, like me, and have seen what's possible. Who disagree with the guard's policy of political and technical neutrality. We— they—believe that the people of Virga deserve the right to choose their own fate. The guard is arrogant and ultimately only serves the powers-that-be inside Virga. Well, I didn't want to serve the pirates."

Chaison said nothing. She was tying them together in the silver darkness. Soon it would be completely dark and he would be back in the nightmare of his cell.

"After the Outage, some of the members of my group decided to act. We were all looking for the key anyway, but they were determined not to hand it over if they found it. We'd use it, they said, to free Virga from our terrible backwardness.

"I was the extraction expert for Meridian, the only one of our group who knew Slipstream and its neighbors. I had to be the one to sniff out the location of the key. So they came to me, in secret of course, and asked for my help.

"And like an idiot, I refused."

"Why?" He barely heard himself; all sound was absorbed in the cloud, like vision itself.

"I didn't trust the motives of our leadership. —Less than I trusted the leaders of the guard itself. I'd thought . . . well, I never believed we would get the chance for the kind of power these men craved, and in the meantime their stated agenda had fit mine. How was I to know you would plunder a mythical treasure, find something supposedly lost forever, and throw the whole world into chaos with it?"

"Don't blame me," he said. "I'm the one who's tied up here."

"They have my sister. Chaison, you have to believe me, I wouldn't be doing this if there were any other way! I have to, or they'll kill her."

"You have to what?"

"I have to get you to tell me where the key to Candesce is," she said.

"And if I don't?"

"I take you to them," she said, looking away. "They're waiting for us. In Rush."

Chaison gave a long, ragged sigh. Then, despite himself, he had to laugh. "What?" said Antaea, sounding wounded.

"It seems everyone is waiting for us in Rush," he murmured.

"Just tell me where it is," she said. "Then we can head for the city. I can drop you off at some pub; you can find Darius and Richard and laugh about your narrow escape. . . . And never have to see me again."

"You know I can't give you what you want," he told her.

It was, of course, fickle, duplicitous Venera Fanning who had the key. And while Chaison had no idea where to find his wife, and though she was not the proper person to trust with the key, he couldn't bring himself to give her up. He found that he didn't care what she was doing or whether she'd waited for him; the thought of Antaea's people going after her enraged him. He would give them nothing, come what may.

He smiled grimly at Antaea, and they settled in silence to wait.

IT WAS IN the deepest chill of the night that Antaea decided the coast was clear. She unfurled her wings, flicking dew from them, then began to tirelessly pump the stirrups, towing Chaison out of the cloud and into memory.

He knew these skies. Dark as it was, the air was alight with thousands of lamps and lanterns from the many settlements that clustered near Rush. Each had its characteristic shape and coloration and as a boy Chaison had memorized them all. They were the constellations of his youth.

There had been that escapade when he was eighteen, down there in Blanson Township. Funny thing: Antonin had been involved in that little bit of petty theft and vandalism. And over there was the little wheel of Hatfall, where Chaison had briefly (and awkwardly, he now knew) wooed a local girl. Her parents had been overjoyed at his attention, highborn as he was. But one thing Chaison had not been in his youth was an accomplished lover.

Not until he met Venera.

There was a tug on his rope every few seconds, as Antaea's wings made another peristaltic flap. It felt maddeningly like a tug to get his attention, but she wasn't speaking and he had nothing to say to her. He brooded and watched the lights that preserved his memories go by, untouchable and unreachable.

At least Darius and Richard would be all right. Even now Darius might be running in the streets of his childhood home, free for the first time since he came to an awareness of who he was. The thought buoyed Chaison, surprisingly strongly. Wars, whole countries might be lost, but a commander who's saved even one life is a hero to that one.

Despite himself, he smiled.

"Hey," he said into the darkness. After a moment Antaea grunted, and he realized she had been half-asleep. Chaison cursed his luck; had he known he could have climbed up his rope and subdued her . . . maybe.

"What is it?" she said, not pausing in the slow rhythm of her wing-flaps.

"What are you going to do after you've got her back?"

There was a long silence. "Don't ask me that."

"Oh, are you going to gag me now?"

"Chaison, I'll—"

"Do whatever you have to, sure. But you know what, Antaea, if you have any sense of honor in you at all, then one of the things you have to do is treat me fairly. And the least that you can do is not stop your ears to me."

A pained, weary sigh drifted back on the air. "Is this my penance, then?"

"No, it's a conversation between combatants." She didn't answer that, so he continued. "You and I find ourselves on opposite sides here. But I've found that there's two kinds of soldier, Antaea. There's those who can only fight by demonizing the enemy, or belittling him in their own minds. They have to hate you to fight you. But the true soldier can fight without hating.

"I'm just wondering if you always despised me, or whether you've made yourself do it in order to give you strength to do . . . this."

There was another long silence. Then, very softly, "What do you think?"

Chaison laughed bitterly. "Don't. Don't do that. Don't presume to demand that I make some sort of lover's leap of blind faith about what you feel or what you think because I don't know, I have no idea what you're really feeling at this very second and right now, guessing could get me killed. So tell me the truth—and don't lie to save your own feelings or mine, I won't respect that now or later. Did you only sleep with me to put me off my guard?"

This time the silence stretched for over a minute. Chaison decided he knew the answer from that silence, but eventually she said hoarsely, "No. I didn't sleep with you to put you off your guard."

Then, before he could reply, she said, "Why are you doing this to me? You know perfectly well I don't have any choice about this. Chaison, Telen's my *sister*. They'll kill her unless I deliver you."

"Fine," he said. "Fine, I understand that. My question to you is, what about after you deliver me? What happens then? They turn her over to you and you both fly away to Pacquaea and that's the end of the story? Or do you ensure her safety and then come back for me? You're an expert at extraction, after all."

"They're not going to kill you," she said. "Chaison, if I thought that, I—"

"Don't lie to me, Antaea. Because here's the thing: you could have told me about this. You could have explained that your sister's life was at stake and convinced me to talk to these men. I believe you would have tried that, if you'd believed that they wouldn't kill me. But that's not really what you think, is it? You know full well that my secret is worth dying for and killing for, and you didn't believe you could marshal an argument strong enough to convince me to go along with you. You didn't try to convince me to help you save your sister by cooperating because you knew that I would do the math and realize that I'm not getting out of this unscathed, even if they let me live.

"Yet you still could have told me the truth, if you were willing to plan an escape for me. We could have worked on that together—all of us, even Kestrel who wants me alive for his own purposes. Yet you chose not to do that. Why? Because you've decided: once you have your sister you're done here. Done with me. Isn't that right?"

"You've figured that out, have you?" she asked.

"Yes," he said. "I have. But since I've decided not to make any more assumptions, I'll ask just to be sure. Antaea, are you done with me? Are you leaving me to these men without trying to rescue me or soften what they do to me?"

This time there was no answer from her at all.

ANTAEA HAD ALWAYS had a certain fondness for Slipstream, piratical interloper that it was. The people were warm and welcoming aside from that strange political blind spot that permitted them to contemplate and carry out the conquest of the nations they moved through. The paradox was endlessly fascinating.

Under any other circumstances she would have been happy to be approaching Slipstream's capital, Rush. The city was gorgeous even at night. In daylight you could see the huge brightly colored pinwheels that spun from the edges of the city's town-wheels. At night it was the sky-spanning panoply of lights that was enthralling. A few points of brilliance dotted the sky behind her as she flapped wearily through the still-warm air—but ahead they thickened rapidly, becoming swirls and knots of radiance where buildings clustered. Then, two miraculous sights hove into view, warring for attention: Rush city and Rush asteroid.

The city's town-wheels were huge open-ended cylinders, festooned with lights like jumbles and piles of gems. The air glowed around each quartet of cylinders brightly enough that she could have read a book even here a mile out. Hundreds of ships sat in or slowly trawled the skies around the wheels and a low hum reached her, the composite noise of many jets, conversations, machines, and the movement of things small and large through the air.

Rush invited. You could get lost in there, among so many people. It welcomed foreigners in a way that no city in Falcon Formation could. Antaea and Chaison should be heading for one of the late-night bars right now, there to slouch in a corner and listen to the musicians and the laughter, smell the pipe smoke, and share the beer. Then to a cramped but wonderful room together. It was what she wanted; was, in fact, how she had defined *adventure* to herself before Telen introduced her to the home guard and its awesome mission.

She turned resolutely away from Rush, aiming instead for the second miraculous sight in Slipstream's sky. Rush Asteroid carved its dimensions out of the night in shades of reflected city-light, all muted by the foliage of the trees that carpeted it. The asteroid was four miles long and two wide, the single largest concentration of matter in Meridian. From a distance, in daylight, it was a bright silhouette hiding Slipstream's sun. As distance closed you began to pick out details, and each one shattered your sense of its scale. First the green carpet resolved into trees, then you began to make out towers and blockhouses thrusting out at odd angles. Closer, and the many gaps and cracks in its surface became visible.

Rush asteroid was of a stony type, comprised of four main bodies and a lot of gravel like glue between them. Slipstream's industries had mined that gravel for centuries, first digging deep pits into it and lately, carving trenches that threatened to cut the asteroid into several pieces. Nobody wanted that because of centuries of forest growth and building, so scaffolding and heavy girders laced their way across the biggest gaps. Deep inside these wounds cascades of glittering light nestled—buildings and street-lights from the factories and foundries dug into the asteroid's flesh. At night it was these bare pits and trenches that were visible because the forest ate any lights that glowed under its canopy.

At the end of her strength, Antaea flew slowly toward a gigantic stone, hundreds of feet wide, that had been jacked up out of its original socket in the asteroid's side. Spars and beams held it up against the asteroid's microgravity; it was bare of trees and scarred on all sides by decades of mining. Glowing windows and fans of light from opened doors made an intricate diorama at the bottom of the cup-shaped cavity below it. This was where Raham had told Antaea to go.

She back-pedaled her wings, bringing herself and her captive to a stop in the night air. Chaison Fanning had remained silent for the past half-hour; now he laughed bitterly. "Second thoughts? Somehow I doubt it."

"I'm going to untie you," she said. "Things are getting a bit tight here and we're likely to be seen. I'd find it hard to explain why I'm towing a bound man across the sky."

"I daresay you would." He rubbed his wrists after the rope drifted away, while Antaea brought out her heavy pistol and cocked it. "Problem is, I haven't got wings. How am I going to follow you down there?" He nodded at the pit.

"You'll hold onto the rope, like a proper passenger," she told him. She flipped the end over to him and he took it reluctantly. "And don't even think of yanking on it," she added.

He took the rope, but shook his head. "Antaea, you're really not thinking this through. If I wanted to kick up a fuss, shooting me would just bring more attention."

"If you despise me, then go ahead," she said. "You can make things go badly for both of us; or you can cooperate and they'll just go badly for you. That's your choice."

He made no more protest as he allowed her to tow him across the air. Of course not: he was an honorable man.

The underside of the enormous stone was patched with moss, deeply scored by machines and nature, and washed with faint light from the buildings below. They threaded their way between the girders holding it up and descended toward the semicircle of shacks at the bottom of the cup. These were wooden boxes connected by ropeways, some with incongruously normal doors and windows on them. Antaea was familiar with the place, since this mining company was a home guard front. Like Ergez's mansion, it was a safe house and storage depot for any guard operations involving the nations of Meridian. It was seldom used.

As she flapped deeper into the bowl she noticed something new. A gnarled, thickly branched tree stuck out of the stone next to the largest shack. There had never been a tree there before; it was beyond her why anyone should move a mature tree into a place like this, where it would receive little water and not enough sunlight.

As she approached the shack the tree quivered, and then stood up.

Chaison swore loudly, and Antaea heard herself doing the same under her breath. "It's okay," she said. "It's a friend."

I think.

Clearly, the precipice moth was in disguise. The thick branches couldn't completely cover its glittering surface, and its head was free of foliage as it rose to look at her. She recognized that scarred ball. It was one of only a few moths Antaea had seen up close.

"You're the commander of Flight twelve," she said in surprise. Flight twelve was Telen's squadron.

The moth cocked its head, but before Antaea could say any more, a dozen winged human forms took flight from hiding places around the shack.

The seven men and five women quickly encircled Antaea, gesturing her down with drawn weapons. She recognized most of them as Gonlin's people. This was definitely the right place.

But . . . "What's that doing here?" she asked one of the women as they settled next to the shack. Several of the guard members were glancing nervously back at the giant beast, as if afraid it would do something hostile. Antaea saw that Chaison had noticed this too; she exchanged a glance with him that was, for the first time in hours, complicit rather than hostile.

Nobody answered her question. One of the men nodded to the now-opened door of the shack. Mouth dry, Antaea entered, leaving the rope outside.

She hesitated again at the split in the stone floor that led to the mine. This felt wrong. "What, no congratulations for me?" she said to the grim-faced guard members. "What about a 'welcome home' at least?"

One of them, a man named Erik who had once been a close acquaintance, said, "Welcome home." He didn't return her smile.

Chaison sent her another glance, and gave a barely perceptible shake of his head. Antaea forced herself to smile and laugh. "Thanks!" She ducked into the crevasse and the others followed.

Antaea had once heard that places like the one she was in were typically billions of years old. This one might predate life on old Earth. There was a time when such facts might have impressed her; but she'd seen death, and so past and future no longer seemed distant at all. They were as close as the air on the inside of a bubble, reachable by an instant through the simple act of dying.

Still, this place had an eery coldness to it that reminded her of the wall at the world's edge. The crevasse widened beyond the entrance until its side walls disappeared entirely. Antaea moved ahead between two surfaces of rock, only a chain of whirring gaslights indicating which direction to take.

She had been here in daylight once and remembered seeing slivers of light in the far distance. The asteroid was cracked in half at this point; the undulations her raised hand brushed were the mirror image of those her toes touched. There were other ways in and out, suitable for a slender woman but not mining equipment. It was a fact to bear in mind, considering the circumstances.

Ahead was the beginning of the mined area, marked by more lights and shacks. The shacks were just several walls joining the ceiling and floor; some were open on one side, others on two. They were for the most part just places to store tools. But several were fully enclosed, and had lit windows.

"In there." One of the men gestured to one of the bigger shacks with his rifle. Antaea moved reluctantly toward it, hearing the slight scuff of Chaison's feet following her. She couldn't look at him. She felt sick.

"So the precipice moths are part of your conspiracy," Chaison murmured as the shack's door swung open.

"Not my conspiracy," she hissed, feeling herself flush. "Not anymore. And no . . . a moth couldn't be part of it. They don't have loyalties to humans—only humanity."

"Then what—?"

"Antaea! It's good to see you." Gonlin emerged into the half-light outside the shack. The light of the doorway behind him was blocked by several other large men.

Gonlin appeared tired, but relaxed. There had been a time when Antaea had been impressed by his calm assuredness. That geniality struck a false note now as he put out his hand for Antaea to shake. She was so appalled by his brazen hypocrisy that she found herself shaking it. Gonlin beamed at the others as if this proved something.

"Thank you," he said to her with apparent heartfelt sincerity. "Chaison Fanning, indeed! I take it that, since you've brought the man himself, you weren't able to make him talk yourself."

Despite herself she glanced away. "No," she said curtly.

"That's all right," said Gonlin soothingly. "It was a monumental feat to capture him at all—considering that there's two whole nations' worth of troops trying to do just that. You were always our best extraction agent, Antaea, that's why we had to have you do the job."

"Where's my sister?"

"Right over there." He pointed to one of the outlying shacks. She saw a gleam of lamplight in the little box's window.

"Really, Antaea, I want to hear all about how you did it," he said, "but I know you're angry and anxious about Telen. Go see her and we can talk later."

"Talk—? Gonlin, if you've hurt her—"

He looked puzzled. "Hurt her? Antaea, it was her idea."

She just stared at him. Gonlin shook his head in a long-suffering way. "You thought you knew Telen, but really, she knew you. She knew what would motivate you. And she understands necessity, Antaea—in a way that you never did . . ."

Gonlin continued talking but his words were just a gabble. She whirled and jumped toward the shack he'd pointed to.

More words from behind her: it was Chaison shouting, "Careful! He's playing you!" She heard a muffled blow, then a jumbled scuffle. Then a door slamming.

Antaea spun around slowly as she slid between the two gray rock faces. *He's playing you.* What had Chaison meant by that?

"Antaea, wait!" Erik was following her. She didn't wait for him or pause until he said, "Gonlin wanted me to escort you."

She whirled. "Am I a prisoner too, now? Is that it?"

He looked away. "Antaea, I'm sorry. We didn't know this was Gonlin's plan until you'd left."

"Excuse me if I don't believe that," she sneered. "Well? Are you here to keep me from leaving? Or can I take my sister and go, like Gonlin promised?"

He backed away. "Of course, of course." There was a light of calculation in his eyes, but Antaea couldn't tell what he was thinking. She turned again and kicked off from the stone plain.

The shack was just ahead. It was a rough cube of planks ten feet on a side, with a single door and small dust-rimed windows in its other walls. Darkness swallowed any details beyond it.

She had to know if Gonlin was lying. If Telen was in that glorified crate, was she a prisoner or free? What would she say when Antaea confronted her—would she fall weeping into her sister's arms, or would she be cold?

Antaea braked herself against the rock face just outside the shack. She reached for its rusted latch, then hesitated. This unthinking haste was what Gonlin had wanted from her. That was what Chaison had meant: Gonlin had deliberately provoked her to throw open this door without thinking about what lay beyond it.

Why would he do that?

She licked her dry lips. Her fingers trembled an inch from the latch. She was suddenly sure that if she tugged on that latch, she would receive a bullet in the heart or shrapnel through and through. Why would Gonlin bother to leave her alive after his brutal extortion? Yet she had to know whether Telen was here.

She glanced back. Erik was watching her from near the other shack. There seemed no alternative; she wrapped her fingers around the latch.

There was a distant crash and she heard Chaison shouting. Erik turned his head to look and in that brief second Antaea bounced between the rough stone ceiling and floor, around the corner of the shack, and into the shadows. Erik looked back again, paused for a moment, then turned away decisively, moving toward the sound of the fight. As quietly as she could Antaea drifted to the shack's side window. Heart pounding, she looked in.

It was Telen. She hung in the air, perfectly still, her face absolutely expressionless. Her eyes were on the door to the shack.

She was unbound.

Antaea stared at her, looking for some clue about what to do. As she did Telen's stillness began to seem odd. Unnatural, even.

—No, she couldn't be dead— Antaea saw her blink, and relaxed a bit. She waited for her to blink again, just to confirm what she'd seen. The seconds dragged on.

Fully twenty seconds passed before Telen blinked again. This time Antaea counted, and it was exactly twenty seconds again when she blinked the third time.

It was a motion as slow and precise as the advance of a clock's hour hand. A prickle moved up Antaea's neck. It was over a minute since she had looked in the window yet Telen hadn't moved at all. Nonetheless, she was awake, her gaze fixed on the door Antaea was supposed to come through.

Antaea backed away into the shadows. What *was* this? Was Telen drugged? That seemed like the best explanation at first, but if she'd been drugged she would have curled up into the fetal position, as most sleepers did in freefall. It was how Telen slept when weightless, Antaea knew that much. Her muscles were keeping her erect. She was awake.

A kind of supernatural dread had taken hold of Antaea. She realized she was continuing to back away, into the darkened plain that clove Rush asteroid in two.

She had to be missing something, some clue as to what was going on. Antaea pinched her forearms fiercely. "Think, idiot!" she hissed at herself. What would Chaison Fanning, military tactician, do in this situation?

He would put himself in the enemy's mind. So, what had Gonlin been doing just now? Throwing her off balance, of course, and quite deliberately. He couldn't have Antaea forced or compelled to come here because she was still one of his people; it would be bad for morale for her former friends to see her abused. And he'd wanted her to come straight to this place, rather than going . . . where? There was nowhere else for Antaea to go.

Unless there was, and it was so obvious and compelling that Gonlin felt he needed an emotional gut-punch to keep Antaea from thinking of it. He couldn't let her think about it because it worried him—and all his men. Had them frightened, in fact, and . . . bottled up?

She hissed again, this time in angry surprise. Antaea turned away from the mining shacks and began to feel her way along the narrowing rock crevasse. A few minutes later she pulled herself out of a thin crack beneath the roots of a maple tree.

She looked back. Telen was still in there. If that really was her;

yet if it was, surely Gonlin would be willing to let her go now that he had the admiral. Antaea held onto that thought, and looked around herself.

She hovered in a strange twilight world of bark shafts, ceilinged with thick leaves. The long ropelike trunks of the trees sprang hundreds of feet up from the surface of the asteroid before subdividing into branch and leaf. With Slipstream's sun in its maintenance phase, the only light came from the glow of distant windows and little of that made its way through the foliage. It proved easiest to climb along one of the trunks to the tree's crown where at least she could see something. Then she hopped from branch to branch, circling back to the giant suspended stone.

From the lip of the crater she could just make out the furz of green that was the precipice moth's disguise. It was hunkered down among some big black silhouetted boulders. She could see several of Gonlin's people among the lit huts. They weren't taking their eyes off the moth, but unless there was a watcher in the dark on this side, they were unlikely to see her approach. Not that she had the luxury of time; any minute now someone would realize she hadn't kept her appointment with Telen. She only hoped her sister wouldn't suffer for it.

She glided down the dark slope and fetched up behind the boulders. From there it was a simple matter to sidle around the rocks and under the body of the moth. It knew she was there since it had eyes all over its body. Antaea was counting on the fact that it knew who she was.

A quick hop up to its flank and she was next to one of the access hatches. "Let me in," she whispered. For a tense few seconds she thought it wouldn't obey, then the hatch slid to one side. Red light shone from the interior, but she was on the far side of the moth from Gonlin's watchers. There were no shouts of alarm as she climbed inside.

The hatch shut behind her. Antaea wormed her way around a

tight corner—the insides of these creatures were claustrophobic in the extreme—and pulled herself into one of the two command chairs in the moth's cockpit.

They were called command chairs, and it was called a cockpit, but you didn't exactly command a precipice moth. The things had minds of their own, and these tiny cabins were more like protected bunkers for their occasional human passengers. There were view screens and control pads here, but all were currently dark; Antaea doubted she could call them to life this close to Candesce. If what she'd been told about the moths was true, only its pseudobiological systems could be active this close to the sun of suns. Even the red lights were probably biochemical rather than electrical. Still, its brain would be active, and she could talk to it here in private.

The problem was, which of a hundred questions to ask it first.

"Are you my sister's moth?" The sound of her own voice was surprising in this cramped, dead space.

The voice that replied was even more unnerving—loud and clear, easily understood, but lacking in any human inflection. — Not because the moth couldn't mimic human tones, but because its emotions, if it had any, could not be compacted down into human speech.

"For the duration of the present emergency, I am assigned to work with Telen Argyre," said the moth.

"What are you doing here? I thought your kind only patrolled the skin of Virga?"

"I am in pursuit of an intruder."

"A *what?*"

"An entity from beyond Virga has penetrated to this level of the interior. I have it pinned down inside Rush asteroid. I am instructed to wait here until reinforcements arrive or until it moves again."

"Instructed . . . by who? Gonlin?"

"No, by Distributed Consensus." That was the name of the moth's command-and-control organization, Antaea remembered.

"Are Gonlin's people—are you working with the home guard people inside this asteroid?"

"No. I instructed them to bring me the intruder. They have not done so."

Antaea hugged herself. She tried to think of what to ask next—something, anything other than the obvious next question. The seconds dragged on, until she realized what she was doing and gave in. "What does this intruder look like?"

But she already knew the answer.

"It has the appearance of Telen Argyre."

16

THE FAMILY RESEMBLANCE was obvious. Everyone turned to look as Telen Argyre entered the tiny hut and it was not just because she was as exotic as her sister. She was shorter, her face more heart-shaped than the inverted teardrop of Antaea's, but she had the same fine narrow nose and wideset, large eyes. She wore plain traveler's clothes that did nothing to hide her figure.

She was so beautiful that it took a moment before Chaison realized that the sudden alertness among her torturers signaled something quite different than admiration.

Chaison's throat was raw from screaming into the rag they had stuffed between his teeth. His eyes could barely focus, he was shivering but covered in sweat, and his heart felt like it was about to burst out of his chest. After his time in Falcon's prison he had believed he knew all the ways a man could be tortured, but Gonlin's team had hurt him in ways he'd never imagined you could hurt.

Still . . . "He's given us nothing," said the one who'd introduced himself as Gonlin. He was a pallid, froglike man with darting eyes, not the sort you'd picture as a great revolutionary. The others deferred to him anyway—or they had, until Telen Argyre entered the room.

She lifted her fine-pointed chin now and narrowed her eyes, examining Chaison with serpentine detachment. Then her head turned—almost as if it were an object separate from the rest of her body—and she blinked at Gonlin. "Where is the other one?" she asked. "The sister?"

Gonlin opened his mouth. "I thought . . . she was with you—" He whirled on his men, face darkening. "Didn't I ask her to be escorted? Where is Erik?"

Chaison tried to chuckle ironically, but nothing came out. Telen Argyre seemed to hear anyway; her head snapped back and her eyes focused on his. "Why have you not told them what they want to know?" She seemed more puzzled than angry.

He spat blood at her. She ducked it and turned again to Gonlin. "Bring me water. His throat is dry." Past her, Chaison could make out blurred forms of men and women jumping in and out of the hut. They were shouting to each other and the people outside. He tried his best to laugh.

Somebody brought a wine flask and he sipped some water. Licking his lips, he grinned up at Gonlin and Argyre. "W-What if I gave it t-to Antaea?"

Shock washed over Gonlin's face, but Antaea's sister merely shook her head. "You did not. But why haven't you revealed the location of the key? You could die very soon from what they are doing to you."

"What *you* are doing to me." She didn't even shrug, just kept staring at him. Finally he stammered out, "I was tortured for m-months in Falcon. T-they asked me questions they knew I c-couldn't answer. It was g-good practice for today."

He wouldn't tell them the rest: that he had given up on himself dozens of times during that torture, or later in the black emptiness of his cell. He had consigned himself to death, let go of everything except one slender thread that still connected him to life. He had not forgotten Venera.

She was the one unfinished piece of his life, and he had seized the opportunity of his escape because he might see her again. Returning Darius to his home had been a convenient cover story, something he could use to prop up his determination in darker moments—and he really did care for the boy. But it was the hope of seeing Venera again that had kept him going.

To have lost that chance, once and for all, was to be already dead. If he was going to die without seeing her then it didn't matter how much they hurt him; in fact, the pain was so shocking and immediate that he had embraced it almost with joy. It was the most real thing in his life now and as long as it continued he had something to fight, to dread, and to remind himself that he had lived.

Knowing that he was invulnerable, he smiled into Telen Argyre's eyes.

Somebody burst through the doorway. "Erik swears he saw her go into the box. She must have ducked into a shadow or something. She's gotten away."

Gonlin swore. "She hasn't gotten away. She's with the moth!"

Chaison was able to focus well enough to see the look of raw fear that came over Erik's face at the mention of the tree-covered monster. He drifted out the door, eyes wide. "Get out there!" Gonlin screamed at him.

Then Gonlin turned to Telen Argyre. "We may be out of time here," he said. "It wasn't supposed to work out like this." His tone was almost pleading.

She pulled herself over to Chaison, taking up her dispassionate examination of his condition. "He is not responding to pain," she said. "I will try something else." She raised her hand.

In the dim lantern light it seemed to be sprouting cobwebs. Gonlin looked as startled as Chaison felt at the sight of her fingers fading behind a sudden halo of pale gray.

"That . . . works here?" Gonlin seemed awed by what he was seeing.

"The asteroid shields me from Candesce's influence," said Argyre. "I told you that."

"Well, yes, but I didn't realize that . . ." Gonlin swallowed, watching as Argyre reached up to lay her hand on the top of Chaison's head. He felt the pressure for a moment, then a deep coldness like ice water spreading across his skull. Suddenly, all the pain went away, leaving him blinking in surprise.

Argyre tilted her head, bringing her face close to his. "The monofilaments have penetrated your skin and bone, and I am shutting down your pain response," she said. "The filaments will interface with your neurons and learn the emergent language of your brain. In order to do this they must become part of that system for a time. So, for some minutes you and I will not be separable cognitive entities."

Gonlin cleared his throat. "I doubt your sis—Antaea Argyre will be able to convince the moth to try and break in here. But what if she goes to the local authorities? Tells them that we've got the admiral that everybody's looking for?"

Telen Argyre glanced at him coolly. "This will only take a minute. When I'm done, we will give the admiral to Slipstream's pilot."

"Ah," said Gonlin. "And the moth—?"

"It will pursue us," said Argyre. "We will use the city's people as our shield."

Gonlin looked decidedly unhappy about that idea, but Argyre had already turned her attention back to Chaison. "So," she said.

Chaison found himself clearing his throat. "Don't be alarmed," he said.

That was odd. Why had he spoken?

"It commonly terrifies them," he heard himself say, "when the illusion of individual identity is stripped away." Gonlin was staring at him in horror. Chaison felt his own lips moving again, heard his own voice reverberate through his flesh as he said, "This fear is a side effect of the process. We do not really need it because the subject's emotions are no longer a factor."

The terrible truth of what was happening came to Chaison then. He gave in to panic.

QUARTET THREE, CYLINDER two loomed ahead, a half–black arc and half-cup of glittering city lights. The spring-driven snap of her wings drove spikes of pain into her back, and Antaea's thighs were quivering from pushing down on the stirrups—but she was nearly there. Outrider buildings were sail-ing majestically past now, lights blinking, and ahead a vortex of ropes led to the giant town-wheel's axis. Police cruisers and civilian vessels were always in sight. Gonlin's people wouldn't get away with it if they tried something here.

Unless of course they just used a rifle, and shot her from a mile away. Her only hope was to lose herself in the streets below.

She took one more glance over her shoulder at the dark blot of Rush asteroid. It was a leave-taking look—she recognized the odd trembling sensation in her heart from a similar moment on the day she'd left Pacquaea to join the guard. She had thought she un-derstood these moments by now, she'd had enough of them in her life. This agony of mind, though—there was nothing to com-pare it to, though she deserved every second of it. She had trusted the wrong people—no, even worse, she had trusted *herself,* and the result was that she had betrayed everything she'd ever believed in and the only two people in the world she really cared about.

Her tears trembled in the meager headwind of her flight, and tumbled behind her like tiny signposts leading back to the precipice moth.

A traffic cop waved at her and she obediently moved into a channel of air defined by a trio of ropes. The cop was dressed in bioluminescent clothing and had fan-driven lanterns on his head, wrists, and ankles; if Antaea had been prepared to notice she might have delighted in his fantastical shape, like some underwater creature waving its arms to incoming travelers. Instead her eyes were fixed on nothing, her motions automatic as she followed the landing lights in to a platform high above the circling streets of Rush.

The moth had been plain: there was nothing left of Telen Argyre in the body that moved and talked like her. It was some sort of an infection, said the moth, a nanotechnological fever that had overwhelmed her nervous and immune systems. The moth had seen it before, centuries ago. Those who succumbed didn't just lose their minds. Every nerve in their bodies died, withering out of the way of hard replacements that reported back to an iron-cold processor nestling where the brain should be.

Antaea couldn't stop thinking that Telen might have still been alive when she'd left to find Chaison Fanning. She could have stayed. She could have tried to find Telen instead of this foreign admiral. Why hadn't she done that?

And then, when she began to realize just how deeply she could trust Chaison Fanning, why hadn't she told him about Telen? He had felt so betrayed by her actions; and he was right to feel that way. She *had* betrayed him.

She moved like a sleepwalker along a ramp with a dozen or so other late-night travelers. Only when she bumped into someone who'd stopped abruptly did Antaea become aware of her surroundings again. The formally dressed man she'd collided with barely noticed her in turn—he was pointing something out to his perfumed and gowned lady companion.

"That's it there," he said. "Can you believe they're still bottled up? It defies all reason."

The lady shivered. "The mob," she murmured. "It's like a circling shark, waiting to . . ."

Antaea tuned out the woman's vacuous dramatism. On the other hand, the thing they were looking at . . .

It was the *Severance*, pinned by spotlights to an area of clear air out past the other end of this cylinder. Now that Antaea was in the town-wheel's microgravity it looked like it was the *Severance* turning grandly in the distance; the apparent motion belied the stillness of the scene. The ship's portholes glittered now and then from reflected light, but were otherwise dark. There was no exhaust from its engines. It might have been adrift, yet starting about three hundred feet away from it was a diffuse globe of men and weapons, all aimed at the cruiser. It was like an owl surrounded by sparrows—or a still snapshot of same.

Beyond the *Severance*, the pilot's palace wheeled grandly. That particular town-wheel was entirely lit, as if the *Severance* was keeping the government awake. Which was probably true.

"I'm sure cooler heads will prevail," said the man doubtfully. Antaea slipped past them and found her way to a half-empty express elevator. As the elevator operator dragged the telescoping cage door shut she looked again through wrought-iron filigree at the tiny, toylike *Severance*.

Bottled up. Everything good had become trapped, like bees in a jar. The *Severance* was trapped, Chaison was trapped, Aerie's former citizens locked under martial law and curfews; and the whole home guard had been duped and outmaneuvered by Gonlin and his gang. Only she was free, but probably nobody cared. Antaea had done her damage, she was useless now.

Of course, the monster that had eaten Telen was also trapped. There was just one creature in the whole damned world still capable of acting: the precipice moth. And it was too fearful of causing collateral damage to do anything but wait for the monster to poke its head up.

Maybe all it needed was a good push . . .

When they touched down and the doors opened, Antaea found her feet carrying her in a definite direction. Perhaps she'd had this plan in her subconscious all along, else why had she chosen this particular cylinder? She padded between the curfew ropes that blocked off side streets, moving obediently with the rest of the crowd to the designated taxi stands and hostel quarter. As the watching policemen's eyes tracked the other way for an instant she ducked and dove into a darkened alley, racing along on her toes so that her heel-spikes didn't click on the iron street. For a few seconds she was sure she'd gotten away.

Then the sound of shouting caught up to her.

BEHOLD CANDESCE, THE sun of suns. Not so much a thing or even a place, but a region where light and heat swallowed material reality. Candesce dissolved in flame every morning, taking everything within a hundred miles with it. It was as though the sun of suns cried an invocation to the gods of fire and was sacrificed, consumed utterly by their brief entry into the world, to be born again as a physical object at day's end.

Nations consigned their dead to this heat in daily spiraling flights of coffins; legend said that whole nations had in fact been driven into Candesce by warring neighbors, every town-wheel, building, farm, and lake disappearing into that widening whiteness. Countless millions lived their lives knowing only its light. Yet in this moment, Chaison Fanning found himself gazing upon something whose size and grandeur eclipsed Candesce as much as the sun of suns would drown a single candle's flame.

Was this him remembering the star Vega? It couldn't be; he must be experiencing some memory of that thing that had taken the form of Telen Argyre. And yet he was so sure he had seen it— had been there himself.

Virga and Vega. Surely he had known that the one was a toy version of the other, a model at million-billionth scale. Everyone knew that; Virga was the joke of the Vega system. It was a tiny balloon of carbon fiber discarded at the very edge of Vega's gravitational influence. It hovered on the edge of interstellar space, where no one ever went. Everything of interest happened somewhere else.

Or at least, that was the way it should have been. But, in a turn of events as unlikely as Slipstream's, Virga had lately become a key player in a power play of almost unimaginable proportions.

Vega was an infant star, its planetary system unfinished. Its inner circles were full of whirling Earth- and Mars-sized bodies. They collided regularly in cataclysmic explosions that would have destroyed any life within a million miles; none of these nascent planets was old enough to have a stable crust and many glowed as intensely as young stars. They swept vast trains of matter in their wakes, the shifting rings of dust and smoke filtering Vega's light like a kaleidoscope.

Chaison had always known abstractly that water could only be formed by burning hydrogen and oxygen. He had never followed that thought to its conclusion: that an ocean of water could only be made in a world-sized fire. In the bright violent depths of the Vega system, such fires were common.

Or at least, they had been, before the colonization.

The human settlers who took Vega for their home were unconcerned by matters of mere scale. To them, a cloud of gas and dust seventeen Jupiters in mass was just an unusually big pile of building material. They sent trillions of self-reproducing assemblers into every corner of the system, and for a millennium now these had been exponentially breeding, eating fire and light and dust and birthing civilizations.

For all the variety around Vega, its cultures and sovereign individuals shared a common trait: they all operated at the *technological maximum*. This state was achieved whenever a system developed Edisonian AIs capable of evolving any conceivable device or object in their internal simulations. Natural selection had always been the secret engine behind human creativity; it was simply more efficient at generating novel solutions than algorithmic processes. In the pressure cooker of competition that was modern Vega, any intelligence—artificial or natural—knew it had to harness that power. The all-powerful AIs who served Vega's human population cheerfully abandoned consciousness as the inefficient tool it was, replacing their minds with virtual evolutionary environments.

The proliferation of post-human species, artificial intelligences, and collective minds had meanwhile resulted in a Tower of Babel crisis: common communications were proving more and more difficult among millions of rapidly evolving species. Translation systems emerged to fill the breach, but in order to function they had to go beyond interpreting languages, and learn to interpret needs and motives. The intermediaries that survived and proliferated were the ones that would work for anybody.

It wasn't about what could think anymore. It was all about what could *want*. Anything that could desire could harness unimaginable power to its agenda, even if it had no mind to know that it wanted. So, after centuries of human domination, new powers emerged around Vega: polities whose citizens were insects, or trees, or even translators and Edisonian AIs. The new powers contended and fought, and competed and cooperated in a vast spasm of creative world-building no more conscious of a goal than the organisms that had dominated Earth's oceans and lands for billions of years. It was a new nature—artificial nature.

"But what . . ." Chaison's own voice came to him distantly. "What does any of that have to do with us?"

Telen Argyre's face was inches from his own. This woman-shaped thing was an Edisonian AI, he realized. It wasn't conscious at all; rather it explored branching trees of probability, running thousands of parallel simulations of its surroundings and letting only the fittest turn into plans, actions, or words.

Its eyes were fixed on his. "Vega's powers can no longer speak directly," that process said now. "They are too alien to one another. Whatever grows, whatever can want, that thing now has the power of a god.

"Still, some sort of accommodation has to be reached. So we have evolved a place where our forces can contend in safety. A microcosm, an arena if you will, on the very edge of the Vega system. There, we may push and pull, and talk if talk is possible, and gradually . . . come to coordinate our efforts."

He shook his head. "But what does that . . . Are you talking about Virga?"

She cocked her head. "Not Virga. I refer to that vastly larger arena that Virga is a part of."

"I don't . . ." But he did understand, a little—or at least he had flashes of memory that seemed to make sense. These weren't his memories, surely, these impressions of vast curving black outlines obliterating the stars, dozens of them trailing away into unimaginable distance. Or the sensation of coursing like a fish in a vast school through channels of energy between bush-like constructions that glittered like midnight cities, but seemed grown more than built. Chaison remembered—or Telen remembered—complex games unfolding in the darkness as the many species living around Vega learned to cooperate. Out here on the safely distant edge of the star system, they probed one another's weakness, learned each other's desires and goals, and gradually, achieved some detente or pact or standoff that allowed the whole system to move forward. To a human, the place Argyre had called the arena looked liked a vast construction project—and one of its central features was Virga.

"The civilizations and power blocs orbiting Vega form an ecosystem—but it is an unfinished ecosystem," said Telen Argyre, "rife with infections and extinction. Progress in the experimental arena has come to a stop. One of the arena's major powers, Candesce, stopped cooperating centuries ago. The whole project is now in jeopardy.

"I have shown you these things because I am not your enemy," said Telen Argyre. "My faction intends no harm to you or your people. We merely wish to save our own, and Candesce stands in our way.

"I have shown you my secrets. It's time for you to reciprocate."

Chaison braced himself, preparing for some epic battle of minds with this obscene invader. All that happened was that, unbidden, he began remembering things: late-night conversations with Venera about the legend of Anetene and the keys to Candesce; planning the expedition; visiting the tourist center to find the map to Anetene's hoard. They flitted through his mind quickly and effortlessly, images of Venera holding the key up to the light, of her leaving Chaison's flagship for Candesce with Hayden Griffin and Aubri Mahallan.

He frantically cast about for something else—think of anything else—but it was impossible. All he could do was picture Venera holding the key.

"Ah," said Argyre. "Thank you.

"That was all I needed to know."

THEY WERE ALMOST on top of her. Antaea had been ducking between pools of shadow in arched doorways and behind pillars, trying to shake the dogged pursuit of the pilot's police. Crisscrossing streets from shadow to shadow, she entered an area of modest but prosperous shops, their swinging signs mostly unreadable in the dark canyon of buildings. A few upper-story lights were on but otherwise the city seemed weirdly empty. Nowhere under gravity was ever empty of people—weight was just too rare in this world. This silence was almost supernaturally strange.

She wasn't completely sure of her destination, and hesitated for long moments under the swinging sign, peering up and down an avenue she had only ever seen crowded with people in daylight. Finally she cursed and yanked the bellpull next to the shuttered door. The tinkling noise seemed loud, and she imagined shopkeepers up and down the street starting awake in Pavlovian spasms. Her own skittishness made her smile for just a second. Then she hugged herself and waited.

Thumping footsteps, a growing light in the window—and a little talking-door in the center of the portal opened up. "Have you any idea what time it is?" The voice was male, thin, aged.

"I'm looking for Martin Shambles," said Antaea.

The other laughed. "As if that were some sort of justification for waking me up! It's not enough to be 'looking' for someone, and after curfew no less. What could possibly be in it for the one you're looking for?"

"It's me, Martin, Antaea Argyre." He didn't answer and she wondered if, somehow, he had forgotten her. "Of the home guard?"

The little hatch slammed shut, then the main door creaked halfway open. "I know who you are, girl. Don't dawdle, there'll be a patrol along any minute."

Antaea sighed as the elderly man in the wine-colored dressing gown closed and locked the door. Seeing his white shock of hair and thick glasses took her back in time and for a moment, it was as though the past year hadn't happened. Then he turned and she saw new lines of care on his face. She looked at the floor. "I wasn't sure I had the right place," she said.

"I'm still not sure you do," said Shambles. He held up his candle, peering at her face. "Lords and ladies! What's wrong?"

"It's rather a long story."

"Hmmph! They all are, these days. Well come on." He led the way through the shop. The candlelight softened the angles of the hundreds of slide rules that hung from racks on the walls or stood on little stands in glass cases. There were rules for doing trigonometry, rules for calculating rocket trajectories, and others for gauging how much narrower a house's upper floors should be than their foundation. The cheaper ones were made of wood, the finer of ivory or steel.

Shambles noticed her admiring the wares and snorted. "There's been a run on gun sights lately," he said. "Every one I've made in the past year is now aimed squarely at that little boat parked outside the admiralty. It's a fine irony, really."

"I suppose it would be," she said as he led her down a hallway behind the counter. "You being a member of the Aerie underground and all."

"Is that what this little visit is all about?" he asked her. "I seem to remember that the guard doesn't give a damn about local politics. And neither did you. Your concerns are more lofty and global, aren't they?" He chuckled. "Something about reforming the guard itself, if I recall."

"I've come to you because I can't go to the guard," she admitted. "Their local chapter may have been . . . corrupted."

Shambles tripped over his robe. Recovering, he said, "Corrupted? Oh this doesn't sound good. Come in and tell me all about it."

They entered a little parlor that doubled as a workshop and storeroom: exactly half the floor was neat and tidy, the walls on that side of the room clear of clutter and displaying some framed photographs. The other half of the room was a dizzying maze of boxes and benches, with tools, packing material, and paper lying everywhere. The two leather armchairs on the clean side of the room were angled away from this mess.

Antaea had met Shambles through mutual acquaintances. They had similar professions, and used the same network of smugglers and informants, so it was probably inevitable that their paths should cross. Their first meeting was a bit strained, as they tried to stuff two groups of refugees into one set of barrels bound for the principalities. After they avoided bloodshed and worked out a compromise he had tried to recruit her for the Aerie underground, and she had promised him a place in the home guard.

On one occasion, they had stayed up very late together drinking port, and she had confessed her idealistic dream of turning the guard's hoarded knowledge and science over to the people. Gonlin would have been livid had he known she'd revealed these schemes to an outsider—but Gonlin didn't know about Shambles at all, which was why she felt safe in coming here.

Shambles put down the candle and plunked himself into one of the chairs. Antaea noticed for the first time that under his gown he was fully dressed, despite the lateness of the hour. She had no time to think about this as Shambles steepled his fingers and stretched his long legs into the middle of the carpet. "Somehow it doesn't surprise me, having you show up," he said. "Dire portents about the end of the world seem to be the order of the day. There's two kinds of mob roaming the streets, you're either a loyalist or an agitator and neither kind will let you know which they are before they demand to know where you stand. Give the wrong answer and *poof!* The damned police don't care, they've got this theory that the two sides will cancel each other out somehow." He shook his head bitterly. "Ever since Slipstream conquered Aerie my friends and I have dreamed about something like this happening. Now that it's here all I can say is it's making things worse for us."

"Is it really all about the *Severance* refusing to stand down?" she asked. Antaea tried to order her own thoughts as she sat: what should she tell Shambles, and what was too wild or compromising to mention?

"It's not about the *Severance*," said Shambles. "It's about the damned admiral. Fanning."

Antaea couldn't breathe. She fixed her eyes on the innocuous pictures on Shambles's wall.

"Somebody's fomenting unrest in his name," continued Shambles. "And doing a damned professional job of it, too. At first I thought—we all assumed—it was the admiralty. But there's some other force in play here." He sat up and looked directly at her. "Is it the home guard? —No, tell me it's not!"

"It's not," she said.

"Ha! That's a relief." He brooded for a moment. "Well, then. Why *are* you here?"

She discovered that she'd been wringing her hands. Carefully, Antaea placed them on the arms of the chair. "It *is* about Admiral Fanning," she said.

His eyes widened. "Ha! You're joking." He squinted at her. "Not joking? Antaea, my dear, you're not one of those who's fallen under this man's evangelical spell, are you?"

"I know where he is."

Had Shambles been holding a drink he would have spilled it. As it was he sputtered for a moment, then said, "What?"

"I know where he is, he's in trouble. He's being tortured by—by some very bad people in the mines of Rush asteroid. We need to act right now if we're to save his life."

Shambles groaned and leaning forward, put his head in his hands. Antaea stared at this performance, uncomprehending, until she realized that bent over as he was, Martin was now eyeing her with a desperate expression, one finger jabbing toward the hall. *Get out!*

She stood up, but too late as she heard sliding sounds and footsteps from behind the two chairs. Three men wearing the uniform of the Slipstream police emerged from the clutter and shadow of the workshop. Two held drawn swords, one a pistol.

"Politics makes strange bedfellows," said Shambles as he straightened up. He sighed heavily. "Antaea, as a member of the home guard you were completely safe discussing any of your normal business with me tonight. The last thing I expected was for you to tread into the one subject area that might be of interest to my . . . minders, here."

Antaea eyed the three men. "But why?"

"I'm acting as a go-between," said Shambles with a shrug. "A point of contact between the government and the rebellious commoners in the city. I was relaying the terms of a prisoner swap when you arrived."

She glared at him. "Then why did you even let me in?"

He sighed again. "Because it was you, Antaea. Because I believed you were above such things as local politics."

"I am. This concerns the safety of Virga itself, Martin."

"Oh, Virga is safe now, ma'am," said one of the soldiers with a sarcastic tone. "You see, we know where Fanning is, too.

"He's been captured. Right about now he should be on his way to visit the pilot."

17

THEY MARCHED ANTAEA several blocks through dark narrow alleys, to a covered shed hulking between several buildings. One man had run ahead and after a few minutes she heard the unmistakable—but curiously muffled—whine of a bike's jet engine. "The pilot will want to talk to you," said the man who had his gun trained on her back. "Even if we've already got the admiral."

Antaea kept her feet fixed on the ground. She deserved worse treatment than they were giving her. The home guard had the same status as noblemen in most Meridian nations—the only problem was that some of these soldiers had never heard of the guard, or thought it was a myth. Their talking and pointing didn't matter to her at this point; everything had come crashing down around her. She only hoped that Chaison's capture had also resulted in Gonlin's people being rounded up. If she was really lucky, the monster that had taken her sister's form had been destroyed.

They entered the low shed, which turned out to be a hangar. There were clamshell doors of various sizes in the ground, with bikes hanging over two of them, and a twin-engine boat suspended above the biggest set. A gangplank had been thrown down from this and warm light washed out of the cabin to catch rainbow highlights on the oil-soaked ground. Two soldiers stood at attention over a man who sat on the gangplank. He was tall and lean with handsome features and a boyish mop of black hair. Although he was clearly a prisoner he wore the dress uniform of an officer of the

Slipstream navy. He glanced up as she approached, his face far too despondent for someone who was about to be set free.

No one objected when Antaea sat down next to him. "Antaea," she said, offering her hand. He shook it somberly.

"Travis," he said. "Is it true about the admiral?"

She shrugged. "I don't know. Probably."

He looked into the distance for a moment. Then: "You're not the one I'm being swapped for, are you?"

"No," she said with a sigh. "Just a passenger."

They sat in silence for a while, mirroring one another's postures of listless defeat. Then he murmured, seemingly to no one in particular, "They didn't torture me, exactly. Not in a way that would leave scars. I'm still a high-ranking officer in the navy, after all, and my status was . . . delicate. But they asked questions in a very particular way . . . And they threatened everyone I knew—my family. I told them nothing.

"But I suppose all that bravery doesn't matter now, does it?"

A soldier ran up the alley, shouting, "They're ready!" Travis eased to his feet and smiled down at her. "I hope your stay at the palace is brief," he said with a sad smile.

"I suspect it will be," she said as they led him away. Antaea sat there in the renewed silence thinking about what was going on around her. Things were in motion, no doubt. At least she knew that Gonlin's questioning hadn't killed Chaison. That would be up to the pilot, now.

Sunk in these miserable thoughts, she didn't hear the approaching footsteps until a familiar voice said, "I don't believe it!"

She looked up. Antonin Kestrel stood over her, ringed by soldiers. He was rubbing his right wrist with his left hand. In his right hand he held a bulging file folder.

"Kestrel. You look none the worse for wear," she said tonelessly. He said nothing, and she glanced up again. He did look distressed, in fact. It seemed he was deciding what to say to her.

"What's wrong?" she asked, suddenly fearful that Chaison was dead and Kestrel had already heard.

"Come," he said and without looking back he stalked into the boat. One of the soldiers offered her his hand. Now that he was free, Kestrel was clearly in command here.

"So the admiralty traded you for that Travis fellow?" she said as they strapped themselves into seats on opposite sides of the tiny cabin. Kestrel grunted. Annoyed at his silence, she decided to needle him. "And was it a fair trade?" Only two of the soldiers were able to squeeze in next to them; the rest were clambering into the rumble seats on the outside of the boat.

"Me for Chaison Fanning's best staff officer?" Kestrel pursed his lips. "I'd say our two sides come out about even."

"And how did you come to be in the care of the admiralty?"

He ignored her, clapping the pilot on the shoulder. "Get us going. I have to see Himself immediately."

The pilot reached up and yanked on the release lever. The clamshell doors in the ground banged open and the winch holding the boat aloft let go. Instantly they were falling free in the night airs of Virga, surrounded by swirling city lights. The boat's jets thrummed into life and they shot away from quartet three, cylinder two.

The noise of the jets reverberated through the cabin. Kestrel nodded, suddenly losing his unfocused look. He leaned forward, gesturing for Antaea to do the same.

"I need to talk to you," he said in her ear. She reared back in surprise. When he just grimaced and waited, she brought her head close to his again.

Kestrel pitched his voice to a level that would be inaudible to the soldiers. "As I'm sure you've figured out, your friends Richard and Darius found the admiralty rebels pretty quickly once we got to the city," he said. "They were frantic when they found out you'd taken Chaison. At first I thought it was an act, but . . ." he shook his head. "The boy's no player, though he fancies himself clever. They really didn't trust you, and I thought that was odd if you'd been the one who originally rescued them."

Antaea was puzzled. Why was he telling her this?

She thought about what he'd just said. "Darius and Richard weren't expecting to be rescued," she said. "Neither was Chaison." He nodded, but clearly he expected something more from her. Then she got it. "No!" she said. "I was never working for the admiralty rebels. I really am home guard. I broke him out for my own reasons."

Except, of course, that Antaea had not broken Chaison out of jail. Somebody else had done that and she didn't know who. She had been circling in frustration, unable to come up with a plan to extract him, when he conveniently fell into her lap. She hadn't had time to wonder who it was who'd actually freed him, and it was to her advantage to have him think it was her.

Now she wondered if it hadn't been the admiralty who'd broken up the jail. She could tell Kestrel this—but he was nodding already, as if what she'd told him confirmed his suspicions about something. Certainly, whatever he was thinking, he didn't look happy.

Tired of speculating, she said, "What's this all about?"

He opened the file folder. Several black-and-white photos floated out. Antaea took one and examined it in the leaning city light.

It was mostly a blur of oversaturated white and complete black, but she saw a gray oval that might be a ship, and a scattering of little dots across what looked like a cloudscape. She didn't say anything, just flipped the photo around and shot Kestrel an inquisitive look.

"The admiralty gave me these to take to the pilot," he said. "They're on the *Severance*'s paper and while I would like to doubt their authenticity . . . Some of the details . . ." He saw that she still didn't understand and said, "These are photos taken by the *Severance*'s combat recorder. They're low quality because they were taken in cloud and by flare-light. They're from the battle against Falcon's fleet."

She nodded her comprehension, and he rummaged through the folder. "The admiralty wants me to tell the pilot that they'll print up news sheets with some of these images on them unless he backs down. Images like . . . this one." He turned the little square to catch the light.

Antaea gasped. It was a hellish scene of hundreds of men falling. Those at the edges of the picture were just blurs, but those toward the center were clear: arms and legs thrown every which way, some wearing wings or fins but most grabbing at heavy kits and rifles. The air around them was dotted with helmets, canteens, shoes, and unidentifiable bits of debris.

Kestrel leaned in again. "Chaison said . . ." She looked up from the photo. Kestrel's face was contorted with emotion. "Chaison said that the troop carriers were packed with men. That Falcon wasn't just on maneuvers. Was he . . . ?"

"Was he telling the truth?" She handed the picture back. "Kestrel, I can't tell you for sure. I wasn't there. I can tell you that he knew nothing about the *Severance* or the crisis at the admiralty until you told him."

Kestrel took a deep breath. He slipped the photos into the folder and sat back. When he said nothing Antaea leaned across. "What are you going to do?"

He shook his head.

Antaea sat back, frowning. For the rest of the ride she and Kestrel avoided one another's eyes.

"THAT IT SHOULD come to this," muttered Martin Shambles as he padded down the hallway to his workshop. "Working for the enemy . . . giving up friends . . ."

Outside in the alley next to his shop, officers of the palace guard were doing the prisoner swap that Shambles had negotiated. He'd given them Antaea Argyre to take to the pilot, and the fact was bitter in his throat. Right at the moment Martin didn't want to look on any of the faces waiting out there.

Besides, he had very little time and much to do. He swept his writing desk clear, scattering papers and pens on the floor carelessly. Then he sat down and drafted three notes.

The first said, *Tell him things are coming to a head. Move up plans for spectacular demonstration. Tomorrow, or next day. Don't wait for good weather.*

He folded this letter and, kneeling, pried up a loose floorboard. Underneath was a small space containing several brass tubes with capped ends and a section of bright metal pipe that led off somewhere under the house. He uncapped one of the tubes and put the note in it, then slid back a sheath around the pipe. There was a hissing noise as he consigned the message to a secret pneumatic tube the Aerie insurgency had installed the year before.

He had no idea where the other end of that pipe was, but was fairly sure the pilot's people didn't know about it. They thought he had ties to the underworld, which was true enough and was probably the reason they had left him alone all these years: they'd waited for a day like this when they might need his help. Wise, but stupid, since they hadn't bothered to learn about his true allegiance.

His contacts would have the message within hours. Then, events would be set in motion that might tear Slipstream apart—or strengthen it and destroy all of Martin Shambles's careful work, if he had the timing wrong.

That dire prospect made this second message all the more important. He sat down to draft it not just because he felt guilty over having deceived lovely young Antaea Argyre. He'd fed her to the sharks quite unintentionally, but fed her he had. There was more at stake here than her. It was the status of Chaison Fanning that would likely tip the scales one way or the other, not only in the conflict between the pilot and his unruly navy, but between Slipstream and its conquered vassal state, Aerie.

Martin had once believed Fanning responsible for the destruction of Aerie's secret new sun. He'd hated the man as an enemy of reason as well as the people. Only recently had he learned that Fanning had not participated in that crime. Hayden Griffin had told him a very different story about the admiral, and if it was true then Fanning might be one of the few Slipstreamers in high office who might be willing to help Aerie achieve its independence.

Still, Martin's pen hesitated over the paper. He didn't even know who he was writing to, exactly. The pilot would have Fanning soon, and the admiralty rebels would quickly learn about his capture; Martin would make sure of that. The Aerie insurgency knew, in the person of Shambles himself.

Yet there was a fourth faction in the city. Martin privately called them the bankers—shadowy people, some clearly immigrants whose strange accent and shy nature had turned heads up and down Rush. They were incredibly closed-mouthed, forming tight little communities inside apartment blocks up and down the city's town-wheels. They had odd skills—or no skills—but all answered to some central power they wouldn't discuss. The pilot's police had been utterly unable to crack their circle of silence, or to convict any of them of any crime. Shambles knew, though, that they were the source of the mysterious new currency that was flooding the streets.

To whom it may concern, he wrote. By the time you receive this note, it is likely that Chaison Fanning will have arrived in chains at the pilot's palace. This information has been confirmed both by palace troops and one Antaea Argyre, a member of the home guard. The pilot and admiralty may or may not choose to make Fanning's capture public at this time, so I urge you to contact your people in the palace immediately to verify what I'm telling you.

He didn't actually know that the bankers had people in the palace—but Martin was aware that his was not the only secret organization operating in the city. Even before the *Severance* incident he'd been aware that there was another group, though he didn't know who it worked for, apart from knowing that it wasn't for the government. Recently he had decided that it and the bankers were the same entity. Martin had ears to the palace walls; why shouldn't this other group?

One thing he did know for certain: it was the bankers who were spreading the rumor that Chaison Fanning was returning to Slipstream. *He would return, the rumor said, and he would set everything right again.* The news was messianic, and it often came along with whispered instructions and little slips of paper—the rights currency— that left those who received them strangely empowered.

The bankers didn't work for the aristocracy, or the military. If there was any faction in Slipstream that cared about the common people, it would be them.

It was time for the common people to take these matters into their hands.

He was tempted to sign the note "A friend" but now was not the time to be coy.

I am unsure of your resources, so offer my own. I am Martin Shambles, proprietor of the Computing Sticks shop on Bower Lane. I would tell you where to drop letters to reach my network but we are out of time. I am willing to act openly for I think everything will be decided in the next twenty-four hours. Send someone to speak to me. I have people, money, arms, and equipment.

He read over what he'd written, then shivered. For years he'd tended this little store, making a modest income and enjoying the work and his customers, all the while coordinating the cells of an organization dedicated to the restoration of the nation of Aerie. Many of his operatives had been captured, but the network had held and nobody had ever traced it back to him.

Folding and sealing the letter, he threw off the dressing gown and headed for the door.

If he was caught in one of the curfew sweeps then everything he'd worked for would be ended in one stroke. He hesitated before opening the front door, then sighed and rooted behind the shop's counter for the pistol he kept there. It was covered in dust. He slipped it into an outside pocket of his coat and returned to the door.

Voices were coming from the alley. Evidently the prisoner exchange had only just happened.

"Richard Reiss! I can't believe it!"

Martin Shambles peered into the shadows, where a young man—apparently the newly exchanged prisoner—was embracing a white-haired man with a port-stain birthmark on his cheek. The pilot's soldiers had left the alley; it was just the admiralty men now, standing in a huddle outside Martin's shop.

The newly released officer stepped back and stared searchingly into Reiss's face. "The soldiers just told me that the admiral's been captured. Is it true?"

Reiss looked shocked, then crestfallen. "Ah," he said. "Probably. Probably. We had him, Travis. We traveled with him for long days to get here . . . and then that home guard witch, Antaea Argyre, took him from us. No doubt she's turned him over to the pilot for the reward."

"No, she didn't." Martin had spoken without thinking. They looked over at him, startled at his sudden presence. "They just took her away, too. Strange reward if she'd turned in the admiral, no?"

Reiss frowned, his port-stain birthmark stretching grotesquely. "Then what happened?"

"I know the young lady in question," said Martin after a moment's hesitation. He owed her some defense, he'd decided. "She came to me tonight, but the soldiers were already here and arrested her. She said the admiral was in danger—something about Rush asteroid . . ."

"But she kidnapped him from us!" Reiss glared at Martin. "Are you saying someone took him from her?"

"Evidently," he said slowly, "she did give him up, but not to the pilot. She seems to have felt great remorse having done so. That's why she came to me," he said, realization dawning. "The poor thing . . ."

"If the pilot's got him, we have to act fast," Reiss said to Travis. "Come on, lads," he said to the other admiralty rebels, "the boy and I have acted in good faith. We brought you Kestrel! You can see that Travis here knows me. Now is the time to let me into your inner circles. I *have* to talk to your leadership!"

"As do I."

This stopped them all. They turned to look at Martin Shambles. He shrugged. "The time for masks is over. Your side is going to need the help of my side. I want the admiral freed, and I can help you do it."

"And who are you, exactly?" asked Richard.

"I'm a friend of Hayden Griffin."

The name had a definite effect on Travis and Richard—their eyes widened, they looked at each other, and Travis swore. Then both of them started asking questions at once.

Martin laughed, holding up a hand. "You need to deliver your news to your own people. Do that, return here. Say, two hours? Then we'll sit down and, maybe for the first time, all of us will know each other."

Without waiting for a reply he turned and walked away into the shadows of curfew. He heard them whispering excitedly together, then they drifted away. If they had an ounce of sense, they'd be waiting here when he got back.

He smoothed the note in his pocket, speculating. With the right bills in the right hands, his little letter would fly to its destination. With luck, before the night was out he would know who, or what, the bankers were.

FACES SMEARED PAST Chaison, the words dripping from their mouths following a few seconds later. The whole world was melting and running like wax, except for the lights—city lights crystalline and bright, colors solid as stones.

He'd had a fever once after a sword-cut had become infected. Then, as now, Chaison had known he was delirious. Now, as then, knowing didn't help in the slightest.

His mind still rang from what the false Telen Argyre had done to him. The metallic tang of her thoughts and memories lay all through him, a soiled feeling he was afraid would never leave. He turned frantically from thought to thought, memory to memory, looking for something—anything—that might just be his and not tainted by her invasion. He turned round and round inside himself while cool night air washed over his face to the thrum of a boat's engines.

"—he recover?" That was Gonlin, the leader. Who was he talking about?

Artificial nature is here. The conclusion was inescapable. Having seen inside the false Argyre's mind, Chaison knew what was in store for Virga. Everything touched by A.N. must become a tool, a product, a commodity or a consumable. A rose couldn't be left to be a rose, it must be transformable into a lily or an orchid at the whim of its owner. Even experience and memory had to be made flexible, interchangeable. The whole world must be consumed.

It was obvious now that the woman who had taught Chaison about the technology called "radar" had never been human. Aubri Mahallan had arrived in Slipstream, a vagabond traveler claiming to be from the "tourist station" that perched on the outer skin of Virga. Venera had taken an interest in her, and that interest had led his wife to "discover" the location of the key to Candesce. In retrospect, Mahallan must have led her to the discovery. Mahallan had seemed ordinary enough—and she probably thought she was. It was likely, though, that she had never been born, nor been a child, her personality instead assembled out of open-source components somewhere in the roaring data infinity of Vega. It almost didn't matter, until you realized that instead of a human subconscious, the unconscious processes that had driven her had an agenda completely disconnected to her conscious dreams and hopes. The false Telen Argyre's mind made it clear to Chaison: under artificial nature, a human consciousness rarely existed as more than a mask over something alien, unforgiving, and cold.

He just hoped that Aubri never had to find that out about herself.

These few thoughts, strung together for a few seconds, seemed to stabilize Chaison's world. He blinked and realized that he was strapped into a seat in a three-engined boat that also contained Gonlin, Telen Argyre, and several of Gonlin's thugs—former home guard members if you believed Antaea. They were arcing between the giant revolving cylinders of Rush which were just now being touched by flickering dawn light. Directly ahead was the admiralty and, beside it, the pilot's palace.

Was that the *Severance* hanging in floodlit isolation near the admiralty? Shock at seeing it made the world lose its coherence again. He forgot where he was, disconnected images fluttering through him of yo-yos and paper airplanes, of running along iron roadways as a child. He saw the serious faces of other children, staring back at him from weightless hovels near his parents' estate. Chaison heard himself asking a question and he no longer remembered what it was, only that it hadn't been answered.

"Faster!" The word cut through his mind and all the strange images collapsed. He was back in the boat. Gonlin and his men were staring back, past Chaison's shoulder—at what? Straining, Chaison turned his head to look as well.

It rose from the forested curve of Rush asteroid, shaking trees from its wings with contemptuous ease. The dawning light of Slipstream's sun drenched the precipice moth in gold. It hovered in midair for a moment, then exploded into motion.

"*Faster!*" Gonlin's voice held an edge of panic. It made Chaison laugh to hear it. Here was a man who still had much to lose. It was funny to be on the other side, having lost everything, and to realize just how pointless and silly this man's fear was.

—Which thought made him turn again to look forward. Yes, they were definitely approaching the pilot's palace. Was he being turned over for the reward? Then why was Telen Argyre here with Gonlin? Exposing her meant drawing the precipice moth after them. They could only be doing that under desperate circumstances. Their hidey-hole must have been discovered.

He laughed again. "That thing is going to eat you sooner or later, you know," he said to Argyre. She didn't reply, but Gonlin shot Chaison a superior look.

"Not if the pilot's men kill it first," he said.

Chaison looked between Gonlin and the approaching moth. He saw the plan now: lure the moth into range of the palace guns, and be done with it. "You think they're going to fire on a precipice moth once they figure out what it is?"

"If it starts tearing holes in the palace to get at us, yes," said Gonlin. "Because it'll look like it's after the pilot."

"Oh, that won't play well in the streets." Chaison laughed. "A defender of Virga attacking the pilot? He'll look even more the villain than he does now."

"Who here has ever seen a moth? The pilot will just say it was a monster you'd fished out of winter to wreak havoc on Rush. Besides, we're bringing him *you*, aren't we? No, I wouldn't worry about how this plays, Fanning.

"The pilot will destroy the moth for us, and then we'll find your wife and recover the key."

"You actually think you can control *that* once you get there?" Chaison nodded at Telen Argyre, who seemed to be ignoring their conversation. "I've been inside her mind, Gonlin. She has no intention of just 'dialing down' Candesce's protective field. She's going to destroy it."

Gonlin said nothing, and Chaison realized that he knew this perfectly well—had, perhaps, from the day he'd made his alliance with this monster. "Did you give Antaea's sister to them? As a gift, or sacrifice? Surely she didn't volunteer for it."

For the first time, Gonlin looked troubled. "She brought it on herself. After the Outage we fought back incursions from outside. Telen cornered one of the intruders, but instead of destroying it she made the mistake of trying to talk to it. By the time we found her, she was already like that." He nodded to the woman sitting next to them. "We could have put her down right there—we had enough moths—but luckily the only people there were part of our little group. Malcontents. So I decided to take a chance, and negotiate."

"But it's not going to honor any agreement that leaves Candesce intact."

Gonlin shrugged. "I know. I've given up on that. The best plan now is to let artificial nature transform Virga into something new. For those of us who've positioned ourselves right, we stand to become gods when this reality," he gestured around them, "dissolves into the greater universe."

He leaned in close, and said with calm certainty, "Virga is doomed, Admiral. A month from now, none of this will exist anymore."

"And what will replace it?"

Gonlin smiled. "Anything we want."

THE SHOUTING AND sound of heavy-weapons fire started just as Antaea reached the top of the marble steps above the palace's docks. Kestrel was several steps ahead of her, with dignitaries and palace guards converging on him from several sides under the warm lamplight of the opulent reception hall. They all faltered in their tracks as the first deep chumpf of gunfire made the floor shake.

Kestrel looked back at Antaea. She shook her head uncertainly.

Someone shouted "It's the *Severance!*" and a general panic took hold. Kestrel yelled for order but people were scurrying everywhere now—all except Antaea's guards, who moved closer to her. One took her arm, whether protectively or to keep her from running she couldn't tell. Kestrel stopped a man with a tall plumed helmet and demanded that he find out what was going on and report back. The man stammered something, bowed, and raced away.

"It could be the *Severance*," Antaea said as Kestrel walked back to her. "If they've learned that Chaison's been captured . . ."

"Exactly what I was thinking," he said. "Things could get ugly. Gentlemen," he addressed Antaea's guards, "could you escort this lady to one of the secure guest apartments. Make sure she cannot leave." He hesitated, then smiled tentatively at Antaea. "I won't let any harm come to you. I just have to sort out . . . some things . . . with the pilot."

Antaea let herself be led away. Golden statues and rich tapestries adorned even this, a lower entranceway. Their opulence was obscene—they spoke of that heartless divide between rich and poor that Telen had fought so hard to bridge. At the moment Antaea wanted nothing more than to see it all burn.

Was Chaison somewhere within these walls already? Was he hurt? Or was he too to be put up in a "guest apartment" and eventually forgiven because he was, after all, nobility—even as his supporters were executed en masse outside?

She shook her head. He wasn't like that; it was just her grief making her think these things.

There was a shout from behind her. She turned, her guards pausing as well to look back. The man in the plumed helmet was racing back down the hallway, souting something. "—Monster!" was the only word Antaea caught.

The man holding her arm dragged her forward again. "Wait!" she said. "I think I know what's going on."

"Not your business," said the soldier. "Come along."

"But—" She strained to hear what Kestrel and the other were saying. "Not the *Severance*," came across clearly, as did "threatening the palace."

"Kestrel!" she shouted, digging in her heels. "It's a precipice moth! It's here to stop an abomina—" Her guards hauled her through a pair of iron doors which slammed shut behind her with a heavy finality.

A few minutes later Antaea found herself standing alone in the center of a pleasant little sitting room. This place was a prison, but it was a prison for nobles. She imagined the suite had at times held hostages from neighboring nations and local miscreants with power whose crimes had become so excessive that they could no longer be ignored. There were soft settees and divans, carved side tables with floral arrangements on them, and wide doors that led to a polished-stone bathroom and large bedroom, respectively.

There were also two tall windows at the far end. She moved to these, throwing back the heavy velvet drapes to reveal barred glass. Beyond it was the city of Rush—and a sky full with beauty.

Morning light and haze softened everything to pastel delicacy. Far to the left and up, the massive million-ton town-wheels turned four by four with their banners rippling in the wind; their backdrop was long streamers of golden cloud. Rush asteroid was half-painted into the haze to the lower right, a forest folded in upon itself. Its nearer end was surrounded by a puff of its own weather. Above the asteroid the countless outlying buildings and estates of the city's weightless neighborhoods glittered in the limpid air like sparks frozen in midflight.

These points of reference rotated slowly around Antaea as her own town-wheel spun. Dead-center of her view was the besieged *Severance* and behind it, the admiralty. The *Severance* was a scarred can, the gun emplacements surrounding it painted camouflage blue-gray, their interconnected rope stabilizers a faint spiderweb against the air. Then around them, the pilot's own guard-ships and, in a last shell, a cloud of much bigger vessels loyal to Chaison Fanning. Throwing a long black shadow through it all was the wheel of the admiralty itself, which rivaled the pilot's palace in size.

It seemed like every gun and telescope in Slipstream was focused on the *Severance*—yet dozens had swiveled away and more were following, as spotlights zigzagged crazily through the vista and horns sounded among the ships. Flashes lit the air and writhing balls of smoke blew outward as the precipice moth ran a gauntlet of hostile fire straight for the pilot's palace.

Antaea grabbed the bars of her window and screamed, "Come on!" She bounced off her feet, hauling on the cold metal as though she could rip it aside, feeling for a moment as if she could. She felt every motion of its body as the moth spun and dodged the cannon fire and rockets that were raining on it. Antaea had lived inside this moth's brother for long days during the Outage, not so long ago—and this very one had carried her sister.

She could see every detail of its silvery body now, including the terrible wounds from shrapnel that etched it. "Just a bit more! Come on!"

The firing ceased as the moth got within shouting distance of the palace. The gunners couldn't shoot anymore without risking a hit on the palace itself. Antaea reared back, laughing with delight, as she saw the moth flap stolidly up and out of sight—directly above her. She imagined it coming to perch atop the roof of the pilot's bedchamber, its clawed feet squashing the gargoyles and splintering the slate shingles. In fact, after a few seconds some chunks of masonry fell past her window, on their way to disturb the morning of some poor soul in the surrounding city.

"Come on then!" she shouted. "What are you waiting for? Dig the bastards out!" There was only silence, from the guns and from overhead.

The moth had the false Telen bottled up again. As before, at Rush asteroid, it wouldn't risk human deaths to get at the thing. The palace guard wouldn't risk destroying the wheel to get at it, so, for the moment, the situation was a stalemate.

Antaea whirled away from the window. Suddenly all the luxury around her just seemed obscene. She kicked over a side table and it fell with a satisfying crash. Before she knew it she was demolishing everything in the room.

Much to her satisfaction, nobody came to stop her.

"WILL SOMEONE STOP that infernal racket!" Adrianos Sempeterna III, pilot of Slipstream, put his hands on his hips and glared at the painted ceiling. When the muffled explosions finally ceased, signaling the end of the attack on the moth, the monarch nodded sharply and said, "Thank you."

Sempeterna returned his attention to Chaison. Chaison glared back from where he'd been forced to his knees on the familiar marble floor of the pilot's reception hall. His head was clear at last, and he would have to find some way to keep it that way. He couldn't let this simpering dandy see how vulnerable he was.

The pilot was physically unimpressive, with a bleary-eyed face hovering above thin shoulders, and white, spidery hands that twined around one another when they weren't roving about his costume, unconsciously adjusting ribbon, button, or hem. Today, Sempeterna was a vision in turquoise: his hair was invisible under a brocade cap of that color and a stiffly starched train fanned out behind him, rasping across the floor whenever he turned. Chaison was still having strange thoughts and as he watched the pilot move he wondered what small cargo of dust and lost trinkets he was accumulating under that train.

The one thing the pilot did have was a voice. He seldom put the right words into it, but when given a good speech to read he could, as the proverb went, bring even a statue to tears. His eloquence was neatly tied to his sense of self-preservation, and Chaison had often thought that this was the only reason he was still alive.

Kestrel stepped out from behind a lamplit pillar. "Your majesty," he said. "I've returned."

Sempeterna blinked at him. "Why, so you have, Kestrel, so you have. Good job!"

"We have important matters to discuss," said Kestrel as he approached. He was holding a big sheaf of paper in his hand.

"Good heavens! You're a free man for no more than ten minutes and already you're coming to me with *paperwork?*" The pilot's face was an almost cartoonish study in incredulity. "Could you just relish your restoration for a moment, Kestrel? Besides, I have yet to savor my own victory." He smiled at Chaison. "Something I intend to do right now."

He waggled a finger, and a palace guardsman hauled Chaison to his feet. He brought Chaison to stand near Sempeterna at one of the cathedral-like reception room's huge stained-glass windows. Chaison had been in this room many times, but never here; this raised dais would have held a throne in any other kingdom, but in Slipstream it instead held a few divans, side tables, rugs, and potted plants. Slipstream's pilot did not rule from a throne, but from a lounge. Of course no one but him, his ever-present bodyguards, and a few trusted servants could set foot on the deep pile carpet that surfaced the dais, so technically Sempeterna was granting Chaison a tremendous honor by allowing him up here.

He strutted up to Chaison, train shuffling. "So, your little plot finally comes unraveled," he purred. "—No, don't speak!" he said, holding up a hand. "You'll spoil my moment."

"There was no plot," said Chaison. "You know that."

"Ah, as to that." The pilot examined his fingernails. "It's expedient that there should have been one. Oh, don't look at me like that! This is politics, man, and you're falling on your sword for a reason." He bent down, as far as his clothing would permit, to look Chaison in the eye. Pitching his voice almost to a whisper, he said, "Your actions were noble, and maybe someday I'll be in a position to publicly acknowledge them. Probably not, granted the story and example I'll have to make of you. But we both know that the public good is more important here than the truth, don't we? Or isn't it? Chaison, look me in the eye and tell me that it's more important to clear your name than to end this insurrection and prevent the shedding of any more blood."

For a moment Chaison couldn't speak. He was about to say, "We can do both," but Sempeterna had straightened up again and was laughing. "Ah, what a relief!" he said. "You had me a tiny bit worried there for a while, Fanning. Your supporters were so . . . zealous."

He appeared to notice Gonlin and his party for the first time.

"Are these the good folk who turned the admiral over?" Somebody nodded. The pilot walked straight to Gonlin and shook his hand. "My gratitude and that of Slipstream shall be eternal," he said gravely. "Who do I have the pleasure of addressing?"

"Gonlin Mak, of the Virga home guard."

The pilot dropped his hand and stepped back, visibly startled. "Well! So the guard felt it best to intervene, did they? Wise decision, I'm sure. You felt the prospect of anarchy in Slipstream to be too great? Or was it . . ." He glanced upward, and his eyebrows rose in sudden comprehension. "Has Fanning been consorting with monsters? Is it his creature perched atop my palace?"

"Precisely, your majesty," said Gonlin.

"Yes, I'd thought as much," said Sempeterna. "I trust you're here to dispose of it?"

"We may . . . need your help with that," admitted Gonlin.

Chaison snorted derisively. He was having trouble holding on to the thread of the conversation but clung doggedly to what small scraps he understood. He should be telling the pilot something right now, but he couldn't quite figure out what. A helpless rage filled him. He wanted to strike Sempeterna down right here and now, but couldn't even get to his feet.

"An opportunity to help the home guard help me! I'll certainly take that."

Gonlin hurried on. "The monster is not only after you, but us as well. I beseech you to let us take sanctuary here in your palace until the creature is destroyed."

"Of course! That can't be all you want for delivering me the admiral? It is? Well, of course, you *are* the famous guard . . . Good, then!" Sempeterna turned irritably. "Oh, what is it?"

Kestrel stood at his elbow, the sheaf of papers held in front of him like a shield. "It's about the *Severance*," he said quickly. "You must see these."

"The *Severance*, you say?" The pilot eyed the thick folder, which

Chaison could now see held a number of photographs. "Why is that of any relevance anymore? We have the admiral."

Kestrel took a deep breath and said, "The admiralty rebels claim to have evidence that the admiral was telling the truth about the Falcon fleet's intentions. This is a copy of that evidence. They want to open talks with you, or else they'll make this material public."

For a full ten seconds the pilot stood stock-still, gazing at the folder. Then he took it from Kestrel's hand. "What do we have here?" he said lightly. He flipped it open, peering at this and that picture and sheet of paper. "Documentation . . . from the *Severance's* logs and cameras. Clever, clever . . ."

"Particularly worrying, sir, are these images." Kestrel turned them around for him to look at.

"Men in the air," said Sempeterna, bemused.

The words hit Chaison like a shock of cold water. He looked up at Kestrel. Antonin was staring back at him. Chaison nodded at Kestrel, tight-lipped.

"The admiralty claims that no fleet would have any reason to do maneuvers with their boarding craft full of men," said Kestrel. "Waterbags would do for ballast if the operation were to test the fleet's readiness. Boarding maneuvers are best done separately. The only reason for those men to have been there was if they were going to be used. In an actual invasion."

Pouting, the pilot examined the key images for a while. Then he shrugged. "You and I know that," he said to Kestrel. "But the people don't know that. And it's what the people think that I care about right now. Perhaps, after all, Falcon Formation does do fleet maneuvers with their army as ballast . . . We'll come up with a good reason for that. It's not a crisis, Kestrel—not now that we have the admiral himself."

He flipped the folder closed and handed it back to Kestrel. Turning away he said, "Once again, you're distracting me in my hour of triumph. Could you please get into the spirit of the moment, for once?"

Behind his back Kestrel glared at the pilot with murderous intensity.

"I just had a *great* idea," said Sempeterna suddenly. "It'll tie all of this up in a neat little package and restore the people's confidence in me.

"We seem to have an unusually large audience this morning," he mused, squinting out one of the transparent panes in the window. Chaison looked as well, and saw crowds of people—speckled dark clouds in the morning air—beginning to gather near the admiralty. Maybe they had come to gawk at the precipice moth, but somehow he suspected more. Things were coming to a head and they knew it. Maybe news of his capture had leaked out.

"It would be a shame to send them all home without a show," said the pilot. "Kestrel!" He turned to face the seneschal, who had retreated to the marble floor twenty feet away. "What's the plan for getting rid of that thing on my roof?"

Antonin frowned. "We're planting charges in the eaves under its feet, your majesty. It will be blown into the open air and then hit with a precision rocket barrage."

"Very good. Is it ready?"

"Almost."

"Then here's what we're going to do." The pilot smacked his palms together. "I will take out our little pest," he said, jabbing a finger upward. "In full view of our assembled citizens. I need a shoulder-mounted rocket and more visible clothes. We'll take the shot from my swimming pool. You," he said to Chaison, "will come with me. I'm sure your monster won't attack me if you're standing right next to me, eh?"

Chaison shrugged. "It won't attack you at all. It's not my monster, and it didn't come here to find you."

Sempeterna raised one eyebrow in elegant disdain. "What other target could it have?"

"Her, actually." Chaison pointed at Telen Argyre. The home guard members were still here, standing in a little knot by one of the pillars. Gonlin was watching Chaison and the pilot; he narrowed his eyes, but probably couldn't hear them at this distance.

"Chaison, what *are* you talking about?" Sempeterna leaned against an unobtrusive railing that ran along the base of the window. He seemed highly relaxed and only mildly interested, as if this were some court ball and he was discussing dolphin-breeding.

"That monster is a precipice moth, and it's that woman that it's been following, not me. She's not human. She's from *outside*."

"Oh? Like that interesting young woman you used to employ . . . what was her name again? Mahogany?"

"Mahallan. Aubri Mahallan. Exactly. Sir, this entity is a direct threat to the security of Virga itself. I know that sounds ridiculous, but—"

The pilot held up a hand. Turning to face the window, he said, very quietly, "I'm not a fool, Chaison. I know I don't rate a visit by a precipice moth, and you may be many things, but a sorcerer who summons monsters of the deep you're not. Thanks for identifying its real target, I'll make sure she's taken care of."

Chaison turned as well, facing away from the home guard—and Telen's gaze—as he said, "I doubt you have the firepower. Sir."

"If I can kill a moth, I can kill her. Besides, it's a risk I'm going to have to take," muttered Sempeterna. He grimaced, showing for an instant a side to himself Chaison had never suspected was there. Here was someone clever and calculating, almost reserved in his moves. Chaison was reminded that words and appearances were one thing, actions were another—and this pilot had ruled for many years.

"The people need their show, and I need closure on this whole ugly interlude," the pilot continued. "You're one of the sacrificial lambs, and that moth is going to have to be another. That's just the way it is."

He turned, hooking his elbows behind the railing, and called out, "Kestrel! Go make sure things are ready. I want the crowd told that something momentous is about to happen."

"Very good, your majesty." Face blank, Kestrel turned and left the reception room.

"Once the moth is dead, I'll reveal that I have you," Sempeterna said to Chaison. "I'll feed them the story that you summoned the moth out of the depths of winter to attack me, and I personally captured you and dispatched it. That ought to shut the rabble up for a while. The admiralty will come to terms. Who knows? I may even end up letting you live if that turns out to be part of the deal. Either way, though, I'll see *that* thing," he nodded in the general direction of the *Severance*, "scrapped."

Chaison nodded, but he wasn't listening anymore. He was watching Gonlin, Telen, and the other home guard. The humans were deep in discussion, as oblivious of Sempeterna as he was of them. Telen Argyre simply stood hipshot, staring at nothing— unless she was looking through the very masonry at something invisible to any mere mortal.

The pilot was utterly wrong about her, Chaison was sure. Why should human weapons have any effect on something crafted in the nearly omnipotent forges of artificial nature?

There would be plenty of theatrics today, but it would all be just that—a side show. The only actor who really mattered stood blank-eyed, waiting her turn. If the moth was destroyed or even temporarily incapacitated, the false Telen would reveal what she really was—would hunt down and seize the key to Candesce, and then turn her attention on the sun of suns itself.

The pilot grinned, unwinding his arms from the railing, and slapped his hands together.

"Come on, then," he said. "Kestrel, go make arrangements to blow that pesky monster into the air. You," he pointed at some guardsmen, "show the admiral to some comfortable accommodations. As for me," he examined his nails, "I need to pick out my costume for the show."

TIME DRAGGED. CHAISON paced up and down the suite—glorified cell, really—that they had placed him in. He was thinking about Venera—whether she was alive, and if she was, whether she was here in the city. That monster that had the shape of Telen Argyre had made her its next target, and it was his fault. He should have been able to resist it somehow; the memory of its prying into the most private corners of his mind replayed in his head again and again.

Faint hammering noises echoed through the palace. They were either repairing the roof or, more likely, planting charges under it while pretending to. It's what he would have done. But it was three hours now since the pilot had sent Chaison here and there was no word of what the next move was to be. He supposed he'd had his chance to plead for his life to the pilot, and had thrown it away. All decisions were out of his hands now, a fine irony since the fog of pain and shock from last night was finally lifting.

As to Antaea Argyre—well, he swung between wanting to shoot her on sight, and feeling proud of her brave escape from Gonlin's people. Maybe she really didn't give a damn what happened to him and maybe she had simply run off, but he doubted that. She was the guard's local extraction expert, after all. She would be up to something. The crucial question was, had she discovered her sister's fate? Or was she bending all her energies to free Telen, with the result that she would wind up trapping herself again?

There was a knock at the cell door and a servant spoke through its little window. "Excuse me, sir?" he said in a heavily accented voice. "I was asked to prepare a lunch here for you. May I come in?"

The irony of the question dispelled a little of Chaison's despair; he laughed. "By all means," he said. "I'm not going anywhere."

The butler wheeled in a cart. "It's cold cuts, I'm afraid, but there's some orange juice from the pilot's own trees."

Chaison nodded politely. Then the cell door closed and the man's demeanor changed. "Eat it all," he said. "You'll need your energy if we're going to get you out of here."

"Say again?"

"Look, if they choose to move you to the commons prison," said the servant, pointing down, "then you'll never get out. We have a narrow window of opportunity as it is. Are you fit to fight?"

"As well as I will be." Chaison stared at him. "Who are you working for? Your accent is foreign."

The servant bowed. "Gastony Mayfare, late of Oxorn, at your service. As to who I work for, that would be a very complicated question to answer. We are sympathetic to your cause."

"Who's this 'we'?"

"We who owe our lives to the intercession of the lady Amandera Thrace-Guiles," said Mayfare in a portentous tone. "The lady would like to see you safe."

"Never heard of her." But he wasn't going to turn down an offer of help, no matter how obscure the source.

Mayfare took Chaison's arm brusquely and led him to a mirror. He planted the admiral in front of the glass and started holding up tubes of makeup next to his face. He quickly picked out a foundation, blush, eyebrow pencil, and powder. He brought a wig out of the inside pockets of his jacket and handed it to Chaison. "Your job is to look like me," he said. "We'll swap clothes and—"

Chaison laughed out loud. "This is your plan? Hope that I can just saunter out of here looking like you? Do you think these people are mad? Or stupid?"

Mayfare scowled. "Well it's the only plan we've got. Take it or leave it."

"Even if I got out of this cell, I'd never get off the palace," said Chaison. "They'll have every possible exit manned and riflemen watching the air around the place." Mayfare started to protest, but then looked aside and nodded. "So, leave it," said Chaison. "I'll not have you give up your freedom for no reason."

"But what are you going to do?" Mayfare looked frustrated; Chaison suspected he had been itching to act on his successful infiltration of the palace for a long time. "We can't just count down the hours until they hang you!"

"Believe me, I agree with that." Chaison started to pace. "First of all, I need to know who you are and what's been going on in this city. Who are the players? Who will the civilians back? Who do they hate? Who's grabbing for power in all this chaos?"

Mayfare was glad to talk. His own party were foreigners, it turned out, expats from a ruined town-wheel called Spyre. They had been saved from its destruction and brought to Rush by the mysterious Amandera Thrace-Guiles, who had become their patroness. She, it seemed, was intent on toppling the pilot, though for what reason Mayfare couldn't or wouldn't say.

If Mayfare could be believed, Thrace-Guiles had contacts with both the Aerie rebels and the admiralty. She might be very useful.

As Mayfare described the mood of the city and the disposition of the various contending forces, Chaison found himself imagining various maneuvers that this group or that could pull. It was almost a compulsion—the deep habit of the tactician to mentally turn the field of battle around and picture what the opposition might do. Even if there was nothing he could do anymore to influence events, Chaison found himself unable to resist the urge to plan, as if he were still an admiral in command of a fleet.

And maybe he could be . . .

Chaison took a deep breath, and committed himself to what

might be a last act of complete folly. "There is something you can do, Mayfare," he said. When the man eagerly nodded, Chaison held up a cautioning hand and said, "It involves memorizing a very long and very detailed message, and then taking it to the last man in the palace you're going to want to risk revealing yourself to . . ."

THE ROOFTOPS OF the pilot's palace reached above one another, long swooping curves of shingle and lead, some holding aloft platforms and balconies like waiters carrying trays. From a distance the roofs almost seemed like the storm-tossed waves of some terrestrial sea—save that they wrapped into a ring a half-mile across. Sempeterna's palace was a town-wheel, albeit one covered almost entirely by one multiterraced, many-roofed build-ing. Dozens of elevator shafts crisscrossed the empty interior of the ring, and at its axis of rotation were the usual docks for official and pleasure craft.

Something else glittered and spun like a golden confection in this freefall zone. Years before, Sempeterna had commissioned a grand swimming pool, one that would be unlike any in the world. Its innovation lay not in the fact that it was weightless—zero gravity water was the rule rather than the exception in Virga. No, it was how the water was shaped that made this chamber unique.

Antaea had felt her weight fading for several minutes as the elevator car rose. When it stopped, she and her guards bounced out into a hexagonal passageway at the palace's axis of rotation. Ornate windows showed views of the city and the wheel that turned grandly around them. "This way, please," said one of the guards.

The corridors were draped in red velvet and included numerous pull-cords and ropes. Since they were so well padded you could zip along such ways very quickly; Antaea's escort preferred a slow deliberate glide. So it was that the full grandeur of the pilot's pool emerged slowly for her around the edges of an entranceway shaped like an open mouth.

The building itself was a glass bulb, vaguely onion-shaped, whose ribs shone with gold. Long spires on its ends pointed into the city, and back through the axis to the docks. Various change rooms and drying nests were attached like cocoons to the rib-work.

A gigantic sphere of water hung at the center of the chamber, itself containing numerous man-sized bubbles, some of which had drinks cabinets and other amenities in them. You could swim through the sphere, poke your head into a bubble, and converse with friends there while sipping a fine liqueur. They reminded Antaea of the time she and Chaison had found a bubble in the flood that devoured Songly.

There was nothing exceptional about this pool. But around it were arrayed dozens of glittering, transparent animals—dolphins, whales, birds, and even humans—the smallest a foot across, the largest twenty or more feet in length. They were sculptures made of water, its surfaces teased into keeping these intricate shapes by nearly invisible nets of waxed hair that master artisans had positioned on gold-filigree racks. It was an art form whose medium was the surface tension of water.

Antaea had heard that Sempeterna swam into and through these animals during his morning constitutional. He would dive into an osprey or shark, making its sides quiver and break free of their delicate cages; he would glide like a fish from one end of the transparent beast to the other, emerging with a splash to arrow toward the next one, as the first beast either collapsed into myriad drops, or slowly righted itself into its fantastical shape.

Antaea had little time to admire the opulence as she was led to the narrowing neck of the structure's city-facing end. There, a glass door had been swung back. She could see a sizable crowd of people waiting outside. "Through, please," said the man at her back; so, Antaea climbed through and onto a vertiginous perch astride the golden flagpole that extended fifty feet past the tip of the glass onion.

Sempeterna was here, hovering limply behind a (presumably bulletproof) glass shield. His bodyguards formed a star pattern in the air around him, their feet oriented toward him, heads and weapons pointing outward. Closer in were various officials, engineers, a driver with an idling bike, a chef with a basket of sweetmeats, two doctors, the palace archivist with two scribes, Kestrel, and shadowed by a cloth screen, Chaison Fanning.

He turned around and saw her. Antaea flinched and looked away before she could see whatever expression came over his face. She didn't want to know.

The city of Rush made a backdrop to all of this. Four immense quartets of grandly turning town-wheels flicked their gay banners in the turbulent noon air; past the swarming outrider buildings the asteroid was like a forested whale trailing sheets of cloud. Past that? Incandescence: the uninhabitable region surrounding Slipstream's fusion sun, its whiteness washing out further detail.

The pilot was holding forth on some topic or other while a tailor adjusted his lime-colored clothing. A photographer looked on, squinting through his lens. The one incongruent element in the scene was the shoulder-mounted rocket launcher hanging near Sempeterna's feet.

Gazing at the palace gave her a chance to avoid looking near Chaison again. The palace wheel turned slowly up and down around the swimming pool. To keep herself from thinking, Antaea counted, measuring its rotation: about one rpm. From here of course rooftops and gardens were all she could see—with one exception. The precipice moth was passing twelve o'clock and heading for two o'clock before she found it, but once located, it was impossible to lose. Its massive silver limbs had partially caved in the roof above the reception hall. Even as Antaea spotted it she saw some slate shingles skitter down the slope of the roof and bounce into freefall, traveling tangent to the wheel.

There was a bright flash; Antaea turned to find the pilot relaxing out of his pose. He held the rocket launcher. With a blithe wave he dismissed the photographer, and turned to address the small retinue perching like birds behind him.

"I'm going to shoot the monster now. When I do, there'll be a big explosion so hang on, please. Kestrel's kindly planted some . . . extra charges, under the roof. Below the monster, you know. It'll be knocked into midair and then the rest of our fire team will take it out." He waved in the general direction of the palace. Antaea looked again, but she couldn't see anybody on the rooftops. Were the pilot's fire teams sitting in windowsills or something?

"After the beast, next on the agenda is revealing Admiral Fanning to the crowd," continued Sempeterna. "We'll gauge their reaction and decide from that whether I shoot Fanning right here, or we take him inside to court. Right? Everybody ready?"

Kestrel was hand-walking along the flagpole, his face grim. He came next to Antaea and paused for just a moment. "I met a mutual friend in the hallway," he said. Then he continued on.

He continued on to where Chaison Fanning waited under guard. Antaea watched him go, puzzled by what he'd just said.

Behind them, the pilot prepared to take his shot.

ANTAEA WOULDN'T LOOK at Chaison, which was damned annoying because he really needed to get her attention right now. The pilot was settling the rocket launcher onto his shoulder, getting a feel for its mass by rocking it gently back and forth. All eyes were on him—all save Antonin Kestrel's. The seneschal glided up to Chaison, his expression stark.

He paused in between Chaison and Antaea and said, "When he takes the shot, close your eyes," just loudly enough for both of them to hear. Chaison saw a wonderful expression of surprise on Antaea's face as she stared at the seneschal. He had to laugh.

"Quiet," snapped Kestrel. "You'll ruin the moment."

"So you got my message?" he murmured. Kestrel ignored him. His eyes were on Sempeterna.

"And . . . we go," said Slipstream's monarch. He pulled the trigger on the launcher and a sudden whoosh! and shower of sparks engulfed him. Chaison closed his eyes.

The light was like a slap across the face, even through his closed eyes. The rapid chain of flashes was accompanied by cries of surprise and dismay from all around. A moment later Chaison felt a hand on his wrist and Kestrel shouted, "This way!"

Chaison opened his eyes. Everyone was pawing at their eyes, except he and Kestrel and Antaea. As one they jumped at the idling bike. Chaison grabbed it and started to swing into the passenger saddle only to find Antaea coming in from the other side. She shrank back. Chaison growled and reaching out took her jacket by the lapel, pulling her to him. "Brace yourselves!" yelled Kestrel as he opened the throttle.

The bike's engine brayed, drowning out the confused shouts of the temporarily blinded crowd. Then before they'd gone ten feet there was a gunshot, then another. Chaison craned his neck to see who was shooting.

The pilot was pawing at his eyes, cursing, as were most of his bodyguards—but not all. Three of them had been dutifully watching for threats from other directions than the moth, and they had enough discipline that none had snuck a peek at the pilot's shot. All three were firing their repeating rifles at the bike.

Still, the little jet made it a good fifty feet before something tore through its fans. The bike screamed and belched a black cloud of smoke, then began to tumble. All three of its riders held on for dear life, their legs flailing outward to form a three-sided star in the air. Helpless, they were nonetheless falling in the general direction of the *Severance*.

"What is he trying to do?" shouted Antaea. "Take us to the *Severance?*"

Kestrel grimaced. "I thought it was a pretty good plan under the circumstances. Damn! Those guards were supposed to be too tempted to look the other way."

Antaea laughed wildly. "Now what? Do we let go?"

"Hang on!" Bullets were hissing past them. The whole city had been watching the pilot's pantomime and knew exactly where to look when he'd fired his missile. This part of Chaison's plan had never been much more than a desperate gamble. Even if nearly everybody was blinded by the fireworks flash-pots Kestrel had planted under the moth instead of explosives, nearly everybody wasn't good enough.

"What about the rest of my plan?" he asked.

Kestrel nodded. "As far as I know it's in motion."

"What plan?" Antaea was staring at them both with something close to horror. "What did you do?"

"I was instructed to oversee the planting of the explosives under the moth," explained Kestrel. "After the first team of engineers placed their charges I sent them on an errand, then sent up a second team to take the bombs down, and then the royal fireworks team to plant flash-bombs. Pretty simple, really."

Chaison looked back at the palace. The moth still sat on the roof, which was gouting a spiraling banner of woozy black smoke into the rotational winds. There were holes and splintered cornices everywhere; the carefully timed missiles that were supposed

to finish the moth off had all missed their marks because it hadn't
been knocked off the roof as planned. Those errant missiles had
mostly hit the palace itself.

He laughed. "What a mess! If nothing else, we've made Sempeterna look like the fool that he is."

Two bikes shot into sight. They quickly looped around the disabled jet, the palace guardsmen on their backs leaning out to aim
their guns at the three would-be escapees. "Prepare to be towed!"
said one.

Kestrel and Chaison exchanged a glance. Kestrel shrugged.
"I'm sorry I didn't believe you, Chaison. You saw . . . Sempeterna
admitted that Falcon had been out to invade us. The photos already made me doubt, and then your testimony during our flight
over," he said to Antaea, "made me even more uncertain. But
when the pilot saw the pictures and just shrugged . . . you were
right, and you did save Slipstream, Chaison. I still find it hard to
believe that you weren't in communication with the admiralty
forces until last night—but—" He shrugged awkwardly.

Chaison grinned at his friend as the palace guard clamped a
hook to the bike and turned to tow them back to the swimming
pool. He looked wistfully at the receding shape of the *Severance*. So
close . . .

"It's moving," he said, surprised even though he had known it
might happen.

The *Severance*'s engines had come to life, blurring the air behind
it. Heavy as it was, it was going to take it a few seconds to clear
the cordon of hostile guns surrounding it—but those guns were
still in disarray, since most of the soldiers manning them had been
blinded like everyone else. Not everyone inside the *Severance* could
have been watching from its tiny windows, though, and Chaison
imagined that within seconds every crucial post had replaced its
dazzled personnel. In all likelihood, by the time Kestrel had the
bike in the air, *Severance* had its sight back. The failure of Kestrel's

breakout attempt had been seen, setting one of Chaison's contingency plans into motion.

"They saw *you*," said Antaea. "Chaison, they're coming for you!"

Explosions suddenly shrouded the *Severance*. If it had recovered from its blindness quickly, so had the other large vessels. The police gunboats and palace cutters were all firing on the *Severance* now, heedless of the danger to the crowds clouding the air in the city beyond. Chaison saw one missile go wild and plow into a mansion on the other side of the admiralty. The building exploded in a roar of shattered glass and wood splinters.

The *Severance* disappeared behind smoke and fire. Hammerblows of sound knocked Chaison about; he lost his grip on the bike and flailed out wildly, finding Antaea's reaching hand. He realized he was swearing wildly and shut his mouth.

Antaea pulled him toward her. "This is the time," he said. "You have to fight."

She said, "Chaison, I—"

"I know why you did what you did," he said gruffly. "And I know you tried to fix it." She closed her eyes for a moment, then smiled tentatively. "Get ready to jump," he continued, not looking at her. "We're going to grab the pilot."

But Sempeterna was already on the move under a huddle of bodyguards, swinging back into the onion-shaped pool building while his retinue variously clung to the flagpole and glass siding, or drifted helplessly in the shocked air.

Chaison was about to say something—maybe just to swear, he could never later remember—when the *Severance* reappeared. It nosed out of a roiling pall of smoke, dripping fire, not a quarter mile away. It was headed straight for Sempeterna's swimming pool.

Deep booms echoed between the palace and the city and some of the pool's glass panes cracked. A full-fledged battle had erupted behind the *Severance*, between the police boats controlled by the pilot, and admiralty ships. Underneath it all was the faint sound of twenty thousand people screaming as they flew for cover.

As the sky seemed to come unraveled all around them, Chaison's doubts and hesitations melted away. He was trained for this chaos. It was his job to create moments like this one and then steer the madness in the right direction. Finally, he was in his element.

He glanced back at the pilot then up at the oncoming ship, assessing what was happening and what to do.

As Kestrel's damaged bike bumped gently against the pool's flagpole and the palace guards dismounted to surround them, Chaison said, "The *Severance* will use the palace as a shield. You have to get to it. I'm going after the pilot."

Kestrel blinked at him. "How?"

"With these fine men as my escort," said Chaison ironically. "They want me, not you. Go!"

Without waiting for an answer Chaison dove for the pool building's hatch. There were shouts and he was caught before he could maneuver through the opening. That didn't matter, because Antonin Kestrel and Antaea Argyre had seized the moment and jumped the other way. The guardsmen had chosen to follow Chaison, as expected.

The guards took several half-hearted shots at the fleeing pair, but they'd already passed over the curve of the onion-shaped building and were just shadows in glass now.

Chaison smiled and turned to his captors. "Do your jobs, then," he said. "Take me to the pilot."

THE *SEVERANCE* WAS holed in a dozen places and chunks of concrete and iron were falling off it as it spun, but its heavily armored engines still worked. It passed not two hundred feet beneath Antaea and Kestrel, but fine traceries of bullet fire still stitched the air near the ship and as it spun it was responding in kind to its attackers. There was no way to get near it, so the two held onto the gold-painted iron framing of the pilot's pool and waited.

Antaea spared a glance behind her. Chaison was being hustled after the departing pilot, but he looked unhurt. It had seemed like folly to leave him but now she was realizing that he'd done the moral and tactical calculation and knew that the safest place for him right now was at Sempeterna's side.

The pilot wouldn't kill the one man who might be able to negotiate a way out of this mess.

The *Severance* was inside the turning ring of the palace now. Antaea had never seen madness like this, not even during the siege of Stonecloud: the admiralty vehicle, bearded with smoke, simply plowed into the suspension cables and elevator shafts that spoked the wheel's interior, snapping and smashing its way through them like a maddened animal. Sections of shaft hit the roofs below and these simply disappeared in clouds of masonry dust and flying, twirling shingles. Accompanying it all was the terrifying noise of ship-to-ship battle taking place between the palace, the admiralty, and the city.

The *Severance* was not built for speed, but squat as it was the can-shaped vessel could turn by simply spinning around its own center of gravity. As it reached the midpoint of the palace wheel it did just this. Antaea saw an axis-to-surface ladder rotating majestically toward it and realized with a start that there were human shapes on that ladder. They began to dive off it seconds before the *Severance* clipped it and flung it away in pieces. Men tumbled through the air, their tangents taking them at high speed toward the rooftops. She looked away.

"Come on," said Kestrel a moment later. "Now's the time."

Nobody was firing at the *Severance* anymore. It had carved out a space for itself inside the turning wheel of the palace and now simply hung there letting the ring-shaped building spin around it. Even though its hull was suspended scarcely a dozen feet above the highest rooftop, *Severance* was still weightless because it was not participating in the rotation of the larger structure. It thundered like a furious cloud past the windows of ladies-in-waiting, rattled the sills of butlers and maids and bureaucrats—but it was they that were moving, not it. Draped with cables and surmounted in smoke, *Severance* waited for the enemy's next move.

That move was pedestrian enough that Antaea would have laughed, if not for Kestrel's obvious distress at the damage being done to the palace. A packed elevator car sank slowly down from the pool on one of the few untouched cables; she could see Sempeterna, Chaison, and a squad of guards all crammed into it cheek-by-jowl.

Kestrel turned away. "How good are you at long jumping?" he asked her. Antaea shot him a confident smile.

"It was the way we got around back home." Much of her days as a child had been spent in freefall, so like most kids Antaea had become adept at accurately jumping between buildings that might be up to a quarter-mile away from one another. A mis-jump could strand you in the air or, worse, leave you open to humiliation by your friends. Tired, hungry, and sore as she was, she knew she could clear the space between this spot and the *Severance* with little trouble.

"As long as they don't shoot us on the approach," muttered Kestrel as he put his feet against the side of the pool building.

"Who?" Oh. Now that the smoke was clearing from around the *Severance*, she could see that its heavily reinforced hangar doors were slowly winching open. A mob of men with guns and swords crowded around the doors, awaiting the right moment to leap off the ship and onto the palace's rooftops.

Antaea returned her gaze to the ship as a whole, concentrating. Then she and Kestrel kicked off, reaching for one another's hands immediately afterward.

Surrounded by flying shrapnel, bullets, with the turning palace roofs ahead, they had consigned themselves to a trajectory they could no longer control. Hand in hand, they sailed slowly toward the smoking *Severance*.

"YOU GOT TO him! I should have known it—you two were always too close." Sempeterna darted out of the elevator forcing his guards to run to catch up. "Kestrel! That he should have betrayed me . . ."

Chaison shook his head. "Maybe it was that time when you tried to kill us both in Hale."

"Well, considering what you've just done, I was right to try, wasn't I?" The pilot stopped and glared at Chaison. "Now what? Is your ship going to blow up my palace?"

Plaster suddenly dropped from the ceiling above Sempeterna's head. Coriolis force pulled it to one side so that it landed in a puff of white three feet away from him. Chaison could hear groaning noises coming through the walls. "It may not have to," he said. "If enough of those cables were snapped . . ."

The pilot scowled, then turned to one of his officers. "Evacuate everyone except the security staff to the safe rooms and seal them, just in case."

"We have to negotiate an end to this," continued Chaison. "Luckily, we *can*."

"We have to do no such thing," snapped the pilot. "You think this," he waved at the building around them, "is a crisis? You and your little band of rebels can have this place. It's just a building. But you'll never get . . ." A captain of the palace guard was running up the corridor, his plumed hat askew.

"Coming down from the roof!" he shouted. "Thirty—forty of them, more behind."

Sempeterna sneered. "And how many of *you* are there? Two hundred? *Get* them!"

The floor shook and more plaster fell. Chaison heard "—Cut the rest of us off!" from the newly arrived guardsman. He nodded to himself.

"The *Severance* is firing its heavy guns into the wings surrounding this hall," he told the pilot. "They've isolated you here. I don't think you have two hundred men to take on the *Severance*'s crew."

For the first time Sempeterna looked truly rattled. He turned to his master-at-arms. "Your highness, the boat docks are below us," said the guardsman. "We need to get you to a cutter and off the palace."

"But . . ." The pilot turned, wild-eyed, to look at Chaison. For a moment it looked like he was about to say something; but then he turned away with a curse.

"Take me to the docks! I'll see this place blown to pieces before I negotiate with these—these pirates."

They hurried along, and Chaison followed. One of the guards glanced over at him and snapped, "What are you smiling at?"

Chaison hadn't even realized he was doing it. Against all reason and expectation, he discovered he was having a very good time.

FALLING AT THE *Severance* gave Antaea plenty of time to watch the unfolding battle in the air around the admiralty. The pilot's honor was being defended by two dozen police and army boats of varying sizes, mostly squat spindle-shapes painted camouflage-gray. Against them were two midsized naval cruisers bristling with guns, and six attack boats with long metal rams on their prows. Despite the noise and explosions, all the ships were refraining from using their heavy missiles for fear of hitting the city. Their short-range ordnance was certainly damaging enough.

Around the big ships roared swarms of bikes and catamarans— ornately plumed palace guards versus dark-uniformed admiralty airmen. They were also refraining from firing their machine-guns and rifles, so their battle had become a joust. Men shot past one another at combined speeds of hundreds of miles per hour, lashing out with their cutlasses in hopes of catching the other rider. Some riders paired up, stringing thin cables between their bikes and hurtling together at the enemy in an attempt to cut them in two.

The city was quickly being obscured both by smoke and a fine mist of blood; so, it took some seconds before Antaea saw what was happening there.

She pulled Kestrel around, pointing. "Look!"

The four quartets of spinning town-wheels were emptying themselves. Thousands of human figures swarmed the air, sprouting all manner of wings, fins, and spinning fans to propel themselves.

Sunlight glinted off metal here and there: swords and rifles carried by the flocking citizens. There was no order to the exodus, but the clouds of people hedged their way around the outskirts of the battle. They had a different destination, it seemed.

Kestrel gaped at the sight. "They're coming here!"

Antaea had no more time to think about what was happening in the city, as the *Severance* was approaching quickly. It seemed magically suspended in the air above the rapidly racing spires and roofs of the palace. Every time the rooftop where the precipice moth perched came around, two or three of the airmen clustered at the hatches of the battered ship would leap into the air, with far more energy than their legs could propel them—they must have rigged some crude catapults. Without that boost of speed, they would have hit the speeding rooftops at over a hundred miles per hour; as it was, they crashed indiscriminately through window or shingled plane, rapidly building their own set of holes next to the ones left by the moth. That creature was watching their performance with an air of easy distraction, apparently unfazed by the battle, the flash-pots, and the fire that continued to smolder right under its feet.

It was clear that she and Kestrel had been spotted because several of the stubby machine-guns poking out of the ship's hull had swiveled to follow their progress across the sky. She also saw some of the airmen pointing at them, so, for all the good she thought it would do, Antaea waved at them.

"You're sure they saw us try to rescue Chaison?" she said in a deliberately light tone. Kestrel shrugged.

"Chaison's friend the butler was supposed to relay the plan to the admiralty. Of course, he's not one of theirs—I don't know who he works for—but whoever it is has contacts. The plan was I would fire the flash-pots, fly Chaison and maybe you if I could out to the *Severance*, and then we'd rally the admiralty and the people."

Antaea glanced back. "Well, somebody got to the people."

"Brace yourself," said Kestrel. They were about to arrive at the *Severance*.

Nobody'd shot them yet, but if the captain wasn't in the mood to entertain visitors then in about five seconds they were going to bounce off the black, scarred hull of the vessel and drift who knew where—maybe right into the heart of the battle.

Faces were watching her from the hatches; and then, without fanfare, a man stepped onto the hull holding a rope, and kicked off in their direction. He held out his hand and Kestrel gripped it, wrist to wrist. Antaea recognized him from the previous night.

"Travis!"

"Chaison's first officer," said Kestrel.

Travis nodded at her. "Captured with the admiral after the battle in Falcon, traded back to Slipstream with the rest of his crew." He squinted at her shrewdly. "You freed him from prison, I hear."

She bit her lip, but said nothing.

The rope tautened and they were hauled into the *Severance*. After all its adventures and the long siege, Antaea had expected the ship to reek of offal and unwashed men. There was a bit of a smell, but it wasn't nearly as bad as she'd expected. She supposed there was no way the pilot could have prevented the admiralty launching buckets-full of water at the *Severance* whenever they wanted.

It was dark, though; they'd probably rationed lamp oil. The ship had a strange shape on the inside, with all its bulkheads wrapped around the central core that held the engines. She could see a little curve of space to each side of the engine shaft, and a little ways fore and aft before her view was cut off by platforms and cargo nets—but that was it. There was probably no clear line of sight through the ship at any point.

Unshaven grim men were lining up by the dozen to climb onto the absurd, home-built catapults that had been mounted next to the open hatches. With time on their hands, the crew of the ship had obviously planned this assault meticulously. They might have known better than anybody else in the kingdom how the siege was going to end. As Antaea watched, a stocky airman with a cutlass in his hand climbed into a legless chair that had been made into a giant slingshot. Four other men hauled back on the straps that bound it as he fidgeted, trying to find his center of gravity in the thing. He said "0—

"—Kay!" as he was shot out of the ship. She watched him put his hands over his head and curl into a ball just in time as a speeding dormer window caught up with him and swallowed him whole.

Travis saw her amazed expression and shrugged. "After a few months in here they'll do anything to get out."

Kestrel shook his head. "But how did you get in? I just saw you last night, in the city—and *Severance* has been ringed with sentries all along."

"We boarded the same way you were supposed to," said Travis. "We were on a bike, circling at speed. The instant the flash-pots went off we aimed for the *Severance*. Made it two seconds before the loyalist machine-gunners opened fire on us."

"'We'?" asked Antaea.

"That's right, ya traitor," said a familiar voice. She turned to see Darius Martor swinging his way, apelike, up the ship's internal rope system. Behind him was Richard Reiss. Darius was grinning, Richard looked his most dignified.

"I . . ." She had no idea what to say to them.

"We were almost home!" barked Darius. "And you stole him from us to turn him over to the pilot—" Richard put a hand on his shoulder, and shook his head.

"Not the pilot, I gather," said Reiss. "The message Chaison relayed through Kestrel said that you were forced to turn him in. Something about your sister's life being threatened?" She nodded dumbly. "I see. Is your sister . . . ?"

She blinked, looking away. "Dead," she said. "After all that, she's dead."

"Oh." Darius was clearly struggling over whether to feel outrage or sympathy. "Ah, that's rough."

Desperate to change the subject, she said, "What are you doing here? Chaison brought you back so you could be free from all this." She gestured at the ship around them.

Now it was Darius's turn to look uncomfortable. "We got unfinished business," he said.

"He's afraid of his freedom," said Reiss, not unsympathetically. "We walked onto the streets of Rush and I said, 'This is it, boy, you're home!' And he stared into the crowds, and then he shrank back against me."

"'Cause you had a death-grip on my shoulder!" Darius glared at the diplomat. "Anyway," he said in a more subdued tone, "what was I to do after all this time?"

Reiss nodded, looking haunted. "What *are* we to do now?"

An awkward silence followed. Finally Antaea shook her head ruefully and said, "If you're going down there," she pointed to the open hatchway, "I'd like to try to make up for what I did."

Kestrel shook his head. "I'll take no more part in this barbarism," he said. "The pilot may have been wrong, but it's not right to compound crime with crime."

Darius grinned. "The admiral's in there and alive?" Antaea nodded. Darius shouldered to the front of the line and climbed into the catapult's saddle, ignoring the protests of the waiting airmen.

"Then let's get him back!"

"A LITTLE LESSON in political expedience," said the pilot as they trotted together down the steps to the dock. "Nothing good would come of the general population knowing that Falcon Formation tried to invade us. What would be served by inflaming hatred against Falcon's people?"

"That assumes that our people are stupid, which they're not," retorted Chaison. "They're fully capable of distinguishing between the government of Falcon and its people."

Sempeterna laughed. "Are they? And what guarantee are you willing to give me that if I go to stand with you on the edge of the palace, and tell the city what really happened last year, that they'll take it well?"

Chaison cupped a hand next to his ear in an exaggerated listening pose. "It's a little late for you to worry about that, isn't it? They don't seem to be taking it well that you're in charge at all."

There were shouts from below and Chaison bumped into the man ahead of him. It was very bright farther down the stairs, and a stiff wind was pushing at him from behind. He craned his neck to see what was happening.

"—Floor! It's gone!"

Standing on tiptoe, Chaison finally made sense of what the guardsman was saying. They were just above the hangar, which was a long building slung under the bottom of the wheel, its floor containing hatches of varying sizes through which bikes or boats could be dropped. Chaison could see one or two bikes still dangling from their chains—but they were dangling above thin air. The floor of the hangar was missing, just a few twisted spars poking out from the walls. Cloud and blue air shot by below and the air funneling down the stairwell shot into it in a steady blast.

As everybody cursed and turned and he was pushed back up the stairs, Chaison smiled. That part of the plan, at least, had gone like clockwork.

For once, the pilot had nothing to say.

They'd come down quite a ways, so by the time they reached the top of the stairs both Sempeterna and Chaison were panting. They could hear the steady sound of gunfire coming from the floors above. The captain of the guard pointed. "The reception hall is a safe room. We'll make a stand there."

"A stand?" The pilot stared at him in shock. "Since when are we making *stands?*"

"Come, sir." The captain hauled the pilot along like a disobedient child. They entered the cavernous waiting room that adjoined the hall. This was windowless, its walls draped with obscenely rich tapestries and its floor dotted with colorful rugs and little furniture clusters. It could hold a hundred people without straining. Just now there were about twenty palace guards there, milling around the tall doors to the hall. These were closed.

Now Sempeterna nodded. "Very good. Yes." He turned to Chaison. "Those doors are bomb-proof if I remember rightly. There's only this entrance and my personal one which is similarly secure. All right," he shouted, clapping his hands to get the attention of all the guardsmen. "We're going to use the reception hall as our base. Ten men stay out here to relay messages and guard the doors, the rest come with me. We're going to demand a cessation to these hostilities, or we will summarily execute the admiral." He scowled at Chaison. "Correction: I will execute him."

"Sir!" One of the men by the inner doors ran over, saluting hastily. "We shut the doors to lessen the noise, sir." When Sempeterna merely raised an eyebrow, the man went on, "the windows at the other end of the hall are broken. The spin wind's howling something frightful in there."

"A little privation we can stand for a few minutes while we sort all of this out." The pilot gestured for them to open the doors. The heavy portals almost pulled the men holding them off their feet as they swung in, and Chaison felt a rush of air from behind him. Howling turned out to be the right word to describe the noise coming from the smashed-in stained-glass wall at the far end. As the party of guardsmen padded into the deeply carpeted assembly end of the hall, some clapped hands over their ears. The pilot sauntered through it all, making a moue of distaste at the tangle of leading and glass that had wreaked havoc with the carpets.

The stained-glass windows extended fully thirty feet from the floor to the hall's ceiling, only the chamber's wraparound gallery breaking their symmetry. The ones at this end looked out on a fan-shaped garden and open sky beyond that. The hall was built on the very edge of the palace wheel, so at the other end, almost two hundred feet away, open air and the city beyond glowed behind Sempeterna's raised dais. Normally the light of Slipstream's sun would shine from behind him, casting myriad colors across visitors and long shadows across the marble floor.

Now, shafts of white light extended the length of the place, making bright smears across the marble floor below the pilot's dais. The stone was strewn with glass.

The guardsmen slammed the doors shut and lowered a bar across them. Sempeterna nodded and strode toward the noisy chaos at his end of the hall.

The hall seemed empty and Chaison cursed under his breath. He knew he needed to run, *right now*, but didn't know which direction to go. He looked around, trying to catch a glimpse of what he knew must be here.

Shouts and shots—and somebody lunged past Chaison. He saw the look in Sempeterna's eye—*oh no you don't!*—as one of the guardsmen tried to tackle him again, then the sovereign of Slipstream dodged out of the way and ran behind a pillar.

The men who'd just lowered the bar across the doors were falling, felled by bullets from the gallery fifteen feet up. The catamarans or bikes that had carried this ambush party were nowhere to be seen; after smashing through the windows of the empty hall and disgorging their passengers, they'd probably been tipped out into the open air again. The invaders had then hidden in the gallery.

Chaison had gambled that Sempeterna would return to this section of the palace. The royal apartments were here and this was the origin of the elevator to the pool. Luck was finally with him.

The guardsmen were all behind the pillars with the pilot now.

Chaison started to sprint for the stairs to the gallery but heard the click of weapons cocking behind him. He glanced back to find at least five weapons aimed at him. The party in the gallery couldn't put down decent covering fire at this angle; Chaison was alone in the center of the floor, completely exposed to the pilot's men. Cursing foully, he raised his hands and walked back to them. All firing ceased as he did so.

Of course his team had been in the gallery. He should have made a break for it the instant he entered the room.

"Chaison?" The pilot stood facing the wall with his back pressed firmly against a pillar. "Are these your people?" He had a wild look in his eye. In the momentary lull, the sound of something massive crashing against the hall doors rumbled under the screech of the wind.

"This is my element," Chaison shouted back. "Chaos. Yes, I set it in motion. But that doesn't mean I can control it." *I just hang on and ride it*, he thought. Hopefully that would be enough.

His moment's hesitation a moment ago might have cost him his life, though. The captain of the guard gestured Chaison over and put a pistol to his temple. He frowned at Sempeterna, who appeared to consider, then shook his head.

"You in the gallery!" he shouted, his well-trained voice blurred but not extinguished by the roaring wind. "We have your admiral. Give up or we shoot him!"

There was a long pause. Then—barely audible—the words, "Then we shoot you."

Chaison could feel the cold circle of the captain's weapon next to his ear. It was jumping about nervously.

The pilot rolled his shoulders and deliberately sighed a long sigh, staring off into the distance. Then he turned to Chaison. "All we have to do is hold them off until the rest of my men break down the doors," he said. "Which shouldn't take long. Then they'll surrender or die."

Chaison glanced at the doors. Sempeterna was right. The palace guardsmen in the waiting room had heard the gunfire in here and were pounding heavily on the doors. Armored though they might be, the doors would have to fall soon.

He looked longingly at the broken windows. Too far to make a break for those. "All right, then," he said. "Let's just agree to end this right now. Then you and I can walk out of here and shake hands in front of the whole city. You'll still be pilot and you can exile me for all I care, as long as you spare the *Severance*'s crew."

Sempeterna looked away for a moment. "What about Falcon?" he asked.

"In case you hadn't noticed, they're being overrun by the Gretels right now. I hardly think Falcon is a problem."

"True . . ." Sempeterna tilted his head back and forth, thinking. Then he said, "It's not so unreasonable. Let's—"

A thunderous crash drowned whatever he said next, as the doors to the waiting room blew out on a fist of smoke.

The pilot laughed. "Then again, maybe not!"

"KEEP YOUR HEAD down, boy!" shouted Richard Reiss. "We didn't bring you all this way to get you killed at the last moment!"

Antaea watched him make an example for Darius by ducking and weaving toward the gallery stairs. Flaming pieces of the hall doors were still in motion as the *Severance*'s crewmen fanned out under the great stained-glass windows. She ran in herself and without discussion went back-to-back with Travis; they aimed their weapons about, looking for a shot.

"Good work, Darius!" she shouted. The boy grinned.

As the *Severance*'s crew had clattered down the final flight of steps to the level of the hall entrance, Darius had raced ahead. Travis cursed and made a grab for him but the boy was too quick. As they reached the main corridor Antaea saw that the guardsmen had made a six-foot-high barricade of furniture across a grand, gold-filigreed archway to the left. If that was a defensive point there should be men atop the pile, but there weren't any. Darius raced up to the heaped chairs and cabinets but staggered to a halt when shouts came from the other side of the barrier.

He spun, a look of terror on his face. He was completely exposed in the middle of the hallway. Just in time he ducked under a chair on the edge of the pile, as three guardsmen surmounted its top.

Antaea ducked back just in time and turned, arms out, to block the way. "Shhh!" she hissed, nodding in the direction Darius had taken. "Twenty feet away."

Travis peeked around the corner. Then he grinned. "Perfect!" He turned to a couple of battered and mean-looking airmen. "Give me covering fire for five seconds."

Antaea watched as the men popped out, firing wildly, and Travis stepped carefully into the hall beside them. He cocked his head, hands cradling something at his chest. Then he bent, one leg sliding back, and swung his arm. Something small rolled swiftly away.

All three men fell back as a fusillade of bullets ripped through the spot where they'd been standing. Travis winked at Antaea. "Rolled a grenade to the boy," he said.

It was almost two minutes later that the barricade blew up. The delay was just long enough for Antaea's body to start to relax, so the explosion when it came shocked her into biting her tongue. The airmen leaped out into the corridor past tumbling wardrobes and spinning chair legs and she followed, spitting blood.

Darius still stood with his back flat against the wall next to the archway. He looked stunned. The *Severance*'s men ran past him into a fierce but brief gunfight. Antaea walked up to Darius and took his head in her hands. He blinked up at her and smiled tentatively.

When the shooting stopped a moment later, his expression hardened and he stepped away from her. Antaea knew in that moment that Chaison's quest to bring the boy home had been pointless. Darius knew nothing but war. He would never leave the navy; and his reckless focus meant his life would probably be short.

Did her devotion to her causes doom her in the same way?

The others had planted explosives on the reception hall doors, and now they were inside. The place was huge, a long rectangle of light and stone currently paved with rubble and glass. Some sort of a fight was developing at the far end and Antaea headed that way.

Under covering fire from the gallery, the Severance's men were mopping up a knot of guardsmen who were making a break for the hall's only other door, which was near a raised dais under a broken wall of stained-glass. Antaea glanced around, noted the figure of Darius walking slowly into the hall with a finger in his ear, and ran for the action.

Suddenly the firing stopped. Antaea arrived to find her men spread in a half-circle around the dais, where only two men still stood. One was the pilot. He had an arm clamped around Chaison Fanning's throat. His other hand held a pistol at the admiral's head.

"I can see where this is going," cried Sempeterna over the roar of the wind. "Your people may win the city, Chaison, but you're not going to see it."

The pilot was edging them toward a big gap in the glass wall. A sideways vortex of wind was billowing out that hole. If he turned and jumped he would be falling free in the air of the city, and gone before anyone could reach the window. Antaea knew that he would kill Chaison on his way out, but though there were sixteen men with rifles trained on the pilot, none had a clear shot.

Chaison looked up and his eyes met hers. He grimaced, a smile of resignation. He didn't seem afraid, just tired.

The two men had almost reached the gap in the window. Chaison scuffed his feet in an attempt to unbalance them, but Sempeterna kept his footing. He glanced at the window, obviously judging whether he was close enough to jump for it. Antaea's heart seemed to stop and her breath caught in her throat as her hand involuntarily reached out.

Then sunlight fell across the scene in a silent thunderclap. The pilot winced and staggered back.

Antaea turned, held up her hand and saw Richard Reiss doing the same. Two hundred feet down the hall, the windows at the far end framed a halo of white in the center of which shone a tiny point of impossible brilliance.

"A sun!" someone cried. "A new sun!" For a moment everyone froze in a state of almost superstitious awe. A sun was a device, yes of course you could build one—but only Candesce could supply some of the crucial pieces. A sun was just a light—but in Virga, radiance like this, silently raging where moments ago the sky had held the deepening blue of uninhabited winter—such radiance signaled the birth of nations.

She heard a sound from behind her. Antaea spun, raising her pistol in time to see Chaison twist out of Sempeterna's grasp and dive for the floor. For a moment the pilot stood transfixed, staring dumbfounded at the eye of brilliance that had opened somewhere on the edge of Slipstream's territory. Then a single shot sounded.

The pilot's head snapped back. He slumped against green and gold panes then slid down the window to lie crumpled on the floor.

Before Chaison could regain his feet Antaea was with him. She drew him up and wrapped her arms around him fiercely, burying her face in his throat. She heard him chuckle and say, "there there," as if it were she who had almost died seconds ago.

Antaea disengaged just enough to look around, and saw some admiralty airmen staring at her and Chaison—and some looking up.

A deep shadow fell through the light of double suns as someone dived from the gallery rail. The figure spread giant wings and touched down gracefully a few feet away.

Those wings were black as a crow's; she was dressed in black leather breeches and a jacket of crimson brocade. The woman had striking features and a fan of black hair. The only thing that marred the perfection of her tanned features was a white scar on her chin.

She held a smoking rifle in her hands.

"I see you've met my husband," she said.

ALL CHAISON COULD see was her. Venera looked careworn but she was alive and her skin glowed with health. Her hair was carefully coiffed, her outfit perfect as always, and rich jewels glowed at the base of her throat—remnants he recognized, as they had plundered them together from the hoard of Anetene. Still, her gaze, direct as always, was nonetheless different somehow. In her eyes was no anger, only a question.

He had to smile at that.

Chaison looked down at Antaea. She smiled at him wistfully, then stepped back. "Admiral," she murmured. "I'm glad I was able to see you home."

"So aren't you going to intro—" Venera wasn't able to finish as Chaison pulled her to him and kissed her fiercely and for a long time. When he let her go she said, "Oh," and that was all.

"Antaea," said Chaison, turning to find her—but she had already passed the riflemen clattering down the gallery steps on her way to the doors. He wanted to run after her, but then what? He felt an awful paralysis as the moment passed and she vanished out of sight.

Venera had been following his gaze. "It's been an eventful time," she said, almost making a question of it.

"Was that your shot?" He nodded to the still form of Adrianos Sempeterna III.

The old Venera would have grinned and preened, but this one had a much more complicated expression on her face as she gazed at the fallen sovereign of Slipstream. "Doubtless this will start something else unpleasant," she said in a resigned tone.

They were suddenly surrounded by cheering people. Richard Reiss stepped forward to shake Chaison's hand. "Capital plan, old man. Went off like clockwork."

"I didn't know if everybody got my messages," he said. "And anyway . . ." He squinted at the unexpected new sun that sent dusty shafts of light the length of the hall. "I didn't plan *that*."

"But we did." A bespectacled man with a shock of white hair stepped carefully through the rubble. Behind him was a sizable and growing crowd of men and women, all of whom were dressed in ordinary street clothes. More were streaming in through the broken doors at the far end of the hall.

The white-haired man stepped up and held out his hand. "Martin Shambles, late of Aerie. That's our sun out there," he said. "Built for us courtesy of a friend of yours, Admiral. A certain young airman who used to work for your wife, here."

Chaison blinked in surprise. "Surely not . . . Hayden Griffin?"

"He sends his greetings from Aerie's new territory, carved out of winter by the light of our new sun." Shambles turned his attention to Venera. "I'm told you are the real prime mover of these events. Amandera Thrace-Guiles, I believe?"

Venera nodded gravely. "That is one of my names."

Shambles nodded quickly. "Of course, of course. You're the one who started the rumors that Fanning was alive—that he was returning. You've been printing propaganda, financing the malcontents . . ." He wound down, looking troubled. "You manipulated public sentiment. Because you intended to pull a coup."

"Of course," she sniffed. "What of it?"

"But the people's will . . ."

"Was always my will," she said with a superior smile.

Shambles looked crestfallen. "So now what? The pilot is dead, so," he looked pointedly at Chaison, "long live the pilot?"

Venera draped herself on Chaison's arm. "That sounds quite delicious, I think."

Chaison had been so focused on survival through all of this that he hadn't even thought of that possibility. He turned the notion over in his head: to be a pilot, which was every boy's dream; to rule from this palace, not just as admiral but sovereign . . .

He pictured the faces of men and women coming to this dais to petition him—and for some reason the face that stood out was that of Corbus. What would the former Atlas have said about this turn of events? He would have nodded in disgust and turned away. Even Antaea had accused Chaison of being just another aristocrat, out of touch with the people.

The more Chaison thought about it, the more the idea of ruling filled him with the same claustrophobic dread that he'd felt in those nights in the cell when he'd drifted away from the walls. To be trapped here, bound by the ultimate bonds of tradition and responsibility, and doomed to be as out of touch with everyday people as it was possible to be.

Venera was watching him, frowning slightly. She had always been ambitious for him, and him taking the pilot's post would be the ultimate career move from her point of view. Knowing how fury and resentment had simmered in her in recent years, what could he expect from her if he said no to this chance?

He took a deep breath and opened his mouth—and Venera put her hand on his heart. "It sounds delicious," she said, "but I believe my husband's answer is no. He has no desire to be pilot."

Chaison stared at her in astonishment. Venera closed her eyes and tossed her hair. "I, on the other hand . . ."

He had to laugh, and she joined in. "No, on third thought, perhaps not," she said.

Chaison looked into her eyes. This was not the woman he'd left at Candesce's border those many months ago. "What—"

"Sir!" He looked up to see a familiar face emerging from the crowd. Chaison shouted, letting go of Venera long enough to clap him on the shoulders. "Travis! Were you part of this conspiracy?"

Venera stood back, pouting—but not entirely unhappily—as the young officer shook Chaison's hand. "Admiral . . . what are we looking at?"

"The future government of Slipstream, I suspect." Seeing the expressions that came over the faces of Travis and his fighters, he frowned. "No, not me. *Them.*" He pointed at the crowd of milling citizens.

"Them?" Venera scowled at the delegation. "I'd make a better pilot than any of these plebeians." Then she caught Chaison's eye with another sly look. "But I suspect that I couldn't rule better than *all* of them." She bowed to the crowd. "The nation is yours. May your reign be long and wise."

Applause started and it seemed to Chaison like the perfect moment for a kiss—but just then a shout echoed down the hall. They all looked up to see the figure of a short, red-faced man in a captain's uniform hopping from foot to foot near the far entrance. It was Airgrove, the captain of the *Severance.*

"My God, what have you *done,* Fanning!" he roared. "We only wanted to talk to the man, not shoot him! If I'd known you were going to—"

A hand of flame and smoke picked Airgrove up and tossed him ten feet. Smoke roiled through the hall entrance and a slender form staggered out of it. She fell to her hands and knees.

Coughing, Antaea tried to rise, but fell back. She spoke, but the wind snatched away her words. She tried again: "Chaison, I tried to keep them out—"

The thing that looked like Telen Argyre strode past Antaea as if she wasn't even there. It froze Chaison's blood to see her again. The human-shaped AI's clothing was torn, her skin dotted with black bullet holes, but there was no blood. She scanned the vast room once and her eyes fixed on Venera. She broke into a run.

"Chaison, who is—?"

He grabbed Venera's arm. "Do you have the key with you?" She stared at him and he shook her in frustration. "The key to Candesce! Do you have it?"

"I . . . I always have it." She glanced down at her jacket.

"*Shoot!*" He pointed at Telen Argyre as he dragged Venera toward the window. "Shoot that woman!"

Townspeople screamed and dove for cover as the *Severance*'s airmen opened fire. Shreds of cloth, hair, and skin peppered the air behind Argyre; her features distorted as bullets impacted her nose and forehead. Still she kept coming.

Chaison looked around. They had retreated as far as they could and were now standing over the body of the pilot. Bullets wouldn't kill this thing; there was only one way he could see to end it but the Argyre-monster would be too smart to fall for that. Unless he gave it exactly what it wanted . . .

"Sorry, dear," he said, and pushed Venera into its path. Venera shrieked as Argyre reached out clawlike hands to paw at her jacket. She ripped free the white key to Candesce and held it up triumphantly.

Chaison tackled her.

It was like running into a wall, and if not for the powerful suction of the broken windows Argyre might have been unmoved. As it was she staggered and a moment later she and Venera and Chaison were through. All the breath left Chaison and his vision blurred as the palace's rotation shot them away at more than a hundred miles per hour. He glimpsed a red-and-black form and angled his body toward it. A moment later he was clutching Venera's waist, and she opened her wings and they began to brake.

He looked behind them in time to see something silver flash in the light of two suns. The precipice moth dove at Telen Argyre and she screamed, a weird and inhuman noise like a failing siren, before disappearing in a whirl of talons.

Chaison and Venera held each other tightly as her wings shuddered above them. Gradually, their rushing wind became a tolerable breeze. They were still falling—had already left the palace a mile behind—but their speed was no longer fatal.

Endless skies surrounded them, sky above and below, sky to left and right. White clouds dotted the blue in an infinity of receding patterns. Free and alive in that sky were all the birds and fish, the habitations of men, and men and women themselves, of Chaison's childhood and youth. His sun still shone, even if it had a new companion.

The precipice moth finished its work of destruction. It had left a smear of debris on the sky, but as it flapped stolidly away he saw that it clutched something small and white between the points of two talons. "So much for the key," he said.

"It's for the best," said Venera. She hugged him tightly as the warm air slid by. They stayed like that for a long time, until she suddenly frowned.

"None of this would have been necessary," she accused, "if you'd just stayed put like you were told to."

"Stayed put? What are you talking about?"

"At the prison. When I came to rescue you. It was a brilliant plan if I do say so myself, but you blew it all to hell when you insisted on rescuing your men . . ."

"That was you?"

"Of course it was me. Who did you think it was?"

"You searched for me afterward?"

"High and low. I just missed you at that ruined town, Songly, and then again at Stonecloud . . ."

"You spread the rumors that I was returning."

She nodded.

"This alias of yours . . ."

"From Spyre. I stayed there a while." She brightened as if remembering something. "I would have brought you a horse . . . but it fell off the edge when the world ended."

"What?"

"I'll explain later."

There was a long silence.

"So you like women with big eyes?"

"Uh, Antaea's just a . . . well, she handed me over to that monster, actually."

"Since when has a woman's duplicity given you pause?"

"Actually . . . I'm partial to one particular duplicitous woman, who has a history of saving my life."

"Hmm, yes," she said breezily, "I never did regret blackmailing my father into letting you marry me."

"*What?*"

"I'm sorry, did I say that out loud?"

There was another long silence. Then:

"What's so funny?"

"You and I, Miss 'Thrace-Guiles,' " he said as he laughed, "clearly have a lot of catching up to do."

About the Author

Karl Schroeder lives in Toronto, Ontario, Canada, with his wife and daughter. Although he has a reputation for being knowledgeable in many subjects and has been erroneously described as a physicist, he didn't finish high school (because he was too busy writing his first novel) and is almost entirely self-taught. In addition to writing science fiction and blogging for sites such as *WorldChanging.com*, Karl consults on the future of technology and culture for clients such as the Canadian government and army. His Web site is www.karlschroeder.com.